BIG

....

BEGINNINGS

GREYSON BRYAN

Magneto Books
New York, New York

Magneto Books
Ansonia Station
PO Box 230535
New York, NY 10023
magnetobooks.com

Publisher's Note: This is a work of fiction. Names, characters, places, and incidents are a product of the author's imagination. Locales and public names are sometimes used for atmospheric purposes. Any resemblance to actual people, living or dead, or to businesses, companies, events, institutions, or locales is completely coincidental.

Book Layout ©2013 BookDesignTemplates.com

Ordering Information:
Quantity sales. Special discounts are available on quantity purchases by corporations, associations, and others. For details, contact the "Special Sales Department" at the address above.

BIG: Beginnings/ Greyson Bryan. -- 1st ed.
ISBN 13: 978-1530680771

For my Parents

*"If you know the enemy and know yourself,
you need not fear the result ..."*
–Sun Tzu

PROLOGUE

··

FRIDAY, DECEMBER 3
LOS ANGELES

No one paid attention to the well-built jogger in the charcoal tracksuit and black Adidas baseball cap heading up the southeast end of the Santa Monica Pier. To the hundreds of people on that windy Friday afternoon, the jogger looked like any of the men who might stop after his morning run along the beach to enjoy the expansive Pacific Ocean view. For a studious observer, the expensive pair of Leica binoculars dangling from his neck may have seemed odd, but most would have barely noticed him since he blended well with the other men hanging around the pier, searching the horizon for whales or ogling the stream of scantily clad runners and Roller bladers moving up and down the promenade parallel to the beach.

Slowing his gait to a walk, the jogger marched past the ornate carousel house and stood by the metal railing as a recording of "Always Look on the Bright Side of Life" sputtered from a weather-beaten speaker. To his right, a stiff ocean breeze whipped the Pacific into a December whitecap frenzy. Below, a concrete path snaked like a sidewinder from beneath the pier along the sand toward Venice. Ignoring the screams of small children on the merry-go-round, he trained his binoculars on a spot about two hundred yards south, where a shapely blond woman in a tight yellow skin suit was offering a helmet to a tall, silver-haired man wearing a trendy Lycra suit emblazoned with a skull and cross-bones.

The jogger snorted at the sight of the old man preening like a teenager while he smoothed his suit over his narrow shoulders and bulging midsection. Then the man grabbed the helmet and tried to strap it on, but it was too small. He shook the helmet at the young woman and threw it back at her. Pivoting abruptly, he began to blade southward toward Venice at a steady clip.

Pointing his binoculars a hundred yards farther south down the esplanade, the jogger spied an unkempt, unshaven young man in worn skates, gray sweats and a dirty navy hoodie, gazing back at the pier. He stood out against the expensively outfitted Westside residents who had the leisure to exercise that morning, looking as if he'd just stumbled out of one of the dingy hotels that populated Venice Beach. When the older man skated near him on the path, the young man turned and pushed off in the same direction and slowly increased speed until the two were neck and neck. He lifted his left hand in a mock salute and said something. As the older man turned to glare at the kid and flip him the bird, the jogger observed a fine mist shoot out from the kid's left hand. The kid immediately slowed, allowing the older man to speed ahead, then bladed off the path and into a parking lot just as the blonde skated past, waving the helmet in the direction of her mate.

The jogger followed along with his binoculars and watched the silver-haired man glide a few more strides. Suddenly, the man gripped his chest and veered into the oncoming lane. A bicyclist speeding north swerved to avoid a collision, but clipped the older man. Struggling to regain his balance, the man tripped over his skates and flew backward, head first, into a concrete barrier that separated the bike path from the beach.

The jogger smiled faintly, lowered his binoculars, and moved into the crowd milling around the amusement park. Reaching the end of the pier overlooking the gray Pacific, he joined a group of whale watchers and took a long, deep breath of the briny Pacific air.

ONE

....

FRIDAY, DECEMBER 10
LOS ANGELES

Duncan Luke drove south on Lincoln Boulevard until he reached the entrance to Loyola Marymount University. He had agreed at the end of the summer to become a visiting professor at the LMU business school, beginning December 15, and teach one seminar during the spring semester. But winding down his white-collar practice and the acrimony at home since he had accepted the LMU position had kept him from visiting campus again until today. As he climbed the hill where the campus was perched, he could see the brilliant midday sun poised high above the Pacific Ocean. Despite his somber mood, he felt an almost physical release, a lightening of the body as if he were a traveler on a spaceship escaping Earth's gravity.

Inserting the key to his office in the Hilton Center for Business, he unlocked the door and pushed it open, nearly dropping the file box he carried along with his briefcase. The musty scent of stale air filled his nose. He flipped on the light switch with his elbow and bright fluorescent light illuminated the room. A slightly chipped laminated wood desk sat to his left. Matching faux cherry built-in cabinets and shelves stood behind his black vinyl desk chair and a narrow window ran from floor to ceiling on half of the wall opposite the door. Two gray stainless-steel stackable chairs faced his desk and filled the remainder of the tiny room. Duncan felt sure someone had selected the chairs for maximum discomfort to discourage student visitors. He laid his box and briefcase on the desk and took a step back. His old office, in his stately law firm, had four times the space, with heavy mahogany furniture and shiny leather chairs. He knew the contrast would give Gracie, his wife, yet another reason to criticize his decision to leave his flourishing practice. Duncan chased the thought away and dug into the box to set up his desk. He pulled out the obligatory calendar, an array of pens and pencils, and a gift from a grateful client, a clock with an image of the scales of justice and the inscription, "I'm trusting in the Lord and a good lawyer." Only a fool would trust either to achieve justice in this world, Duncan thought to himself. He arranged these on his desk and then pulled out his copies of Black's and Mellinkoff's legal dictionaries, which he placed on one bookshelf, and a binder full of possible reading material for his course, "Strategic Intelligence for International Business," which he deposited on the other.

Finally, Duncan retrieved two carefully wrapped bundles from the box. He removed the newspaper around each and held up his two favorite pictures of his son, Sam. In one, taken three years ago when his son was about seven, Sam wore a Dalmatian costume and a cap with black ears. Someone had painted dark whiskers on his chubby cheeks. He looked sideways at the camera with a worried smile as if to ask, I'm not really a dog, am I? In the other, taken two summers ago, Sam peered out of a tube in a playground at Venice Beach, eyes sparkling with delight that he had found the courage to enter the dark hole at the top and slide into the light at the bottom.

Duncan polished each frame with the tail of his polo shirt and placed them directly in front of him on his desk. He slumped down in his chair, put his feet up on the desk, and gazed out the window at the inner courtyard of the Hilton Center. By giving up his lucrative law partnership to devote time to his family and finally follow his dream of teaching, Duncan had jumped down his own rabbit hole. He had never dreamed the ride would be as bumpy or bewildering as it had been.

Three hours later, Duncan left his office at LMU filled with frustration. Months before, when he had proposed to teach the course, the objective for the class had been crystal clear: instruct future business leaders on how international businesses should organize the gathering and analysis of information to reduce risk and create competitive advantage in their long-term planning. Much of his experience in private practice involved working with investigative firms, data analysts, and forensic accountants to develop intelligence for clients to use in resolving immediate crises. He had handled every type of international corporate "complication," from getting rid of a corrupt partner or an employee-turned-terrorist recruiter to investigating foreign affiliates for exploiting child labor, discharging toxic pollution, or financing narcotics traffickers. He saw the course as a simple extension of lessons he had learned, but with a positive spin: transform his experience of crisis management from tactical to strategic, giving his students the tools to design better futures for their businesses. After reading a dozen articles and trying to hammer out a syllabus, however, the concept—once so clear—had become opaque. Memories of last night's battle with Gracie over his decision to leave private practice, an argument that had ruined their weekly dinner out once again, didn't help his clarity.

Steering his five-year-old white Acura toward their home in Santa Monica, he decided to drive along the coast rather than take the 405 and Santa Monica Freeways. If the dinner last night had gone differently, Duncan would have chosen the faster ride home to spend the late afternoon shooting baskets with Sam, but he dreaded another heated confrontation with Gracie and chose the longer route to clear his head. Traveling up Lincoln Boulevard, he stopped on the side of a narrow bridge to look over the brown bulrushes and vernal ponds of the Ballona Wetlands. A pair of Mallard ducks, a gray male with a bright green head and a mottled brown female, circled over the marsh and settled down on one of the few grassy spots. He knew that ducks generally mated only for a single season but found himself hoping these two would be the rare exception and remain partners for life.

Duncan pulled back onto the bridge and turned off Lincoln to wind his way through Marina del Rey. When Sam was younger, they had spent many Sunday mornings brunching on the patio of the Jamaica Bay Inn and building sand castles on nearby Mother's Beach. On a whim, he swerved left on Mindanao Way and parked at Burton Chace Park, a thick finger of lawn and trees sticking out into the waters of the marina. As he watched the sailboats and yachts glide by, he wondered whether there was anything he could do to ease the tension with Gracie, at least for this one evening. Then it came to him: a half Portobello mushroom and half chicken-sausage pizza from Abbot's. Sam and Gracie both loved the thick, crunchy poppy seed bagel crust and, after months of negotiation, had finally arrived at a compromise over toppings: as long as Gracie, who disliked the spicy sausage, could have mushrooms on one side of the pizza, Sam, who detested vegetables of all kinds, especially mushrooms, could have his sausage on the other. Duncan had no doubt that the treat would delight Sam; but would it distract Gracie enough to spend the evening in peace? Could a quiet evening turn into a peaceful week, a week into a month?

After placing his order at Abbot's, Duncan wandered down to Hal's for a beer. As he examined the enormous canvases of modern art on the walls, he wondered whether, after all, he was just as responsible as Gracie for the rending of their emotional bond. He knew he could be quiet, even withdrawn. Gracie had said at the end of the previous week's date night she felt as if she were living with a corpse; he had stifled an angry retort about her lack of empathy, which had only made him more sullen and soured their ride home. Christ, why couldn't she understand that his periodic bouts with melancholy were one of the by-products of the unrelenting pressure of his practice? Who wouldn't be hard to reach from time to time with all the travel and deadlines? Duncan started to fume again but stopped. A couple of beers at Hal's would cheer him up and release some of the grinding anxiety he felt about returning home. Maybe if his mood were buoyed, Gracie's would lighten too and they would make love tonight for the first time in months. Yes, he told himself as he finished the first glass in a gulp, he was sure they would.

The sweet and spicy scents of oregano, mozzarella, and Italian sausage filled the Acura as Duncan pulled to a stop outside their extensively renovated 1930s Spanish-style home on Seventeenth Street. Juggling his briefcase in one hand and a steaming two-foot-square box in the other, he tiptoed up the flagstone pathway. Gracie was sitting in the filtered light of late afternoon on the Spanish Colonial wooden bench that squatted on the flagstone of their front porch. An enormous book hid her face but not the swan's neck below or the curly auburn hair above. The rapid plucking of strings from the "Winter" movement of Vivaldi's *The Four Seasons* poured out the window like icy rain. Gracie put her book down, revealing her fair, pretty oval face and emerald eyes. When they first met, he had imagined Modigliani had made her just for him. He caught his breath at the sheer perfection of the scene: a smart, beautiful wife, a treasured son, a lovely home. He was certain they would find a way to be happy after all.

"I've brought a mushroom and sausage pizza from Abbot's," Duncan announced, as he held up the oil-stained box like an offering to placate the gods.

"Thanks. I'll put it in the oven to keep warm. Could you wait for me here?" she asked in a clipped voice. "I'd like to speak with you."

"Sure," Duncan replied, trying to sound upbeat, even though Gracie's tone made it clear another confrontation was coming. His heart sank. With the effects of three beers clouding his mind, he was in no shape to fend off Gracie's verbal onslaught. "Where's Sammy?"

"He's studying the *Lakers Yearbook* again; remember, the one I begged you not to give him? I'll be right back." A few moments later, Gracie returned, carrying the two large brown suitcases they used for long trips. "Do you want to sit?" she asked, releasing the suitcases so that they landed with a thud in front of Duncan.

"No, I don't want to sit! What's going on?" he gasped, suddenly short of breath.

"Please don't shout. You'll alarm Sam," Gracie commanded. She sat down on the bench, back straight, legs crossed, hands in her lap, and stared passed Duncan out at the street.

"Remember five years ago when I received an average review at Goldman? How upset I was because I had never before in my whole life been average at anything?" she asked in a calm, almost disembodied, voice.

"Yes, of course. We spent hours discussing it, how it wasn't fair, how you had done a superb job for them."

Gracie closed her eyes for a second.

"What I remember is you coolly deliberating over my despair like a fucking Supreme Court Justice—like I was just another one of your cases. You never had a clue, did you? You never realized how *small* you made me feel. All those years, we both worked long

9

hours, but you were an Assistant U.S. Attorney trying cases that filled the newspapers and then a partner at a prestigious law firm making more than a million dollars a year and traveling the world on assignments so sensitive you couldn't even tell *me* about them. And me? I . . . I had become just *average*? I couldn't bear coming home every night to someone who loved his work and was highly regarded for it while I loathed what I was doing and was judged as just . . . *average*. So I *quit*. And you didn't even care!"

"Of course I cared!"

"Let me finish," Gracie commanded chopping the air with her left hand. "So I left Goldman and spent months reading everything written about Asperger's and autism, going to conferences and meeting with researchers. The board at Sam's school asked *me* to join. Parents began to call *me*. Conferences invited *me* to speak," she exclaimed jabbing her right index finger into her chest. "I finally loved what I did and was recognized for it. Then you started pestering me about going back to work. As if what I did for Sam wasn't *work*."

Duncan put his briefcase down and sat on one of the suitcases. He rubbed his hands through his hair. The bitter, bready aftertaste of beer filled his mouth. "But we had agreed when you stopped working, I mean, when you left Goldman, it would only be for a few years. You would find something to bring in money so I could leave private practice and teach."

"Why should I find a job where I would have to start over and be treated like crap," Gracie interjected, "when I have a doctorate in caring for Sam? I'm good at this. It makes me happy and it's critical for *our* son. You certainly aren't going to do what I've done for Sam. You want to teach, not take care of him."

"I want to do both," Duncan objected.

"Right." Gracie snorted. "But how do you think we're going to pay for Sam's therapies and special education if you give up prac-

ticing law? Don't you care about your son's well-being? I've dedicated my life to him. What have you done? You've dedicated your
life to yourself."

Duncan felt nauseated. Some of the oil from the pizza box had
congealed on his hand. He wiped it on his jeans. The old olive
tree on the side of the house captured his eyes. All the branches
needed trimming and one decrepit limb needed a brace. He'd
have to get Juan to come out for the job.

"Duncan? Are you listening to me? Focus, goddammit! Focus!
You've been drinking again, haven't you? You asshole! Tune me
in!"

Duncan blinked twice and faced Gracie. "If we both worked, we
could make ends meet. We might have to move to a smaller
house, but we'd have more time together as a family."

"You just don't *get* it, do you? Sam doesn't need more family
time, not if it means there's no money to pay for the *professional*
help he needs, not if it means that *I* won't be available whenever
he needs me." Gracie stood up and put her hands on her hips. "I
warned you I would never forgive you if you insisted on being so
selfish. But you didn't listen and you left your practice anyway. So
here we are." Gracie looked directly into Duncan's eyes. "I've been
advised that I have to file for a divorce while you're still a partner
if I want to protect our right to the support that Sam and I will
need. The divorce papers went in today. I've also been counseled I
should allow you to see Sam here for an hour on Wednesday and
Saturday evenings until we work out a custody agreement. Please
come by at seven o'clock. I'll get Sam now so you can talk with
him." Gracie headed to the door.

"*Wait.* What are you *doing?*" Duncan shouted. "This is my
home, too. I'm not going to meet Sam at the front door like some
. . . some magazine salesman!" Duncan tripped on his way toward
the entrance nearly stumbling into Gracie. She stepped aside with

a laugh. He twisted the handle in vain. He took out his keys. None of them would turn in the lock. He slammed his fist against the wooden door.

"Yes, a locksmith came while you were gone. And, a male paralegal from my lawyer's office, a former college football player as big as you, two decades younger and sober, is inside. If your temper gets out of control, he has the number of the Santa Monica police department programmed into his cell. I wish I could say I'm sorry, Duncan, but I'm not. In fact, it's been years since I've felt this good. You have ten minutes with Sam. Please try not to upset him," Gracie ordered as she unlocked the wooden door, walked in, and closed it behind her.

Duncan kicked both suitcases over and threw his briefcase across the lawn toward his car. For an instant, he imagined starting the engine and ramming the car through the front door. Sweating heavily, he slumped down on the bench and tried to control his breathing so Sam wouldn't feel how upset he was. The front door swung open. Sam, a slight boy with creamy skin peered out at him. He wore a Dodgers T-shirt, flip-flops, and khaki shorts. Curly black hair spilled out the sides of a Dodgers cap like an overturned bowl of squid-ink spaghetti. Sam stepped out and sat next to Duncan. He stared intently at the dog-eared copy of the *Los Angeles Lakers Yearbook* that Duncan had given him only a few months ago. A warm tide of tenderness swept away his anger.

"Hello, Sammy," Duncan said as he placed his hand on his son's leg and struggled to keep his voice from cracking. Sam did not reply.

"How are you?"

"Did you know that the Lakers lost on Friday to the Bulls? Kobe had twenty-three points and seven assists. Gasol had twenty-one points and eight rebounds. I like Gasol. He has hair like mine.

Odom had eighteen points and eight rebounds. Ron Artest only had two points. He stinks."

"Sam?" Duncan asked gently, knowing his son often took refuge from feelings in facts. "Are you worried about something?" Sam looked up from the *Yearbook*.

"Are those yours?" Sam asked, pointing at the suitcases lying on the lawn.

Duncan rubbed his forehead and swallowed a sob. He whispered, "What did your mom tell you?"

Sam turned his eyes to the *Yearbook*. "She said you guys decided it was best if you would live somewhere else. Are you going to live in Washington or Tokyo? Who will bring us pizza when you're gone? Who will watch games with me?"

"No, Sammy," Duncan said, blinking his eyes to keep the tears away. "I'm not going to live in Washington or Japan. I don't know exactly where I'll be but it will be close, I promise you. Someplace you'll like." Duncan put his arm around Sam's bony shoulders. "We'll have pizza together. We'll watch games together. You'll have a bedroom there, just like here. I promise."

Sam put the *Yearbook* down. He wrapped his arms around his knees and began to rock back and forth. "I don't want a new home," he insisted quietly. "I like this one. All my things are here. You can visit me here, but you can't make me move."

"You don't have to move, sweetheart," Duncan said as he rubbed Sam's back. "You'll have two homes: this one and our new home. That's all. Not many boys get to have two homes. Want to sit in my lap for a bit?" Duncan asked, longing to hold his son.

"No!" shouted Sam as he jumped up from the bench. He paced back and forth in front of Duncan, gesturing wildly and screeching. "I don't want a new home. I don't want a new home. I don't want a new home."

"Sam, just listen to me," Duncan pleaded.

"Noooooo! You can't make me! I hate you!" Sam screamed and sprinted to the bench, grabbed the *Yearbook*, and dashed to the front door. He banged his fist against the wood. The door opened and a muscular young man stepped out. Sam ducked around him and into the house.

The young man broadened his stance in front of the entrance. "I'm sorry, man. But I think you'd better go now."

Duncan watched, transfixed, as the door closed. His world had spun out of control.

....

TWO

SATURDAY, DECEMBER 11
LOS ANGELES

The celebration of the life of Robert Bingham was concluding as a wan December sun settled below the horizon. After two hours of greeting her guests, Ghislaine Bingham could not stomach another compliment for her late, almost ex-husband or condolence for his demise. When the last guest had wandered inside from the growing chill of the backyard, she remained behind to stroll among the pear trees scattered around the rolling lawn. The once verdant leaves had turned to pale gold and red, complementing the stucco walls and roof tiles of her Mediterranean home. Planting those trees was the first of many changes she had made to the house on Beverly Glen twenty-five years ago during the first month of their marriage. For the young Ghislaine, the trees had symbolized not just how much she hoped her love for Robert would flourish but also her decision to root herself in Los Angeles far from her Brussels home. A cool fall breeze rustled the leaves. Ghislaine gazed back on the three arched French doors leading into the living room. Installing those doors had sparked the first fight of their marriage. Robert's business had been struggling and he had accused her of being extravagant, but her Flemish stubbornness had insisted. When Robert saw how the glass panes of the new doors lightened the living room, he had taken her in his arms and kissed her.

As she recalled that tender moment, regret at the loss of so many years welled up inside her. She had been so sure of her love for Robert and of her future with him that she had defied her maman for the first time in her life to marry the older American. But after a few years, their passion ebbed, leaving a married life with only two shared emotions: joy in raising their son, Robbie, and pride in building their company, Bingham International Group Inc. or BIG as it was—much to Ghislaine's annoyance—often called.

After twenty-five years of marriage and twenty years as a successful business team, Robert had deserted her for a Russian Roller blade instructor and threatened to remove Ghislaine from Bingham International. She had for a long time felt vulnerable to his capricious character but never allowed herself to believe he would cast her aside from the company. She knew her marriage was a charade, but her success in business was not. She had been Mrs. Robert Bingham, Executive Vice President of Bingham International, for almost her entire adult life. She had sacrificed so much of herself to preserve that identity and battled countless times with Robert to ensure their company maintained a reputation worthy of their family's name. Aside from Robbie, the company and the people who gave it life were the sun and moon to her, and then that bastard of a husband tried to eclipse them.

Four months of despair and agony later, a freak accident crushed Robert's skull. No longer could he ruin her moments of happiness with an angry outburst, a sudden command, or a withering complaint. Now this beautiful house and a controlling interest in the company belonged to her alone. Fate had given her a chance to sculpt a new Ghislaine Bingham, one who would never again entrust her sense of self to a man. The news of Robert's death had numbed her at first; soon, however, she felt reborn, wanting to run barefoot in the grass, as she had done when she was a girl in Belgium.

Stepping through the French doors into the living room, Ghislaine saw with relief that only a few guests were lingering. The muscles in her shoulders relaxed for the first time since the event had begun. Thank God Taro Takayama had departed with apologies shortly after the reception had begun, saying he was obligated to return to Tokyo that evening. President of Aoki, a Japanese trading company that owned 20 percent of Bingham International, Takayama had always dealt directly with Robert and seemed ill at ease around Ghislaine, mispronouncing her name as "Jeeren" rather than the French "Geelen," an irritating habit Ghislaine forced herself to endure without comment. He seemed acutely sensitive to titles—as an executive vice president, she was beneath his status—and uncomfortable with the idea of a woman filling an important position in a partner enterprise. She had ignored his chauvinism before, but now she *had* to care. For the company to thrive under her direction, she had to learn to work with Aoki and gain Taro Takayama's respect. Anxiety began to bore a hole in her stomach. *Stop it.* Worry about Takayama-san on Monday.

She walked to the end of the living room where her son stood chatting with his father's lawyer. Was this tall, muscular twenty-three-year-old the same boy who, at ten, was short and skinny and lost at school? The tan from his recent trip to Panama accentuated Rob's blond good looks. Even Ghislaine couldn't help admiring the resemblance to his father. He glanced at her with his soft eyes, eyes that came from her maman, as if to ask, "How are you doing?"

"I'm fine," she mouthed as she passed the two men, touching her son on the arm. Robbie patted it briefly and smiled down at her. He may resemble his father, Ghislaine thought, but his soul is Maman's. More than anything in the world, she wanted to find the strength to lead the company to even greater success and then pass the company to him as her legacy.

"Hello, Ghislaine," a deep voice with a slight Russian accent sounded at her side. Ghislaine turned, startled, and then smiled.

"Andrei. *Dear* Andrei." She murmured, her husky voice catching on his name. She took his hands and squeezed them. "It is so good to see you. I didn't think you could come."

"My flight was canceled. Snow in New York." He pulled her to him and kissed her on both cheeks. Lingering by her right ear, he whispered, "You look so much better than the last time I saw you. I hope you're happier *now*."

Ghislaine flushed briefly and looked down to her right, not quite sure how to respond. Andrei Kronsky was several years older than her, a charming companion, and, after Robert had left her, sometimes more. He was not quite as tall as Ghislaine, but had the broad shoulders, narrow waist, and light step of a former world-class gymnast. A Russian military doctor who immigrated to the United States, Andrei had founded a biomedical company that had made him into a billionaire. He was unaccustomed to waiting for anything or anyone.

Ghislaine sensed that she had become his current goal. But his persistence, while flattering, was sometimes uncomfortable.

"I've missed you so much," Andrei continued. She inhaled the familiar spicy scent of Andrei's aftershave. Then she leaned away.

"Robert's death shocked me, but, yes, I *am* happier now," she breathed. "Thank you. As for the rest . . ." She paused and shook her head slightly. "I . . . I told you I need time to think it over. Please don't rush me."

"I won't. Just know you can ask *anything* of me, anytime," Andrei pledged with a slight bow.

"I know. Thank you." She touched Andrei's shoulder and turned to wander into the music room. In the corner rested a glossy black 1928 Chickering baby grand piano, which Robert had given her to celebrate her first Bingham deal, their investment in a Dutch winter sportswear company whose clothes she had worn as a figure skater. Ghislaine had anticipated that athletic wear would become a sportswear trend years before the idea became mainstream. She had loved the piano, of course, but longed for Robert's embrace and praise for her contribution to their company. She realized now Robert's elaborate gift was the first time she had begun to question whether he loved her for herself or viewed her as an object he could exploit. She had pushed the uncertainty from her mind at the time, but now after two decades she was struck by how long she had lived with a lurking sense of insecurity. *Salaud.*

At the far end of the music room just off the front hall she saw her stepson, Ward, Robert's son by his first wife, Leila. Ghislaine had never met Leila, who had died in a tragic car accident a year before she was introduced to Robert. The stories she'd heard described a petite woman with flawless skin, sea-green eyes, a sharp mind, and a famous temper. Ward, who was only five years younger than his stepmother, had inherited his mother's dark good looks and wiry, athletic frame, as well as her volatile temperament. He could be curt, even contemptuous, which Ghislaine knew well from working with him at Bingham, where Ward now served as president. She anticipated he would make her assuming control of the company as difficult as possible.

Dressed in one of his half-dozen black Armani suits, he stood facing away from Ghislaine, his right arm encircling the waist of a young woman who had draped her left arm over his shoulder. Ghislaine squinted. Ward seemed to have an inexhaustible supply of Armani suits *and* blond girlfriends. She did not recognize this one. Cursing the vanity that kept her from wearing her glasses, she moved toward them. She would welcome Ward and his guest and escape up the long stairway leading from the entryway to her bedroom on the second floor. As Ghislaine approached, the woman rocked with laughter at something Ward had whispered in her ear, gave him a playful shove in the chest, and turned abruptly toward Ghislaine.

Stunned, Ghislaine stared at the beautiful young woman with the same face and form as her own, but twenty-five years younger. It was as if Ghislaine had stepped out of the sterling frame of her wedding picture. A chill ran down her back.

"Hello, Ghislaine." Ward smiled and ran his hand through his black, slicked-back hair. "I don't believe you've met my guest. This is Katrina Petrolova. Katrina, this is my stepmother."

Ghislaine glared wide-eyed at Ward. "Excuse us for a moment, Ms. Petrolova," she said without looking at the Russian. "Could I have a word with you in private?" Ward patted Katrina on the arm and followed his stepmother into the near corner of the music room.

"Now, don't insult my guest," Ward chided Ghislaine. "Katrina and Robert were engaged. You could at least be cordial to the fiancée of the man whose memory we're here to celebrate. You can't begrudge Katrina for trying to emulate you, can you?"

"You know that your father was a widower when I met him. Your poor mother had been dead . . ."

The smile vanished from Ward's face. "You have no right to say a word—not a word—about my mother," he interrupted. "Do you understand me?! You were no different than Katrina is today. All you wanted then and all Katrina wants now is a green card and a passport to riches."

Ghislaine straightened her shoulders and held her head erect so she could peer down at Ward. "I know that you don't care what this woman did to my marriage, but you're a fool to defend someone whose escapade with your father destroyed the business partnership that was the lifeblood of the company you work for."

"Don't call me a fool," Ward snapped. "And I don't work for the company. I own it."

"Robert and I were still married when he died, Ward. Both the company and this house belong to *me.*" Ghislaine took a deep breath to contain herself. She would not lose control in front of her guests. "Now leave and take your *friend.*"

"Yes, ma'am." Ward smirked and started to step toward Katrina and then turned back. "By the way, I've asked that a copy of Robert's *updated* estate documents be sent to your lawyer on Monday morning. They're complicated, but I'm sure Monica will explain them so even a second-rate actress like yourself can understand."

Ghislaine started to bark a French curse but stopped. Ward took Katrina by the arm and led her to the front door. Ghislaine stood, arms folded against her chest, willing him out of her home. Ward turned and with mock formality bowed at his stepmother. Opening the door, he laughed loudly and walked out.

Updated estate documents? Her stomach muscles tightened. What had Robert done to her now?

THREE

SUNDAY, DECEMBER 12
LOS ANGELES

Ward slipped quietly out of bed, not wanting to wake Katrina. Warm, tousled, and naked, the young Russian lay snoring softly in his bed. He had insisted they shower before sex last night, and, naturally, he needed to cleanse himself this morning of the smell of her sweat and stale perfume. Katrina was an enthusiastic and inventive lover and he felt renewed by their coupling, but not enough to change his mind. She had served her purpose and needed to disappear.

While he quietly showered and dressed in his Italian marble bathroom, Ward recalled the improbable chain of events that had brought Katrina into his bed. He had been sitting at the bar of the boisterous Factory Nightclub in West Hollywood last June sipping a Grey Goose on the rocks and mulling over the predicament he was facing at work. He had known for years that his father and stepmother had a marriage that hinged solely on their love for his half brother and their fear that a divorce would destroy the success of Bingham International. For almost as many years he had labored to ingratiate himself with his father so Robert would leave the company to him rather than Ghislaine. He'd often recount to Robert with feigned pleasure his days at the

Catholic boarding school where Robert and Ghislaine had banished him as a teenager and his time at the same WASP fraternity at USC where Robert had been a member. Ward emulated Robert's fancy clothes, flashy cars, and penchant for full-figured blondes, trappings he knew his beloved mother would have despised. Ward had always loathed Robert for what he did to his mother, but each time his groveling failed to capture his father's attention, his rage against Robert would grow. Still Ward never allowed his anger to burst through the surface. When self-doubt would sharpen into self-loathing, he would chase away his qualms with even more expensive food and liquor and the company of fair-haired women whom he would later toss aside like an empty bottle of Courvoisier. *Nothing*, he would assure himself, not even his growing appetite for Robert's lifestyle, would have mattered more to his mother than reclaiming Bingham International for her family.

Five years ago when Rob left for college, Ward felt sure Robert and Ghislaine's mutual antipathy would finally break them apart and Robert would declare him his sole heir. When they remained together, he cursed his father's weakness and his stepmother's guile. Redoubling his efforts at work, he brought in profitable deals and new investors to show Robert that Bingham International would thrive under his direction. For all his effort, he had been rewarded with a few bonuses, a meaningless title, and a measly 20 percent of the company.

Then, earlier this year, Ghislaine surprised and infuriated him by persuading Rob to return to Los Angeles and work at the company. He knew his scheming stepmother would convince Robert, nearing seventy years old, that his tongue-twisted half brother deserved a share of the company equal to Ward's. Even if she didn't, she would inherit Robert's sixty percent if his father were to die still married to her. Ward cursed at his fate. After two decades of sacrificing himself on the altar of Robert Bingham and five years in which he practically carried the company on his back, he would end up working for the daughter of a Brussels barkeeper, the woman who had usurped his mother's place at home, cast him out to boarding school, and insinuated herself into the company Robert had stolen from his mother's family. The dread that he had not only failed his mother but betrayed her values in the process sickened his soul. He should have sabotaged Ghislaine years ago . . .

Ward remembered gulping the vodka so fast it burned his throat. As he raised his empty glass toward the bartender, a gorgeous, leggy, honey-blonde with high cheekbones came into sight. The glass nearly slipped from his hand. My God, it can't be. Sliding off his stool, he walked, mesmerized, across the room toward the mirror image of Ghislaine when he had first met her twenty-seven years before. "Hello, beautiful," Ward crooned. "My name is Ward Bingham." The woman looked at Ward, giggled, and started to back away. "I'm president of Bingham International Group. Perhaps you've heard of it?" The giggling stopped. The doppelganger of the young Ghislaine cocked her head and raised an eyebrow. "May I buy you a Cristal?" Ward asked. The blonde smiled broadly and nodded. When Ward returned with the two flutes, he handed one to the blonde, gazed into her eyes, and murmured, "Cheers."

"Thank you. I introduce myself, yes? My name is Katrina Petrolova," the woman said with a thick Russian accent. "I am from Leningrad . . . sorry, Saint Petersburg. I trained with the Mariinsky Ballet, but not so good. I came here. I like your California very much. So warm in winter!"

As Ward listened to Katrina talk, an idea formed in his mind. What better way to invigorate an aging man than to offer him a chance to bask again in the glow of a young, blond Ghislaine look-alike, who would pretend to be thrilled by Robert's success and enraptured by his charm? Bedding the lovely Katrina would trump any anxiety his father might feel over the breakup of his marriage. His plan was set. He would offer her money to seduce his father and drive Ghislaine out of his life.

Later that night, after they had returned to his Century City condo, showered, and made love, Ward lay beside Katrina stroking her baby-soft arm. In his most soothing voice, he whispered, "I have an idea that I want to share with you."

After listening to Ward's scheme, Katrina shook her head and shouted, "We have just met and now you ask me to have sex with your father for money? This I do not believe!" she cried, jammed her fist into Ward's chest, and started to leap from the bed. Ward grabbed her arm.

"Wait. Please! It will only be for a little while," Ward cooed. "Once he divorces my stepmother, you will return to me, my darling. I will be rich and we will have a wonderful life together. I am not employing you; I am making you my partner." Katrina picked up a pillow, held it against her chest and looked away.

"I will give you ten thousand dollars a month whether you succeed or not," Ward offered, running his hand along the inside of her thigh. Katrina dropped the pillow and turned to him.

"Okay, Ward. I do this for you . . . and for us, so we can be together," she said as she wrapped her arms around his neck. "May I have my ten thousand dollars now, please?"

His strategy had succeeded brilliantly. Katrina had captivated Robert from the moment they met in a feigned Roller blading collision on the Venice Beach bike path. By mid-August, Robert had left Ghislaine and filed for divorce. It took little effort for Ward to convince his infatuated father that he should alter his estate plan to reflect his estrangement from Ghislaine.

Everything went exactly as Ward had hoped until late November when Katrina called unexpectedly. "You promised we would be together," she whined. "I am sick of his face of wrinkles, his stringy hair of silver."

"But, dear Katrina," Ward purred. "If you leave Robert, he could go back to Ghislaine. Everything that we've worked for would be lost. You have to wait until the divorce is final."

"This will take how long?"

"Six months, perhaps more."

"No!" she howled. "I will be crazy. Please, Ward, you are smart man. You must have some good plan."

"There is no other way out, my love. Unless, of course," Ward laughed, "his heart failed from trying to satisfy you."

"What? If Robert is dead, then we could be happy together?"

"Yes, of course," Ward replied impatiently. "But he's in great shape. Put it out of your mind, darling."

Four days later, Robert died in an accident on the same beach path where he and Katrina had first met. Alarmed, Ward called Katrina as soon as he heard the news. She swore she had begged Robert to wear a helmet, but he had reacted like a sixteen-year-old on a dare and took off without protection. She had chased after him with his helmet, but before she could catch him, a bicyclist sideswiped him into a cement wall, crushing his skull.

"I am so sorry. I am so sorry. But now we can be together," she repeated like a mantra.

Her words reverberated in Ward's ears as he finished dressing and crept over to the side of the bed where Katrina lay curled around a down pillow. He placed a cashier's check for $20,000 and a one-way ticket to New York in her name on the bedside table. He set the alarm for eight thirty to make sure she didn't oversleep. After softly closing the door to his condo, he stopped just outside the elevator bank to send her a text message warning her not to miss the flight at noon. He would inform the *Los Angeles Times* reporter who had covered his father's death of her illegal status no later than one o'clock. Ward had little doubt that Katrina would go, although he expected to find his apartment a wreck when he returned that evening. A small price to pay to restore his mother's legacy.

As Ward stepped from the elevator into the ground-floor lobby, he wondered again whether his father's failure to wear a helmet and the encounter with a speeding bicyclist were as coincidental as Katrina implied. But Robert's impulsiveness was well known and no one questioned the accidental nature of the death. Of course, twenty-eight years before, no one had suspected his mother's death was anything but a horrible accident. But he knew better, didn't he?

FOUR

·····································

SUNDAY, DECEMBER 12
PANAMA CITY

"**A**re you threatening *me*, my friend?" Rodrigo Salduba hissed into his cell phone. "I would very much advise against it. I am a proud Panamanian, a former high-ranking government official, and a prominent lawyer in good standing with the bar. Besides, if I thought you were threatening me and you were foolish enough to come within a thousand miles of Panama again . . ." Salduba paused and then began to shout, "I would put your microscopic *cojones* in a vice and crush them to make bird feed. DO YOU UNDERSTAND?"

"But Salduba-sensei, Aoki hired you to be its lawyer. You cannot represent a competitor in bidding for the concession. That would be . . . uh . . . that would an act against your moral obligation to us." Salduba, a dark bull of a man dressed in an elegant white linen suit, laughed.

"Aoki *was* my client, Señor Emoto. But when you failed to reimburse my expenses as I requested, my relationship with Aoki terminated. Good-bye, Señor Emoto, and good luck in the future."

"But . . . but . . ." Emoto sputtered as Salduba ended the call. He had been expecting Emoto to call in protest, but the timing was inconvenient, coming the same night he had planned to deal with Magdalena.

Ah, Magdalena, Rodrigo sighed and ran his fingers through his black hair. Almost eight years had passed since she had arrived at the Golden Island. A destitute and desperate university student from Colombia, she was nearly six feet tall and her slender frame swayed when she walked like a palm frond in a light wind. She had the face of a Latin Madonna: high cheekbones, large almond eyes, and a patrician nose. Her coffee-colored skin glowed and her long mahogany hair cascaded over her shoulders and across her breasts. Rodrigo considered himself a connoisseur of gorgeous women. What he admired about Magdalena's beauty was its authenticity; natural, like the seas of his country's San Blas Islands, not the product of a doctor's knife like so many of his other Colombian girls. She was a work of art made of flesh and blood and he knew from first glance he could not bear to share her. So, he had kept her in an apartment not far from his own, and bought her Gucci, Dior and Fendi and a fire engine red Ford Mustang convertible to drive. Wanting her on his arm before clients and friends, he paid for her English lessons and decorating classes. She astonished him with her progress. She had a brain like a computer, able to process pages of information and understand everything. He had never before known the mind of a woman to fan his physical desire but the flashes of brilliance she so casually displayed made him want to possess her soul not just her body. He pampered her even more by escorting her to resorts on the Caribbean coast and ranches in the countryside where she learned to ride and shoot. What spirit she developed! When angered, she was a *jaguar*. Head held high and eyes flashing, she often behaved more like his wife than a kept woman. Well, tonight he would remind her who she was.

Salduba glanced at his watch. He had asked Magdalena to come to the club at six but knew she would be at least fifteen minutes late. He walked from his office, rode down the elevator, and strolled through the warm evening along the Avenida Aquilino de la Guardia. He ignored the blaring horns and exhaust spewing from the evening traffic to focus on the task at hand. He never enjoyed teaching these lessons, but they were necessary to running a successful business.

When he approached the club, a beefy security guard saluted him and swung open the ornately carved wooden door. A blast of the air-conditioning assaulted him as he stepped past the entryway and into the main room. He could tell immediately business would be slow tonight. A languid *salsa* flowed from the trio on stage to the nearly empty dance floor, where three girls were swaying and thrusting to entice one of the few customers watching to join them. At least two *Norteamericanos* sat perched at the bar buying drinks for several of his girls, the usual prelude to a more lucrative negotiation. In the far left corner, he was surprised to see Magdalena waiting for him at a cocktail table sipping water. She looked ravishing in a cream-colored cotton piqué pants suit. When their eyes met, she rose and smiled hesitantly.

"Rodrigo, *querido*. Why have you asked me here?" she asked, her eyes searching his for some clue why he would have her come to the Golden Island, a place she had not set foot in for eight years.

"Please come with me, *querida*," he replied brusquely and took her by the arm through a red velvet curtain to a locked metal door at the back. He opened the door with a key and, gripping her arm tightly, began to descend the steep staircase into the pitch-dark basement. The air was warm and reeked of sweat and urine. A dog-like whimper echoed up the concrete walls that lined the stairs. When they reached the bottom, Rodrigo switched on a single light bulb hanging from a wood beam. Two wire-mesh cubes about four feet on all sides rested side by side on the floor. One of the dog cages stood empty, its gate open. In the other a naked teenage girl lay curled up sucking her thumb. When she raised her head and saw Magdalena, she cried out.

"*Magdalena! Gracias a Dios! Salvame! Salvame!*"

"*Silencio!*" roared Rodrigo. The girl began to sob. Rodrigo carefully removed a cigar and a packet of matches from the inside pocket of his coat. He bit off its end, struck a match, and lit the cigar, thoughtfully sucking on it until a sweet smoke billowed out. "There, so much better smelling than your little Panamanian friend. So, *querida,* is it shock I see on your Madonna's face? You wish to know how we could treat Anna, *tu hermana pequena,* like this? The story is simple. One of Anna's roommates called last night when she returned and found Anna had disappeared. We caught Anna this morning at the central bus station trying to run away."

"But, Rodrigo, she left money to pay her debt to you, had she not? *Querido,* was she not then free to return to her village?"

"Ah, *querida,* yes, of course, Anna would have *told* you she had repaid her debt. But where did she get the thousand dollars I paid her family two years ago? *That* is the question. What I pay her for her services barely covers what it costs me for her bed, her food, and her clothes, and what is left each month I send to her poor parents. So the only possible answer is she stole it from the club or its customers, which means she stole it from *me.* How could she do such a thing after all I have done for her family—for *her?* Because of my generosity, her father has a donkey to help plow the field, her mother has chickens to give the family eggs, and her brother has books for school. She repays my kindness, thanks me for my beneficence by STEALING FROM ME?" Rodrigo roared.

"*Magdalena me lo dio. Magdalena me lo dio!*" screamed Anna. "*Oh, Magdalena, dile por favor!*"

"*Silencio!*" Rodrigo shouted and kicked Anna's cage. He held his cigar over the wire mesh and tapped ash over the girl's head. Anna wailed in fear.

"You see, *querida,* how she lies, how she accuses you, who is like her older sister, of giving her the money? But that could not be, could it?" he asked as he moved to stand by the open cage. "After all," he said, lifting his foot to rest on the wire mesh and leaning on his knee, "the only money you have is *mine* and you would not steal from *me,* would you, *querida?*"

Magdalena glanced at Anna, who lay moaning in a fetal position on the floor of her cage. Then she stared at the open gate of the second cage for several seconds. Finally, without looking at Rodrigo, she murmured, "No, of course, I would not . . . *querido.*"

"So, Anna, whom you loved like a sister, is lying?" Magdalena looked up at Rodrigo, who was now standing by Anna's cage, grinning.

"Yes, she is lying," Magdalena whispered.

"I could not hear you, *querida.*"

"Yes, she is lying," Magdalena spat out the words.

"Good, *querida.* I was sure of it. But she begged me to bring you here. You understand. You know I wish to be fair."

"Yes. I am so sorry you have been troubled," Magdalena mumbled. "What will happen to Anna now?"

"She cannot return to work here, no, not after stealing from me. And I could not sell her to another club in Panama without risking my business reputation. What if she stole again?" Rodrigo puffed on his cigar. "Still, I have invested money in her and must be repaid. I think I will sell her to a business that provides women to the camps of men working on the expansion of the canal. Yes, there will be little to steal in such a place. Still, she must be punished, but not in a way that would decrease her value, don't you agree?" Magdalena remained silent, her eyes riveted on Anna. "Good, I see you agree," Rodrigo smiled. He leaned down, quickly unlatched the gate and grabbed one of Anna's bare feet.

"*Ay, no. No,*" the girl pleaded and kicked out but could not loosen his grip. He lifted her foot up and pressed the glowing end of the cigar against the middle of her sole. The smell of burnt flesh wafted up as Anna shrieked in pain and went limp. Rodrigo dropped her foot back into the cage and latched it shut.

"Shall we go now, *querida?*"

"I am so sorry to have troubled you," Magdalena muttered as she turned to climb the concrete stairway.

"I know you are, *querida,*" Rodrigo said gently, supporting her arm as they walked away. "In the future, however, you must be careful of those you spend time with. Always remember, I am the only one who truly cares for you, the only one you can trust."

"Yes, I know, *querido.* I know."

FIVE

....

MONDAY, DECEMBER 13
LOS ANGELES

At eight fifteen, Duncan trudged out of the Holiday Inn Express near Los Angeles International Airport, carrying his two suitcases. Before he climbed into his car, he glanced up at the dark clouds and pulled the collar of his Eddie Bauer rain jacket up around his neck. The roar of landing jets fading behind him, he drove northwest on Sepulveda through a dilapidated commercial district and then turned on Centinela, passing a Salvadoran bakery, a *mariscos* restaurant and several auto repair shops. When he reached Mar Vista, he turned on to Grand View Boulevard, slowed, and found a parking spot just across the street from the shaded entrance to Pacific Western, Sam's school.

Duncan looked out at the beige, one-story complex of buildings that occupied almost a whole block. Not having visited since last June, he had forgotten the school was situated among apartment buildings and tiny, ill-kept bungalows. He sat in his car and stared at the schoolyard. Kids were chasing each other and scrambling over the climbing structure. Duncan began to lose his nerve. This was not the right setting to see Sam, not after all that had happened Friday night. He knew Sam needed time to process his emotions. Hell, who *didn't* need time to process this mess? Still, though he knew an unanticipated visit might upset Sam even more, he couldn't bear waiting until Wednesday night to see him, to let him know how much he loved him.

He stepped from his car, walked past the school's sea-green iron gate, and rang the bell at the front door. At the buzzing sound, he opened the door and turned left into a small security office.

"Hello," Duncan greeted the well-built Hispanic man behind the desk. Noticing the black metal nameplate, he continued. "Hello, Arturo. My name is Duncan Luke. I'm Sam Luke's father. I . . . I was hoping to see Sam for a moment before classes started."

Arturo raised his bushy eyebrows. "May I see some identification, please?" Duncan handed over his driver's license. After examining it and scrutinizing Duncan's face, Arturo returned it to him. "Let me just check the list of approved visitors," he said as he ran his finger down a white sheet of paper. "I'm sorry, Mr. Luke, Gracie Lewis is on the list by Sam's name but you are not. And there's also a note that says we'd need a letter from her allowing you on the approved list of visitors or a court order. Do you have either one?"

Duncan's heart began to race. "Bullshit," he shouted, raising his right hand in protest. "She kicked me out Friday night. How would I know I'd need a letter to see my own son? There's no court order yet; we haven't even had a custody hearing. He's my *son,* for God's sake." Duncan pounded his fist on the counter.

Arturo slowly elevated his large frame, leaned forward, and glowered at Duncan. "If he's your son," he declared slowly, "you should have sent back the registration form with your name on it in September like all the other parents did. Not my problem you screwed up, man."

Duncan's shoulders sagged like punctured balloons. "Okay, sorry for shouting at you," he mumbled and turned to leave.

Arturo hesitated a moment before he yelled at Duncan's back, "Hey, I'm a divorced dad, too. I know how you feel, man." Duncan stopped and spun around to face Arturo.

"I can't let you in the front, but you can see whether he's still on the playground. Stand outside the fence, okay?"

"Thank you," Duncan gasped and ran out the door. He raced back to the street and veered left to a spot just outside a tall, black iron fence that separated the yard from the sidewalk. Children jostled to line up for roll call.

Sam sat alone at a sun-bleached lunch table in the far right corner of the play area. Dressed in his beloved Lakers sweatshirt, he was staring at the dog-eared copy of the *Los Angeles Lakers Yearbook*. God only knows what statistics Sam was memorizing now, Duncan smiled to himself. Suddenly, Sam looked up and peered out toward the fence. Duncan couldn't tell whether his son saw him or not. He felt an urge to yell out Sam's name, to tell him he was there watching over him; he would always be there. Duncan swallowed the words before they could form. What if he frightened Sam? Sam did not react well to surprises. A teacher standing at the head of a line of students called out, "Sam?" Sam twisted around to look at the teacher and stood up. After stuffing the yearbook in his backpack, he slung the pack over his left shoulder and joined the line of students moving into the school.

As Duncan watched his son disappear, he grabbed two rods of the iron fence, and squeezed until his hands were white. If he didn't fight for time with Sam, looking through bars would be the only way he'd see his son in the light of day again. He'd need a divorce lawyer, and Web Allen was the best. But how in the world could he pay Web's fees? With a sigh, he turned back toward his car to leave when he spied Gracie in the schoolyard. She was strolling between the school director and Terri Hubert, the school psychologist, toward the entrance of the administration building. As they approached the double glass doors, Gracie took Terri by the arm and swiveled to say something to the school director. All three women stopped to laugh before continuing into the school. Duncan swallowed hard. He realized now that there was one person who didn't need time to process the calamity that had struck his family. Gracie had been planning the separation for months. Winning time with Sam would require everything he had.

SIX

....

MONDAY, DECEMBER 13
LOS ANGELES

Although Ghislaine had been out of the office for the ten days since Robert's death and was anxious to return, this morning she lingered in her nightgown at home to calm her nerves. She was still rankled by the confrontation with Ward at the reception and needed to steady herself. If she was going to assume command of Bingham, now was not the time to appear weak or distracted at work.

She practiced her yoga routine, holding the poses for a few extra breaths to force the tension from her body. She took a steamy shower, working her favorite shea butter soap from L'Occitane over her body. After she had toweled herself dry, she massaged honey almond moisturizer into her skin. She breathed deeply and donned her soft, alpaca-blend bathrobe. Now I'm ready, she thought. Sitting at her antique pine desk situated by a large window in her spacious second-floor bedroom, she phoned her lawyer, Monica Burns, to tell her to expect Robert's revised estate plan from Ward's lawyer. Trying to keep her voice steady, Ghislaine asked Monica the question that had kept her up all night.

"Can he actually do this to me? Monica, you know how much I've invested in the company. You know how often I've had to clean up the mess from Ward's stupid decisions. Can he really have the power to push me out *now*? What legal recourse could he have?"

Monica hesitated. "Ghislaine, I won't know until I see the documents. But if Ward convinced Robert to change his estate plan, anything is possible. I can't speculate."

Ghislaine pursed her lips. Typical lawyer.

"Doesn't twenty-five years of marriage and my two decades at the firm count for anything?"

"Let's not jump to conclusions. As soon as I review everything, I'll call. Probably around three."

Ghislaine hung up. *Merde,* she cursed to herself. It was worse than she thought.

Ghislaine gazed out the windows at the heavy black clouds. She didn't need Monica Burns to tell her that Ward hated her despite all that she'd done for him. She had always treated Ward like a wayward younger brother and not the spoiled brat that he was. She had begged the USC dean to reinstate him after the drunken fraternity rampage. She had paid off young blondes with black eyes and bruised arms, bailed him out of jail for pulling a knife at a party, and negotiated a suspended sentence conditioned upon rehabilitation. When he finally sobered up enough to graduate, she helped him get into USC's business school by convincing Robert to pledge one million dollars to its endowment. When the bastard got his MBA but no offers, she had insisted to Robert that they employ him. And when he finally started to perform, she had argued in favor of giving him shares in the company, putting him in charge of the new Middle East and Africa division and making him president and a director. She wondered now whether

Ward despised her not in spite of her attempts to help him but because of them.

She looked down at the cars passing beneath the sycamores lining Beverly Glen. Raindrops began to speckle the asphalt. She loved the smell of grass after a rain. Perhaps Ward was bluffing. Perhaps she had nothing to fear. *Stop it.* Stop fooling yourself. A bitter fight loomed ahead just as surely as the rain would turn from drops to a torrent. Did she have the strength for a fight with Ward? Ward lacked the carnival-barker confidence and physical magnetism of his father, but he had the devil's cunning. He would be ten times more formidable than Robert.

Feeling a new surge of self-doubt, Ghislaine strode to her closet, reached inside the top drawer of the built-in cabinet, and fished around for a Christmas sock she'd received as a teenager. From inside the sock she extracted a nearly full, red-and-white pack of Belga cigarettes and a scarlet lighter. She walked into her tiled bathroom, closed the door, and opened the window. Then she lit up. Ghislaine had begun smoking more than thirty years ago to calm herself before skating competitions and she continued the habit during her brief acting career, sneaking a Belga or two before a particularly difficult scene. She despised herself for not being able to give up such a loathsome habit and did everything she could to hide it, first from Maman, then Robert, and now from Rob. But, as she inhaled and the sweet smoke filled her lungs, she closed her eyes and felt not guilt but relief. Her shoulder muscles, stiff as steel bars, began to melt. After each glorious puff, she stood up and carefully blew the smoke out the window. Halfway through the cigarette, her cell rang. Rob was calling. She reflexively flushed the cigarette down the toilet, as if he had knocked on her door, and then answered.

"Rob, darling. How are you doing today? I was just getting ready for work."

"Mom, I'm *fine*. How are *you*? I want to give you a ride to the office. I know it's your first day back and thought you might need some support."

"You are sweet, but, no, darling. I'll be okay. There isn't anything I can't handle, you know that."

"I know, Mom. But I'd like to help, if I can."

"Well, you can," she said and paused for a moment to choose her words. "I've been meaning to ask you. Does it bother you that I . . . that I'm not more upset, you know, about your father?"

"Mom. I loved dad, but his decision to leave you must have felt incredibly cruel. You're human. I *understand* why you're not more upset."

Ghislaine considered this for a moment. Despite his reassurance, she wondered why Rob wasn't more upset at her for not grieving Robert's death. Now was not a good time to probe.

"Listen, Robbie. I've got to get going. I'll see you later?"

"Of course. Mom, I love you."

"I love you, too, sweetheart."

To purge the taste and smell of tobacco, she gargled with Listerine and sprayed her Givenchy cologne over herself and in the air. Stepping from the bathroom, Ghislaine felt a sudden tide of confidence flow inside. Support? She didn't need anyone's support. She needed to get back to work. Bingham was where she would find the fortitude to fight Ward, not sulking in her bathroom. She remembered seeing *Gone with the Wind* for the first time and understanding intuitively what Tara meant to Scarlett O'Hara. Her past, her future, her fortune, her legacy, Bingham International was her Tara and she loved the company and drew strength from it just as Scarlett had loved and drew strength from Tara.

She dressed carefully, knowing that fine clothes imbued her with greater confidence. An hour later, she stood in front of the full-length mirror on the bathroom door. A fit, attractive woman gazed back at her. The elegant black pants suit and dark-gray silk blouse suited her tall frame; the single string of gleaming pearls and matching earrings offered perfect contrast. Her golden-blond hair, which normally fell just below her shoulders, was tied back in a bun to accent her high cheekbones and large turquoise eyes. A subtle, pinkish beige lip color complemented her skin tone without drawing attention to her full lips and wide mouth, which Ghislaine considered her worst feature. Ghislaine nodded with satisfaction that only a few laugh lines ran from her eyes. When she noticed new wrinkles flowing across her forehead, however, she frowned. The creases deepened. *Merde!*

Around two o'clock, Ghislaine steered her black BMW 720i through the pounding rain and down the steep, tree-lined drive-way of her midcentury home. A few minutes later, she turned left on the recently widened Santa Monica Boulevard, passed the de-serted Westfield Shopping Center, and then headed right be-tween the rows of office buildings that lined Avenue of the Stars. In a hundred yards, she escaped from the downpour into the gar-age of the forty-story modern granite-and-glass building in which Bingham International had its offices. Swearing at the speed bumps that made her crawl through the garage to her reserved spot, she parked and stepped out of the sedan with her black leather briefcase. A few seconds later, standing in the black gran-ite and pink limestone elevator lobby, Ghislaine closed her eyes briefly. She knew the layout of the Bingham office as well as the curve of her son's chin, but she wanted to anticipate each person she expected to meet between the lobby of the twenty-second floor and her office. She would need them on her side and she had to assume that Ward would have already begun to turn some of them against her.

The receptionist greeted her with a big hug. "We're all sorry about Mr. Bingham, but so glad to have you back," she whispered.

"Thank you." Ghislaine returned the embrace. "It means so much to be back. I've missed you all. How are Scott and Natalie? Did you have fun celebrating Natalie's third birthday?"

"Yes, we did. Thank you for asking," the receptionist said with a beaming smile.

Ghislaine pushed through the glass door in the wall behind reception and made her way through the honeycomb-like cubicles that stood in the middle of the back office. She waved to the young analysts and administrative assistants, greeting many by their first names. More than a few stood to hug her and extend their condolences. She ducked into each of the three exterior offices that lined the far wall and spoke briefly with the managers of the firm's Asia, Latin America, and Russia and Eastern Europe funds, all of whom she had recruited. She glanced to her far right at what had been Robert's corner office and saw Ward had already taken it over. With a shrug, she moved toward her own darkened office in the far left-hand corner, stopping briefly to greet Alan the harried office manager, who mumbled his sympathies. Anna, the firm's bespectacled accountant, who occupied a small office next to Alan's, came out and embraced Ghislaine.

"Whatever you need. Please let me know." Anna wiped tears from her eyes.

"Thank you, Anna. I'm grateful." Ghislaine secretly exhaled as she turned toward her office. Ward might be a skillful manipulator, but she felt confident now he couldn't undo the bond with her colleagues she had formed by caring for them over the years as human beings and not just as numbers on an expense report.

Pushing open her office door and flipping on the light, Ghislaine felt adrenaline course through her body. This place would give her the strength she needed. The only child of a single mother, Ghislaine had grown up without much family around her. She realized now that, after Rob, her employees were her family, an adopted family who *believed* in her, sometimes more than she believed in herself. It would be with their support and encouragement that she would defeat Ward and forge a new path for the company.

She sat down at her desk and began to sort through the stack of mail. Maman, a strong-willed, big-hearted woman, had always said, "Success smells more of sweat than perfume." Now more than ever before, Ghislaine knew her mother was right. She had been an athletic but ungainly figure skater and a photogenic but wooden actress. What success she had won always flowed from hard work. Her twenty-year business career proved it. She wasn't well educated, which Robert had often pointed out when she attempted to contribute to business discussions. *Use your smile to land the investors and leave the thinking to me,* he had said. But she had ignored Robert and instead remembered Maman, spending countless hours in business meetings listening intently and taking voluminous notes.

Years of tabulating customer's checks in her head at her mother's Brussels wine bar had given her a facility for numbers. But it was her smart questions, no matter how unappreciated at the time, her dogged research, and her growing body of knowledge from each successive deal that shaped her business acumen. Robert never acknowledged it, but over the last fifteen years, she knew they had become equal partners in Bingham's success. If she could teach herself how to structure international business deals, she could certainly beat back Ward's power play. The employees were behind her, Robbie was behind her; all she needed to do was lead. Did she have the audacity leadership required? The knot in her stomach told her she wasn't sure.

SEVEN

....

MONDAY, DECEMBER 13
LOS ANGELES

"*Sac a merde!*" Ghislaine shouted as Monica Burns finished explaining the estate plan.

"I have no idea what you've called him, but I'm sure it's right on. Robert made Ward his executor and directed that his shares in Bingham be divided between Ward and Rob. And he has given you a year to live in the home before it is sold and the proceeds divided between them."

Ghislaine was reeling. Not only did Robert's new estate plan disinherit her, but the papers explained that Ward intended to direct the $6 million dollars the company would receive from an insurance policy on Robert's life toward purchasing Robert's 60 percent of the company.

"At least now we understand what Ward is up to," Monica continued. "A six million dollar current value for Robert's shares would mean a value for the company of ten million dollars and no appreciation over the twenty-five years of your marriage. Your half of Robert's appreciation, which is the least I believe you're entitled to under the law, would be worth nothing. Half of zero is zero. Rob and Ward will each receive three million dollars, and

Aoki and Ward, as the only remaining shareholders of the firm, would each own half of the remaining shares. Not bad at all."

"*Fils de salope!*" Ghislaine bellowed into the phone. "Aoki doesn't want to run Bingham International, so Ward gets half the company but all the control! Of *my* company. How do we stop this?"

"We go to court and argue that Robert's shares are community property and cannot be sold without your consent. Since he acquired the shares before marriage, we may well lose. But, even if they're not community property, we argue the six-million-dollar valuation is bogus and you have a right to one-half of the increase in their value during your marriage."

"And demand the court stop the sale of the shares until a correct value is determined," Ghislaine interjected.

"Yes. We can make that demand," Monica said slowly. "But it's more likely that a judge will conclude your interest would be protected by whatever money damages he ultimately orders paid to you and won't stop the sale."

"That's bullshit," Ghislaine snapped. "I spent twenty years helping Robert build the firm and protecting its reputation. I'm an EVP and a director. No amount of money can compensate me for the loss of my reputation, my family, and my livelihood. "

"I understand how you feel, but Ward is the executor of Robert's estate and has the right to sell the shares. And Ward, as executor, now controls sixty percent of the company and individually owns another twenty percent. He can force the company to buy the shares."

Ghislaine pounded her desk.

"Yes, but in this case, valuation *is* control. If the value of Robert's sixty percent were, say, sixty million dollars, the increase since our marriage would be fifty-four million dollars and my share would be twenty-seven million dollars. The firm doesn't have sixty million dollars to buy Robert's shares from the estate and so the estate wouldn't have the cash to pay me my twenty-seven million. Ward would be forced to give me twenty-seven percent of the company and split thirty-three percent with Rob. Rob and I wouldn't have outright control, but *neither would he.*"

"Yes, but is the firm really worth a hundred million dollars now?" Monica asked.

Ghislaine shook her head in silence.

"No," she admitted finally. "It's not worth a hundred million right now, but it's worth more than ten million, especially if Rob's new Panama project has any value."

"Ghislaine. I know you're upset—you have every right to be—but you need to be realistic. We need to pick a fight we can win."

"Wait a minute. Aoki has certain veto rights as a minority shareholder. They can veto a buyback of company shares. Even with eighty percent of the company, Ward can't act without Aoki's approval."

"But why would Aoki refuse to support Ward?" Monica asked. "If Ward's scheme works, they end up with half of the company without investing a penny more."

"I don't know, but I have to try everything. We'll work on two tracks. You work on preparing the papers to be filed with the court. I'll meet with Ward to find out how he justifies the low valuation and somehow get him to postpone taking any action."

"How?"

"I don't know. I don't want to attack and push him to implement his plan quickly. I'll find a way to stroke his ego. I need time to approach Aoki. I don't know Taro Takayama well, but neither does Ward."

"Taro Takayama? Wasn't he accused of sexual harassment years ago?"

"Yes, why?"

"My partner has a new client who knows him extremely well."

"Who?"

"Duncan Luke. He's the lawyer who got Takayama off. A high-profile white-collar lawyer in town, specializing in international law and . . . tricky foreign situations."

"Can he help me with Takayama?"

"He just quit his practice to teach at Loyola Marymount, and I can tell you—since it's a matter of public record—he's going through a divorce so he may need the money."

A newly separated, unemployed lawyer, Ghislaine thought. Not promising.

"Maybe not. I'll have to figure this out on my own."

Monica cleared her throat.

"I'm sorry to bring this up at a delicate time, Ghislaine, but the ten-thousand-dollar retainer is almost gone. My partners have asked that I get another twenty-five thousand from you before we take on any more assignments."

"Monica, I don't have that kind of cash. My main assets are the house, the business, and my share of Rob's company in Panama. Can you take a note of some kind?"

"I would, of course, but my partners . . . well, I'm sorry."

"I see," Ghislaine exhaled. Her fingers fiddled with the pearls around her neck. A great deal of money was at stake, but this fight was about *more* than money. Ward wouldn't give a damn about tarnishing the company's reputation—*her reputation*—if it meant making a few dollars. She would fight for her company, for Rob's future and that of her extended family at Bingham. She set her jaw.

"I have some jewelry," she said at last. "A Thai sapphire-and-diamond necklace Robert gave me for our fifteenth anniversary worth at least a hundred thousand dollars."

"Ghislaine. I don't mean for you to sell things of sentimental value."

"*Sentimental value?* After what Robert has done to me, I'll sell it to the highest bidder. You'll have your twenty-five thousand. But I want a firm cap at fifty thousand through the court hearing."

"Fine. That seems fair. Thank you."

"I don't care about fair. I care about *winning.*"

"Well, if you really want to win, I think you should speak to Duncan Luke. He's quirky, but from what I've heard, he has a reputation for being able to fix just about any sticky situation."

Ça me fait chiers! Ghislaine fumed to herself. Another lawyer. Why do lawyers *always* recommend more lawyers when there's a problem to be solved?

"Fine. Get me a background report on this Duncan Luke so I can decide whether he can really help me with Takayama."

"Okay. I'll be in touch."

Ghislaine ended the call with a silent curse. She hated the idea of staking her life on a man, especially a lawyer. She scrolled through her cell phone to find the name of her jeweler. At least selling the necklace would feel good.

EIGHT

....

TUESDAY, DECEMBER 14
LOS ANGELES

Duncan Luke strolled across the sunken garden at LMU just after four in the afternoon. The sun bathed the grass and trees in a golden filigree of light. He stretched out his six-foot-four-inch frame on a bench under a towering palm tree and grimaced as he strained muscles already aching from the move yesterday into his new apartment. He tried to go over in his mind the draft outline for the first seminar and file away questions his students were likely to ask. After a futile few minutes, he shifted to what needed fixing at his new apartment in Playa del Rey, but could not focus. His desire to see Sam again consumed him.

He had often been away from Sam on business trips, and he was scheduled to see Sam tomorrow night, but he had never felt so cut off from his son. Duncan missed the squeak of his voice, the smear of ketchup on his cheek just beyond the reach of his tongue, the smell of fresh grass stains on his faded jeans. Longing for Sam turned to rage at Gracie, and his pulse began to race. He closed his eyes and tried to modulate his breathing to clear his mind. As a young wrestler he had learned deep-breathing techniques to prepare for a match. The breathing helped to calm his nerves, but he had little doubt Gracie would be a formidable foe.

Chimes from his BlackBerry startled him awake. It was Web Allen, Duncan's newly retained divorce attorney. Web was a stump of a man who looked like he had played high school football and been hit in the nose one too many times. His voice, a hoarse baritone, did little to dispel the impression of a man with more strength than smarts. But Duncan knew Web was a brilliant lawyer who had an intuitive feel for the vulnerabilities of his clients and their opponents, the emotional pressure points that he needed to protect or exploit. He was grateful Web had agreed to represent him on short notice.

"Hello, Web. How are you?"

"Fine, thank you," Web replied on speaker. Duncan could hear the din of traffic in the background. "Beginning to enjoy the cloistered life of contemplation and co-eds?"

"At least the former; unless you are a miracle worker, I'm still married. How did the meeting go?"

"That's why I called. Look, I'm on my way back to Manhattan Beach. Why don't we meet at Outlaws and discuss over a beer? I'm buying."

For Christ's sake, the news must be awful. Web had never invited him for a drink, let alone offered to pay.

"How bad is it?"

"Duncan," Web sighed. "You know your wife better than I do." Then he cackled. "Or, at least, you were supposed to before you got married. But, there's some good news, too. I'll see you at Outlaws at five?"

"Okay." Duncan looked at his watch. It was 4:45. The warmth of the offshore wind had given way to the chill of the onshore breeze. He rubbed the spot in his back where he had been slammed to the mat more than thirty years ago in the state wrestling finals. He had survived that match, so he knew he could get through the next months no matter how painful. Duncan raised himself from the grass and ambled to his car.

Duncan had never been to Outlaws, but he had heard of it over the years. The restaurant owed its reputation to its location, minutes from the beach, as well as to a large weathered sign of a reclining cowboy holding a frosty mug overflowing with beer. Inside, the bar was dark and smelled of stale beer. A solitary strand of white holiday lights hung near the windows. Two television sets suspended from the ceiling soundlessly broadcast the UCLA basketball game. Duncan felt his mouth go dry when he saw Web sitting at one of the tables near the front. This was a bad sign. Web was almost certainly counting on their proximity to the bar crowd to make sure Duncan would control himself.

"Hi, Web," Duncan croaked.

"Have a seat, my friend. Sounds like you could use a beer. What can I get you?"

Duncan cleared his throat. "A Sierra Nevada draft. Thanks."

Web caught the eye of the waitress, and a few minutes later a Sierra Nevada draft and a bottle of Negra Modelo for Web sat before them.

"How's your course prep coming along?" Another bad omen, Duncan thought. Web's trying to avoid talking about his meeting with Gracie's lawyer.

"Not well, but I have a title: 'Strategic Intelligence for International Business.'"

"Business intelligence?" Web snorted. "Sounds like an oxymoron."

"Very funny. It's the application of the principles and practices used in military and national intelligence agencies to global business. How a company gathers and analyzes information can generate a competitive edge or reduce risk or both."

"Public information?" Web inquired as he poured the dark beer into his glass.

"Not all, no. Some of it comes from private investigative work, some of it from non-public sources in industry and government."

"Sounds like a course on corporate espionage."

"I admit the line between corporate espionage and the gathering of competitive intelligence is blurry, but my strategies are completely legal—*and* ethical. Think of business intelligence as the sword and shield of any enterprise, a sword to obtain advantage and a shield to protect against risk," Duncan explained. "But you didn't offer to buy me a beer to learn about my seminar, did you?"

"No," Web replied as he sipped from his glass. "How's Sam doing?"

"I don't know," Duncan replied. "I haven't been with him since I was kicked out on Friday. I called him Saturday, Sunday, and last night and we talked for a minute or two but he seemed distracted. I spoke to Jenny Rice, his therapist, yesterday and she says it may be a few weeks more before he'll come around. The separation caught him completely by surprise, and surprise is never a good thing for Sam."

"I'm sorry," Web said as he drew circles with his finger in the moisture on the table in front of him. "It must be hard on you."

Duncan lowered his eyes. "Four days ago Sam screamed that he hated me. For each of the past four nights, I've had nightmares where Sam is frantic, desperate to get away from me. He runs into the ocean and swims away. I race after him but I can't move fast enough. I don't reach him until he's drowned."

Web asked quietly, "But the therapist thinks that your relationship with Sam is fundamentally sound?"

"She does and if she didn't then she'd be out of her fucking mind," Duncan snapped. When he saw Web's raised eyebrows, he continued in a quieter tone. "Yes, she believes the bond between us is durable and as Sam gradually feels better about himself and the world, our relationship will heal. It will take time, but seeing him tomorrow night and Saturday will be a good start." Duncan hesitated and then added quickly, "I want more time with him, though. As soon as possible. An overnight or two each week."

Web looked down into his beer mug.

"Can I give you some free advice?" He asked looking Duncan in the eye. "Sam will be your son forever. Don't get caught up in placing too much importance on any single day. The quality of your relationship with him is important, not the number of hours or days. Okay?"

Duncan stared at Web for a moment and then nodded.

Web sipped at his beer and folded his hands on the table. "I need to report what Gracie's lawyer said today. But, before I do, you know this is only their opening bid. Don't take it as a final result. Remember, you told me just to go and listen and not prepare a statement of our own position to save money."

Duncan felt his shoulders tighten. "I've litigated before so, *no*; I didn't want to spend any money before hearing what they had to say."

"I know you've had plenty of litigation experience, but it's a huge difference when you're the client. Anyway, on Sam, Gracie wants sole legal and physical custody."

"What the *fuck*," Duncan exclaimed and pounded the table so hard that his glass rattled. The bartender, a massive young man with a handlebar mustache, glared at Duncan.

"I know that this won't be easy to hear, but you've got to let me finish," Web said. "Gracie maintains that she is the primary caregiver and has become an expert on Sam's condition, an expertise critical to Sam's well-being and one which she says you lack. She believes that Sam's distancing himself from you is not a reaction to the separation but a consequence of the years you spent caring more about your career than your family."

Duncan threw up his hands. "I was working to support my family. Gracie knows how it is; it's only been five years since she left Goldman Sachs. For Christ's sake, she worked longer hours than I did when she was there."

"Her lawyer gave me a list Gracie put together of times over the past five years that you missed school conferences or meetings with therapists or after-school performances. They total fifty-five. She also gave me a report from Terri Hubert, the child psychologist at Sam's school. You won't enjoy reading it. Gracie is a model mother and you are . . . well, you won't enjoy reading it."

Good God, Gracie, Duncan thought. You are nothing if not thorough.

"Yes, I missed some conferences and meetings and a few performances. My practice required a lot of international travel. When Gracie quit her job to devote more time to Sam, we agreed that she would cover meetings and performances when I was away so one of us would always be there for Sam."

"You don't need to persuade me," Web said holding his hands up. "But you had better come up with a reason that you moved to Playa del Rey rather than stay in Santa Monica. You can be sure they will raise that, too. I would."

Duncan leaned back in his chair and folded his arms.

"Dammit, I had no warning that I was being kicked out of my house and would need to scramble to rent an apartment. I was lucky that an unfurnished, two-bedroom in Playa del Rey was put on Craigslist and Goodwill was open so I could move some furniture in yesterday. Christ, Web. Gracie wouldn't even let me take a stick of furniture from the house - too unsettling for Sam, she said, as if Sam cared more about losing an old couch than his father! Besides, PDR is near Sam's school, which is where I assumed that I would pick him up and drop him off after his visits. And he loves the beach as much as I do."

Web raised his eyebrows.

"Okay, okay," Duncan waved his hands. "And, it's close to LMU and far away from Gracie."

"Well, two out of three isn't bad," Web chuckled. "We'll have to work on your responses if you ever get deposed."

"Did you point out the fact that I gave up my practice primarily to spend more time with Sam?" Duncan asked as he leaned forward. "Was that putting career before family?"

"No, you asked me just to listen, remember? But Gracie's lawyer contends that you gave up your partnership to avoid paying support, not so you could spend more time with Sam. Gracie wants twenty-five thousand dollars a month based your compensation as a partner."

Duncan sputtered, "Twenty-five thousand a month is crazy, isn't it? My salary at LMU is based upon seventy-two thousand a year, and I have no guarantee I'll be hired full-time. Gracie has a couple of million dollars in her trust and will get half of the million dollars in my retirement account. Up until five years ago, she was making two-fifty a year plus bonus at Goldman. A judge wouldn't really order that amount, would he?"

"If a judge were to find that you intentionally gave up your partnership to avoid paying support, then, yes, he could. Neither one of you will get any money from the retirement account for many years so that's irrelevant. Gracie hasn't worked for five years and you can bet she will argue no mother of a child like Sam should be forced to work, not while there's a father capable of making over a million dollars. As for the two-point-five million dollars in Gracie's trust account, you know you have no claim on it—it's separate property. And you can be sure that the trustee will not distribute any money to her until all this is over."

Duncan looked up at the row of beer bottles lining the shelf just below the ceiling. Negra Modelo, Guinness, Tiger, Imperial were all there, but most were completely unknown. He wondered how long some of them had been there. What sad souls had placed them on the ledge?

Web reached over and touched his arm. "Duncan?"

"Yes. Okay. She wants sole custody of Sam and twenty-five thousand dollars a month. Let me guess," Duncan snapped. "Gracie wants the house, too, right?"

Web removed his glasses and rubbed his eyes. "You resigned from the partnership effective tomorrow. When Gracie filed for divorce on Friday, you were still a partner. They contend that at the time of filing the partnership interest was a community property asset owned half by Gracie and half by you just as the house is community property. Bottom line, Gracie is willing to trade your half of the house for her half of your partnership interest."

"So, let me get this straight," Duncan barked. "Gracie wants sole custody of Sam, twenty-five thousand a month in support out of my monthly salary of six thousand dollars, and the house including all of its furnishings and art in exchange for a partnership interest I will, effective tomorrow, no longer own? Does this sound like a reasonable offer to you?"

"Gracie's lawyer is reasonable, but I'm not sure she's ever had a client as smart and driven as your wife. One other thing. Ben Teller has relocated to the Valley. Fran Cooper is our new judge."

Duncan remembered Fran Cooper. Before going on the bench, she had been a plaintiff-side labor lawyer who specialized in representing women in sexual harassment or gender discrimination cases. He had never litigated against her but knew her by reputation as an aggressive advocate on behalf of her clients. Hadn't she been briefly, but unhappily, married? He was screwed.

Duncan took a deep breath and asked, "What's your advice?"

"We have been friends for a while. I have a lot of respect for you as a lawyer and a person. On the custody issues, I think we can get joint legal custody. I also think there's a good chance we can get joint physical custody, but much will depend on the views of Sam's personal therapist and whether they're consistent with the report of the school psychologist."

"Jenny Rice won't want to get involved," Duncan said with a shake of his head. "She'll be scared of hurting her reputation, costing her future clients. She'll claim privilege."

"Well, in that case, maybe you'd be better served by giving up on joint physical custody in return for greater visitation rights. We'll see how it looks in a week or so."

"What's your cheery advice on the support and property issues?"

"It's pretty common in these types of cases for courts to find that the non-working spouse keeps the house and the working spouse keeps the interest in the business. Their case for twenty-five thousand a month has more problems. Not easy to prove you gave up your partnership to avoid paying support. Still, the circumstantial evidence isn't good. Your resignation wasn't effective when Gracie filed for divorce and you must have known that your marriage was failing before you started looking for teaching jobs." Web took a long drink from his glass before continuing. "I would summarize my advice with one question: Do you think there's any way to get your partnership back?"

Duncan turned away from Web and gazed out the window at the blackening sky. Could he go back to a life of constant travel, clients expecting immediate results any day, any time, partners squabbling over compensation, offices, and clients? Divorce would mean he wouldn't see Sam every day but returning to practice wouldn't give him any more time with his son. Less, in truth. Besides, would getting his partnership back change Gracie's mind about ending their marriage? On Friday she seemed so happy to be rid of him.

Web rubbed his hand across his chin.

"Okay. I'll take your silence as a 'no.' Do you want to hear the good news?"

If Gracie ran away with a billionaire who hates kids...*that* would be good news, Duncan thought.

"Sure. I could use some good news."

"Look, I know between Sam's therapies, home improvements, and the retirement account, you didn't save much. I also know that Gracie withdrew half of the fifty thousand dollars in your joint securities account and half of the ten thousand dollars in your joint bank account. That leaves you with about thirty thousand dollars, max. You're hurting for cash."

Duncan gave Web a withering look.

"Okay, okay. The *good* news is that I may have an opportunity for you to make some money. It's a short-term gig and you could charge your old hourly rate. Whatever you decide to do, you're going to need some resources."

"To cover legal costs?"

"Yes," Web said, rapping his knuckles on the table. "We're giving you the friends and family rate, but friends and family pay on time. You owe us a ten-thousand-dollar retainer already, and it will take at least that much just to prepare a counterproposal."

Duncan stared at Web. "Okay. What's the job?"

"My partner, Monica Burns, has a client who may need your services. Her name is Ghislaine Bingham, EVP at Bingham International Group. BIG, as some call it."

"What's BIG?"

"It's a family-run investment management firm that specializes in private equity investments in emerging markets. Their main office is in Century City and they have about sixty employees."

"Emerging markets?" Duncan grunted. "Where?"

"Check out their website. They have four funds for investments in Asia, Latin America, Russia and Eastern Europe, and the Middle East and Africa, respectively. I recall seeing investments in an Indonesian textile company, a Russian shopping center concern, and a South African telecom company."

"Indonesia, Russia, South Africa? Someone has a healthy appetite for risk." Duncan shook his head. He doubted anyone at BIG had a clue how to identify let alone manage risks. "What's the problem?"

"BIG's voting shares are held by the family except for the Japanese company, Aoki, which holds a twenty percent stake."

"Taro Takayama's company?" Duncan interjected. "That shouldn't be a problem. He's a reasonable businessman."

"No, Aoki isn't the problem, the Bingham family is. Robert Bingham, BIG's founder, chairman and holder of sixty percent of the company just died. His wife—or almost ex-wife—and his son, who owns twenty percent, are fighting over control of the company. Ghislaine Bingham, the estranged widow, thinks Takayama is the key to her winning the fight."

"Which is why she needs me." Duncan sat back in his chair. He had an excellent relationship with Taka, particularly after he saved his friend from a sexual harassment suit that would have destroyed Aoki's U.S. operations. He could count on Taka being willing to listen to him, but he didn't see Taka wanting to get involved in a family dispute.

"I know it's not exactly how you envisioned spending the winter break, but will you at least meet her? I think you'll be surprised by how strong her case is," Web said. "Besides, I can't say it any other way. You need the money."

Duncan looked up from his drink at Web, remembering his own parents' broken marriage. His father, a distracted professor of organic chemistry at UCLA, somehow found the wherewithal to make sure Duncan and his brother knew they were loved after their mother ran off with a rich guy when Duncan was eight.

"Sam is my life and I will do *anything* to make sure he feels loved by his father. If helping Ghislaine Bingham gives me the money I need to fight for Sam, tell me when and where and I'll be there."

NINE

TUESDAY, DECEMBER 14
LOS ANGELES

Afte a day spent fielding condolence calls and redecorating his father's office, Ward needed a hot shower and a nice meal. Maybe he'd call the waitress at Spago he met last week. But he couldn't leave yet. His assistant had said Ghislaine wanted to discuss Robert's estate plan. Urgently. As he stepped into a small outside conference room at Bingham, he expected a tirade from his stepmother and couldn't wait to shout her down.

He found Ghislaine staring out the conference room window overlooking Constellation Avenue. When she turned to greet Ward, the look on her face shocked him. Her skin was pale and her slight smile was weary, even resigned. She looked down unable to hold his gaze. A predatory smile crept across Ward's face.

"Hello, Ghislaine," he said. "How are you holding up?"

"Oh, I'm doing pretty well. Thank you. Listen, I apologize for the way I behaved at the celebration."

"Apology accepted. Shall we sit down?"

"Oh. Of course," Ghislaine muttered. When they both had settled into their seats, she continued. "I'm sorry to trouble you but, even after speaking with Monica, I'm just so . . . well confused.

Robert and I are still, or, at least, at the time of his death, were married, weren't we?"

Ward folded his hands on the table before him. This was going to be easier than he thought. "Let me see if I can explain. Just stop me if you don't understand something."

Ghislaine lifted her eyes. "Oh, excuse me, what did you say?" She paused. "I haven't been sleeping well."

"I'm so sorry to hear that," Ward said. "Let me summarize quickly so we can both go home. Under my father's new will, his sixty percent in the company is to be divided between Rob and me. You have the right to stay in the house for a year rent free, after which the house will be sold and the proceeds split between Rob and me. We'll sell the art and personal property and you'll get half of that, of course. Perhaps a half million dollars or so."

"But I don't understand," Ghislaine said. "Monica said that Robert and I were like partners, that any judge would award me half of the increase in the value of his shares as—What did she say?—common property. Have I somehow got that wrong?"

Ward studied Ghislaine's face for any sign of a fight. All he saw were her swollen eyes fixed on the table in front of her.

"Well, I think you mean *community* property. In any event, that's an interesting theory, but the last two years have been awful for business, haven't they? The recession has diminished the value of our funds as well as our share of any appreciation. Our own investments suffered. But we didn't reduce staff or benefits or stop making donations to your charities, did we?" Ward continued, his voice rising. "We even added a new investment strategy looking at low-profit development projects to persuade Rob to return to work with us, against *my* better judgment. You insisted that we protect our reputation in the community and think long-term. Well, now," Ward slapped the table, "the consequence of *your* bad decisions is this: I am going to use the six million dollars from Robert's life insurance to buy his sixty percent interest from the estate."

"But that can't be right," Ghislaine murmured softly. "We were offered a hundred million dollars for the whole company just a few years ago."

"What a difference a few years makes." Ward laughed. "Six million for sixty percent is fair. But to appease you, I'll discuss the valuation with our independent accountants to make sure they can support it."

Ghislaine rose unsteadily from her chair. She massaged her left temple.

"I'm sorry, but my head is splitting and I can't follow the numbers you're giving me. Could we continue this discussion when I'm feeling better?"

"Of course," Ward replied as he rose and escorted Ghislaine to the door. He knew a beaten woman when he saw one.

"I have to travel to London, and when I get back I'll be inundated with holiday parties. Let's reconvene in early January. I'll make sure that we have the lawyers and accountants with us so we can address Monica's more creative arguments. In the meantime, I'm always available if you have any questions."

"Thank you, Ward," Ghislaine said. "I know we haven't always been in agreement, but I think we owe it to your father to work this out." Ward nodded as Ghislaine stepped out the door and disappeared down the hall. Taking over the company would be even easier than he had anticipated.

TEN

··

TUESDAY, DECEMBER 14
PANAMA CITY

For the third night since Rodrigo had led her down into the basement of the Golden Island, Magdalena lay staring up at the ceiling above her bed. She could not erase the image of Anna writhing as Rodrigo pressed his cigar against the sole of her foot. How low she had fallen! Magdalena rose abruptly from her bed, threw on her silk nightgown, and walked out of the bedroom. She gazed across the dark living room at the dim outline of her furniture, the green glow of the surge protector softly lighting the new audio system and television set. A pale white orchid sat on the teak dining table. All gifts from Rodrigo, whose generosity knew no bounds. The source of such unselfish munificence could not be responsible for what happened to Anna. Magdalena alone was to blame.

She turned and entered the small kitchen. She removed a long, thin carving knife from its wooden stand and examined the blade. She ran it lightly over the veins on the underside of her left arm, not as a butcher might run a blade over a leather strap but lightly, like the caress of the mother she had never known, like the tender touch with which she had often stroked Anna's cheek. And now Anna was gone, or worse, because of what Magdalena had done.

Unbearable guilt suffocated her soul. She leaned over the sink, plugged the drain, and turned on a stream of warm water. When it was half full, she extended her left wrist into the gathering pool and felt the warmth embrace her skin like a bath, cleansing, purifying. She closed her eyes and raised the knife.

A soft knock at the door broke her concentration. "Magdalena?" whispered a high-pitched voice. It was Luz, a young Colombian woman who lived with three other girls in an apartment down the hall. Luz knocked again and called more loudly, "Magdalena? Are you awake?" Magdalena sighed and turned the water off. She placed the knife on the counter and walked to the door. Magdalena adored Luz. They had met about two months ago at the elevator, discovered they both came from Cartagena, and had become fast friends in only a few weeks. Magdalena loved Luz's bawdy sense of humor and wicked laugh. She switched on the lights and opened the door.

"*Hola!* Am I disturbing you? Do you not wish my company tonight?"

"No, my friend. Come in. You are home early." Magdalena slowly closed the door behind her friend, a short, sultry twenty-two-year-old.

"Ha! A farmer from Nebraska with the face of a goat and the skin of a pig brought me back to his room," Luz explained in rapid Colombian Spanish. "When I threw off my dress, his eyes bulged like eggs. Can you imagine? The poor man had never seen a naked woman before! His wife insists that they make love with her clothes on and their eyes closed. Anyway, the mere sight of me had him spouting like a fountain," she said gesturing upward with her hands. "He paid extra and let me leave early, so I thought we might sit and talk about Cartagena. I am so homesick. I miss my children."

Suddenly Luz stopped, examined Magdalena, reached up and cradled her face. "Your eyes are dull and your skin is pale. Magdalena! Are you sick?" demanded Luz. "If you are not well, I will make you some tea to soothe you," the Colombian girl clucked and strode into the kitchen. When she saw the carving knife on the counter and the pool of clean, warm water in the sink, she spun around.

"Magdalena, what has happened?" Luz took Magdalena's hands and led her to the couch. They sat down and Luz stroked her forehead. *"Dime, Magdalena. Dime,"* she whispered.

"I am not sick, but I have not been able to sleep or eat since Sunday. Oh, Luz, I did something terrible to a Panamanian girl who befriended me." Magdalena began to sob and told Luz what had happened on Sunday.

"But why in the name of God do you blame yourself?" Luz demanded when Magdalena had finished. "Rodrigo is the *bastardo.*"

"No. The money I gave Anna *did* come from Rodrigo. And he has been very generous to her family and to her. I should have known he would be enraged. I should have known what would happen to her."

"Do you really believe the money Rodrigo gives you is not yours to do with as you please? That he has been *generous* to Anna and her family? You tried to help a friend return to her home. You are no more responsible for the horrible things Rodrigo did than if Anna had been attacked by wild dogs."

"Rodrigo is *not* a wild dog!" Magdalena objected. "Look," Magdalena swept her arm over the room. "Look at how much he has given to me."

"Oh, Magdalena, I see only things, not feelings. They are lovely things. But make no mistake, Rodrigo believes he owns everything in his club and in this apartment, including you." Magdalena sobbed harder. Luz hesitated and after a moment continued.

"Dear one, do you not know? We are both whores—only I know what I am and you . . . you live in some fantasy. Do you not realize that someday he will tire of you and send you back to Colombia?"

"No! Rodrigo would never do that to *me*. He knows what would happen if I went back to Cartagena. No, he would never send me back. Not after I have been with him for so long. I am like a wife to him."

"*Magdalena*. For one so very smart, you sound completely crazy. There is a knife on the kitchen counter and a sink full of water. Why? Your dream has become a nightmare and you are too terrified to wake up. Cutting yourself so you sleep forever is no answer. God forbids it! *I* forbid it," Luz cried. "Anna is not your fault. Wake up! Before it's too late." Magdalena started weeping again and Luz held her until she stopped.

"So, you are right," she finally took Luz's hands into hers and clasped them against her chest. "I am a whore. But Rodrigo *saved* me when I came to Panama. I had lost faith in God and done terrible things. Oh, Luz, there are things I have never told you about my life in Cartagena."

"Let me share your burden of grief. Tell me what happened to you."

Luz took Magdalena's hand and sat with her until dawn as she recounted the story of her life in Cartagena.

Ten years ago Magdalena stood before Sister Margarita's worn wooden desk in her brown plastic sandals, American blue jeans, and aqua-blue Beatles "Yellow Submarine" T-shirt, all gifts of Catholic missionaries who had visited the orphanage. The only store-bought dress she had ever worn was her confirmation dress, which she shared with two other girls. Sister Margarita, a tiny, leathery woman dressed in a habit, beamed at Magdalena over her black spectacles.

"We are so proud of you. *God* is so proud of you. You are the first orphan from *Casa Corazon* to pass the entrance examination to the university here. When God brought you to us almost eighteen years ago, only He could have known what joy you would give us all. You have been like a little Sister, helping us care for the young ones during the day and studying late into the night to improve your mind so that you might better serve Him when your time came." Sister Margarita stood and walked over to Magdalena, taking her face in her hands and looking up into her almond eyes.

"We prayed that you would pass your examination so, God willing, you could go to university and someday return to run our school. When our prayers were answered, we prayed again that He might provide the means to send you to the university." Sister Margarita let her hands fall from Magdalena's face. She glanced up at the cross hanging on the wall to her right and pressed her lips together. "And our prayers have been answered, *querida*," she said turning to face Magdalena. "A week ago, I spoke to one of our benefactors about you and he has agreed to meet you tonight. If you impress him, he has agreed to pay for your education. Is that not wonderful news?" she asked as tears began to fall from her cheeks to the concrete floor.

"I am so grateful to the Sisters and you for what you have done for me," Magdalena whispered, eyes lowered to her feet. "But why can't I stay here and attend university? Why must I leave?"

"You have no place here among the Sisters right now. You have abilities that only living in the outside world can develop. Do not be afraid," Sister Margarita replied rubbing the moisture from her eyes. "God will protect you until you return to us. *Vaya con Dios mi hermana pequena.*" She hugged Magdalena and sent her back to her room.

Magdalena spent the next two hours scrubbing her body, ironing the hand-sewn white cotton dress she wore to Mass, and combing her hair until it shined. As she prepared, she imagined her benefactor as a gray-haired man with a wrinkled face who would test her with question after question to determine whether she was worthy of his help. She set to memory a long speech to persuade him that helping her to attend the university would serve God and the orphanage.

A driver picked Magdalena up that evening and drove her to a townhouse in the old city behind Santo Domingo Church. The man was waiting for her on a shady terrace that looked out across the old city to the ocean.

"Please, come sit down here beside me," he waved to her. Magdalena obeyed and waited for his questions with a straight back, her hands folded in her lap. The man said not a word, but reclined in his chair and smoked a cigarette as the sun faded into the sea.

"You are even more beautiful than Sister Margarita had led me to hope."

Was this a test? "All children are beautiful in His eyes," she replied. Forgetting the speech she had crafted, the words tumbled out of her mouth. "Sir, please believe me, my only desire in life is to be educated so I can help God and the orphanage. How can I persuade you to help me?"

The benefactor laughed softly. "I do not need proof of your intelligence. I have already decided to help you but," he said looking into Magdalena's eyes, "on condition that you help me in return."

"I do not understand, sir. I would be willing to do anything, but how could an orphan like me help a rich man like you?"

"I live in Bogotá, but I come to Cartagena frequently on business. I am often lonely and desire company. The university is within walking distance so you could easily attend classes," he paused and then continued, "while you stayed with me." The benefactor reached over and stroked Magdalena's hand.

Magdalena stared down at the benefactor's hand touching hers. She felt sick. He was not gray and wrinkled, but she had never kissed a boy, never even held a boy's hand. She moved her hand away. "Thank you, sir. I . . . I do not wish to offend you because I know how generous you have been to the orphanage and I have no greater desire than to attend the university, but I am certain that Sister Margarita would find out if I were to stay with you. I could not bear to break her heart," Magdalena pleaded.

The benefactor smiled and took Magdalena's hand in his. "You are an intelligent girl. Why do you think Sister Margarita asked you to come here tonight?"

Magdalena's mouth dropped open. After a moment she began to shake. Holding her head in her hands, she wept. The benefactor took out a handkerchief and dried her tears. He stood up and held out his hand. Magdalena gazed up at him. Her lips trembled and, despite the warm night, chills ran through her body. The benefactor leaned down, took her hands, and led her up to his bedroom.

He placed a pink silk robe on the bed, lowered the light, and left the room. When he returned, Magdalena lay on top of the bed dressed only in the silk robe, hands folded over her chest, eyes fixed on the ceiling directly above. She would do as Sister Margarita had commanded and place herself in God's hands.

"Close your eyes, Magdalena," the benefactor whispered. He took his clothes off and lay next to her, letting the warmth of their bodies flow together. He ran his hand gently over her neck, her breasts, and finally between her legs. She shuddered as a strange glow grew where he touched her. "Do not be afraid, Magdalena," he whispered. He lifted her arms from her chest, untied her robe, and mounted her.

After six months, the benefactor's business in Cartagena failed. He found Magdalena an apartment, kissed her farewell, and left her with enough money to live for half a year. During that time, Magdalena enjoyed her freedom and continued to do well with her studies, hoping to graduate in three years and return to the orphanage. As the money dwindled, however, she grew more and more fearful she would fail. She wrote to Sister Margarita asking for money but received only a short reply, "We do not have enough money to serve our orphans, your little brothers and sister. Remember, dear child, God helps those who help themselves." Magdalena looked for work but could not find a job that would support her and her studies. Just after her nineteenth birthday, she found herself in the cathedral praying for guidance. As she prayed, she caught her reflection in a mirror on the candlelit altar and realized God had given her the gift of beauty. She would use that gift to finish her studies and serve Him.

One night, a year later, she strolled to the Café del Mar as she had done two nights a week for months since praying in the cathedral. The café had a spectacular view of the setting sun and attracted wealthy men, rich university boys, and the occasional *Norteamericano.* Magdalena always wore a simple white linen dress and a magenta shawl. She would order a *café con leche* and wait, staring out at the sea. Some nights, no one would approach her. This night, however, she had taken only a few sips before a handsome young man walked up.

"Forgive me for intruding, *señorita,*" he began. "But would it be too much of an imposition if I joined you?" Magdalena did not recognize the young man, but he was well dressed and had good manners, unlike some others whose approach she would have refused. She indicated with a slight nod of her head that she did not object to his company. He ordered a Bavaria beer and, as they drank and talked, she learned that he was the son of a general in the army and that he, too, studied at the university. She marveled at his stories of having visited Panama and Miami and so, when he asked her to dinner, she accepted provided that they would dine at the Café del Mar.

As they ate, Magdalena hinted, as she had learned to do, at her difficult circumstances and her desire to graduate so that she could return to the orphanage. "But *señorita*," the young man said, "I cannot allow such a beautiful woman to endure any hardship. Please tell me how I might assist you," he begged. Magdalena looked the young man in the eyes for several seconds. She took out her pen and wrote "US$250" on the paper napkin beside her *café*. The young man smiled and reached for his wallet. When he had placed the money underneath her napkin, he raised his eyebrows and tilted his head forward slightly. Magdalena hesitated for a moment. Finally, she shrugged, wrote her address and the time, nine o'clock, on the napkin beside his beer. Folding her napkin with the money in it, she placed it in her purse. She rose and the young man kissed her hand as she departed.

At nine o'clock, Magdalena heard a rap on her door. She peered through the peephole and saw the young man holding a bouquet of roses. When she opened the door for him, several other young men jumped out from around the corner and pushed her into the apartment. The handsome young man threw down the roses and put his hand over Magdalena's mouth to stifle her scream. She bit his hand hard, drawing blood. He picked her up and threw her onto her bed. As he straddled her, Magdalena kicked out and caught her betrayer between his legs. He yowled, grabbed her right hand, and struck her just above the left eye. Stunned by the blow, Magdalena resisted no further. When the young men had finished raping her, they closed her door and scampered away laughing.

Magdalena lay on the bed as they had left her until the night air grew cold. How could He allow this to happen to her? Whether she was so unworthy or God so uncaring made little difference to her fate. She felt abandoned and would no longer dedicate her life to His service. She left her apartment days later, only after the bruise had healed, but she always wore a scarf over her head and dark glasses. She was terrified of seeing the general's son.

One day an older Spanish woman who was a professor at the university approached her as she was buying fruit.

"I have heard, my dear, that you had an unfortunate accident and you have no family to help you. If I may speak as one who cares for young women who have been treated as you have, I fear for your safety if you stay in Cartagena. I can arrange for you to travel to Panama, where you could make thousands of dollars a month just for dancing and entertaining *Norteamericanos* in a nightclub." When Magdalena objected, the Spanish woman held up her hand. "I wish only to protect you and to make you rich so you no longer have to depend on men like the general's son. I hope you will think of me as you would your mother just as I think of you as my daughter. I promise you, dear daughter, that in Panama your employer will keep you safe."

The rape had filled Magdalena with terror. The offer to leave Colombia and seek a better, safer life in Panama was too tempting. Still, she was afraid the general's son would do to other young women what he had done to her. When she told the Spanish woman her fear, the woman grinned. Two nights later, the general's son was walking home from a bar in the Walled City. Three thugs attacked him, raped him with a wooden police stick, and cut him between his legs so he could no longer torment girls. As they walked away, they threw money on him and told him it was from Magdalena. When Magdalena heard what had happened to the general's son, she knew she had to leave Colombia immediately. And never return.

ELEVEN

....

WEDNESDAY, DECEMBER 15
LOS ANGELES

G hislaine sat at a window table and stared out at the grassy terraced courtyard behind the CAA building. She loved the food at Craft Los Angeles, but she could only pick at her lunch. She tried to focus on the complaints of a wealthy investor in their Latin America Fund about the poor quality of after-school programs at her children's private school, but the memory of her conversation with Ward distracted her. Six million dollars is absurd! Her contribution to the company had been worth *nothing*? She fumed as she spooned more roasted cauliflower on her plate and pushed the florets around in their olive oil, coriander, and cumin. The halibut *crudo* bathed in oil, lemon, and red pepper flakes stared up at her. She couldn't stomach any of it, no matter how good it looked.

Ghislaine's cell phone rang, interrupting the woman's diatribe about the merits of piano over violin instruction.

"I'm so sorry," Ghislaine said. "I better take this. It's my lawyer. We have so many details to handle with Robert's estate. I'll be just a minute." She excused herself from the table and headed to the ladies room. "Monica, I've been waiting to hear from you. Do you have the report on Duncan Luke? I don't have much time. I need to figure out my strategy with Aoki."

"Yes, we have it. Should we go over it now?"

"I can't. I'm at a lunch with one of our investors. Could you send it to my private email address? I'll call as soon as I've read it."

Ghislaine returned to her lunch and managed to focus long enough to wrestle a bigger commitment to their next Latin America fund before running back to the office to print and read the report. Then she called Monica.

"I'm ready to discuss Duncan Luke," Ghislaine said and closed the door to her office.

"Good. What are your impressions?"

"He seems unstable. Why else would his wife leave him and file for sole custody of their son? And why would he leave private practice to *teach*?"

"Let's address the second question first. I don't know him personally, but I think it's possible he just burned out. Remember, he practiced law for twenty-five years, including five at the State Department, thirteen as an Assistant U.S. Attorney prosecuting international criminal activity, including some high-profile sex trafficking cases, and seven years as a partner at Burton, Engelman and Conley working on highly sensitive cross-border criminal and civil matters. A lot of lawyers dream of escaping. Luke might be one of the few who actually makes it out."

"And you think I should hire someone who wants to run away from the kind of work I need him to do?"

"Look, you'd be asking for a week of his time, tops, not a lifetime commitment. Besides, he has a good pedigree—Berkeley International Relations and Stanford Law—and he's known as an excellent lawyer. I think he's worth a meeting."

"What about his wife? The divorce? What's that about?"

"I don't know her motivation, but she filed just before his resignation became effective, so I can speculate she did so to strengthen her argument for support and a favorable property split. As for seeking sole custody, she states in her court filings that his practice took him away from home often and their boy, Samuel, who will be ten later this month, has a form of autism. She argues that their son's well-being is completely in her hands, which means she can't work either."

"I see," Ghislaine murmured. Rob's learning disability had been difficult to manage, but *autism*. "Whenever I hear about a child with such a severe disability, I feel fortunate Robbie is so healthy and then feel guilty to feel that way."

"I know how you feel," said Monica in a brisk tone. Ghislaine rolled her eyes at the fake sympathy. No one except a parent could possibly understand how it felt to watch her child struggle. Even now, it was impossible for Ghislaine to find the words to describe the torment of feeling profoundly responsible and yet completely helpless at the same time.

"Monica, I still do not see why you think I should talk to Duncan Luke about Aoki. Taro Takayama doesn't even trust me, and he's known me for years."

"In 2002, when Takayama was an executive at Aoki's U.S. subsidiary, Luke defended him in a sexual harassment suit brought by his female assistant. She claimed Takayama had created a hostile work environment by asking her to arrange for business meetings at hostess clubs in Little Tokyo and Koreatown and then requiring her to accompany him to those meetings."

"Hostess clubs are a part of business culture in Japan," Ghislaine interrupted. "Even I've been taken to a club."

"Yes, but an American jury wouldn't understand that, so Luke had to come up with something convincing. During the discovery process, he found evidence the assistant had worked part-time as a hostess at the Blue Moulin in Tokyo. He produced pictures of her smiling and posing with three other hostesses holding a sign that read, 'Winners of 2000 Blue Moulin Beauty Contest.' Luke persuaded the jury, made up of eight women and four men no less, that Takayama's assistant could not claim hostess clubs in Los Angeles were abusive if she had willingly immersed herself in the same environment in Tokyo. I usually disdain male lawyers who blame female victims in order to get their male clients off, but I think Luke did well by Takayama. I'm not sure I would have unearthed the pictures or realized their significance."

"So he's a good lawyer and I should ignore his personal life?" Ghislaine probed.

"Former colleagues have described him as 'intelligent,' 'hard-working,' 'relentlessly curious,' and a 'lawyer with a creative, un-conventional mind.' Those who have opposed him in court have said he's 'quirky,' 'distractible,' 'not strong on the law,' and 'quick-tempered.' There are a few reports that he sometimes drinks too much, but that's hardly disqualifying for a lawyer. He could be brilliant or he could be a bust. But, to be blunt, Taro Takayama probably trusts Luke more than he trusts you. You'll just have to meet him to decide whether you can trust him, too."

"Fine, but I don't want to wait in case he doesn't work out. Can we do this at my house at four this afternoon? I need to keep this discreet."

"I'm available, but I'll confirm with Web Allen for Luke. I'm sure it will be fine. Web says Luke is highly motivated to move forward—he needs the money."

"Ha! Who doesn't? Maybe he should have stuck with private practice. Thank you, Monica. See you at four."

Ghislaine hung up, gathered her things, and turned to shut down her computer. She stared at the picture of Duncan Luke attached with the report. He seemed tall, even taller than Rob, but heavier. His curly black hair, deep-set eyes, and pale skin reminded her of someone who spent too much time in libraries. She examined his face. He had the faraway look of a six-year-old boy staring out a classroom window on a sunny day. This was the Duncan Luke who was going to help her? *Merde!*

TWELVE

....

WEDNESDAY, DECEMBER 15
LOS ANGELES

Duncan Luke exited the 405 at Sunset and headed east. He told himself to calm down. He didn't appreciate being summoned to meet a potential client, particularly two hours before he was to see Sam for the first time since he'd been kicked out, but he needed the money and Web seemed to think Ghislaine Bingham would pay full fare. He exhaled and glanced to his left where the roads wound up the wooded canyons of Bel Air. As he drove up a hill, the snow-capped peaks of the San Gabriel Mountains came briefly into view and the red brick buildings and leafy campus of UCLA spread out below to his right.

Just before reaching Beverly Hills, he turned right onto the wide, Sycamore-lined South Beverly Glen Boulevard. When he reached the driveway at 220, he pulled up to the large, iron gate and punched the speaker button.

"Duncan Luke to see Ghislaine Bingham."

"Yes, sir, Mr. Luke. Mrs. Bingham is expecting you. I'll open the gate."

The gate slowly swung open and Duncan continued up a concrete driveway bordered by sandstone pavers. Large wide-leaf maple trees shaded the driveway, which gracefully curved up to stop before a grand, two-story 1950s Mediterranean home. Three other cars sat in the driveway, including Web's, all BMWs. He parked his Acura next to Web's black Beemer, grabbed his briefcase and strolled over to the entrance. An elderly Hispanic housekeeper clad in a white apron was waiting by the front door.

"Welcome, Mr. Luke." She smiled. "Please, follow me."

He nodded and followed her into a red-tile entry hall over which hung a magnificent Mexican iron chandelier. A carpeted stairway led up to the second floor. Prints by Robert Rauschenberg, Jasper Johns, and Sam Francis dotted the staircase wall.

Before Duncan could orient himself, the housekeeper turned abruptly into a large rectangular room on the right and he hurried to keep up with her. The room was filled with a soft glow from handsome floor-to-ceiling windows that looked out onto the shaded driveway. A glossy black baby grand piano rested in the far left corner. The end of the piano room opened into a sunken living room that was as large as his Playa del Rey apartment. Light streamed in from three French doors on the left, which led to a backyard. Five people sat around three sides of an enormous rectangular pine coffee table.

Web rose from a chair to Duncan's right. A stocky woman with copper-colored hair and a dark-green-and-tangerine scarf sat to Duncan's left and nodded. This must be Monica Burns, Duncan thought.

"Hello, Duncan." Web greeted him and they shook hands. "I'd like you to meet Ghislaine Bingham."

A tall, slender woman with shoulder-length hair the color of butterscotch stood up from an elegant sofa across the table. She wore a cream-colored blouse and a highly tailored, navy-blue pants suit, a businesswoman's attire but elegant nonetheless. Duncan was startled. He hadn't pictured Ghislaine Bingham as a stunningly beautiful woman.

Ghislaine smiled warmly and extended her hand horizontally, palm down.

"Welcome, Duncan, if I may call you that," she said in a low, gravelly voice. Duncan took her long graceful hand in his large stubby one. He felt a strange compulsion to kneel before her like a knight before his queen. Ghislaine released his hand.

"I'm very grateful to you for agreeing to meet on such short notice. Let me introduce you to my son, Rob."

A handsome, well-built young man with short-cropped, sandy hair stood at her right. His light-gray suit, blue button-down shirt, and crimson necktie could have come directly from a Brooks Brothers catalogue, but he had an easy-going smile, an athletic bearing, and his ruddy cheeks glowed—from a recent ski trip, Duncan guessed.

Rob gripped his hand firmly. "Nice to meet you."

"And this is my assistant, M. D. Corrales." Ghislaine turned to her left where a petite young woman in a black pinstriped suit stood holding a yellow pad in one hand and a pen in another. Duncan thought she seemed overly serious, but her lovely heart-shaped face and thick, glossy, shoulder-length black hair spoke to something softer.

She shook Duncan's hand without a word.

The stocky woman rose and introduced herself.

"Duncan, I'm Monica Burns. Nice to finally meet you. I've only known you by reputation." Duncan cocked his head to the side and was about to make a self-deprecating joke about his reputation but thought better of it. Out of the corner of his eye, Duncan could see Ghislaine drumming her fingers on crossed arms.

"Please everyone, have a seat." Ghislaine pointed Duncan to a particularly overstuffed armchair opposite her. "Duncan, would you like anything to drink? Perrier? My housekeeper makes a delightful strawberry iced tea."

"No. I'm fine. Thanks."

"Well, then, I know you must be very busy so shall we begin? Have you been briefed on my case?" Ghislaine asked as she and the others sat down.

Duncan let his briefcase drop to the floor with a thud, but did not sit down. He knew pointing out problems wasn't the best way to start a relationship, but part of his job was to protect clients from themselves.

"Before we start, I'd like to confirm who would be my client, that is, if I were to take this assignment."

"You would be representing me," Ghislaine replied.

"Then, why are Mr. Bingham and Ms. Corrales here?"

Ghislaine furrowed her brow, leaned back, and folded her hands in her lap. "Rob is my son and M.D. works for me. May I ask why you're concerned?" she inquired, her voice betraying frustration.

"Are they employees of Bingham International?"

"Yes, M.D. and I are, but I don't see why that's important," Rob interrupted. "My mother and I have no secrets. And M.D. is a valued member of my mother's team."

Out of the corner of his eye, Duncan could see M.D. flush briefly and regain her composure. Ghislaine smiled warmly at Rob and faced Duncan.

"Rob is absolutely correct. They both have my absolute confidence."

"Mrs. Bingham," Duncan began.

"Please, call me Ghislaine."

"All right, Ghislaine. From what I've been told, I believe that your personal interest and the interest of your company may well differ in this matter. If so, I don't think we do Ms. Corrales or your son any service by having them participate in this conversation. What if, for example, your stepson asked them to report to him, as president of the company, and tell him what was said here? Would they be able to refuse? Would you feel comfortable having them lie?"

Ghislaine straightened her back. "There is no reason whatsoever why Ward Bingham should find out about this meeting, unless," she added, leaning forward, "*you* plan to tell him."

"Hold on, hold on," interrupted Web, raising his palms up as if to quiet a noisy class. "Whatever is said here is a matter of client confidentiality that Duncan would never reveal without your permission. Isn't that right, Duncan?"

"Yes, that's right. Mrs. Bingham, I mean, Ghislaine, I have no idea how Ward might learn of this meeting, but I would advise you, based on two-and-a-half decades of experience helping clients protect secrets, it would be wise to assume he will. Protecting yourself from your stepson will be difficult enough without handing him another weapon to use against you."

"Thank you for your lecture on the difficulty of preserving confidences," Ghislaine declared through a stiff smile. "But I'm not hiring you to advise me on how to run my business."

Duncan sighed. Maybe this wasn't a good fit, he thought as he glanced up at the decorative moldings on the ceiling and wondered why anyone bothered with such things. Who decided whether they should be vines or flowers or ropes, whether they should be painted or not? And, if painted, then what color? Duncan looked again at Ghislaine Bingham. Her eyes were the same sky-blue color as the moldings.

Ghislaine tapped her foot impatiently. "Are you still with us, Duncan?"

"Yes, I'm sorry," Duncan replied, a trace of irritation creeping into his voice. "When I represent someone, my advice is not delivered wrapped in neat packages of my client's choosing. Problems tend to be fluid and messy and have the habit of spilling out in unpredictable ways. Either you accept that I will give you all the advice I think necessary to address the problem you've asked me to help you with or . . . or you can find someone else."

Ghislaine stared wide-eyed at Duncan. She puckered her lips like a little girl who had been asked to eat some detested vegetable.

Rob's eyes glanced at his mother and then focused on Duncan. "Well, thank you for coming, Mr. Luke. I think that concludes our discussion." Duncan shrugged and reached down for his briefcase.

Web stood. "Wait, Duncan. I think we're working at cross-purposes here. I don't think Rob understands you're just trying to protect his mother."

"Yes, I agree with Web. Rob, darling," Ghislaine intervened. "It may be better if you and M.D. were not here. We don't want to spook Ward into accelerating his plan and certainly don't want him to have any justification for firing either of you. I need you both with me."

"But mother . . ." Rob started to object.

"Please go, Robbie. M.D., would you please wait with Rob in my office?" M.D. nodded at Ghislaine, rose abruptly, and strode out of the room ahead of Rob.

"Perhaps, *now,* I can tell you what I need done?" Ghislaine demanded. Gone were the warm smile and welcoming handshake. Duncan lowered himself into the soft armchair and immediately struggled to find a comfortable spot for his bulky body. Finally, he leaned back, rested his hands on his thighs and nodded.

"My stepson is trying to cheat me out of my interest in Bingham and remove me as an officer and director in the business that I spent the last two decades building with my now-deceased husband. I plan to fight him over his valuation of our company," she declared with a flip of her wrist, "but to buy back Robert's shares, he needs Aoki's consent. I want you to use your influence with Taro Takayama to persuade him to support me and vote against Ward. It's that simple."

Duncan marveled at Ghislaine's crisp delivery. She has a good brain, he thought, although perhaps not quite as good as she believes. But something about her seemed brittle, too, as if she were trying too hard to demonstrate her command of the situation. Beauty could be a curse as well as a blessing, Duncan thought, as he coughed slightly to clear his throat and shifted his body forward.

"I'm afraid it's not simple. I would offend Takayama-san if I tried to use our friendship to obtain a favor for a client. You would not get what you want and I would lose a close friend. More important, he does not own Aoki. He *is* president, but he is subject to the oversight of a board of directors. He could not act against the interests of Aoki even if I asked him to, which I would not, and he wanted to oblige me, which he would not."

"Well, then," Ghislaine blurted. "What is the purpose of this meeting if you knew you couldn't help me? Forgive my impatience, but I have no time for *this*." She rose abruptly.

Duncan leaned back and put his hands behind his head. "I didn't say I *couldn't* help you. I said I wouldn't ask Takayama-san to act against the best interests of his company. I can get a meeting with him at any time. He trusts me, and he will listen to what I say. Two key aspects to my relationship with him which I would guess you lack."

"Lawyers and meetings." Ghislaine threw up her hands. "What good is a meeting? I need action. I need results. I need them *now*," she insisted, chopping the air with her slender right hand. "You don't understand, Duncan Luke. Bingham is my *life*. I can't lose it."

Duncan squinted up at Ghislaine. Were those tears in her eyes? The last few days had taught him all too well what it was like to fear losing someone you loved. Could Ghislaine Bingham possibly love her company the way he loved Sam? He sank deeper into the armchair as if her frustration had pushed his body backward.

"I know you're anxious to move quickly, but we will have only one chance to persuade Takayama-san," he replied. "Acting without good intelligence is like cooking in the dark— you're more likely to burn yourself than to make a good meal. As I've told many clients, good business intelligence is the sword and shield of any enterprise."

Duncan paused to see if anyone was listening. Web and Monica shifted uncomfortably in their seats. Ghislaine stood across from him staring at the floor. He realized he needed to be more specific. "To persuade Aoki to help you, we have to gather and analyze intelligence on Aoki's business and develop an argument why supporting you would either reduce Aoki's risk or, better yet, create a competitive advantage."

"Yes, but we don't have weeks for fact finding. I need Takayama's support *now*."

"I understand. If you want me to represent you, I will contact Takayama-san and tell him you have retained me on a matter concerning Aoki's investment in Bingham International. He will guess my visit concerns Robert Bingham's death and control of the company."

"Then you'll meet with him this week?"

"No, I could leave tomorrow midday but I wouldn't arrive in Tokyo until Friday evening, too late for a meeting and, besides, we need time to collect intelligence. I think it would be better to leave Friday. I'll arrive in Tokyo on Saturday evening, have Sunday to prepare and meet with Takayama-san first thing on Monday. I'll schedule my return for late Monday afternoon." Duncan paused for a moment to think. "I will need a report on Aoki and its relationship with Bingham International and Bingham's current business plans for the funds you oversee."

"That would be Russia and Eastern Europe, Asia, and Latin America," Ghislaine declared and then continued. "So I won't know until early next week if this plan of yours will actually work?"

"No," Duncan replied.

Ghislaine looked down at Duncan for a moment before lowering herself back onto the sofa. "All right. M.D. is the only one I would trust to do the report. She graduated top of her class at USC's Marshall School of Business last year. She's extremely well organized; she thinks and writes clearly. I recruited her personally and in a year she has never disappointed me. If we can't use her, perhaps we could get an outside consultant to do something. But it wouldn't be as good or as fast."

"M.D. would be fine," Duncan replied with a shrug, noticing that Ghislaine had not mentioned Rob. "Please send me the report no later than Saturday at noon so I will have it early Sunday morning in Tokyo."

"Now I don't understand," Ghislaine countered. "You just said you didn't want to involve M.D. Have you changed your mind so soon?"

"No, I haven't," Duncan responded, conscious that Ghislaine was trying to catch him in a contradiction. "Tell M.D. you want the report to look at potential investment opportunities. Studying Aoki's current business might generate ideas about opportunities for Bingham and Aoki to work together. That's certainly within your purview as an executive vice president. If Ward were to ask M.D. why she was preparing a report, she could answer truthfully and even show him the report without alerting him to what we hope to accomplish."

Duncan felt Ghislaine's stare bore into him. She didn't seem particularly enthusiastic about his plan of action. Did he even have the energy to travel to Tokyo right now?

"All right," Ghislaine said after a long silence. "We'll have the report prepared as you suggest. Make your travel arrangements through Monica's firm since they now have a substantial retainer from me. I'd also prefer that you bill Monica so that I don't have any of your paperwork around."

Monica nodded to Web and Duncan her agreement.

"And let me be clear about communications. I can't afford any missteps so I need *daily* reports about progress on your discussions with Takayama-san. Not in writing but on my cell. I don't want to leave a written record of our plans for Ward to stumble upon."

"Okay. I'll do my best given the time difference." Quick study, thought Duncan as he got up to leave. Or, maybe she did know how to keep secrets after all.

Ghislaine rose and extended her hand. "I trust this will be a fruitful partnership."

Duncan took her hand and shook it firmly. Partnership? More like a short-term rental.

"Like I said, I'll do my best." He moved toward the door back through the piano room. He was eager to get going. He didn't want to be late to see Sam.

"Oh, Duncan?" Ghislaine said to Duncan's back. "You know your sword and shield image?"

"Yes?" Duncan grunted and turned to face his new client.

"It's been used before. In the Soviet Union. It's the emblem of the KGB."

Duncan considered this for a moment and then delivered a vague half smile to hide his surprise. Interesting woman, Duncan mused to himself. He waved to Monica and Web and walked to his car. Why would Ghislaine Bingham know anything about the KGB anyway?

....

THIRTEEN

WEDNESDAY, DECEMBER 15
LOS ANGELES

Rob sat with M.D. in Ghislaine's office. While she silently studied her BlackBerry, he shifted uneasily in the chair behind his mother's desk. He finally got up to pace around the room, uncomfortable with the silence. Although he knew his mother thought highly of M.D., and he had seen her around the office from time to time, he knew little else about her. When he found out that she would be in the meeting with Duncan Luke, Rob had asked Bingham's office manager what she was like. Alan's description hadn't clarified the picture at all.

"M.D. is an interesting woman," chuckled Alan. "She uses her initials instead of her given name, Maria Dulce, because she thinks it makes her sound too feminine and conveys the wrong impression that she lacks drive and ambition—not that anyone would make the mistake once they met her. She has always been extremely professional with me, if a little defensive. But don't get into a debate with her. She's armed with a vocabulary bigger than Merriam-Webster."

"Why would she be defensive? She's smart and has a good career going."

"I don't really know, but from what little she's told me, she didn't have it easy growing up," Alan explained. "Her mother raised her by herself and I don't think they had a lot of money. I met M.D.'s mother once when she came to the office. She's a hardworking, no-nonsense woman, just like her daughter."

"She just seems so delicate—tiny and pretty—like a porcelain figurine."

"Don't let her hear you say that! She has a black belt in karate. I've heard rumors that when she was in Colombia for a year between undergrad and graduate school to perfect her Spanish, she practiced her self-defense skills on men whose advances were unwelcome."

Rob paused mid pace to consider what M.D.'s self-defense moves might be. He imagined a quick kick in the gut. His stomach muscles instinctively tightened.

"May I ask you a question?"

M.D.'s voice startled Rob.

"What? Oh, sorry. Of course. Sure. Fire away."

"Your mother told me you spent high school skiing the Tahoe backcountry and kite boarding off Zuma Beach. I would assume you slept through your classes at Brentwood," M.D. added as if to herself.

"Then you surprised everyone when you aced your SATs and got into Harvey Mudd, where you graduated with honors in civil engineering and went on to receive a master's in developmental economics from Columbia. Is that right?"

"Well . . . well," Rob stammered. "Uh, scigh hool, shit, I mean high school teachers were hard to understand. I escaped the frustration I felt in class on the beach and the slopes." Rob glanced at M.D. and quickly continued. "Anyway, as for the SATs, I had a lot of help preparing for them and my verbal scores weren't all that hot. But once I started at Harvey Mudd, everything changed. The classes had less talking and more projects, you know, figuring out how things work in the real world. By Columbia, I was more confident. And my professors let me do a lot of independent work. Rob gazed past M.D. out the bay window behind his mother's desk. "I know I'm . . . I'm not a brilliant person by any means, but I *am* good at visualizing solutions even though I can't always describe what I'm seeing. Oh," he stopped himself suddenly. "Sorry to have talked so much."

"Not at all. Not at all. Okay. So, you're good with practical problems. That's great. I have a predicament you might be able to assist me with."

"Really?" Rob exclaimed, a wide grin breaking across his face. "Of course, I'd be happy to help."

"Here's my quandary," M.D. began as she folded her arms and started to pace in front of Rob as if she were delivering a particularly important lecture to a class. "I came to Bingham International because I couldn't stomach the country-club culture at the big Wall Street firms. During the interview process, their disdain for me as a Latina scholarship student was obvious. My MBA classmates snickered at me when I leaned toward working for your mother. They warned me she was a socialite not a businesswoman and I'd end up branch manager for a local bank in the Valley. But I liked Ghislaine and didn't want to be the affirmative action token among scores of Wonder Bread snobs, so I took the job at BIG. I've worked with your mother for almost a year and my regard for her has grown tremendously. During your father's shabby tryst, she maintained her dignity. Personally, I would have shot the idiot for nearly ruining the business. She is the woman I would like to be in twenty years. I have staked my career on your mother and I want more than anything her respect in return."

"Oh," Rob gushed. "I know she thinks the world of you." M.D. stared at Rob for a moment.

"Well, I'm gratified to hear that," M.D. declared. "So what would you advise me to do? As the son of the woman I most admire. Should I swallow your insult or confront you?"

Rob felt as though he were struggling to keep his head just above the torrent of words flowing from M.D. "Again, I'm sorry. I didn't mean . . ." He shook his head and took a long breath. "I apologize for being dense, but how did I insult you?"

"Your mother and you have no secrets, implying Ghislaine doesn't trust me as much? I'm a *valued* member of your mother's team? From someone who just joined the company? Do you realize how *condescending* you sounded? How that makes me look in front of Ghislaine?"

Rob stood wide-eyed. How could he have been misinterpreted so thoroughly?

"I . . . I didn't mean to be, uh, condescending. Of course, my mother trusts you. I was trying, uh, to compliment you." M.D. glared at him as if he had swung a snake in her face.

"As if I want *your* compliments. Do not *presume* to compliment me!"

Rob should have taken Alan's advice to heart and just apologized from the beginning. No matter how little sense her argument made.

"I'm sorry. I really didn't mean to insult you or whatever else I've done to upset you. I'm, I'm used to being in the field, not in a business meeting."

M.D. turned and walked over to the Shaker chair behind Ghislaine's massive antique desk. She sat down, folded her hands in her lap, and studied Rob for what felt like hours.

Finally, she spoke.

"Apology accepted."

Rob breathed a sigh of relief. As he was clearing his head from the confrontation, Ghislaine strode into her office. M.D. sprang up from the desk chair.

"Ghislaine. I'm sorry . . ." Ghislaine waved her off.

"No, I'm sorry about excluding you two, but I had no choice. I hope you've had a chance to become better acquainted. I trust you both explicitly and expect you'll be working closely together in the next two weeks."

"We have an excellent understanding of each other *now*, don't we?" M.D. glanced at Rob.

"Uh, sure."

"Good. M.D., I have an assignment to discuss with you right now." Ghislaine looked over at Rob.

"Rob, let's talk over dinner tonight—about the valuation of the company—because tomorrow I'd like you to call our accountants. As one of the two beneficiaries of your father's estate, you have a right to know what Ward is up to. Maybe you can get some information out of them if they think you're calling on your own behalf and not mine. In the meantime, would you go back to the office and keep an eye on things for me?"

"Okay . . ." Rob said. As he left, he heard Ghislaine begin to issue M.D. some sort of instructions. He turned around and saw M.D.'s face glowing with admiration as she listened to his mother. Suddenly, a new and completely unexpected sensation came over him: the strange desire for M.D. to look at him in the same way.

FOURTEEN

....

WEDNESDAY, DECEMBER 15
LOS ANGELES

Exhausted by his meeting with Ghislaine Bingham, Duncan pulled his white Acura into the driveway of his former home. His head slumped against the steering wheel. He knew Ghislaine Bingham wouldn't be an easy client and dreaded the long plane ride to Tokyo and the fog of jet lag he'd have to endure for the three days he would be there. But he needed the money. Besides, it would only be a week and he could get back to his new life at LMU.

Just as Duncan was about to turn off the engine, he caught himself, sighed wearily, and backed the car out onto the street in front of the house. At precisely seven, he walked up to the front door and punched the doorbell with his stubby index finger. Gracie opened the door and pointed to the den.

"Sam's just finished dinner and is waiting for you in the den. I'll be upstairs and will come down in an hour. Please try not to agitate him like you did on Friday," she commanded. Duncan gritted his teeth. The night of his first visit with Sam would not be a good time to tell Gracie to go fuck herself. But her attitude was *exactly* why he had no choice but to do the job for Bingham. He couldn't let his relationship with Sam be dictated by someone so self-righteously blind to her own contribution not just to upsetting Sam on Friday but to the destruction of their family.

He turned through arched doors into the cramped room that was his former den. An ancient brick fireplace was sandwiched between floor-to-ceiling bookshelves and a small, tattered brown sofa sat against the opposite wall in front of a TV hanging above the mantle. He had loved the coziness of the room where Sam and he had spent hundreds of hours watching sports; now the small space felt slightly oppressive.

Sam, in his jeans and worn Dodgers sweatshirt, sat on the sofa holding his knees against his chest and stared at the blank, flat-screen TV. Duncan slid down beside him. He smelled of Parmesan cheese and butter, which made Duncan smile.

"Hello, Sam. How are you?" Duncan asked as he tousled his son's black curls and then wrapped his left arm around his son's narrow shoulders.

"The TV's broken and the Lakers are on," Sam grumbled not moving his gaze from the silent flat screen. "And I haven't had dessert yet."

"Well, then, let's play a game. There must be a pack of Uno cards around here. Would that be okay?" Duncan asked. Sam did not respond.

"Sammy? Is that okay . . .?" Duncan squeezed him affectionately, but Sam refused to speak.

***

When his mom told him at dinner that his dad would visit him for an hour tonight, Sam felt excited and scared, like when his dad threw fly balls to him and he would stick his mitt out as far as he could to try to catch the ball before it hit him in the face. Sam loved the thrill of catching a ball and hated the fear that it would hit him on the nose. When he finished his pasta with butter and Parmesan, his mom said that his dad would arrive soon and he

98

would have to wait for dessert until his dad left. He got mad and stomped around the kitchen. He waved his arms and yelled for dessert. He had seen the chocolate ice cream cake in the freezer and couldn't wait to spoon a big, sweet bite of frosting into his mouth and let it slowly melt. But when his mom told him he wouldn't get any cake at all if he didn't calm down and go wait in the den, he stood still like a statue. After a moment, he tromped into the den and threw himself onto the couch.

He tried to turn on the Lakers game. He *loved* the Lakers and the Dodgers. Watching games on TV made him feel safe. He knew all the rules and liked keeping score. He knew all the players' numbers by heart. His dad said that he had a good head for figures and he knew he did. Then he remembered the TV didn't work. He threw the remote on the floor and waited, rocking himself on the old brown couch, thinking of dessert.

Suddenly his big old dad was sitting next to him. He felt his dad's huge hand run through his hair and his dad's heavy arm weigh on his shoulders. He smelled his dad's warm body. It smelled good, like his pajamas after he had worn them for a few days. He told his dad the TV was broken and he hadn't had dessert yet. His dad asked him a question, but he didn't answer. Then his dad took a long breath and let it out very slowly like a balloon with a hole in it. Usually Sam didn't like being held too close, but tonight he felt different. His dad's arm felt good. His dad's body smelled good. He crawled up onto his dad's lap and threw his arms around his neck. "Where have you been, Dad?" he asked. His dad's body began to jerk and he felt tears splash on his hair. His dad held him tight, too tight.

"Not so tight," Sam complained and wiggled out of his dad's arms. All of a sudden, Sam heard the Lakers game on the TV upstairs. He walked over and opened the den door to hear more clearly. His mom didn't like sports the way he and his dad did, but tonight she was watching the game!

"Sorry, Sammy. Want to play Uno?" His dad asked as he wiped his eyes. Sam didn't reply. The Lakers were behind ninety-five to ninety-two with three minutes left! But Kobe Bryant had the ball! Sam ran out of the room and froze before the staircase.

"Come on, Dad, let's see the game! It's almost over!" he shouted and waved his hand for his dad to follow him.

"I'm sorry. I . . . I can't go upstairs."

"Why not?" Sam cried, arms outstretched. Before his dad answered, Sam heard the announcer say, "Kobe makes a three and it's ninety-five to ninety-five with two minutes to go." Oh, no! Sam looked back at his dad sitting on the couch, ran his eyes back up the stairs to where the TV was and back again to his dad. Then he thought of the ice cream cake.

"Bye, Dad," he yelled and bolted up the stairs.

FIFTEEN

....

THURSDAY, DECEMBER 16
LONDON

Ward normally lodged at the Connaught when in London on business, but the Savoy had been renovated and the new Edwardian and Art Deco interiors had caught his eye in a recent *Architectural Digest* spread. When he had mentioned how much he enjoyed the article to the front desk, they upgraded him to a junior suite overlooking the Thames.

The hotel was also on the Strand, within easy walking distance of the office, although Ward anticipated spending more time than usual working in his room. He hadn't heard from their accountant yet but was determined to get the valuation he wanted. After checking in, he showered and ordered room service, a light lunch of poached Scottish salmon in dill sauce with a strawberry-and-cucumber salad. He avoided the sauce.

While he ate, Ward called the London office administrator to confirm his meeting the next day with the professional staff. He then called the accountant asking for a report on the valuation. He didn't care that it was five in the morning California time, and left a message to that effect.

The remainder of the afternoon, Ward, clad in the hotel robe, worked on his presentation to the staff concerning the previous quarter's uninspiring performance. He relished the thought of knocking heads tomorrow, particularly those of the analysts in Ghislaine's floundering Russia and Eastern Europe division. He doubted many would last long after he'd taken control.

As night fell, he chatted with his assistant, Elaine, in the Los Angeles office. Ron Danko had canceled their meeting tonight, rescheduling for Friday at five, but on the phone, not in person. Ward swore to himself. Danko had promised a status update on their application to the São Tomé and Príncipe government for its approval of their deal. A Ukrainian-Canadian with a degree in geological engineering from Arizona State, Danko had spent several decades in the oil industry in West Africa, acquiring friends and investment opportunities in Nigeria and São Tomé and Príncipe. Ward admired the oil man's rough charisma but didn't trust him an inch. For a finder's fee of $1 million, Danko had given BIG the exclusive right to invest $10 million for a 10 percent stake in Gulf of Guinea, a company Danko owned and whose only asset was a São Toméan oil concession.

If Ron rescheduled their meeting it meant he was stalling for time, which was never good news. He was about to lay into Elaine for not getting more information from Ron when a call came in from the accountant.

"Elaine, I'll call you back. I have to take this." He hung up abruptly.

"Well, hello, Matthew. I don't need to hear excuses for your incompetence. I asked for that report *yesterday.*"

"I have been working all night. I didn't want to call you back without some numbers. But I still have questions."

The veins on Ward Bingham's neck pulsed.

"Look, Matthew, I'm in London on important business and don't have time to explain basic accounting to you. I'm losing patience with your lack of creativity. The firm can't be worth more than ten million dollars, and if Levy and Maxwell wants to keep our business, you'll find a way to make that number."

"I'm an accountant, not a screenwriter," Matthew Levy countered. "We have worked the value of the four funds down from about a hundred and fifty million in unrealized gains to fifty million. But even at fifty million dollars, the company's twenty percent share is ten million. Add to that BIG's own investments, which we've managed to get to ten million or so, we're still at twenty million dollars without accounting for goodwill. There's no way to get to ten million."

"I didn't hire you to explain basic math," Ward roared. "I *hired* you to make the numbers do what *I* want them to do." Ward pounded the bed. "Find a way to make them work."

"All right, but I'm compelled to remind you that you *may* regret having to defend a low valuation for the company. It might affect the company's ability to borrow or to raise funds from investors in the future."

"I'm not concerned about the future," Ward snarled. "Get me a report by Monday morning valuing BIG at ten million dollars, or you're fired!"

Ward hung up and unconsciously began to stroke the back of his neck as he paced around his hotel room. He should never have promised his stepmother he would wait until early January to finalize the sale of his father's shares. When his opponent is exposed, he always goes for the jugular. "Speed is the essence of war" was his favorite Sun Tzu quotation. Ghislaine's weakness had distracted him, but he was clearheaded now. He didn't see how she could frustrate his plans in the next three weeks, but it wouldn't hurt to find something to show her that fighting him would be futile—and painful. He dialed Elaine again.

"Any other messages?"

"A few more condolence calls. Oh, and Gracie Lewis called."

"Who?"

"Gracie Lewis. You worked together six or seven years ago when she was with Goldman. They helped finance one of our investments. Anyway, she wants to see if BIG would contribute to a charity event for her son's school. Her kid is autistic."

He remembered her now. Not a blonde, but attractive and sharp. Married to a lawyer. Perhaps they'd split up?

"Call her back and tell her I'm in London. Ask her to call me when I'm back. And get her current contacts. Tell her I'd be happy to hear more about her son's school." Ward laughed to himself. Who had time for *charity?* Then he remembered. Ghislaine did.

"Elaine? Transfer me to Alan. And reconfirm the call with Ron, will you? Don't let him off the hook again."

"Yes, Mr. Bingham. Good night."

As Alan's line rang, Ward felt his stress evaporate. He would enjoy running Bingham by himself.

"Alan? It's Ward. I reviewed some recent requests for expenditures and found that Ghislaine had approved a twenty-five thousand dollar contribution to the holiday benefit for Children's Charities of Los Angeles. I want it canceled immediately. And don't worry about notifying her. I'll tell her myself." Ward grinned as he imagined the look on his stepmother's face when Children's Charities of Los Angeles called asking about their money.

Feeling more like himself, Ward decided to dine downstairs at the Savoy Grill. Sitting at the back corner table with a Macallan 18 and a splash of water, he ordered a pork, veal, and pistachio pie to start and a roasted duck breast with braised endive and bacon as his main course. The sommelier recommended a 2005 Chateauneuf-du-Pape with the duck. He would not deny himself the fine food and drink he felt he was owed after a long day, but to stay ahead of any weight gain he vowed he would work out an extra day when he returned to Los Angeles.

With dinner and a twenty-seven-year-old Armagnac warming his body, Ward walked out of the restaurant planning on a good night's sleep. As he approached the elevators, an elderly woman passed him and smiled. She had a slight build, emerald eyes, fine, olive skin and stepped lightly for someone her age. He turned reflexively to watch the woman move away, stifling the impulse to call after her. If his mother had lived, she would be this woman. Ward shook his head. He drank too much. He needed to get to bed and sleep off the jet lag.

Hours later he awoke in a cold sweat and bolted upright in bed. His heart was racing and his head was throbbing. He had dreamt again that he was running after his mother to prevent her from leaving the house. In the dream, his legs churned but he could not move; his mouth opened but he could not speak. He heard her car roar down the driveway. A few agonizing seconds later, the boom of her car crashing had jarred him awake.

That woman in the lobby must have triggered the dream. He fell back in his bed racked with grief, as if he had just lost his mother all over again. If he were in Los Angeles, he would call Khala, the tiny woman who had been his nanny, his mother's nanny, and the caregiver to his grandparents. Khala's reminiscences about Leila would remind him of his childhood and ease Ward's anguish. He tried to suppress the dream by remembering the fun they had had together in the park, watching ducks, eating ice cream, laughing with his mother. But Khala had also witnessed every one of his personal tragedies. She had been there when he was sent away to boarding school. She had been there when his mother died. She had been there the first time he had witnessed his parents' marriage erupt in a vicious fight. Ward tried but couldn't stop visions of the past flooding back into his mind.

Leila had picked Ward up from Warner Elementary and they had walked home hand in hand. She had made him scrub his hands thoroughly as she always did before he went to the kitchen to greet Khala and have his snack. His mother had sat with him as Khala, who was like Leila's older sister, only darker, rounder, and with a nose like a camel, poured a glass of chocolate milk. He remembered sitting between the two women feeling enveloped by the warmth of their love. He remembered thinking their love and the glow he felt surround him would last forever.

"Drink, my little Lion of Judah. Become stronger," Khala cajoled, stroking the birthmark on the back of Ward's neck.

"Don't call him that," Leila commanded. "The birthmark will fade away in a few years. You'll see."

"But his Hebrew name is Judah and the mark has the shape of a lion! It is God's sign that Ward will be powerful and brilliant like the great kings David and Solomon!" Ward's eyes widened over the rim of his glass of chocolate milk.

"Don't fill his head with your silly superstitions," Leila retorted. Khala bowed and left mother and son alone. With a hug and a kiss, Leila told her son to go up to his room to play with the model King Arthur's Castle his father had given him.

"Try to nap my sweet boy," she said stroking his hair. "Your eyes are heavy."

After a half hour of playing with his knights, Ward washed his hands and face and curled up with his blanket and closed his eyes. The sound of glass shattering woke him abruptly. The sun had gone down and his room was cold and dark.

"You forged my name on the mortgage, didn't you?" he heard his mother shout, followed by another loud pop of breaking glass. Ward grabbed the plastic sword his mother had given him, crept out of his room, and crawled along the hall to where he could look down on the entryway through the iron railing. He could see his mother standing by a table full of his father's favorite wine-glasses. His father was crouched by the door with his hands over his head.

"I did it for us, baby," he cried. His mother shrieked and threw a glass. His father ducked and it crashed against the front door.

"Don't give me that bullshit! You got the mortgage to buy my parents out just before you closed your first deal, didn't you?" She hurled another glass that just missed his father's head. "After all they've done for you. All the money they've given you for your company. You cheated them!"

"I didn't cheat them. It was business, that's all. But the profits from the deal paid off the mortgage, darling. The money from your trust that we used to buy the house is safe. Please, stop." His mother howled like a goblin, reached for another wineglass, and flung it at his father. He deflected it with his left arm and it splattered on the tile floor.

"You used the trust money *I* put into this house to defraud my parents and enrich *yourself.* Have you no conscience?" Another glass missile crashed against the door.

"They don't need the money. They're rich as Rockefeller, for Christ's sake."

"They came here from Egypt with nothing and earned every penny, you prick. You know they intended to give their shares in the company to Ward. But you couldn't bear to share the company with anyone. Not even our son!"

Without another word, his mother launched all of the remaining glasses, one by one, at his father, who ducked and leapt from side to side. When the last glass had shattered, his father leaned back against the door, panting like a dog, while his mother spun around and ran up the stairs. Ward raced into his room before she reached the top of the staircase. He heard his parents' bedroom door slam shut.

His father had stolen from his grandparents? His father's company was to be his one day? Ward twisted a lock of his black hair until it burned his scalp. He looked at the model castle and felt sick to his stomach. Seizing his sword, he swung as hard as he could at the fortress, scattering its towers, walls, and moat. He rushed into his bathroom and scrubbed himself clean again to make his mother happy. Feeling better, he climbed back into his bed and held his blanket close to his chest. Stroking the birthmark on the back of his neck, he waited for Khala to come for him.

Nine years later, Ward sat with his father on a platform at the far end of the back lawn. His grandparents slumped in armchairs on the other side, faces as gray as their hair. Khala, who now cared for his mother's parents, stood behind them, eyes cast to the ground. In front of the podium sat a black-clad audience of mourners. Ward had listened for over an hour as speaker after speaker had praised his mother's love of family and passion for justice. They had used phrases like "unspeakable tragedy," "unforeseen calamity," and "terrible misfortune" to describe the car accident on Sunset Boulevard that two weeks before had claimed her life.

Now it was his turn to speak. Ward moved to the podium, but could not feel his legs. His mouth opened, but he couldn't make a sound. The words he had scribbled lay silent on the paper he clutched in front of him. A wave of rage at his father overwhelmed his grief. His parents had fought before his mother had run out that night. They had circled each other in the front hall like wild animals snarling and shouting for what seemed like hours. His father accused her parents of sabotaging his reputation and destroying his business; his mother screamed that he had ruined himself by cheating others the way he cheated her family and his own son.

"Get out!" he had ordered at last.

"With pleasure!" she had bellowed, grabbing her coat and dashing out the door. Ward had started to run downstairs to stop her but was not quick enough. He watched the door slam and heard her car race away. It was the last time he saw her.

He longed to tell the world who had murdered his mother, who had stolen his mother and the company from his grandparents and from him. But he knew his mother would not want him to speak openly of her private troubles, so he held his anger inside. At last, he managed to mutter, "I'm so sorry," and returned to his seat, where he covered his face with his hands. The crowd murmured its understanding. Robert got up from his seat without pausing to comfort Ward and strode to the podium. Ward heard him say, "Thank you, my dear friends, for coming to my home today to share in my grief," but he could not bear to listen to another word.

Several hours later, Robert drove off with two business friends to dine at Spago, and Ward pried open the liquor cabinet. After thirty minutes, with half a bottle of Bacardi burning through his body, he climbed into his father's BMW and inserted the key he had stolen from his father's desk. As his driving instructor had recently taught him, he slid down the driveway with his foot tapping the brakes and steered right onto Beverly Glen. He stopped at the red light at Sunset and exhaled slowly. When it flashed green, Ward turned right again, straightened the BMW, and forced the accelerator to the floor, racing around the tight right turn. Feeling the car swerve into the oncoming lane, he jerked the wheel farther to the right, skidded off the road, and slammed into the trees at the southwest corner of Sunset and Mapleton.

The next year had been spent in a haze of grief that only Khala and visits to his grandparents could lift. Then Ghislaine Palet came into his life. He remembered the first time he saw her, talking with his father in the entrance hall. She was breathtakingly lovely, not much older than himself, and had long legs and honey-colored hair flowing down to her shoulders. He had dared not speak for fear his sixteen-year-old voice would crack. He hated the sight of her standing where his mother had once stood. And then Ghislaine's eyes found his.

A smile spread across her face and lit up her sky-blue eyes. She stepped away from his father and walked toward him, holding out her hands. Ward tried to resist taking her hands but he was weak, and the warmth of her embrace was intoxicating. As she hugged him, he drank in her soft scent and could not stop himself from uttering, "I am so happy to meet you, Ghislaine."

Later that evening, Robert called a friend from the entryway telephone. His drunken voice boomed into Ward's bedroom. Ward groaned and buried his head between his pillows.

"I've just met her but I know that she's the one. She just needs time to get to know me, but that's nearly impossible with Ward here." Ward put the pillows down and sat up in bed, holding his breath.

"He's either moping around the house or out someplace careening completely out of control. He got dead drunk at the school's spring party last month and had to be hospitalized. Even though he's a star on the soccer team, the school won't take him back. I'm thinking that Villanova Prep, a school up in Ojai, would be ideal." Ward felt nausea rise in his throat. "It's Catholic, good academics, a great soccer program, and no cars so he can't wander back here. Best of all, I'll have the space I need to pursue Ghislaine. What? No, I haven't told her yet, but I'm sure she'll be delighted to have more time together without a snot-nosed boy around."

That night, Ward had sat up, unable to sleep, staring at the darkness of his room, trying to soothe himself by rubbing the back of his neck. He despised himself. How could he have embraced the woman who would replace his mother? His father would marry her. Ghislaine would have a son to take his place. She would steal the business that his mother had promised to *him*. He ran to the bathroom and showered in scalding hot water scrubbing her scent from his body.

Now Ward lay awake in his London hotel just as he had so many years before. Tortured by the loss of the love he had assumed would always be his, infuriated by the memory of Ghislaine's duplicity, he swore to himself, *never again*. Pounding his fist over and over into his pillow, he yelled to the empty hotel room, "Never again!"

SIXTEEN

....

THURSDAY, DECEMBER 16
LOS ANGELES

Duncan returned to his apartment around six o'clock. He had spent all day in his office at LMU getting his syllabus and class assignments into shape. He knew he wouldn't have much time to focus on the course over the next week. Ghislaine Bingham would make sure of it; she had already called him twice today. After switching off his car, he tried to rub the stiffness from his back. The money would be worth the stress of the upcoming trip, he reminded himself. Money to pay for a life with Sam. Oh my God, *Sam*. Dammit! *Saturday.* He would be in Tokyo when he was supposed to be with Sam. *Fuck.* He had to ask Gracie to switch nights. But first he needed to hear his son's voice. Sitting behind the wheel of his Acura, he called the house on Seventeenth Street.

"I asked you not to call between six and seven thirty," Gracie barked. "You're completely disrupting our dinner. I'm entitled to sit down with Sam without you bothering us."

"I'm sorry." Duncan clenched his teeth. "The time got away from me. But for God's sake, when *can* I speak with Sam? When I called Tuesday, you told me not to phone before dinner either, because that's when he needs to concentrate on his homework.

Can't I just speak with him for a moment or, at the very least, can't you ask him to call me when you're finished with dinner?"

"I'm not going to tell Sam to call you. If he doesn't want to speak with you, I'm not going to push him. You can call back if you want, but no later than eight since he has to get ready for bed. I have to go now."

"Wait! Gracie! I . . . I have to go to Tokyo over the weekend on business. I'll be back on Monday. I'd like to see Sam on Monday night rather than Saturday." A seething silence poured from the phone.

"You've *got* to be kidding," Gracie finally responded. "I thought you took the job at LMU so you wouldn't have to travel. Don't you realize how this will upset Sam? But if you care so little for your son you'll miss your first Saturday evening with him, *fine*. Your problem, not mine. You know how important consistency is to him. I'm not going to scramble his schedule. Use your time or lose it, Duncan. *Good-bye.*"

Duncan squeezed the steering wheel until his hands hurt. Sam was his boy just as much as Gracie's. He pressed redial on his BlackBerry. No answer. He hung up and dialed again. No answer. He slammed his fist down on the dashboard. He tried Gracie's cell phone. She picked up after five rings.

"If you don't stop harassing us, I'm getting a restraining order," she warned. "From now on, if you want to speak to Sam or to me, send an email proposing a time and I'll see what I can do. But I'm certainly not paying for calls to Tokyo. Don't bother us again or, so help me God, I'll go to court." The cell phone connection went dead.

"Fuck you!" Duncan screamed into the dead cell phone. Sweating despite the cool of the night, he closed his eyes. Cracking open a window, he drank in the salt air and listened to the roar of the surf. After a couple of minutes, he climbed out of the car and plodded up the two flights of exterior wooden steps to his top-floor apartment.

He entered and turned on the light. Throwing his briefcase down, he muttered, "Welcome home," to himself and slammed the door shut. A cold silence chilled his spirit. He moved through the combination living room–dining room to stare out the floor-to-ceiling windows over the sandy beach of Playa del Rey to the ocean beyond. The lights of a tanker glowed in the dark. He spun around, his eyes falling on the small kitchen lying beyond the waist-high counter that separated it from the living room. He deserved a drink. He bounded into the kitchen, pulled out a new bottle of Sauza. He preferred cheap tequila to the expensive stuff. Messed you up the same, anyway. He unscrewed the cap and poured himself a large shot. The caramel-colored liquor streamed down his throat and lit a fire in his gut. Suddenly he didn't feel quite so lonely. Let's inspect the bedrooms! Perhaps they had grown larger, he chuckled to himself. But another shot first. He poured two more inches and, glass in hand, ventured down the hall leading to the back of the apartment.

He glanced in Sam's bedroom. He had given Sam the south-facing room since his son was so sensitive to noise. A small bed, bedside table, and reading lamp stood waiting in the otherwise empty room. At least the furniture was painted various shades of blue, the color of Sam's beloved Dodgers and Lakers. Duncan didn't bother looking at his own bedroom at the end of the hall. He had seen all there was to see out the small window looking over the street and the lumpy mattress on the floor only reminded him how alone he was. He drained the tequila in one gulp.

Returning to the kitchen, he snatched up the bottle of Sauza and flopped down on the scratched, faux-leather brown couch he had bought from Goodwill on Monday. The couch and a matching armchair sat in the living room facing the windows and ocean beyond. He sloshed a little tequila into his glass and threw down another gulp. Then he put his feet up on the small wooden coffee table and switched on a lamp perched on the side table. Swiveling around, he reached back and lay the tequila bottle on the butcher block dining table behind the couch.

Lying back on the couch, he stared up at the stucco ceiling. How had his life with Gracie turned to such shit? He had adored her when they first met. And, to his constant surprise, she had worshipped him, a lanky, goofy-looking young prosecutor with none of her San Francisco sophistication. Duncan shook his head at the mysteries of love and life. He pushed himself off the couch and walked over to his stereo system near the kitchen. He rummaged in a box of CDs and found *One Kind Favor,* B.B. King's recent album. He put the CD in the player and scanned to the track, "World Is Gone Wrong."

Duncan splashed more tequila in his glass and went to his bedroom. He sipped the Sauza as he packed for Tokyo. In ten minutes, he was done. Years of international travel had taught him exactly what he did and didn't need on a business trip. He planted the suitcase by the door for an easy exit in the morning. Then he emailed Taka that he was coming to Tokyo over the weekend on a matter for Ghislaine Bingham and "would be grateful for an opportunity to meet at his earliest convenience." Duncan added his contact information at the Peninsula Hotel.

Finished with his preparations, he lay back down on the couch. His buzz was wearing off and gloom began to fill Duncan's head again. The Sauza bottle called to him from its perch on the dining table. All right, he decided. He would skip dinner and have one last big blast as he listened to some music. He wanted to lose a few pounds anyway. He poured tequila halfway up his glass and decided on Clapton. He dug into his CD box again looking for *Chronicles* and inserted the CD in his stereo. Swallowing half the tequila, he returned to the couch and let his mind wander through "Blue Eyes Blue" and "My Father's Eyes." Maybe it would all be okay. Maybe once she calmed down, Gracie would be more reasonable and would remember how important he was to Sam. As the first few chords from "Tears in Heaven" drifted from the speakers, Duncan's eyes filled. Then the Sauza turned on him and he broke down sobbing.

SEVENTEEN

....

FRIDAY, DECEMBER 17
LONDON

The bedside radio startled Ward awake at nine. He had finally fallen asleep at five after tossing around in his bed for hours alternately mourning his mother and damning Ghislaine. Disoriented by his strange surroundings and jet lag, he pulled back the sheets and stumbled into the bathroom. Gazing at his grizzled reflection, Ward contemplated returning to bed for more sleep. No, he thought. He'd work out his jet lag in the gym. Ghislaine's team in the London office would learn today that he was their real boss.

Several hours later, Ward gazed out at the small group of bankers gathered around an oval conference table. "The performance of our team here in London has been dismal this year," Ward began. "With the exception of the two of you working for the Middle East and Africa division, the results have been terrible." The faces of the three women and three men who sat around the conference room table blanched. Ward continued.

"I will run through the numbers with you, but I must be honest. I don't see how we can justify keeping twice as many professionals working on Russia and Eastern Europe as we have on the Middle East and Africa."

A young woman raised her hand.

"Mr. Bingham, does Mrs. Bingham—Ghislaine—concur with your assessment? She gave me the impression she was pleased with our work. Isn't she responsible for our Russia and Eastern Europe investments?"

"What Ghislaine thinks about the numbers is *irrelevant,*" Ward barked. "Her expertise is giving parties, not managing a business. Now, please, hold your questions until I am finished." The bankers looked at one another uneasily and stayed quiet.

Ward concluded his review, answered the few questions anyone dared ask, and then dismissed them. As the bankers glumly filed out of the room, a tall woman with short, white-blond hair lingered, fidgeting by the door.

"Excuse me, sir, my name is Azra Begic," she said approaching him. "Could I have a word with you?"

Ward studied the young woman's brilliant blue eyes before responding.

"Of course." Her skin was so milky and fine he couldn't help wondering what she would look like naked. As she drew near, he noticed the pad of paper she held in her right hand quivered.

"Thank you, sir," Azra said, her light soprano quavering slightly. "I'm sorry to take your time but I don't believe we've met," she said, holding out her hand. "I'm the youngest analyst on the Russia and Eastern Europe team. Ghislaine hired me a year ago right out of London University. I have degrees in German and International Business."

"Ghislaine hired you? I see. Well, I'm pleased to meet you." Ward smiled as he shook her small, smooth hand. "What can I do for you?"

"Well, to be honest, sir, I was a little shocked to hear you say that there might be a redundancy in the Russia and Eastern Europe group due to low business levels," she said, averting her eyes from Ward's gaze. "One of the reasons I came to Bingham was the perspective I thought the company had on generating profits. Rather than emphasizing quarterly statements, Ghislaine stressed the need to take a long-term view of investment in emerging markets, a vision I very much share."

Azra raised her eyes to Ward's.

"I support myself and my family in Bosnia. So my job here is very important. If it wouldn't be too much trouble, I'd like to have your advice on how to succeed at Bingham."

Ward laid his hand lightly on the pale-blue silk blouse covering Azra's left arm. She was beautiful, he thought. "I'm so glad that you introduced yourself. Unfortunately, I don't have a lot of time to chat right now, but I am free for dinner tonight. We could eat at my hotel, the Savoy. It's near the office. I'd love to discuss your career plans—and your vision."

Azra drew the pad against her chest.

"Oh, that's . . . that's a lovely invitation, sir, but . . . but I'm afraid I have other plans. I attend services at Regent's Park Mosque on Friday evenings."

"You're Muslim?" Ward blurted out. "But you look, you look Scandinavian."

"I know, but I *am* Muslim. From Bosnia. Perhaps the next time you're in London we can arrange a lunch?"

"Oh, of course," Ward said patronizingly patting her arm. "Let's try to do that. But you asked for advice, so let me give you some. Many qualities lead to success, but when competition is severe and business is in a state of constant flux as it is now . . ." he paused to lean forward and whisper in her ear. "A willingness to be *flexible* is critical."

Ward felt Azra flinch as his lips lightly grazed her ear. She nodded at him without making eye contact and darted out of the conference room.

Ward spent the rest of the day making sure everyone in the London office would feel his displeasure. He sat in a spare office pouring over the quarterly reports and called each banker in one by one to grill them on their personal performance. When it was Azra's turn, however, he asked only one question and then dismissed her with a wave of his hand. Before five, he abruptly left and hurried back to his hotel for the call with Ron Danko.

As Ward reclined in an Edwardian armchair waiting for Danko's call, he mulled over his two conversations with Azra Begic. Was that panic he had seen flood her eyes at the end? Too bad. Bingham couldn't afford young bankers without the confidence to take risks. At five after five, the phone rang.

"Hello, Ward," Ron Danko greeted him. "Sorry about the delay, but good news is worth the wait, don't you think?"

"I'll be the judge about whether or not it's good news."

"Very good news, as I see it. I've been assured by my friends at the Ministry; we'll have approval early next week. Then we can close Bingham's minority investment in Gulf. When we take Gulf of Guinea public, we'll reap a fortune."

"Thanks, Ron. That *is* good news. Let me know as soon as final approval comes in, will you?"

"Will do, will do. I'll be back in touch early next week."

Ward was considering where he would go to dinner to celebrate the Gulf triumph when his cell phone rang. Matthew Levy. His jaw tightened at the prospect of another argument over valuation.

"Matthew? What's the problem now?"

"Rob called last night after we spoke. He wants to know the status of our valuation."

"Did he say *why* he was asking for the information?" Ward tightly gripped his phone.

"Yes. He said if the company was going to buy the shares his father had left him, he wanted to make sure the value would be fair.

"*Fair?* And what did you say?" Ward struggled to keep the anger out of his voice.

"I told him I understood his position, but we hadn't finished our analysis yet and he'd have to get a copy of our report from you, as executor of the estate."

"Good, Matthew. Exactly right." Ward exhaled with relief. "I'll deal with Rob when I get back. Are we down to ten million dollars yet?"

"Not yet," Matthew admitted. "But we'll be there over the weekend, I promise."

"Excellent. I look forward to your report."

Ward hung up. His good mood recovered. He decided a light workout and steam bath in the hotel gym would smooth out the remaining jet lag. He made a dinner reservation for eight, quickly changed, and hurried out the door.

Just before eight o'clock, Ward had dressed for dinner and was heading down to the hotel restaurant when the room phone rang.

"Mr. Bingham? It's the front desk. You have a visitor here in the lobby."

Ward heard several clicks over the phone and waited, drumming his fingers impatiently. Who could be so rude as to visit at the dinner hour? Finally, a high-pitched voice wavered over the line.

"Hello, sir."

Ward didn't recognize the voice immediately. Then he smiled hungrily.

"Hello, Azra."

EIGHTEEN

....

FRIDAY, DECEMBER 17
LOS ANGELES

Duncan's mouth felt like an old Pendleton sweater when he rolled over to stare at his clock. Seven. Time to catch a flight. He groaned, vowed for the tenth time in the last month never to drink tequila again, and trudged to the shower. A dousing and several glasses of water revived him. He dressed in his travel uniform: baggy jeans, a light-brown T-shirt, a dark-blue sweater, and his worn black-and-blue New Balance running shoes. He had been wearing the same type of clothes on long flights for years. Comfort trumped style and a little routine helped him deal with the disorientation of international travel.

After gulping down a glass of orange juice, Duncan ate a banana but skipped the coffee he normally craved. It was midnight in Tokyo and he didn't want the caffeine to slow the process of adjusting his body to the time change. Besides, the Sauza had dehydrated him enough.

Taka's assistant had responded to Duncan's message. Delighted to learn that his American friend was coming to Tokyo, he offered to have Duncan picked up at his hotel on Sunday afternoon and driven to Hakone where they would have dinner at a Japanese inn with a view of Lake Ashi and Mount Fuji. Taka would also make himself available for a meeting at the Aoki offices on Monday morning at ten. Duncan responded he was overwhelmed by the hospitality and looked forward to seeing Takayama-san on Sunday.

Duncan had selected Singapore Airlines for his flight to Tokyo. The flight attendants were particularly attentive in business class and he liked having a choice between Western and Asian food, which were both as good as first class fare on any other airline. But his favorite feature about flying Singapore was the seat, which reclined with the touch of a button into a narrow but completely horizontal bed. He had booked an open aisle seat in the upper deck of the Boeing 747. Some experienced travelers hated riding in the narrow business-class space above the first-class cabin, but Duncan enjoyed flying in what felt like a private compartment with only two seats on each side of the aisle.

As was his practice on long-haul flights, he ordered a plate of appetizers, two glasses of red wine, and a double Courvoisier to be served just after takeoff and asked that his main meal be ready about six hours into the twelve-hour flight. To minimize jet lag, Duncan planned to begin his adjustment to Tokyo time by sleeping for several hours, since it was already early Saturday morning in Japan. No one took the seat next to him, so he spread out once the plane took off. After the light meal, he downed the cognac in one gulp. Reclining the seat completely, he closed the window shades near him and put on his eye mask. Too tall to be able to stretch out fully, he turned on his side and brought his knees up. The low buzz of the aircraft and the warmth of the Courvoisier soon lulled him to sleep.

He came through the door and threw his briefcase down. Sam greeted him by wrapping his arms around his legs. He picked Sam up, tipped his baseball cap back, and kissed him on the forehead. His son squealed in protest and delight. Gracie called out from her office that Mila would have dinner ready in an hour.

At dinner, he asked Sam how school had been. Sam turned to Gracie. Gracie replied that it had been okay. He asked Sam whether math was still his favorite class. Sam again looked at Gracie and Gracie replied that it was. A knot in his throat began to swell, constricting his breathing. He reached over to stroke Sam's head, but his arm had inexplicably grown too short to touch his son. He asked Sam question after question, but each time Sam turned to Gracie and Gracie replied.

When Sam went up to get ready for bed, Duncan asked Gracie whether he could tuck Sam in. Gracie smiled and said, "Of course you can." The thought of putting Sam to bed untied the knot in his throat. But just as Duncan rose to go upstairs to Sam's room, the head of his firm called to ask Duncan to talk to a new client. Then Ghislaine Bingham came on the line and her husky voice started to dictate to Duncan how to persuade Takayama-san to support her. Time passed but Ghislaine wouldn't stop talking, and whenever he tried to break away she said it would only take another minute. More time passed and finally Ghislaine finished. Duncan raced up the stairs. The door to Sam's room opened and Gracie stepped out. She smiled and shook her head. The light was off and he could hear Sam breathing softly.

He had trouble sleeping that night. Gracie was again lying at the far edge of the bed with her back toward him. Tonight, however, he ached to touch her. As he did so, the nightgown she was wearing melted away. He moved his hand toward her and began to stroke the curve where her neck met her shoulders. But as he caressed her, her skin mottled under his touch. He yanked his hand back, but too late. Boils were forming at the spots where he had traced his fingers. They spread across her neck, shoulders, and back. He gagged as the boils burst and pus spread out from the ruptures in long thin dribbles. The dribbles turned to worms; the worms became snakes. He screamed and jumped out of bed.

Duncan woke with a start. A light sweat covered his entire body. Duncan stared around at the darkened interior of the plane. He still had almost seven hours before arrival but felt like he'd been on the flight for days. He lifted himself from his seat and walked up and down the aisle twice. After stretching, he asked for his meal, two more cognacs, and some bottled water. He nibbled at the seared chicken breast and snow peas and then tried, without success, to sleep again before the plane landed in Tokyo. He usually could not remember his dreams, but this one refused to leave him. What did it mean? Somewhere deep inside him a battle raged. His hope that his marriage could be saved and his family restored was under relentless attack by the reality that his wife didn't want him in her life anymore. The nightmare was hope waving its white flag. The past was over. The fight for his future, for a life with Sam, had begun.

NINETEEN

······························

FRIDAY, DECEMBER 17
PANAMA CITY

Magdalena stared through swollen eyes at the turquoise water of the Marriott Hotel's patio pool as she waited for Luz to arrive. She had spent the past three days in turmoil, her world flipped from white to black by Luz's insistence that she stop lying to herself. She had come to realize Rodrigo was not the benefactor she had convinced herself he was. He was a beast. His presence physically revolted her. Yet she trembled at the thought of what he would do if she left him. She could not erase the image of the open dog cage from her mind.

"*Hola!*" shouted Luz as she strolled up behind Magdalena. "I am so sorry to be late. I could not decide which cocktail dress to wear to the club tonight. Not that I expect to spend much time with it on," she said as a crooked grin split her wide, pretty face. Then her eyes met Magdalena's. "Oh, Magdalena, have you been crying?"

"We have no time to talk tonight. It is already six thirty. You need to go to work soon," Magdalena protested.

"Oh, it is Friday night, if I am at the Golden Island by eight, there will still be plenty of *Norteamericanos* with small cocks and big wallets. Tell me what is in your heart. Have you thought about what I said Tuesday night?"

"In my soul, I now know what you said is true. But I am paralyzed. How I envy you. You make your own money. You have a visa. If I were in your position, I would not be so frightened to leave Rodrigo."

"*No seas loca!* If you were in my position, you would spend most nights on your back with some sweaty stranger pounding his dick into you. Your two little children would live with your mother back in Cartagena and you would see them only for a week or two every three months. You envy *me?* At least you have been protected by a powerful man for eight years, even if he is a *bastardo.*"

"But you are free to do as you please!"

"Ha! Is that what you think?" Luz grabbed Magdalena's arm in anger. "So, yes, I am free to go home and raise my children to be as poor and ignorant as I am—or worse. Is *that* freedom? Do you think Anna's mother wanted to sell her to Rodrigo? I suck the smelly cock of a different man every night so my daughter will not end up like your poor friend, so she will not end up like *me!*"

"But what am I to do? If I leave Rodrigo, he might not treat me like Anna, but he will have the immigration police deport me to Colombia. You *know* what the general's son would do to me."

"Yes, I know." Luz sighed and released her friend's arm. "You are right. If you left Rodrigo now, he would have you deported. But he thinks you are still his lover, no? Have you not asked him to get you a resident visa? If you had one, you could not be deported, even if you left him."

"Perhaps you are right. But . . . but the memory of what he did to Anna . . . I could not stomach his hands on me. "

"Do not think of Anna. She is dead or wishes she were and your thoughts cannot help her. Listen to me, Magdalena. If I can fake an orgasm while being screwed by a fifty-year-old *Norteamericano* whose prick goes limp every five seconds, you can pretend like you love nothing more than to feel Rodrigo's hands on you. Do not lose yourself in dreams *or* in despair. Live *in* the world, Magdalena. You are so bright and still very beautiful. Your life lies ahead."

Luz stood up and straightened her dress. "Now, I must go to work. *Promise* me. Think only of your future tonight when Rodrigo comes to you."

"All right," she agreed and kissed Luz on both cheeks. "I will try." As Magdalena watched Luz walk away, she tried but failed to think of her future. Instead, she weighed the choice that confronted her: the despair of a life with Rodrigo or the dread of living with no one to protect her. As the setting sun cast its last rays over the pool, Magdalena felt hope fade with the light. Did it matter which way the balance would tip?

TWENTY

....

FRIDAY, DECEMBER 17
LOS ANGELES

Ghislaine was dining in a back booth at the Brentwood Restaurant with two friends from her earliest days in Los Angeles. Camille Marceau Petersen had made her acting debut in a 1980 French film about a sixteen-year-old girl who was the mistress of a middle-aged pianist. Like Ghislaine, she had migrated to Hollywood and appeared in several mediocre films before her career faded away. She married a wealthy plastic surgeon and gave him two sons who were now in their twenties. When her husband could not stop having affairs with grateful patients, she divorced him, received a $10 million settlement, $350,000 a year in alimony, and a graceful Italianate home in the Beverly Hills flats.

Ghislaine's other friend, Lydia Armstrong Feinstein, had moved to California in 1984 from Texas to model swimsuits. She had married and divorced two prominent corporate lawyers, neither of whom, as Lydia often smirked, had been particularly good at closing the deal. She had done very well from both divorces, although not quite so well as Camille, a fact that she blamed on all six of the lawyers whom she had at one time or another retained and then fired for incompetence. Both women were investors in Ghislaine's Asia fund.

"How could you have gotten yourself into this terrible situation?" Camille asked in a lilting French accent as she sipped her Kir Royale. Camille had been in the United States as long as Ghislaine but still spoke with a heavy accent, which Ghislaine attributed to the fact that Camille spent most of her time talking rather than listening. "How could you have left yourself so dependent on the good faith of someone like Robert?"

"A businesswoman like *you*," Lydia exclaimed with a hint of a Texas twang to her voice. "Why the hell didn't you think to be as careful and thorough for yourself as you have been for your investors? Why didn't you go to Monica when things got bad with Robert? Why did you wait until he filed? Didn't you learn anything from the horseshit I had to wade through to get out of my two marriages?" Lydia raised her eyebrows as she lifted her Cosmopolitan to her lips.

"I was so busy and the business was so successful that it never occurred to me to protect myself." Ghislaine shrugged, wanting to appear cool and in control in the hope her friends would soon drop the subject.

"And this Russian girl," Camille began, "you had no idea that Robert was seeing her?"

"Not until he asked for the divorce," Ghislaine replied, shaking her head. "I never imagined that at sixty-eight, Robert would wreck a marriage and jeopardize our business. God knows I wouldn't have cared if he had had another discreet affair." Ghislaine sat lost in her thoughts for a moment. "Time passes so quickly," she murmured half to herself.

"Well, if you ask me," Lydia proclaimed, "the guy on the bicycle who bumped Robert deserves a medal. He should do the same to that bastard stepson of yours. Did they ever find out who the bicyclist was?"

Ghislaine looked briefly from left to right to make sure no one could overhear her, and then glanced down at the table. "No," she replied quietly. "No one saw him well enough to describe him. He probably didn't even know he had hit Robert let alone knocked him into the cement barrier."

"Well, dear Ghislaine," Camille said after a moment. "You are still young and attractive. It's time to think about finding a man, someone who can protect you from the craziness Ward is planning."

"Yes, someone rich enough to make Ward eat shit and leave the company to you! Or, even better, allow you to enjoy life without *worrying* about the company," Lydia said. Then she added with a wink, "What about Andrei Kronsky? He's head over heels for you, rich as Midas, and tough as nails. A friend of a friend told me she saw the two of you at the Biltmore in Santa Barbara not so long ago."

Ghislaine froze.

"We did bump into each other at the Biltmore. Andrei was there for a biotech conference and I was attending that wedding in Montecito," she replied as smoothly as possible. "I respect Andrei a great deal and I'm grateful to him for being such a significant investor in our funds, but I don't really find him attractive."

Lydia rolled her eyes and smirked at Camille.

"Well, screw *respect!* You need a man who gets your blood boiling, gal. Listen," she said to Ghislaine, "I know a couple of lawyers you might like."

Good God, Ghislaine thought, did some women really think having a man could solve any problem in life? How could her friends possibly understand? She loved the work she did, the thrill of landing a big investor, the rush of finding just the right deal for a fund. She was fighting for that work, but also for the strong, resourceful, intuitive leader she knew she could be if given the chance. She believed she could lead the company to triumphs far greater than Robert had or Ward could. Relying on a man, *any* man, to prevail in that struggle would be as great a defeat for her spirit as if she succumbed to Ward without a protest.

"Well, thank you both," she said quickly. "But, I . . ." she paused, "I'm not emotionally ready for that right now."

"Of course, it is only two weeks since Robert died." Camille gushed and touched Ghislaine's arm in sympathy. "Let us know when you are ready. In the meantime, if you ever need anything, you can count on us."

Ghislaine looked at Camille and saw the gentle conviction in her eyes and was grateful for it. She turned to smile at Lydia, but Lydia was eyeing a couple of men at the bar.

"Thank you, Camille. Thank you both. I hope I never have to call on your generosity, but your offer to help means so much to me."

Now let's change the subject, Ghislaine thought.

"Have either of you been seeing anyone interesting lately?" she asked. Camille and Lydia exchanged glances, giggled, and then both started talking at once.

An hour later, Ghislaine made excuses to her friends and began her short drive home. As she turned onto Sunset, her cell phone rang.

"Ghislaine? This is Sarah Wilmer with Children's Charities."

"Hello, Sarah. I'm looking forward to seeing you tomorrow night at the gala. Why are you working so late?"

"Well, we're trying to finalize the program for tomorrow night. Ghislaine . . . you know Bingham is among our top givers. When we didn't receive the check today, I called your office. Around six thirty, someone called back to say your company wouldn't be fulfilling its pledge."

"*What?!*" Ghislaine cried. "That can't be right. There must be some mistake. I approved the check myself on Monday. Are you sure?"

"I spoke with your office manager. A man named Alan? I told him you had personally made the pledge on behalf of the company. He was very apologetic. He said he thought your president had informed you the pledge had been canceled."

Ghislaine felt the air rush out of her chest. A dozen friends who were investors in Bingham would attend the gala. Even worse, several competitors would be there. She pulled onto Loring Avenue to avoid swerving into oncoming traffic.

"I'm sorry. You've always been such a supporter of ours. There's something else, I'm afraid. The programs have already been printed. We're doing our best to cover your name and Bingham International Group, but you can still see your names through the sticker. We had no intention of embarrassing you or your company. I just wish we had been told sooner."

Ghislaine sat in silence for a moment. She would be personally humiliated but, more important, she knew her competitors wouldn't miss the chance to question aloud at the party whether Bingham International, which did not make good on its pledge, was in some financial distress. How soon would her investors ask about the safety of their money? She didn't have the cash to make good on the pledge herself. She couldn't keep hocking her jewels, not when she might need them to fund her fight with Ward. So this is how it will feel if Ward wins, she thought bitterly. Her reputation and her company's sacrificed on a selfish whim.

"I didn't know. I'm sorry, Sarah. I'll speak with Alan on Monday to see what happened. I'm . . . well, I don't know what I am."

"We'll miss you at the head table tomorrow night."

"Yes, of course. Thanks for calling, Sarah. Good night and good luck tomorrow."

Ghislaine turned off the motor and headlights. Her stomach churned with apprehension. This was Ward's shot across her bow. He was reminding her just how vulnerable she was. It was easy to thirst for a fight when she was chatting comfortably over drinks with Camille and Lydia. Did she really possess the determination, the force of will, to engage her stepson in a long battle she could not win by charm or manipulation alone, as she had so many others? And where would she get the money? Reaching over, she opened the glove compartment and extracted a tiny crimson purse embroidered with spring blossoms. She loosened the drawstrings and removed a navy-blue lighter and a half-consumed red-and-white pack of Belga cigarettes. Lighting up and inhaling, she felt the tension begin to drift away. Blowing the smoke out her window, she took four puffs, opened the door, and put out the cigarette on the asphalt. Closing the door, she felt the night's cold creep around her. She swore at herself for being complacent. Her performance in the conference room with Ward had bought herself a few extra days. That was all. If she didn't win this fight, Ward would make sure her name, the person she hoped to be, and the legacy she wanted to leave Rob would be buried underneath a cheap sticker. She would *not* allow that to happen, she vowed to herself. She would *not* let Duncan Luke fail.

TWENTY-ONE

....

SATURDAY, DECEMBER 18
TOKYO

When Duncan emerged from the immigration and customs area into the cavernous waiting hall at Narita Airport, he spied a driver from the Peninsula Hotel holding a sign with his name printed on it. Slumped in the backseat, his mind faded in and out of sleep as the car sped by fallow rice paddies and suburban shopping centers before finally slowing as it encountered the flashing neon and pulsating traffic of Tokyo. Not a second after the limousine pulled up in front of the hotel, a bellboy in a brimless black cap and red vest opened the door and chirped, "Good evening, sir. Welcome to the Peninsula Hotel. How many bags tonight, sir?" Still drowsy, Duncan motioned wordlessly to the single piece of carry-on luggage in the trunk. He grabbed his briefcase and stepped out of the car. The bellboy led Duncan through the lobby to the front desk where he checked in. Five minutes later, Duncan stood in his room on the twenty-second floor overlooking Hibiya Park.

Duncan glanced at the digital clock on the bed stand. It was six o'clock on Saturday evening in Tokyo, but one o'clock Saturday morning in Los Angeles. Sighing, he stripped off his traveling clothes, tossed them in a laundry bag, and turned on the shower.

The warm water poured over his body and shoulders and washed away the haze in his head. As he dried himself, he began to feel hungry and his thoughts turned to Yurakucho Yakitori Alley, only a short walk from the hotel. He dressed quickly in wool pants and a sweater, put some yen in his pocket, and headed out the back door of the hotel toward Yurakucho Station. A cold, clear December night greeted him.

Just before he reached the station, he veered right through an intersection lit up by blazing neon signs and walked below the elevated Yamanote Line for a few minutes until he reached a tunnel running under the tracks. He turned into the opening and immediately his eyes watered as a cloud of smoke enveloped him. In the tunnel, and the alleys beyond, stood countless stands and open-air grills serving *yakitori* to the salary men and office ladies who worked in the skyscrapers in nearby Yurakucho, Hibiya, and Ginza. A *yakitoriya* called Tanuki caught his eye, undoubtedly because of the enormous wooden carving of a raccoon dog that hung on the wall above the grill. Duncan recalled from Japanese folklore that the Tanuki possessed eight special traits that brought good fortune, including large testicles for financial luck. That's what I need, Duncan chuckled to himself: the balls to persuade Taka to stand up to Ward.

He squatted on a red plastic stool at one of the five or six small communal tables. Ignoring the shock on the faces of the gray-haired Japanese men at his table, Duncan squinted at the menu scrawled on a blackboard above the grill. A young waiter offered an English menu, but Duncan had already decided what to order. In heavily accented Japanese, he ordered a bottle of hot *sake,* two skewers each of chicken livers, chunks of breast meat and balls of ground chicken, and, for good measure, two skewers each of grilled green onions and shiitake mushrooms. He asked that the meat be prepared with the sweet sauce called *tare* and the vegetables with plain salt in the *shio* style. When the waiter brought the *sake* bottle and small cup, he began to pour himself a drink. Before he could wet his glass, however, one of the old men reached for the bottle in Duncan's hand and said, "*sumimasen ga, yoroshikereba . . .*" Duncan accepted his offer to pour the *sake* for him, as is the custom, and immediately offered to pour a drink for the old man and his two friends. A half dozen bottles of *sake* and innumerable skewers of grilled food later, Duncan thanked his new friends for their kindness and staggered back to the hotel through the chilly night air.

The phone rang and roused Duncan from a dreamless sleep. The hotel room was pitch-dark. His eyes felt swollen, his hair smelled of charcoal, and his lips tasted of *tare*. Where the hell was he? Then he remembered: Tokyo. He looked at the clock by the bed. It was 3:30 a.m. He picked up the phone and switched on the nightlight.

"Hello," Duncan wheezed, his voice still heavy with *sake*.

"Oh, Duncan," a low raspy voice said. "It's Ghislaine Bingham. I am so sorry if I've disturbed you." She apologized in a way that made it clear that disturbing him was exactly what she had intended. "How was your flight?" Her voice resounded like it came from the next room.

"Do you have any idea what time it is here?"

"Well, yes, of course I know what time it is. It's three thirty Sunday morning Tokyo time and ten thirty on Saturday morning here. But you didn't call after you arrived in Tokyo, did you? I need to go out for several hours and I wanted to hear from you. Besides, I thought you'd be up by now. I always am when I travel to Asia. Have you heard from Takayama-san yet?"

When you travel, Duncan thought, you probably don't stay up drinking with a bunch of retired executives. If you did, perhaps you'd sleep better when you do. "I have nothing to report. I won't see him until later today. By the way," he asked as his mind began to clear, "has M.D. sent her report yet?"

"No, but she will have it done by noon today. I'll forward it to you as soon as I get it."

"Okay. Good-bye. I'm going back to sleep now."

"All right, but don't forget. I expect a report after your meeting with Takayama-san Sunday evening. Speak with you then."

Duncan replaced the phone and turned off the nightlight. He closed his eyes, breathed slowly, and counted to one hundred. To five hundred. Thirty minutes later he cursed Ghislaine fucking Bingham, got out of bed, and turned on CNN International. He checked his emails and saw that the report on Aoki had arrived. The email read simply, "Hope this helps you get back to sleep. Ghislaine."

TWENTY-TWO

....

SUNDAY, DECEMBER 19
TOKYO

Dressed in a blue-and-white *yukata* robe that failed to cover his bony knees, Duncan sat in front of his HP laptop at the built-in wooden desk in his room. He sent an email to Gracie, asking whether he could call Sam at seven o'clock Saturday night in Los Angeles, which would be noon on Sunday in Tokyo.

Then he opened M.D.'s report and scanned it quickly. He noted its four sections, General Background on Aoki Co., Ltd., Aoki's Relationship with Bingham International, Aoki's Current Business Strategy, and Opportunities for Enhanced Cooperation between Bingham International and Aoki. A final section contained lengthy appendices, including Aoki's latest financial statements, newspaper articles on Aoki's business, and analyses by securities companies of Aoki's current and projected performance.

Having represented Taka, Duncan knew the history of Aoki as an intermediary between commodity-poor Japan and the commodity-rich emerging nations of Asia, Latin America, Africa, Eastern Europe, and Russia, so he glanced at the first section and quickly turned to focus on the history of Aoki's relationship with Bingham International. Aoki had approached Bingham in 2006, proposing a relationship whereby Aoki would pay cash for a 20 percent stake in return for priority access to deals in areas of Aoki's principal interest, namely, agriculture, energy and mined commodities, and related infrastructure. The report confirmed that Aoki received certain veto rights over actions affecting the financial status of Bingham International, including the purchase of Bingham International shares and the right to designate one director, currently Taro Takayama. Duncan smiled and nodded to himself. The deal perfectly reflected the man Duncan knew as Taka: a brilliant strategist and an indefatigable negotiator.

M.D. described Aoki's primary strategic goal as supplying the Japanese market with commodities, but unexpectedly she noted a newer objective: feeding the growing appetite in China and, to a lesser extent, India for energy and mined commodities. M.D. concluded by mentioning a special project designed to fulfill both strategic ends, a novel underwater venture in which Aoki, under license from the Japan Agency for Marine-Earth Science and Technology (JAMSTEC), was building prototype robotic submarines for use in mining copper, lead, silver, gold, zinc, and nickel from sulfide deposits located on the seabed within Japan's territorial waters.

Duncan skimmed ahead to the last section on strategic opportunities for Aoki and Bingham International. His shoulders sagged at the pessimistic assessment. None of the investments made by Bingham after Aoki became a minority shareholder had been in a sector of principal interest to Aoki. M.D. speculated that Aoki was likely to be disappointed in its overall relationship with Bingham International. M.D. offered two new ideas to create opportunities for Aoki that struck Duncan as unimpressive. He hoped Taka would have a different view.

It was eleven o'clock when Gracie replied to his email. She and Sam were having dinner with friends tonight. Perhaps he could propose a time on Sunday evening? Good, he thought, the con-frontation of a few nights ago seemed to be behind them. Duncan tapped out a reply that he would call at seven o'clock Sunday evening. After switching off his laptop, he ordered room service, showered, and dressed. He scanned the *International Herald Trib-une* as he ate lunch, a cup of hot cream of corn soup and a soggy turkey sandwich. At three thirty in the afternoon, the phone rang. The car to take him to Hakone had arrived. He only had a few hours before he would be dining with Taka, trying to persuade him to help Ghislaine. Given M.D.'s bleak assessment, he decided that he would ask for a bonus of $50,000, if he were to succeed. Surely fifty grand would be enough for Web to hammer out the main points of a compromise with Gracie, perhaps even by the end of January?

TWENTY-THREE

....

SUNDAY, DECEMBER 19
HAKONE

The driver informed Duncan that the trip to the Hakone Onsen Inn would take a little over two hours. On a Sunday afternoon, as the black limousine headed southwest through the Tokyo districts of Shibuya and Setagaya and on to the Tomei Highway, they encountered little traffic. Duncan found himself mesmerized by the endless urban sprawl pressing up against the ribbon of road, the electronic billboards offering everything from noodles to massages to adult education classes. The driver had tuned the radio to a sports talk show. Two commentators argued in rapid Japanese whether Hakuho, the Yokozuna who had won five sumo tournaments in a row, or Ichiro Suzuki, the Seattle Mariners star right fielder who had tied Pete Rose's record of ten straight 200-hit seasons, was the greater Japanese sports hero.

Just under two hours later, the driver pulled into a driveway of crushed white stone. At the end of the driveway stood a single-story, traditional Japanese building made of Japanese cypress pillars and beams, white plaster walls, and a dark-blue tiled roof. Two older women stood at the entrance dressed in black silk kimono around which milk-white brocade *obi* sashes were wound. They greeted him with a bow.

"Takayama-san has arrived and waits for you in your room," the taller of the two women said. "Before you join Takayama-san, we would be honored if you would bathe and change your clothes. Please come this way." She motioned toward the open sliding doors in a way that made clear she was not offering Duncan a choice. Duncan slipped off his shoes, squeezed the front half of his feet into a pair of black vinyl slippers, and dutifully followed the two women as they shuffled down a dim wooden corridor to the baths at the far left of the building. Steering Duncan into a small, warmly lit locker room, they made sure he understood to wash himself thoroughly before entering the communal *ofuro*.

Duncan undressed, folded his clothes neatly and placed them in a wooden cubicle. He left his slippers on the floor below the cubicle, took a small towel from the stack resting on a stand next to the washing room entrance, and slid into a pair of dark-green plastic sandals used for the bath. Naked except for the green sandals, he opened the door to the washing room and found four washing stations, each with a faucet and hand shower. A sky-blue plastic stool and a red plastic washing bowl waited before each place. Soap, shampoo, and conditioner dispensers stood on the shelf above each station; a razor leaned against a small mirror for shaving. He carefully lowered himself onto a tiny plastic stool, adjusted the water temperature, and washed and rinsed himself several times. Picking up the razor, he stared at the foggy mirror and saw a creased face with sunken eyes that he could hardly believe was his own. He shaved quickly, nicking himself slightly on the chin.

When he was certain that no soap remained on his body and the small cut had stopped bleeding, he turned off the shower and walked over to the opaque glass door marked Ofuro in both *kanji*, pictograms used in the Japanese language, and *hiragana*, one of two phonetic Japanese alphabets. He slid the door open and stepped out into a tiny outdoor garden enclosed on three sides by a bamboo fence. Across a narrow floor of slate-gray tile, steam rose from a stone sunken bath that ran ten feet along the fence. At the far right corner of the bath, hot water from the Hakone *onsen* trickled down craggy rocks into the pool. Duncan eased himself into the clear, burning liquid and closed his eyes.

After ten minutes, he raised his lobster-orange body out of the bath, dried off, and returned to the locker room. His clothes had vanished, replaced by a crisp blue-and-white *yukata* robe and soft cloth slippers. He put them on and ambled up two flights of stairs to his guest room. Opening the outer door, he stepped into the anteroom and stood facing a Japanese sliding door leading to the main room. "Duncan-san! Come in! Come in!" bellowed Taka. Duncan slid the door open, stepped out of his slippers and into a spacious *washitsu*, a traditional *tatami* mat room. In the *tokonoma* alcove to his left hung a somber black-and-white calligraphy; before the calligraphy stood an *ikebana* flower arrangement made of dark-green pine and thin, curled willow branches. A low, square table occupied the middle of the room. At the far end was a large window looking out at the darkening waters of Lake Ashi and, beyond, a snow-capped Mt. Fuji silhouetted by the moonlight.

Beaming at his friend, Taka greeted Duncan with a boisterous, "Welcome, welcome!" Taka had graying black hair that covered his huge square head. His dark eyes were small relative to his face but constantly searching. His voice had a smoker's rasp, but he was as healthy as ever. Duncan was amazed that, even though they were the same age, Taka's short, thickset frame seemed as fit as when he had played rugby at Waseda University.

"It is very good to see you again, my friend," Duncan said with a slight bow.

"Good evening," Taka replied bending slightly at the waist. Taka motioned for Duncan to sit on one of the cushions next to the table. As Duncan lowered himself onto the cushion, Taka pushed the buzzer on the table and immediately a woman clad in a silver kimono and night-blue *obi* shuffled in to take his order for food and drink.

Two hours, four bottles of *sake*, an excellent *kaiseki* meal, and many stories later, Duncan felt that it was no longer impolite to raise the question of Aoki's relationship with Bingham and its position, if any, in the fight between Ward and Ghislaine for control of the company. "I am very sorry to repay your hospitality this evening by mentioning business," Duncan began, "but I am, as you know, here to speak with you about Bingham International Group and my client, Ghislaine Bingham." Duncan paused, hoping that Taka would say something to give him a hint as to how to proceed. However, Taka just raised his eyebrows and nodded to Duncan to continue.

Duncan took a deep breath and began. "I do not believe that Aoki or you have any personal relationship with either Ward or Ghislaine Bingham and so I would respectfully suggest that the important question for Aoki is what course of action would most benefit Aoki's business interest. I understand you have recently learned of Ward Bingham's plan to have the company purchase the shares held by Robert Bingham's estate and also readily understand that the prospect of Aoki owning half of the company without the outlay of any further money would seem appealing. But it is, I believe, *mikake daoshi,* a proposal that is not as good as it looks."

"Really, your Japanese is quite impressive. Is it the *sake* or have you found a Japanese girlfriend to help you recover from your terrible marriage?" Taka asked with a straight face. Before Duncan could object, Taka burst out laughing. "Have some more *sake*," he offered as he poured more rice wine into Duncan's cup. "Now, please continue your excellent presentation. I am most curious as to why becoming half-owner of Bingham for doing nothing is *mikake daoshi*."

"Thank you for your patience," Duncan said as he took a sip from his replenished cup. "Ward Bingham's strategy is not as good as it looks for Aoki because Ghislaine Bingham has been and remains critical to the success of Bingham International in Asia, Latin America, Russia, and Eastern Europe. She has generated most of the business opportunities in those regions. And those regions will continue to account for more than three-quarters of the company's profits. It is simple mathematics. Fifty percent of a company that will soon be worth twenty-five percent of its current value is much less than the twenty percent of the company you have now."

Taka gazed over at the *tokonoma*. "Ghislaine-san is a very attractive and . . ." Taka paused to find the right word in English, "a very energetic woman," he offered. "But she is only an Executive Vice President and Ward Bingham is President.   Besides, as you know, our interest is limited to what it can do for us in the commodity segment. Africa and the Middle East, which are Ward-san's responsibility, are equally if not more important to us than the rest of the emerging markets put together."

"That may be so at the moment," Duncan replied. "But I am sure that Aoki has not missed the rapid rise of China and India and the importance to its business of finding customers in those markets with the Japanese demand for commodities diminishing. Ghislaine Bingham, not Ward Bingham, has been responsible for the company's success in those countries and has excellent contacts that I'm sure would help Aoki find the buyers it needs."

Taka cocked his head to consider what Duncan said and then snorted. "Yes, we need both new customers and new sources of supply. Do you know we have built a deep-sea robot that we hope one day will bring many valuable minerals to our country and others?" Taka shook his head in amazement but, after a moment, his expression grew serious. "I will tell you frankly, Duncan-san, Bingham has disappointed us. They have taken our money, but they do not understand we want more than dividends in return. We want a partner who understands us and will provide opportunities for our business to grow."

"I understand," Duncan nodded. "Perhaps if Aoki had one of its employees seconded to work at Bingham, not just to learn from Bingham but to be available to explain Aoki's capabilities and priorities, the relationship might be more beneficial to both companies? Ghislaine Bingham would be very much in favor of such an arrangement."

"Perhaps, perhaps," Taka said rocking his head left and right, trying to ring the tension out of his neck muscles. Pouring Duncan and himself another round of *sake,* he continued. "And I suppose that you believe that Ghislaine-san would manage an employee assigned to Bingham more successfully than Ward-san?"

"I would not presume to tell you what you already know," Duncan smiled with a slight bow of his head toward his old friend.

Taka's eyes narrowed. He frowned briefly and then chuckled. "It is late and I must return to Tokyo tonight. Please stay here and rest. My car will come for you tomorrow morning at eight and bring you to my office for our meeting. In the meantime, I will consider what you have said tonight and consult with others at Aoki."

"But I did not expect to stay here tonight," Duncan objected. "Could I ride back with you to Tokyo?"

"You are suffering from jet lag and need your rest," Taka insisted. "You are not like our robots, which can work night and day above ground and underwater and never complain! Besides, I have ordered a special dessert for you, a particularly delicious variety of Japanese persimmon. I am sure you will find the fruit ripe and succulent. Good night, Duncan-san. *Oyasumi nasai.*" With another resounding laugh and a slap on Duncan's shoulder, Taka stepped through the screen door and slid it closed.

Ten minutes later, a young Japanese woman in a luminous orange-and-brown silk kimono came to ready the room for the night. Thank God, Duncan thought, they've forgotten the dessert.

With a smile, the young woman gracefully moved the table to one side and motioned for Duncan to remain lounging on the cushion while she prepared the bedding. She took out a large futon, two pillows, and a futon cover from the cabinet on one side of the alcove. She placed a small lamp by the head of the bed and turned it on low. After she turned off the overhead lights, she faced Duncan, whose eyes were barely open. She bowed to Duncan and gestured toward the ready futon. *"Dozo,"* she said.

Fighting off sleep, Duncan smiled gratefully and stepped toward the waiting bed. *"Arigatoo Gozaimasu."* Duncan thanked her and then continued in his rusty Japanese. "By the way, that is a beautiful kimono. What colors are they?"

"The same as my name," the woman replied. "I am called Kaki."

"Kaki?" Duncan asked. Japanese had so many homonyms, *kaki* could have ten different meanings and he was too tired to decipher this one.

"Yes, Kaki. In English, you say, 'persimmon.'"

"Oh," Duncan uttered, as he blinked his eyes trying to focus. So *she* was his dessert. Duncan looked again at the young woman waiting by the futon. She beckoned him to lie down with a wave of her hand. His mind leapt back to the nightmare on the plane. His heart raced and the muscles of his stomach tightened. Goddammit, he thought. I didn't ask for this. I'm not ready. Taka had *no* right. Duncan felt a cold knot grow below his waist; an icy numbness spread around his loins. He glanced at Kaki again. Puzzlement filled her eyes, though she managed to hold her smile in place. Maybe Taka was right, he thought. Sleeping with this lovely Japanese woman might help heal the wounds from his bruising marriage. Even if not, how could he refuse Kaki without offending her and, worse, Taka, who would surely be told that his guest had failed to accept his generous gift?

Kaki looked at the huge American with the sad eyes stand hunched over, unable to move. She had experienced this before, but only with very young men whom she was hired to introduce to the world of lovemaking. The American was certainly not young. Nor did he look inexperienced. Did he not like her? Was he afraid she would break under his weight? Whatever the reason, she didn't have time to waste. She had a date with her new boyfriend in two hours.

Kaki stepped over to take the giant's hand and led him to the futon. She loosened the belt on his *yukata* and, with an expert tug, pulled the robe from his shoulders. When he did not lie down, she gently pushed him onto the bed. But instead of lying on his side so that she could lie next to him or on his back so she could mount him, the American lay face down. What a strange man, she thought. He seems as tightly wound as a skein of yarn. Perhaps a massage would help him to relax? Kaki untied the belt to her orange-and-brown kimono and let the kimono and the cotton undergarment fall to her feet. She sat astride the saddle of his lower back, leaned forward, and began to knead his neck muscles with her tiny but practiced hands. The American groaned and started to breathe deeply. After a few minutes, she massaged his shoulders, and, after a few minutes more, slid down onto his buttocks so that she could rub the muscles of his back. She could feel him relax beneath her touch. His breathing fell into a steady rhythm. He is ready, she thought. She dismounted and stretched her diminutive frame out alongside him. Her feet reached only to just below his knees. His eyes were closed.

"*Daijoobu? Yaritai no?*" she asked softly and then in English. "Are you all right? Do you want me?" She repeated her question in a slightly louder voice. He did not stir. He was asleep.

"*Mottainai,*" she muttered with a shake of her head. Kaki sighed and dressed quickly. She would have plenty of time now before her date to shower and put on her favorite red silk blouse and black satin miniskirt. She looked forward to a night of dancing and drinking with her boyfriend at a local club. Before leaving, she took a small, beautifully wrapped box from her kimono sleeve and placed it on the table. She always left her clients the same gift, a white cotton handkerchief with the *kanji* for love embroidered in red in one corner. Opening the sliding doors, Kaki stepped through and turned to bow toward the futon where the American slumbered. Then she closed the doors behind her.

TWENTY-FOUR

....

SUNDAY, DECEMBER 19
LOS ANGELES

Three hours after Duncan fell asleep in Hakone, Ghislaine Bingham woke with a start. She switched on the light by her bed and immediately turned on her BlackBerry. It was six in the morning. She checked her voicemail for a message from Duncan Luke. Nothing. Growling through clenched teeth, she scrolled through the emails that had come in overnight. There was one from the manager of the Asia fund reporting on a meeting with an Indian telecommunications company and another from the London office sending quarterly financial information on the Polish department store chain Bingham International had invested in, but nothing from Duncan Luke.

"*Salaud.*" Ghislaine spat out.

She sat up in bed and looked at her watch. Thirty minutes after six in Los Angeles was half past eleven on Sunday night in Tokyo. Screw him, she cursed as she dialed the Peninsula Hotel. "Hello? Yes, please connect me immediately to Mr. Duncan Luke's room. Luke. L - u - k - e. Luke. Thank you."

She let the phone ring for almost an entire minute until the hotel operator came back on. "I'm sorry. No one is picking up. Would you like to call back later?" the young man asked.

"No I do not wish to call back later," she barked. "Please send someone to Mr. Luke's room and wake him up. This is an emergency. His mother is very ill."

"One moment, please."

Ghislaine put on her silk robe and paced her bedroom for five minutes, five minutes during which she tried and failed to calm herself down. Finally, an older voice came on the line. "This is Tanaka, the night supervisor. May I ask who you are?"

"I'm Mr. Luke's sister. Our mother is very ill and I need to speak with him immediately," she shouted into the speaker.

"I'm sorry but we have checked his room and Mr. Luke is not there. The bed has not been slept in. Perhaps he is still out with friends?" Tanaka-san offered. Several seconds passed. "Hello? Hello?" asked Tanaka-san.

Ghislaine loosened her jaw just enough to mutter, "Thank you, Mr. Tanaka. Could you put me into his voicemail, please?"

"Fils de putain!" she hissed to herself. She waited for the tone. "Duncan. This is Ghislaine. It is Sunday morning here and Sunday evening in Tokyo. You will have met with Takayama-san by now or something has gone terribly wrong. Either way, I've heard nothing from you contrary to what we had agreed. Call me as soon as you pick this up, do you understand? AS SOON AS YOU PICK THIS MESSAGE UP," she bellowed into the phone.

TWENTY-FIVE

....

SUNDAY, DECEMBER 19
LOS ANGELES

Ward devoted the morning to a long workout in the gym at his condo building. He had gained three pounds on the London trip and was determined to sweat them off. Wearing a black Adidas training suit, he began with thirty minutes on the bike to warm up, moved on to fifteen minutes of stretching, and finished with an hour doing sets on seven of his preferred weight machines. Before using each piece of equipment, he made a practice of wiping it thoroughly with an alcohol swab; he knew gyms bred germs like petri dishes. When he had finished his workout, he studied himself carefully in the mirror, noting where his muscles needed more firming and toning. Satisfied that at forty-three he retained the body of a much younger man, he returned to his condo.

After carefully scrubbing to remove any lingering contamination from the gym, he spent the rest of the morning surveying the Sunday *New York Times* and the weekend *Wall Street Journal*. Running errands that his trip to London had left unattended to and napping briefly to dissipate the haze of jet lag consumed the early afternoon.

At exactly four o'clock Ward picked up the phone, as he had almost each Sunday for nearly twenty years, dialed the Sephardic Home for the Aged on La Brea Avenue and asked to speak with Khala Sawari.

"Certainly, Mr. Bingham," the receptionist replied. "But, first, if you wouldn't mind, our director would like to speak with you. Please hold on." Ward drummed his fingers on the glass of his dining room table.

"Hello, Mr. Bingham? This is Rebecca Schwartz. We've talked before several times?"

"Yes, Rebecca, I remember you. How can I help you?"

"Oh, Mr. Bingham, you *have* helped us already so much. Your contribution to our annual giving campaign was incredibly generous. I just wanted to thank you personally."

"Well, that's very kind of you. I hope to be able to do even more next year. Now, could I speak with Khala? I don't want to keep her waiting."

"Certainly. Good afternoon and thank you again!"

A moment later the reed-thin, watery voice of the woman who had cared for his mother and for him and finally for his grandparents wobbled over the line. In her late eighties now, Khala was his only family. "Who is calling, please?"

"Hello, Khala. It's Judah, Leila's son," Ward crooned as he absentmindedly stroked the back of his neck.

"Oh!" his old nanny exclaimed. "Judah? My little lion? How my days are filled with visions of your lovely mother." And without further prompting, Khala proceeded to retell story after story of Leila as a lively girl, as an alluring young woman, and as a doting mother. At the end of the long march of memories, she halted and asked, as she often did, "Now, tell me about your business, you know, the one Leila's family started, the one Leila promised would be yours one day."

"It's doing fine, Khala. Thank you for asking. You'll be happy to know it will finally be mine soon."

"Oh, that *is* good news. Your mother would be so proud of you," she said in a raspy tone that faded away as she finished congratulating him. Ward heard the fatigue clouding her voice.

"It's been wonderful to speak with you, dear, dear Khala," he enthused. "I'll call you again next week and come to see you soon, I promise."

"Oh, thank you," Khala replied. "That would be wonderful. Will you take me to lunch?"

"Yes, of course," Ward promised. "In the garden, as we always do," he murmured, his voice thickening with emotion.

"Good-bye, then," Khala said, "and bless you, my boy."

An hour later, Ward was seated on his charcoal couch reading the weekend *Los Angeles Times* when he received an email from Levy and Maxwell. After a detailed review, they had concluded that the firm was worth $10 million. Ward slapped the glass-topped coffee table in triumph. In a reply email to Matthew Levy, he thanked him for his report and asked him to send a copy to Rob no later than eight o'clock on Monday morning. Tomorrow he would deal with any objections Rob might raise.

His thoughts drifted to dinner later that evening at the Grill on the Alley in Beverly Hills with his current girlfriend, a sandy-blond aspiring jazz singer named Julie Wharton. He knew it would be tedious to listen to her moan about how no one appreciated her talent and complain of the treachery of club owners and music executives. But it would be a small price to pay for the pleasure of exploring her generous body. Besides, she never complained about showering before having sex. To the contrary, unlike the weepy Azra, she seemed to enjoy washing him.

TWENTY-SIX

....

MONDAY, DECEMBER 20
HAKONE AND TOKYO

"*Ohayo Gozaimasu!*" Duncan's eyes sprang open. He looked around the unfamiliar room. After a momentary panic, he recalled that he was in a Japanese inn in Hakone, where he had met Taka the night before. He saw the small box on the table and remembered being undressed and massaged by Ka-ki. Did anything else happen, he wondered. No, he had fallen asleep under her touch.

"*Ohayo Gozaimasu,*" he called out to let the woman know he was awake and she should bring breakfast shortly. Two hours later, Taka's driver rolled up, crunching the white rock in front of the inn. The two old women who had welcomed him stood there to see him off with a deep bow. He nodded his head in their direction, climbed in the black limousine, and was soon lost in thought as the limousine sped back to Tokyo.

By the time the car pulled up in front of the DN Tower 21 Building, Duncan had replayed the previous evening's conversation many times. Each time he went over the exchange, he felt more certain that he had failed to persuade Taka it would be to Aoki's benefit to keep Ghislaine at Bingham. It wasn't M.D.'s fault, but he suspected her suggestions, which pointed to Ghislaine's importance to Aoki, would be unconvincing in the absence of an overarching strategy to make the partnership flourish. He did not look forward to having his fears confirmed at the meeting this morning and relished even less conveying the bad news to Ghislaine Bingham.

The Aoki offices were located on the fifteenth floor of the massive gray-stone tower attached to the rear of the colonnaded building, made of the same gray stone, where Douglas MacArthur was headquartered during the American occupation of Japan. An office lady in a blue uniform and white blouse led Duncan from the spacious black marble reception area into a long conference room that looked over the moat surrounding the Imperial Palace and the almost three square miles of the park-like Palace grounds. A minute later, the door opened and Taka entered with two younger Japanese executives. Taka introduced Duncan to Takei-san, a thin, high-strung man with a Chaplinesque mustache who oversaw the relationship with Bingham International, and to Emoto-san, a chubby clean-shaven man who supervised Aoki's operations in Latin America. The men each exchanged business cards with Duncan. The office girl served tea as the three Aoki executives sat down facing him.

"I sincerely hope you had a good rest last night," Taka said with a straight face but a twinkle in his eye. "Our Japanese persimmons contain much nourishment that can cure jet lag."

"Yes, thanks to your hospitality, I slept more soundly than I have for several months. I am very grateful for your kindness, as always."

"Not at all, not at all; it was my pleasure," Taka declared with a wave of his hand. And then he paused to indicate that the introductory pleasantries were over and the business discussion was about to begin. "You will excuse me for being so direct, but I must tell you, after discussions with Takei this morning, we reached the conclusion that it is not in our best interest to intervene in the internal affairs of Bingham International. Quite frankly, we do not know either Ward-san or Ghislaine-san well. We do not believe we could evaluate their relative contributions to the company either in the past or the future, despite your most interesting presentation at dinner last night. Also, we consider Aoki's relationship to have been with Robert Bingham. Although he died, which is regrettable, it seems clear he intended Ward-san to control the company after his death. We do not see any reason why we should interfere with Robert-san's choice."

Duncan looked beyond Taka to the Impressionist painting that hung on the wall directly behind him. The painting portrayed the French countryside in the foreground, with what looked like a woman standing before a cow, and a small village of red-and-blue rooftops in the background. Was it a Pissarro, Duncan wondered, or an early Seurat? What would it have been like to live in such a village more than a hundred years ago?

"But then just by chance," Taka continued, snapping Duncan back into focus. "Emoto came to me this morning with a problem that requires urgent and perhaps unconventional action. Please explain the situation," Taka ordered with a curt nod toward his colleague.

"Yes," Emoto-san said in high-pitched but flawless British English. "As you may know, in 2006 an expansion of the Panama Canal was approved by the Panamanian people. The work on the expansion project is expected to be completed by 2014 or 2015. The Colon Free Zone is located at the Atlantic mouth of the Panama Canal. The expansion of the canal naturally led the CFZ administration to consider further developing the CFZ. Multiple opportunities to bid for large-scale construction projects are available. The total value of these projects is estimated to be between five hundred million and one-point-five billion dollars. In order to participate in these bids, however, a company must qualify with the CFZ administration. We, Aoki, believe we can be very competitive in bidding for several of these projects and have been working for more than a year to become qualified." Emoto-san stopped and asked, "Do you follow me so far?"

"Yes, go on," Duncan replied, not quite sure where he was being led and somewhat irritated by the young executive's condescending tone.

"Good. Because we did not have any experience in Panama, we retained a lawyer to assist us in passing through the qualification process. This lawyer is a former official of the CFZ administration, who came highly recommended. We worked diligently to provide him with all of the materials necessary to prepare our submission. The submission was made in mid-November as planned. A week later, our lawyer asked for an additional fifty thousand dollars to cover what he called 'special expenses.' When he refused to provide us with any explanation of these special expenses, we rejected his request. Then, earlier this month, we learned, to our shock, that our lawyer had also been assisting one of our Korean competitors. Naturally, we confronted the lawyer with this information and demanded that he stop working for the Korean company. He refused our request, saying that there was nothing in our contract with him or in Panamanian law that prohibited him from working for the Korean company. He also insisted he had fulfilled the terms of our agreement when our submission was made and our failure to reimburse his expenses meant he could terminate our legal relationship with him." Emoto-san stopped for a moment and looked at Taka for permission to continue. Taka glowered back at him.

"Early this morning, we received another shock. The CFZ administration emailed us saying that they had reviewed our qualification submission and rejected it because of several unspecified deficiencies. You must understand. Our submission is many hundreds of pages long. We reviewed it carefully after receiving the CFZ email and found some minor omissions or discrepancies but nothing that justifies rejection of the entire application. We strongly suspect our former lawyer may have negatively influenced his friends at the CFZ administration or perhaps he promised his friends some bribe which, when we did not pay the special expenses, he did not make and so they rejected our application."

Duncan ran his hand through his hair. What could be the significance of Aoki's Panama project? Was jet lag dulling his mind? "I am very sorry for your misfortune, but I am confused as to how this relates to Bingham International."

"Ah," Taka interjected. "Perhaps you have heard of the Japanese proverb, *inu mo arukeba bou ni ataru*? In English one meaning would be something like, 'the dog who walks around long enough will sometimes be hit by a bone.' Well, you have been hit by a bone. We have a severe problem in Panama that must be solved by Wednesday at noon, the deadline for approval of all qualification submissions. Naturally, we will do everything we can to rectify the situation ourselves," Taka said as he glared once again at Emoto-san. "But I asked Takei whether Bingham had any contacts in Panama who might be helpful to us. He told me that they had recently invested in a new Panamanian company that has a concession from the government to improve navigation on part of the Panama Canal by removing old trees. While Bingham has a minority stake, the company is controlled by Ghislaine Bingham, so we wonder whether she may have some, shall we say, experience in working successfully with the Panama Canal authorities."

"So," Duncan said slowly, "you want Ghislaine to assist Aoki in solving its problem with the CFZ?"

"Yes, that's right," Taka replied crisply. "And, if she does, it will be taken by us as a strong indication of the importance of Ghislaine-san to the future success of the company." Taka paused. "As a result, we would be forced to seriously consider your suggestion that it would not be in our best interest to consent to Ward-san's plans. If she does not, well . . ." Taka raised his eyebrows and shrugged. He did not finish his sentence. He did not have to.

"But you said the deadline is the day after tomorrow." Duncan sputtered. "How in the world can we resolve your problem in two days?"

Taka's mouth curled into a slight smile, but his eyes were cold. "When you are hit with a bone, my advice is that you bite it quickly before it is snatched away by another dog. Besides, it is only Sunday afternoon in Panama and Los Angeles. You have more time than you think." Duncan began to object again but saw impatience flash across Taka's face. Duncan shut his mouth without uttering a word.

"I see. In that case, please excuse me." Duncan apologized as he rose to leave. "I must return to my hotel. I have a four p.m. flight from Narita and an important call to Ghislaine Bingham before I leave."

"My driver will take you back to the hotel and on to Narita. Good luck," Taka said as he escorted his friend to the elevator. "And enjoy Panama." He clapped Duncan on the back. "I don't believe they have persimmons there, but I understand that the mangoes are most enjoyable." A familiar roar of laughter followed Duncan as he stepped into the elevator, turned to face Taka, and bowed.

Duncan returned to the hotel, packed quickly, and then noticed the blinking message light. He listened to Ghislaine's blistering message and erased it. After checking out from the hotel, he climbed into Taka's car. It was one o'clock in Tokyo on Monday afternoon and eight on Sunday evening in Los Angeles. He asked the driver if he could make international calls on the car phone. The driver handed him the phone.

"Hello, Ghislaine? It's Duncan."

"Why didn't you call me last night as we agreed?" she demanded.

"Yes, I'm sorry, but I was involved in negotiations with Taka-yama-san until very late. And, yes, I know that you asked me to call regularly."

"You have no right to leave me in the dark. This is *my* life that's at stake."

"Again, I'm sorry, but," Duncan lied, "I will arrive shortly at Narita and must get through security to catch my plane."

"Now you listen to me . . ."

"I can't right now," Duncan cut in. "I will be in Los Angeles around eight thirty Monday morning. We need to meet around eleven at your home, if that's at all possible. In the meantime, do you have anything in your files that describes your Panamanian company and its operations?"

"The only thing I can think of is the report Rob prepared for our board," she replied. "But why do you need *that*? What does Panama have to do with my problem?"

"Perfect," Duncan said. "Please send it to me by email to review before we meet. Panama may be the key to unlocking Taka-yama-san's support for you."

"You're not making sense."

"Just send me the report. I'll explain everything tomorrow. And ask Rob and M.D. to join us around noon. We may need their help. I've got to get out of the car now. Speak with you when I arrive."

Duncan terminated the call just as Ghislaine shouted, "Don't you *dare!*" After two deep breaths to clear his mind, he asked himself what else needed to get done before he boarded the plane at Narita. He had accepted his current assignment without much thought and now it appeared likely he would be working with Ghislaine and her son on the delicate task of intervening with the Panamanian government on behalf of Aoki. There was nothing illegal in representing clients before foreign government agencies. But if a client secretly greased the wheels with backdoor payments, the lawyer's reputation could be destroyed. Could he trust Ghislaine and Rob Bingham? He would need good intelligence on them before continuing. Duncan called a friend who was an investigator and owed him a favor for all the business he had sent his way while in private practice.

"Hey, Jim. It's Duncan Luke. Sorry to bother you at home on Sunday evening, but I'm calling from Tokyo and don't have much time. I'd like a report on a woman named Ghislaine Bingham, her son, Rob Bingham, and her firm, Bingham International Group. And I need it quickly, Jim, by first thing tomorrow morning. Can you do it?" Duncan half listened as Jim explained the scope of what he could do on short notice. He was already exhausted. How could he possibly find the energy in the next two days to save Taka's Panama project and preserve Ghislaine's chance to beat back her stepson?

"Great. Email or call me when you have it done so we can talk the results over before you send me the report. Thanks, Jim. I owe you drinks and dinner."

Duncan exhaled and sank back into his seat. But for some reason he couldn't relax. He felt uneasy, as if he'd forgotten something important. Oh my God, he thought, bolted upright and slapped his hand down on the seat beside him. *Sammy!* He had forgotten to call Sam when he'd promised! Fuck it. He would just call now. He punched in Gracie's number. As the phone rang, he realized it was already eight thirty Sunday evening in Los Angeles, exactly the time when Gracie would be putting Sam to bed. You're one thoughtless asshole of a father, he swore at himself and terminated the call. How would he explain himself to his son?

....

TWENTY-SEVEN

MONDAY, DECEMBER 20
LOS ANGELES

"Bzzzzzzz," vibrated the BlackBerry on Ward's nightstand at two in the morning. Fuck! He had forgotten to set it on silent mode. Ward knew it would take at least an hour to fall back asleep since his body was still half on London time, so he decided to check his messages. Ward scrolled through his email and discovered, to his surprise, that the communication was from Mr. Takei at Aoki. He asked Ward to call him on his mobile phone as soon as possible. Ward slid from his bed and slipped on his gray Thai-silk robe. Leaning back against the pillows, he called the number Takei-san had provided.

"Hello?"

"This is Ward Bingham," Ward's voice, husky with sleep, announced. "You asked me to call?"

"Ah, yes, this is Takei from Aoki. Please forgive me for disturbing you so early on Monday morning. And thank you for calling me on my mobile. I wanted to speak with you in private. I have some information for you, information that I am giving as a friend."

Ward rolled his eyes in disbelief. No one in business gave information as a friend, least of all Mr. Takei, who served as Aoki's liaison with BIG. For the past two years, Takei-san had nagged him weekly about the dwindling pipeline of deals and chided him whenever the list of possibilities lacked an opportunity in which Aoki might have an interest. Ward opened his mouth to bark a sarcastic reply, but he stopped himself. The Japanese executive was ambitious and seemed to chafe under the control of Taro Ta-kayama. Perhaps this was an unexpected opportunity. He forced warmth into his voice.

"I appreciate the courtesy, Mr. Takei. What kind of infor-mation?"

"Are you familiar with a lawyer named Duncan Luke?"

"No, who is he?"

"He represented Mr. Takayama during the sexual harassment incident several years ago. He was very successful, and Mr. Taka-yama respects him very much."

"Thank you, Mr. Takei," Ward said as his foot began to tap on the floor, "but what does this have to do with me, especially at two in the morning?"

"Duncan Luke met with Mr. Takayama this weekend and visit-ed our offices this morning to discuss BIG."

"BIG?"

"Yes, he represents Ghislaine Bingham. He is proposing that Aoki should not consent to the purchase by BIG of the shares formerly owned by Robert Bingham."

Ward slammed his fist down onto the bed. That *bitch*. She had taken advantage of his good will and accepted his generous offer of more time all the while working to screw him. He should have known.

"But Mr. Takei," Ward objected as he struggled to grasp the consequences of a meeting between Takayama-san and this Dun-can Luke. "My stepmother is not a businesswoman. She's an ag-ing, has-been actress. Besides, Aoki's consenting to the purchase of shares would more than double Aoki's interest in BIG without Aoki having to provide any financing whatsoever. The purchase of shares from the Robert Bingham Estate is an unparalleled opportunity for your company. And I'm sure you realize it would be a considerable success for you personally."

"Yes, you are, of course, correct. In fact, I met with Mr. Takayama this morning to discuss whether Aoki should refuse to consent to the purchase of shares. Although he has a personal relationship with Duncan Luke and would like very much to assist him, he agreed with my recommendation that we should not interfere with your plan. In my view, you are the best person to lead the company and to assist Aoki, and also me, in the future."

"Excellent, excellent, Mr. Takei," exclaimed Ward. "I can't thank you enough. I am confident that we will have many opportunities to work together more closely in the future."

"Unfortunately, the story is more complicated. After my meeting this morning with Mr. Takayama, a problem arose. Aoki is very interested in participating in certain infrastructure projects in Panama, and my colleague Emoto learned today that the administration of the Colon Free Zone had rejected our submission because of deficiencies in the materials, defects which they declined to specify. The deadline for a decision by the CFZ on the qualifications of potential bidders is this Wednesday at noon. We also suspect that the lawyer we hired to shepherd the application is corrupt and working for one of our competitors."

Panama, Ward thought. *Damn.* I don't like where this is going.

"When Mr. Takayama learned this morning of Emoto's blunder, he ordered Emoto to remedy any defects in our materials and resubmit the application by Wednesday at noon. But he also asked me if BIG had contacts in Panama. I told him about Rob Bingham's company. In the meeting this morning with Duncan Luke, Mr. Takayama said he would view any help Ghislaine Bingham could give in resolving our Panama difficulty as a strong indication of her business skills and importance to the future of Bingham International."

Ward squeezed his free hand into a white-knuckled fist. *Fuck.* "I understand, Mr. Takei. And, again, thank you for the information. I will confront Ghislaine in the office today and tell her I will proceed immediately with the buyback plan."

Ward could hear Mr. Takei suck his breath in through his teeth. "I am afraid that you cannot do that."

"Why can't I?"

"Because Mr. Takayama would surely learn of such a conversation with Ghislaine Bingham and would conclude that you must have spoken with me. Only he, Emoto, and I know of the meeting with Duncan Luke and only I have any relationship with you. My career would be finished, and Mr. Takayama would not view favorably any attempt by you to prevent Ghislaine Bingham from helping Aoki in Panama. No, although I appreciate your *samurai* spirit, we must be more subtle."

"All right." Ward breathed. "What do you propose?"

"I understand that our lawyer in Panama is a very resourceful person. I imagine he also has reason to wish Aoki's submission to fail. I suggest that you speak with him about how to prevent Ghislaine Bingham from solving Aoki's problem, without mentioning me, of course."

Ward nodded in silent agreement. Perhaps there was more to Mr. Takei than he had given him credit for.

"Mr. Takei, please give me the lawyer's contact information. I will reach out to him when business opens today."

TWENTY-EIGHT

....

MONDAY, DECEMBER 20
LOS ANGELES

Ward arrived at his corner office by eight o'clock dressed in one of his three light-gray Armani suits. To go with it, he had selected a lightly starched white dress shirt and a black-and-silver-striped tie with a matching silk pocket handkerchief. Although he had at first sought out expensive clothes to curry favor with his father, he had come to enjoy wearing Armani and had acquired Robert's disdain for anyone who either could not afford or lacked the sense of style to dress well. Someone like his Brooks Brothers half brother, for instance.

Having donated to the Sephardic Home the antique oak and pine American pieces with which Ghislaine had furnished Robert's office, he gazed in satisfaction at the contemporary Italian furniture in various shades of black and white that adorned his new office. Sitting down at his desk, he sipped his Nespresso coffee and examined the information he had received from Mr. Takei: Rodrigo Salduba, Salduba & Asociados, Via Espana, Torre Delta, Piso 10, Panama, Republic of Panama. Tel: (507) 269-9177. Email: Rodrigo.Salduba@Saldubayasoc.com.

Ward pecked at his computer keyboard to search for Salduba's English language website. He learned that Rodrigo Juan Salduba had founded Salduba & Asociados in 1999. The firm touted itself as specializing in administrative and immigration law; offshore banks, trusts, and companies; and affiliations with other high-quality law firms in the well-known tax havens of the British Virgin Islands and the Cayman Islands.

Ward clicked on the link to Salduba's biography. A handsome, swarthy man of fifty with slicked-back black hair, a broad face, and a hawk-like nose smiled confidently at him. Ward could not gauge the size of the man, but he appeared solidly built. A 1987 graduate of the Law School of the University of Panama and a 1990 graduate of the tax law program at Tulane University, Salduba had worked briefly with a firm in Miami, after which he returned to Panama in 1991 to become chief of the legal department at the CFZ. He became deputy general counsel of the Panama Canal Authority by 1995 and left four years later to start his own practice.

Ward confirmed that Panama was three hours ahead of Los Angeles and considered how to introduce himself. Then he picked up his cell phone and dialed Salduba's number.

"Salduba & Asociados," a woman's voice said in Spanish and repeated in English, "Salduba and Associates."

"Hello," Ward enunciated slowly so that the woman would know that he spoke only English. "I would like to speak with Rodrigo Salduba. My name is Ward Bingham. I am president of Bingham International Group in Los Angeles."

"May I ask what the nature of your business is, sir?"

"I have a legal problem and wish to speak with Mr. Salduba about retaining him to assist me."

"I see. One moment, please, sir."

After about ten seconds, Salduba came on the line. "This is Rodrigo Salduba. Mr. Bingham? How might I help you?" He spoke excellent English, but the words flowed in the syncopated rhythm of his native Spanish.

"Mr. Salduba," Ward began, "I am president of a boutique investment firm based in Los Angeles. The founder of the firm, my father, died suddenly in an accident several weeks ago."

"I am terribly sorry."

"Thank you," Ward brushed aside the condolence. "In any event, I am also executor of my father's estate. The estate owns sixty percent of the company, I hold another twenty percent, and a passive investor holds the remaining twenty percent. I have planned for the company to buy back the sixty percent with the proceeds of insurance on my father's life, and my stepmother is attempting to prevent the purchase."

"May I ask what interest your stepmother has in the estate?"

"My father filed for a divorce from my stepmother shortly before his death and changed his estate documents to disinherit her."

"And, the price that you, I mean the company, is offering to pay the estate reflects only a small increase in the value of the shares since the marriage?"

Ward snorted, impressed by Salduba's intuition. "Our outside accountants have approved the price as fair and reasonable, but, yes, the offered price would mean that my stepmother's claim based upon California community property law, even if it had merit, would be worthless."

"I see. So, your stepmother, I assume she is unhappy?"

"Yes, she is unhappy. She is attempting to frustrate my father's wishes by persuading the passive shareholder to withhold its consent to the company's purchase of the estate's shares."

"Well, this is a very interesting story. I am confused, however. Why have you called me?"

"My stepmother has an investment in Panama and the passive investor in my company has encountered a problem with the CFZ that they have asked my stepmother to help resolve. If she succeeds, the investor may take my stepmother's side and withhold its approval of the plan that my father had put in place." Ward could feel through the phone line that Salduba's interest had quickened.

"And who is the passive investor, if I may ask?"

"Aoki."

Several seconds passed before Salduba exhaled. "Ah. I see now why you have contacted me." Several more seconds later, Salduba inquired, "How do you know of your stepmother's plans and of my work for Aoki?"

"Let's just say that one of my stepmother's employees has divided loyalties," Ward lied smoothly.

"So you know that Aoki retained me to manage its submission to the CFZ to qualify for the bidding process, and I performed my obligations to my client in full, yet they terminated the engagement and refused to pay my expenses as they had agreed?"

"Yes, that is what I heard."

"You must also know that the CFZ rejected Aoki's submission because of errors Aoki made?"

"Yes, that is the problem that Aoki has asked my stepmother to resolve. A lawyer by the name of Duncan Luke is flying to Panama, possibly tonight, to sort out the submission with the CFZ administration. He is working on behalf of my stepmother."

"Do you know how they intend to do so? The deadline for qualifying is this Wednesday at noon. I think it would not be too easy for them."

"I really don't know," Ward said. "All I know is I want you to ensure that they fail."

Ward could hear Salduba breathing slowly as the Panamanian lawyer considered the situation. "I believe the problem can be managed to your benefit," he said finally. "If you wish me to do so, I would require a nonrefundable retainer of fifty thousand dollars wired to my account immediately."

"I had imagined a fee more in the range of ten thousand."

"I regret to disappoint you. However, this matter would require my *personal* involvement. I do not wish to boast, but no one else in Panama has the expertise to ensure a successful outcome for you. Besides, I am sure that protecting your father's legacy must be worth at least fifty thousand to you."

Bastard. "For such a fee, I would expect a guarantee of a successful outcome," Ward bargained. "Would you give such a guarantee?"

"Yes, I would."

"So I would receive a refund if you are not successful?"

Salduba laughed. "Let us not haggle like two old men over a scrawny chicken but agree as friends that I will refund one-half if I am not successful. But do not expect any money back, my friend. I do not fail my clients."

"Agreed, then; you can expect the fifty thousand dollars by wire this afternoon."

"Excellent, excellent. I will be delighted to assist you."

"Thank you," Ward said before hastening to add. "To make the payment, I will need an invoice for fifty thousand dollars for . . . for what shall we say?"

"Would 'General Legal Advice on Panamanian Tax and Investment Laws' be sufficient?" Salduba offered. "I can send you several memoranda we have already prepared on the subject as a kind of cover."

"Yes, excellent idea. One last thing: I don't need to know *how* you plan to stop my stepmother's lawyer from succeeding, just let me know that you have. Understood?"

"Yes, of course." Salduba grunted. "Panama can be a dangerous place for inexperienced foreigners."

"What?" Ward blurted out. "Look, I don't know what you mean by 'dangerous,' and I do want them stopped, but I don't want anyone hurt either." Salduba remained silent for an instant.

"No, no, my friend. I think you misunderstood me. After all, I am an officer of the court."

"Good," Ward concluded and terminated the call.

Fifty thousand dollars is *outrageous,* Ward fumed after hanging up with Salduba. But it would be worth every penny if Ghislaine failed. He longed to strike back today, to confront her and accelerate taking control of the company, but Takei was right, it wouldn't be prudent to upset Takayama-san at this critical moment. Canceling her pledge to the charity obviously hadn't rattled Ghislaine enough. He would have to find another way to intimidate her, to threaten that which she most valued. Deep in thought, Ward glanced at his BlackBerry and saw a reminder to call Rob today to discuss the accountants' report. A wolfish grin spread slowly across his face.

TWENTY-NINE

....

MONDAY, DECEMBER 20
TOKYO AND LOS ANGELES

D uncan scoured the duty-free shops at Narita for a present for Sam and finally found what he was looking for: a blue Yokohama Baystars baseball cap with the team's logo, a gold starfish, on the front. Sam didn't know much about baseball in Japan, but he loved Takashi Saito, a closer who used to play for the Dodgers, and would be thrilled to have a cap like the one he once wore.

After takeoff and a light dinner, Duncan downed several glasses of wine and a double Courvoisier, stretched out, and wrestled a five-foot blanket over his six-four frame. Before the exhaustion of the past few days carried him to sleep, Duncan's thoughts returned to Sam. He damned Gracie for refusing to allow him to swap his lost Saturday time for an hour on Monday. What harm could it do her? What if he dropped the baseball cap off at the house late Monday afternoon, gave Sam a hug and a kiss, and told him he was sorry to miss so much time with him, that he'd make it up to him soon. Gracie couldn't object, could she? He saw no reason to tell her he might have to travel to Panama. He wasn't certain Ghislaine Bingham would ask him to go and, if she did, he could call Sam from Panama on Tuesday night and be back in time for his Wednesday night hour with him. After all, the deadline was noon Wednesday in Panama, which was three hours ahead of Los Angeles. He would surely be able to return to Los Angeles by seven. Yes, that was it. It would all work out, he assured himself, just before he drifted off to sleep.

Duncan's flight from Tokyo arrived in Los Angeles a half hour early. The Southern California sun glinted off his sunglasses as he hailed a cab. The prospect of a few moments to rest at his apartment, not to mention a shower, renewed his strength. On the way to Playa del Rey, he sent Gracie an email to apologize for missing the call with Sam on Sunday and suggest he drop by around six with a present for Sam. He tried to make his request sound natural but couldn't prevent his stomach muscles from clenching as he pressed Send. Reviewing his other emails, he saw one from Ghislaine with the report on their Panamanian interest. She had it marked as highly confidential and extremely urgent with two exclamation points for good measure. Good God, *everything* seemed to be highly confidential and extremely urgent for this woman.

When he stepped out of the cab, the onshore wind, carrying the scent of salt and seaweed, rejuvenated his spirits and filled his lungs with fresh air. The songs of gulls rang out above him and three kites glided effortlessly overhead. For so many years, he had taken his happiness for granted, as if it were as natural a sensation as sight or a sense of smell. Now, achieving moments of contentment seemed Sisyphean. He dropped his bags and stretched out his arms toward the sun, yearning to release from his shoulders the immense, unremitting tension of impending divorce, separation from Sam, and this new work for Ghislaine Bingham. He lowered his arms and gazed at the kites floating ever higher above the Earth. Recalling a moment last summer when he had taken Sam to Will Rogers Beach to fly kites, he suddenly felt weighed down by the gravity of his troubles. The dream of flying kites with Sam again one day was the only thing that made life bearable.

After a last look over his shoulder at the morning sky, he tramped up the stairs to his apartment. Opening the front door, he felt stale air rush out to welcome him home. Once inside, he saw that everything remained as he had left it three days before. He hung Sam's present on the doorknob to his son's room and glanced at the kitchen clock. It was nine. He took several quick breaths to pump oxygen into his brain, put on some coffee, and fired up his laptop to print the Panama report. As it was printing, he went to his bedroom, stripped off his clothes, and showered. When he returned to the kitchen, he grabbed a cup of coffee and the report and sat down at the small dining table to read. His BlackBerry rang.

"Hello, Duncan. It's Jim Brooks. Is this a good time to talk about Ghislaine Bingham?"

"It has to be quick but, sure."

"Okay. Ghislaine Bingham is a naturalized American citizen born in Brussels on September 3, 1962. She is an unmarried widow. Her husband of twenty-five years, Robert Graham Bingham, died in a Roller blading accident earlier this month. He had filed for divorce about six weeks before, but the divorce hadn't been finalized. She has a son with Robert, who is also named Robert, but everyone calls Rob. Rob is twenty-three. She also has a step-son, Ward, who is forty-three. She was raised by her mother, Monique Palet, a Belgian citizen who ran a successful wine bar in Brussels until her death in 2000."

"Did you see any connection between Robert's death and his filing for divorce? Any incentive to hurry him along?"

"The police looked into that question. Spurned spouses are prime suspects. But they concluded his death was an accident.

Witnesses testified that he was Roller blading without a helmet and a passing bicyclist clipped him. He lost balance and rammed his head into a concrete barrier. They never found the bicyclist but concluded that what killed him was his failure to wear a helmet—something Ghislaine Bingham, who was nowhere nearby, could not have possibly influenced."

"All right, then. What about her childhood?"

"She was raised and educated in Brussels and became a world-class figure skater, winning first place in the Belgian National Championships in 1981 and, in the same year, coming in tenth and twenty-fifth in the European and World Championships, respectively. In 1982, she came in fourth in the World Championships, but the competition was marred by a judging controversy, an unusually high score was given to the third-place finisher and an unusually low score to Bingham by a French judge. The French judge, it turned out, was a close friend of her former coach, whom she had fired for making unwanted sexual overtures."

"Not the only time that's happened, I'll bet," Duncan shook his head. "Sorry to interrupt. Go on."

"No problem. Her skating career stalled with the controversy, but Bingham was offered modeling and acting opportunities in Europe and the United States. She appeared in a half-dozen low-budget films in 1982, 1983, and 1984. While making one of them in 1983, she severely twisted her ankle, ending her skating career. She gave up acting in 1985, after she married Robert Bingham."

"I'm really more interested in her business experience," Duncan interjected. "How did a former skater and failed actress get involved with Bingham International Group?"

"She joined Bingham International in 1990. Up until then, Robert Bingham had run it as a boutique private equity firm that invested in California companies. The business model changed radically when Ghislaine Bingham began to work there. Through her contacts in Europe, in the 1990s she generated investment opportunities first in Holland, France and Belgium and afterward in the newly emerging markets of Eastern Europe, the former Soviet Union, and Russia itself. Bingham developed a reputation as the only West Coast investment firm specializing in emerging markets. Twenty years later, Bingham has four fifty-million-dollar funds for investments in the emerging markets of Eastern Europe and Russia, Asia, Latin America, and the Middle East and Africa, respectively. The company often invests alongside the funds and, of course, both the funds and the company borrow from banks to finance part of the purchase price to create leverage and enhance profitability."

"Was Ghislaine involved in the Latin American, Asian, and Middle Eastern funds, or was that exclusively Robert or someone else?"

"She has been instrumental in finding deals in Latin America and Asia as well as Europe. Apparently, several of her movies enjoyed more commercial success in those regions than they did in Europe and North America. She met figures in the public and private sectors when she toured to promote her films and, over the years, cultivated those contacts for her company. Ward is the one in charge of the Middle East and Africa fund."

"What's her position?"

"She's a Director and Executive Vice President, External Relations, of Bingham International Group, Inc., sometimes called 'BIG.' She is described as responsible for Business Development and Government Relations."

"Is she clean financially?"

"She has no outstanding credit card or bank debt. She has hocked some jewelry recently, about seventy-five thousand dollars' worth. Her only significant assets appear to be the home, some art, and whatever interest she may have in the company."

"Drugs, alcohol, arrest record?"

"Aside from a tendency to accumulate speeding tickets, the police records reveal no arrests or other incidents. No drugs or alcohol of which we're aware. She's apparently an exercise fanatic who is quite knowledgeable about fine wine but oddly enough doesn't like to drink it. Hard to imagine, isn't it? Anyway, let me add a little flesh to the skeleton. First, as a recently separated man, you'll be interested to hear that the newly available Ghislaine Bingham is a gorgeous woman."

"I appreciate the information, but I've met her. She's not my type. Anything else?"

"Okay. Okay. Yes, two other things. First, she is a well-respected philanthropist. She has a reputation for giving back to the community, which, of course, doesn't hurt her business either. Second, and more troubling, one source implied pretty adamantly that BIG's success in emerging markets might stem from its habit of throwing lavish parties for foreign government officials, complete with goodie bags, as well as its practice of making contributions to charities sponsored by those officials."

Duncan stood up from the table and began to pace. "Hold on, Jim. You mean this source is saying that BIG bribed foreign officials to get business?"

"As I said, the source just implied it. No one else had a bad thing to say about Ghislaine Bingham."

"Okay. I think I've got it all, but it would be helpful to have the written report by email. Thanks again. I really appreciate your help."

"Let us know if you need more."

He sat back down, Rob's unread report staring up at him. Tapping his index finger rapidly on the table, Duncan mulled over the information he'd just learned. The report of thinly disguised bribes bothered him, but there was no solid evidence to stop him from going forward with the Panama trip, as long as he made it clear to both Ghislaine and Rob that he would be the one calling the shots.

He glanced at the clock, it was almost 10:45. *Shit.* No time to do anything but skim Rob's report for relevant information. BIG invested $200,000 to acquire 20 percent of Canal Environmentally Sustainable Development, S.A., a Panamanian company in which Ghislaine also owned 60 percent and a Jorge Rodriguez owned 20 percent. CESD's only asset was a twenty-five year concession granted by the Panama Canal Authority to harvest timber from submerged forests in Lake Gatun, part of the Panama Canal.

Nothing useful here, he thought.

A sentence caught his eye: "Partnering with a prominent Panamanian family should lead to more investment opportunities in the future."

Duncan tore through the materials attached to the report. When he found the biography of Jorge Rodriguez, he grinned. Stuffing the report and its attachments in his briefcase, he sprinted down to his car. It was eleven o'clock. He was already late.

As he was getting into his car, the red message light on his BlackBerry caught his eye. Gracie had responded. He flinched and forced himself to open her email. "No, you may not 'drop by' today at six. I told Sam yesterday that you would call him last night at seven," she wrote in a tone that felt no less strident than if she had been sitting next to Duncan. "When you didn't telephone *as you promised,* Sam became *extremely* upset. It is *beyond my comprehension* how you could hurt your son by both missing your time with him on Saturday night and then failing to call on Sunday! What were you *thinking?* In any event, he will be expecting your calls tonight and tomorrow and to see you this Wednesday at seven. *Don't* disappoint him again."

Duncan's head dropped to his chest. He understood that Sam might be upset at him. Shit, he was angry with himself. He called Gracie at home and on her cell. No answer. He spiked his cell phone into his briefcase pocket. Maybe Gracie was lying. Maybe Sam *did* want to see him and *that's* why Gracie refused to let him even stop by for a moment—to keep Sam away from him. He punched his forearm twice into the steering wheel. All right, all right, he slowed his breathing. Remember, you're the one who screwed up, not Gracie. What a *fucking mess.* He needed this job so he could afford to fight to be a father to Sam, but what good would the money be if earning it drove Sam further and further away?

THIRTY

....

MONDAY, DECEMBER 20
LOS ANGELES

Ward waited until ten o'clock before calling Rob and asking him to stop by his office to discuss the Levy and Maxwell report. While he was waiting for his half brother to appear, he opened his top drawer, took out the shoe-shine cloth he kept there, and reached down to polish one of the chrome legs of his desk. The building's custodial service was getting sloppy again. A few minutes later, Rob knocked and walked in, his navy-blue pinstripe suit jacket slung over his shoulder.

"So nice to see you," Ward greeted Rob without rising from his seat. "Please sit down. I assume you've seen the report from Matthew Levy?"

"Yes, I've seen it and, no thanks, I'm more comfortable standing," Rob replied throwing his suit jacket on the gray leather couch facing Ward's desk.

"All right," Ward shrugged. He leaned back and wrapped his hands around the back of his neck. "Well, I can tell you I found the ten-million-dollar valuation for the company a little shocking. I was certainly hoping to get more than three million dollars for my fifty percent of our father's shares."

"Don't bullshit me," Rob interrupted, holding his right hand up. "At Matthew's value, you walk away with three million *and* fifty percent of the company. My mother and I are the ones who get screwed and you know it." Ward's mouth formed a thin smile. His eyes remained fixed on Rob.

"I'm sorry you feel that way, but I'm the executor and, in deciding upon a value for the shares, I'm entitled to rely on the expert opinion of the firm's independent accountants. I don't view that as *screwing* anyone."

Rob's face reddened. "We'll hire our own experts to give a vaccurate aluation," he roared, "and we'll take you to court if that's what we have to do to get some justice."

Ward studied his half brother. What was the nickname that he had given Rob so many years before? Oh, yes. Dudley Do-Right, the strong-chinned, weak-brained Canadian Mountie of Saturday-morning cartoon fame. People never change, do they?

"I think you meant 'accurate valuation,' didn't you? Anyway, I'm not sure you see the point," Ward continued pedantically.

"Even if Ghislaine and you were to get another set of accountants to give a much higher value, the issue will not be whether a judge thinks your accountants are better than Matthew Levy. The issue will be whether a judge thinks it was unreasonable for me to rely on the firm's auditors, auditors whom your mother as a director has voted to approve every year for the past decade. I think a judge would have a hard time finding my decision to be *unreasonable*," he concluded, folding his hands in his lap.

"But, look, you're my brother," Ward declared opening the palms of his hands and in a tone filled with as much warmth as he could muster. "I don't want to waste time and money fighting with you when there's so much *good* that we could do together. Here's what I propose: if you agree not to contest the value at which the company purchases Robert's shares, I promise I will continue to support your Panamanian project and fund, within reason, other development projects you bring to me. On the other hand, if you do fight me." Ward slapped both hands down on his desk. "I will pull the plug on Panama and never give you another dime for your development work. Sound fair to you?"

Rob stared at Ward. "My parents promised me the company would support my Global Development Division for ten years if I came back to work at BIG. I don't give a shit about the company except as a means to help people who didn't have the advantages we had growing up. That's why I gave up the job at the World Bank and returned to L.A. That's what I want to devote my life to."

Ward snickered, learned back in his chair once more, and put his feet up on his desk.

"Dear father is dead, Rob, hadn't you heard? And, just before he died, he stripped your mother of any power she might have had over BIG. If anyone has broken a promise to you, our father has, not me. But, hey, I want you to succeed. I agree with you that BIG shouldn't be just about enriching our clients and ourselves. I'll be happy to agree to a ten-year deal for development projects up to a cap of, say, five percent of company profits. My offer is better than the one your parents made you, don't you agree?"

Rob folded his arms and examined Ward's impassive face. "I want a week to think this over and talk with my mother."

"Certainly," Ward replied with open arms. "Take a week. Just remember. Working together, we can do a great deal of good here. On the other hand, fight me and I will turn your dreams into nightmares. Understand . . . *brother?*"

THIRTY-ONE

....

MONDAY, DECEMBER 20
PANAMA CITY

agdalena spent the weekend with Rodrigo at the Decameron Golf and Beach Resort in Playa Blanca. He played golf during the day and, with Luz's words ringing in her ears, she made love to him at night. Early Monday morning, he dropped her at her apartment and kissed her passionately before speeding off. For the first time in months, he told her he wished to make her happy. She did not, of course, speak of the resident visa, but she now felt confident he would grant her wish.

As she crawled into her bed, happy to be alone and feeling more secure than she had in months, she thought of Anna again but only with the dull regret one feels after a loved one who had been sick for many years finally succumbs. Her phone rang. After a moment's hesitation, she lifted the receiver.

"Magdalena! Thank God you are home," Luz's terrified voice boomed over the phone. "The police and immigration authorities raided the Golden Island last night and arrested me! They are threatening to deport me."

"But they can't! You are here legally, aren't you?"

"I have a tourist visa, but it does not allow me to work. They have arrested me for prostitution."

"Oh, Luz. I will call Rodrigo immediately. He can help I am certain."

"Thank you a thousand times!" A few minutes later, Magdalena reached Rodrigo.

"*Querido,* what happened last night? My friend Luz called. She said there was a raid on the club!"

"Yes," he acknowledged nonchalantly. "An inconvenience, surely, but a necessary one. Fortunately, it was a Sunday night."

"But Luz has been arrested! She will be deported unless we help her."

"I have told you before, *querida,* my business is none of your concern."

"Rodrigo, please. You know I cannot go to the police, but you can send someone from your office to have her released. *Please.*"

"You try my patience but, if you insist, I will speak to you of business this one time, because you were so good to me over the weekend. If your friend Luz had worked for me, I would have supplied her with the proper visa and she would not have been taken. It is therefore her fault she has been arrested, not mine."

"But, Rodrigo, *querido.* She is my friend, from Cartagena, my home."

"*Querida,*" Rodrigo spat the endearment out like a rotten piece of meat, his voice rising as he spoke. "The only girls arrested were those who came on tourist visas and work for *their* profit in *my* club competing against *my* girls. Your friend Luz *stole* from me and must suffer the consequences. You are not a fool. Do you think the police would raid my club without my permission? Of course not. I was the one who asked them to come."

"Oh my God. You asked them to raid your *own* club? But they will stamp her passport so she cannot return for *five* years. She has two children, Rodrigo. She must work for them. Have pity on her!"

"Have pity on *her?*" Salduba roared. "If she were not deported, do you think any girl would work for me again? Of course not. My business would be ruined, a business that not only pays for *your* clothes and car, *your* food and apartment, but a business that employs dozens of poor girls so they can feed *their* families, *their* children. Did your friend consider what would happen to those who prosper from my generosity if the club failed? Did she have pity on *them?* No! Your selfish friend is a filthy parasite who sucks the blood from the body that feeds her, a leech that must be burned away! Besides, I am sure she will find something to do in Cartagena. But enough now. I enjoyed your company over the weekend, but you have become tiresome again. Goodbye!"

The phone went dead, but Magdalena's heart continued to pound. As an *ilegal,* there was nothing she could do to help poor Luz herself, and Rodrigo would not lift a finger. Even worse, she had heard the exasperation in his voice; she had become "tiresome again." The sense of security she had begun to feel just moments before had evaporated. She had to persuade Rodrigo to obtain a resident visa for her now while he still remembered their weekend together, or the next time she offended him he would rip her from her life in Panama and send her back to Cartagena with no more consideration than he gave Luz.

···

THIRTY-TWO

MONDAY, DECEMBER 20
LOS ANGELES

Ghislaine was working in her home office when Duncan called to say that he would be forty-five minutes late. "Don't be any later, because Rob and M.D. are arriving at noon and I want to speak with you before then," she commanded and hung up. *Merde.* Since Duncan had called her on Sunday evening from Tokyo, she had asked herself a hundred times why he needed information on CESD and how that would win her Takayama-san's support. She detested the feeling that Duncan Luke was intruding on completely unrelated aspects of her life when he had been hired to solve one discrete problem. He was like a defective spot remover that not only failed to remove the stain but ruined the entire carpet.

Oh, stop complaining and start planning, she admonished herself. She could not expect others to follow if she did not lead. Turning to gaze out the bay window behind her desk, she pondered how she should conduct the meeting with Luke. She wanted to send an unmistakable message that this was not a friendly encounter between equals. His irritating habit of failing to keep her informed was something that she would forgive, provided he did not disappoint her again. She would be concerned, even mildly annoyed, but in command. She would stand with her back to the door he would enter and turn forty-five degrees toward him as he came in. She would not say anything until he spoke first. When she did speak, she would neither return his greeting nor ask him to sit down nor even acknowledge his apology, if he made one. She would smile slightly, and quietly, but firmly, order him to report.

At eleven forty-five, Ghislaine's housekeeper, Inez, called her to tell her that Mr. Luke had arrived. Ghislaine asked Inez to bring him to her office. A few moments later Duncan Luke stepped through the door. She immediately turned her back to him.

THIRTY-THREE

....

MONDAY, DECEMBER 20
LOS ANGELES

Duncan observed Ghislaine gazing out a bay window at the back of her office. He opened his mouth to greet her but stopped himself. A quick glance around her sanctuary might give him a clue to the strong-willed woman who needed protection from her stepson and from herself at the same time. He immediately admired her rustic pine desk and walnut-stained Shaker armchair with a dark leather cushion. Two identical, armless chairs sat between Duncan and the desk. A carved wooden armoire stood to his left and served as a bookcase and a cabinet for a television and audio equipment. A southwestern-style pine bench with a worn leather seat and a back cushion of faded red and yellow textiles, which looked like a desert sunset, lined the opposite wall. The woman clearly loved beautiful things, but her taste—and he knew instinctively it was her style not some designer's—was eclectic and understated, one that whispered but did not shout wealth.

Ghislaine turned slightly toward him without saying a word, arms folded against her chest. The fragrant, slightly musky scent of her perfume wafted around him. The light from the bay window gave her hair a caramel hue. She wore a light-blue pants suit that perfectly matched her eyes. A large turquoise pendant adorned her neck. She seemed to be posing like a model for a photo, or was she waiting for him to say something?

"Hello," he finally offered. No response. "Well, if you don't mind, I'll sit down. I am bone tired from the trip." Duncan slumped down onto the bench. Misjudging the location of the wall behind him, his head thudded against the wood paneling. Rubbing the back of his head, he noticed that Ghislaine started to say something and then stopped herself. Instead, she leaned on the back of her chair.

"When you are comfortable perhaps you would be good enough to tell me what Panama has to do with Aoki?"

"Absolutely," Duncan said, feeling suddenly as if he were ten years old standing in front of Mrs. Maguire, the principal, trying to explain why he tripped the irresistible Melanie Marks in the pick-up soccer game during recess. He could hardly say to Mrs. Maguire it was the only way he could think of to get Melanie to notice him.

Before Duncan could start talking, however, the phone rang. "Please ask them to come to my office," Ghislaine said. She turned to Duncan. "Well, so much for our *private* chat. Rob and M.D. are here. Is there anything that you'd like to tell me before they arrive? If not, I don't see any reason to ask them to wait, do you?"

"None," Duncan replied. "In fact, it's better that they're here so we won't have to repeat everything before agreeing on a course of action."

When M.D. and Rob had settled themselves in Ghislaine's office, Duncan described his conversation at Aoki, emphasizing that Taka had decided, before learning of Aoki's problem in Panama, not to side with Ghislaine in her struggle with Ward. When he finished, he studied the three faces turned toward him to see whether anyone had any questions. Ghislaine sat erect in her chair with her hands in her lap. M.D. was in one of the armless chairs facing Duncan. She looked thoughtfully first at him and then at Ghislaine. Rob had not bothered to turn the other armless chair around but, straddling it backward, was leaning forward against the back of the chair toward Duncan. He, too, twisted to face Ghislaine.

"So, Takayama-san promised to *consider* helping me if we were able to solve his Panama problem?" She snorted. "If we succeed, what assurance do we have that he will be able to persuade his board at Aoki to veto Ward's plan?"

"I admit we have no assurance," Duncan replied holding his mitt-like hands up. "On the other hand, based upon my experience, saying he would consider helping you is about as strong a statement as he would make given the circumstances. I think the real question for you is: Do you have any alternative but to try?"

"All right, then. Let's say that this is the best option we have. I still don't see how Takayama-san, or you for that matter, can expect me to help him in Panama."

Duncan looked down at the ground. The handmade burnt-red Mexican terra-cotta tiles were almost a foot square. They were stained and pocked and scraped. Were they really part of the original house or had they been distressed to make them look old?

Ghislaine rapped her knuckles against her desk like a grade-school teacher trying to get the class's attention. "Did you hear what I said, Duncan?"

Duncan raised his eyebrows slightly, pursed his lips, and shrugged.

"I'm not sure he does expect you to help him. But he is giving you a chance for three reasons. First, he has a crisis and is grasping at any means to resolve it. Second, he may not expect you to be able to help him, but I did make a pretty good case that you were critical to the company in large part because of your connections in Latin America, Asia, and Europe. So he has an open mind. And third, he trusts me to manage whatever we do in Panama so our actions do not harm Bingham International or Aoki, even if they may not help either one."

"Ah. I see," Ghislaine said, lacing her long fingers together and placing her hands on the desk in front of her. "In order to persuade Takayama-san to support me, you exaggerated my importance to the company's success in Latin America and, for good measure, you maneuvered yourself into whatever effort we might make to help him."

Duncan sighed. "He made it clear that he wanted me to be part of your team. I think he'd be disappointed, perhaps even alarmed, if I were not. Of course, it's ultimately your decision."

"Takayama-san may trust you," Ghislaine declared, "but I've known you for less than a week and in that short time learned that I cannot rely on you to keep me informed so I can make sound decisions. Yet . . ." She exhaled slowly and looked down at the desk. "Yet," she repeated to herself and looked up at Duncan. "Takayama-san obviously would not have given me this chance unless he assumed you would be involved." Ghislaine shook her head slowly at the unappealing choice she confronted. "All right," she said finally. "What's your plan?"

Duncan looked out the bay window past Ghislaine. He half-hoped she would have fired him. She was presumptuous and temperamental, and going to Panama risked doing further damage to his shaky relationship with Sam. Still, he needed Ghislaine's money and had to admit he was warming to the challenge of solving Taka's problem. Perhaps he wasn't ready to give up practicing law altogether? As long as he was back in time to see Sam Wednesday night, it would all work out.

"I don't have a detailed plan yet," he conceded, lowering his eyes to Ghislaine's. "But Rob and I would need to fly to Panama *tonight* to accomplish anything before Wednesday. I assume there's a red-eye. I'll send an email to Rodrigo Salduba asking for an urgent meeting tomorrow to discuss Aoki's situation and solicit his help in resolving the application problems. He may or may not be willing to assist us, but we need to try him first."

"And if that doesn't work?" Ghislaine asked pointedly. "What then?"

Duncan shifted his weight on the bench and leaned forward. "At the same time I contact Salduba, I want Rob to ask Jorge Rodriguez to speak to his uncle about arranging a meeting with us."

"What the hell?" Rob exclaimed shooting to his feet and nearly tipping his chair over. "What does Jorge have to do with any of this? CESD has zero involvement with the CFZ. We're a small company trying to help the people of Panama improve their lives and generate some jobs in the process."

"Jorge's uncle, Fernando Rodriguez, is the General Manager of the CFZ. You *know* he is because it's in the biography you attached to the CESD report *you* authored. And Jorge's father is a prominent businessman and a member of the National Assembly from the Panamenista Party, one of the two leading parties that govern the country. If Salduba can't or won't help us, I would guess that Jorge could at least get us a meeting with his uncle. Asking Jorge for a favor is probably the best chance we have to assist Aoki."

"I won't ask him," Rob insisted. "He's my friend and my partner. He cares about helping the poor people of his country, not about getting a sweet deal for some Japanese multinational that has absolutely no concern for the well-being of the people they are exploiting in the developing world."

Duncan felt the hairs on the back of his neck tingle. He twisted himself into an upright position on the bench. "Let me make myself clear. I am *not* proposing Jorge attempt to influence his uncle one way or the other regarding Aoki's problem. I would resign rather than ask him to persuade his uncle to benefit a client. But I am suggesting that his uncle would listen to him explain the situation and make up his own mind about meeting with us. After all, I would think it would be in his interest as General Manager of the CFZ administration, as well as in his country's interest, to have as many qualified companies as possible bidding against one another."

"My friendship with Jorge is based upon mutual trust and respect," Rob insisted. "Asking him would destroy that trust and risk CESD's future." Rob turned to Ghislaine. "You understand, mother, don't you? If a meeting with Jorge's uncle is so important, why can't Duncan arrange it on your behalf?"

Ghislaine looked at Rob before facing Duncan. She opened her mouth to speak just as M.D. sprang up from her chair. "How can you reject Duncan's suggestion that you know will help your mother? Without her, CESD wouldn't exist. And if Ward ousts Ghislaine from the company, how long do you think it will be before he decimates CESD? Sure, you have a concession from the government, but you will need more capital to implement it. Where do you think that will come from if he expels Ghislaine?"

"You're wead drong." Rob cut her off with a wave of his hand. "I mean, oh, dammit, you're . . . you're dead wrong. Ward promised me that he would *support* CESD and my development projects for ten years if I didn't challenge the buyback of the shares. If I ask Jorge to help us and we fail, Ward will abandon CESD and refuse to fund the development work I came home to do."

M.D.'s ebony eyes widened. She looked back at Ghislaine. Ghislaine closed her eyes briefly then opened them and cleared her throat. "When did Ward speak with you, Rob?" she asked quietly.

"He called me this morning to discuss the Levy and Maxwell report. I blew up at him for trying to cheat us. That's when he made the offer and the threat. I . . . I was going to discuss it all with you after this meeting."

"You *must* know Ward will betray you as soon as he wrests control from Ghislaine," M.D. said, practically growling at Rob. "Do you think Jorge will commend you when CESD founders because you didn't confide in him? Are you really so . . . so obtuse?!" A cloud passed quickly over Rob's face as he appeared not to understand what M.D. had said, then his confusion cleared and he flinched as if slapped. He slumped down beside Duncan on the bench. Out of the corner of his eye, Duncan saw Ghislaine's face blanch briefly. She turned to M.D.

"I know you have all of our interests at heart," she said softly. "And I appreciate your loyalty to me, but you don't know Rob well. If you did, you'd realize he not only has a good head, but more important, a warm heart. I understand how he could feel conflicted when he spoke to Ward." M.D.'s mouth opened to object, but she closed it quickly and nodded.

"I'm . . . I'm sorry," she murmured to Ghislaine. She straightened her shoulders and addressed Rob. "Sorry, Rob. I get carried away sometimes. Sometimes I talk faster than I think. I apologize." Rob, who was staring at M.D., shook the dazed look from his face.

"Thanks, Mother, but . . . but M.D.'s right. I guess I wanted so much to believe Ward would honor his commitment, I lost my bearings."

"No need to apologize. You know Jorge well and I trust your judgment. Whether you decide to speak to Jorge or not, please don't base your decision on a promise that Ward made to you. I think you know what kind of man he is."

"Yes, I do. As long as we're only asking Jorge to tell his uncle about Aoki's situation, I don't have a problem speaking to him. Perhaps, before I call, Duncan and I should discuss exactly what and what not to say?"

"I think that's a good idea, Rob," Duncan said, trying to diffuse any residual tension. "So we have a plan. Rob and I will travel to Panama tonight in the hope of meeting tomorrow with Salduba and, if necessary, Jorge's uncle. Rob, perhaps you can arrange the flights for us, a pick-up at the airport, and a hotel room for Tuesday night? I need to be back in Los Angeles no later than five thirty on Wednesday."

"Sure, if you want to arrive tomorrow morning, we have to take the Copa Airlines flight late tonight. It arrives in Panama City about ten thirty. I'll arrange the pick-up. We'll stay at the Marriott. As for the return, you'd have to be on the twelve thirty flight back to Los Angeles in order to make it here by five thirty. Do you think we can finish by then? The next flight is at seven."

"The deadline is noon on Wednesday so, yes, I think we'll know one way or the other by late Wednesday morning."

"And if you don't?" Ghislaine interrupted. "If there's still work to be done at the last minute, you can't just pick up and leave. I want your promise that you'll stay until we know for certain that Aoki's bid has either been accepted or rejected."

Duncan felt his mouth go dry. Did he dare risk disappointing Sam again? If he couldn't pay Web, he would lose more than just one night with his son.

"All right, you have my promise," he finally replied. He turned to Rob. "Why don't you make backup reservations for the flight at seven? While you're contacting Jorge, I'll email Salduba. Tell Jorge we'll be available Tuesday, late afternoon or very early Wednesday morning, if his uncle is willing to meet with us. Remind him, please, of the noon Wednesday deadline. I'll try to set something up with Salduba for Tuesday around midday. Does anyone have anything else?"

"Just a second," Ghislaine interrupted. "I haven't given my consent yet."

Rob and Duncan stared at Ghislaine, who was now standing behind her desk.

"I will agree to this plan on the condition that M.D. goes with you. She is fluent in Spanish and can translate in meetings, if that's necessary. More important, I trust *her* to communicate with me on a regular basis." Ghislaine glared at Duncan.

"M.D., I'm sorry to ask you to do this at such late notice, but would you go with them?"

"I will. I was hoping you would ask me. My career is on the line too. I'll go home, pack, and meet Rob and Duncan at the airport around midnight."

"Excellent, thank you," Ghislaine said. "*Now* we have a good plan. Best of luck in Panama, M.D. and Duncan. Rob, let's discuss the report from Levy and Maxwell and see if we can find any flaws in it."

Duncan rose slowly and ambled to the door.

"I'll see you two at the airport tonight," he said over his shoulder to M.D. and Rob. As he opened the door and stepped out, he muttered just loud enough so he was sure Ghislaine would hear him, "I will want to discuss a fifty-thousand-dollar bonus with you if by some miracle we succeed in Panama and persuade Takayama-san to support you."

Swinging the door closed, he glimpsed out of the corner of his eye Ghislaine Bingham's face flushing a brilliant red.

THIRTY-FOUR

....

MONDAY, DECEMBER 20
LOS ANGELES

After M.D. had followed Duncan out, Rob closed the door to Ghislaine's office and faced his mother. "I'm sorry I even considered supporting Ward."

Ghislaine looked into Rob's kind eyes, so like her maman's.

"Do you remember the last time your grandmother visited us?" she asked, sitting on the edge of her desk. "It must have been in early two thousand, a few months before she died?"

"Yes, I remember. She hugged me so tightly I thought she would break my back. She always smelled of . . . a kind of sweet, smoky scent. What was it anyway?"

"Ah, she loved lavender and would bathe with lavender soap every morning. When I was growing up, she would sprinkle lavender oil on my pillow at night to help me sleep before a test at school or a skating competition. Whenever I smell lavender, I think of her," Ghislaine whispered with a slight break in her voice.

"You must miss her terribly," Rob said as he walked over and put his arms around his mother. "What made you think about her?"

Ghislaine looked up at her son and smiled. "Do you know that when your grandmother died she was owed tens of thousands of francs by friends who had drunk her wine and eaten her food for years on credit? Sometimes when I worked at the bar as a teenager I would count up all the debts in my head and go to her, furious she would allow her friends to take advantage of us. Do you know what she would say? She would take me in her arms and whisper, *'l'amitie vaut plus que l'or.'* Friendship is worth more than gold. You have her heart, Rob," Ghislaine said, feeling her throat constrict with emotion. "That's why I thought of her. I know that you don't care about the company the way I do . . . I hope that you might someday, but I know you're only here now because you want to use the company to help those less fortunate than we are."

"You're right," Rob admitted. "I've never thought of the company as an end in itself. I know what it means to you, but for me it's only a means to do something good with my life."

"I know. And I wouldn't change that about you for anything in the world, but . . ." Ghislaine hesitated and returned her son's gaze.

"Even in seeking to help others—no, *especially* in trying to do good—you must be careful to whom you give your trust and friendship."

Ghislaine stood up and grabbed Rob's hands. "Anyway," she said, "it's time we stopped talking of ghosts and started working on the problems of the living." She returned to the Shaker chair behind her desk and, with a furrowed brow, started to read through the Levy and Maxwell report.

Rob watched his mother, as she pored over the report, for several seconds before interrupting.

"I've already studied the report, although I'd like your opinion, of course. With one exception, I didn't see any factual errors. We can question their assumptions, especially the one that excludes any unrealized appreciation from the firm's value, but once they make them, they get to ten million dollars without any trouble."

"Ward won't take us seriously. He doesn't care if we challenge assumptions made by the firm's accountants. What's the one factual error?"

"Well, I'm not sure it's a factual error so much as an omission. They didn't include in the list of assets the Gulf of Guinea deal that Ward has been working on. You know he's been telling everyone that it's only a matter of days before we gain government approval and finalize our investment."

"Even if the government consents and our initial investment immediately skyrockets in value, Levy wouldn't include the appreciation in the company's value. So why would the omission make a difference?"

"Technically, it wouldn't," Rob agreed. "But Ward has bragged both within the company and to investors that the Gulf deal will immediately soar in value. If we ask him to include it in the valuation of the company, won't that make him uncomfortable? Ward might worry a judge would question the report if it ignores a large gain Ward himself has been claiming as evidence of his ability to lead the company."

Ghislaine lowered her head and rested her chin on her thumbs for a second. She looked up at Rob.

"It's a clever idea," she smiled, "to hoist him on his own petard. Perhaps you have a little of my deviousness after all. Why don't you contact Ward this afternoon and ask him why the Gulf deal isn't included? Push back if he claims the deal is held up waiting for approval since you know consent is due in a couple of days. Tell him you want Levy to make it part of his analysis as soon as approval comes through. I don't see how he could object. It might help us if we can't get Aoki to veto his scheme. But our real hope lies in Panama, Rob. Good luck there. And be careful, please. No unnecessary risks, okay?"

Rob looked at his mother and grinned. "Who? Me?" he asked in mock seriousness.

THIRTY-FIVE

....

MONDAY, DECEMBER 20
LOS ANGELES

Rob returned to the office Monday afternoon and knocked on Ward's open door. "Do you have a few minutes?"

Ward looked up from a letter and gestured for Rob to step into his office. "Of course, I do. Come in. What's on your mind?"

"I looked at Matthew's report again and noticed that the Gulf of Guinea transaction isn't included in the analysis. Do you have any idea why it would be omitted?"

Ward looked down at his left arm and flicked a stray speck of lint from the sleeve of his Armani. "I didn't discuss methodology with Matthew, but I assume he doesn't consider it an asset because the deal hasn't closed yet. Of course, the cash we'll use to make the investment is accounted for. I know you don't have a lot of accounting in your background, but I assume that makes sense to you?"

"Yes, that makes sense," Rob replied, placing his hands in his pockets. "But you've told everyone that you expect approval in the next few days and then we'll close the deal, right? Once the deal is closed, Matthew should revise the analysis to decrease cash and show the new Gulf investment as an asset."

"All right." Ward snorted in frustration. "I agree, he should at *that* time. But you understand, don't you, that it won't change the bottom-line number. Matthew won't include the Gulf deal at any higher value than the cash invested."

"I understand that Matthew won't change *his* analysis," Rob retorted, "but you might want to consider whether his treatment of the Gulf investment ought to be acceptable to *you*, since you've told everyone the Gulf transaction will be an immediate home run."

Ward stared at Rob. "Okay." he exhaled. "If and when the approval comes through and we close, Matthew will revise his report accordingly and I'll ask him whether my past statements ought to affect the value he places on the Gulf investment. Does that satisfy you?"

"Yes, thanks."

"Good. Now, have you had a chance to think over what we discussed this morning?"

"I'm still considering it," Rob said. "You gave me a week, right?"

"Yes, yes, of course," Ward said with a wave. "Let's stay in touch."

After Rob left, Ward rose and began to pace in front of the window overlooking Constellation Avenue. *Shit!* Now he had to call Danko first thing in the morning and tell him to hold up the Gulf deal until he has taken care of Ghislaine and his half brother.

....

THIRTY-SIX

MONDAY, DECEMBER 20
LOS ANGELES

Duncan returned to his apartment around three and tromped up the outside stairs. Out of breath, he paused before entering his apartment to suck in the sea air and slow his pounding heart. Christ! He had sprinted up stadium stairs when he was younger. Scanning the ocean, he saw white caps churning in the distance. Large gray clouds streaked from right to left across the sky. A single cyclist raced south with the wind along the bike path and whooped as he sped away toward Dockweiler Beach. Duncan had hoped leaving private practice would give him time to exercise and lose some of the excess weight accumulated during years of twelve-hour days, long flights, and too much alcohol. Instead, the travel and stress of the past ten days had left him feeling more sluggish than ever before. As soon as I get back from Panama, he promised himself, I will work out every morning.

His apartment was quiet and cold. Switching on the heat, Duncan threw his keys on the dining table. During the drive back from Ghislaine's, he had realized he didn't know anything about Panama, Salduba, Jorge, or his uncle other than what he'd learned at Aoki and what he'd read in Rob's report. Never smart to rely on limited—and likely biased—information. Then he remembered Jed Barbour, a friend at the Department of Justice from his days in D.C. Jed had been posted to the U.S. embassy in Panama as the DOJ representative about a year ago. He felt sure Jed or someone Jed knew would be able to provide the intelligence he needed. Duncan Googled the U.S. embassy's telephone number and clicked on the number of the main switchboard. After a young woman answered and transferred him to the Department of Justice, the phone rang eight times before someone picked up.

"Justice," said a male voice, slightly out of breath.

"I'm looking for Jed Barbour. The name is Duncan Luke."

"It's six o'clock here, so I don't know if he's still around. Hold on one moment."

"Hell's bells, Duncan," Jed shouted in his unmistakable Alabama baritone as he picked up the phone. "What a surprise to hear from you. It's been years, man. How *are* you? You're not in Panama, are you?"

"Hello, Jed," Duncan said, a grin spreading across his face. "It's great to hear your voice too. How are Haley and the girls?" Duncan remembered Jed's most recent holiday card, displaying with pride his pretty wife and two straw-blond girls, the younger with a broad smile bearing what looked to be red, white, and blue braces.

"Fine, fine, Duncan. Thanks for askin', man. Being here is an adventure for them. But they've gone from survivin' to thrivin' in no time."

"That's great to hear. Listen, I'm not in Panama but I'm on my way. Do you have a moment to talk? I would really appreciate your advice," Duncan said as he sat down on the couch and lifted his feet onto the coffee table.

"Sure, sure. Let 'er rip. Haley and the girls left on holiday break yesterday and I'm stuck here until the end of this week."

"Thanks. Let me give you some background." Over the next fifteen minutes, Duncan told Jed of the problem that Aoki had encountered in dealing with Salduba, Aoki's relationship with Bingham International, the investment by Ghislaine Bingham and BIG in CESD, Takayama-san asking Ghislaine and Rob Bingham for their help, and his being retained to work with them. When he finished, he waited a moment for Jed to reply.

"Well, that's quite a tale. I suppose you want whatever I can dig up on Salduba as well as on Fernando and Jorge Rodriguez?"

"You've always been one step ahead of me," Duncan chuckled.

"You can spare the bullshit. We're friends. I could tell you what I know now about Salduba and Fernando Rodriguez, but I'd prefer to poke around a little to make sure I have the full story. Could I get back to you in about an hour?"

"Of course," Duncan said and he gave Jed his cell phone number. "Thanks for your help, my friend."

"You are most welcome. I sure hope we can find some time to get together while you're here and raise a glass or two. It'd be like old times back in D.C. But let's talk about that a little later. I'll get back to you soon, man."

While he waited for Jed to call back, Duncan decided to begin packing now to make sure he had everything that he needed. He checked the weather in Panama for the next few days. He knew the country was situated only a few degrees above the equator, so he wasn't surprised to see high temperatures around ninety degrees and low temperatures in the seventies with humidity hovering above 80 percent. At least the rainy season had ended a month before. He didn't know what business attire was in Panama so he found a business travel website. To his dismay, he read that men were expected to wear a jacket and tie. He packed two pairs of tan slacks, a lightweight blue blazer, a couple of shirts, and a single tie. He also threw in his tan Cole Haan penny loafers, some lightweight wool socks, a couple of pieces of underwear, one pair of swimming trunks, just in case he would have time for a swim in the morning, and his toiletry kit. On his bed, he laid out his traveling clothes: over-size jeans, a light-blue polo shirt, his black-and-blue running shoes, and a lightweight, dark-brown sweater to ward off the California cold on the way to LAX and the air conditioning of the plane.

Duncan put the reports on Aoki and CESD in his laptop case as well as the most recent issue of *The Economist*. He called AT&T to confirm that his BlackBerry and data plan would allow him to access the Internet and send and receive calls in Panama. A male voice with a Filipino accent assured him that it would and wished him a pleasant journey to Panama. What a world we live in, he mused.

Jed called back just before four o'clock. "Well," Jed said, "I have some information for you but, in a nutshell, it looks like you've got your hands full with this guy Salduba. The good news is that Fernando and Jorge Rodriguez seem okay, at least as far as my sources tell me."

"Okay. Give me the good news first, then." Duncan lowered himself into a chair by the dining table and took out a pen and a yellow pad.

"Sure. By way of background, the CFZ is an autonomous agency of the Panamanian government. It's supervised by a board of directors and executive committee, but day-to-day operations are run by the general manager. Fernando Rodriguez was appointed general manager shortly after the elections down here in July 2009. The current government is a coalition made up of two main parties, the Democratic Change Party and the Panamenista Party. They won the election in large part based upon their promise to do away with corruption in government. Of course, we all know that's easier said than done. Rodriguez was a partner in the local

Pricewaterhousecoopers office before bein' appointed and he seems to have a pretty good reputation. He does come from a family well known in local political circles. His brother, the father of Jorge Rodriguez, is a local banker, a member of the National Assembly from the Panamenista Party and reportedly a golfin' buddy of the Vice President's. But there's nothing' wrong with golfin', as you know," Jed laughed.

"As a former star on the University of Alabama golf team, you would be the first to tell me, I'm sure."

"Well, you know, there are *quite* a few good courses down here and they're a lot less expensive than those around D.C."

"I'm beginning to understand why Hayley and the girls have gone from surviving to thriving. You've probably done everything you possibly could to make that happen."

"You always were a perceptive son of a bitch!"

Now it was Duncan's turn to laugh. "Okay. So Fernando seems to be a straight dealer, right? That's good news. Perhaps we can get Aoki's problem settled quickly."

"Hold on, buddy. There's a lot more," said Jed. "But before we get to the main event, Salduba, let me finish up on Jorge Rodriguez. I think you know a little about him already from Rob Bingham? Well, in any event, Jorge is one of a generation of well-heeled and well-educated Panamanians who want to eliminate poverty in their country. That's no small task 'cause poverty stands at anywhere between twenty-eight and thirty-five percent of the population, depending upon whom you ask."

"I'm surprised. I thought Panama was a relatively rich country."

"It is. At least on *average* it is. The problem is income inequality. Panama has the second worst income distribution in Latin America, not a region exactly celebrated for equality in the first place."

"Not that our own country hasn't gotten a lot worse in our lifetimes."

"All too true. But the poverty in Panama, especially the rural poverty, is a major challenge. In any case, Jorge, like almost every other twenty-something, wants to change the world. The company he founded with Rob Bingham is his first attempt. I think you know it received a concession from the Panama Canal Authority to clear submerged mahogany trees and other hazards from parts of Lake Gatun and sell the timber."

"Yes," Duncan said. "Rob Bingham told me about their plans."

"Well, they received their concession in March of this year. Rumors circulated at the time that the only way a start-up company could have received the concession was through, how shall I put it, questionable business practices? But, then, whenever anyone gets anything from the government here there are whispers of backroom deals and money changin' hands."

Duncan drew a series of concentric circles on the yellow pad. Was Jorge a zealous idealist who might regard a bribe as a small price to pay in order to help the poor? And if Jorge were not above committing a small crime to accomplish some greater good, what about Rob? "Did anything ever come of the rumors?" he asked.

"No, nothin' at all. The concession was relatively small and there wasn't much competition. Environmental cleanup and a mom-and-pop timber operation don't exactly attract big money."

"Okay. Now what about Salduba?"

"Ah, Rodrigo Salduba." Jed sighed. "Now, there's one complex fellow. On the surface, Salduba is a well-respected attorney with a good academic background, including graduate study in the United States. He started his own firm in 1999 after serving as deputy general counsel of the Panama Canal Authority for four years and chief of the legal department of the CFZ administration for four years prior to that. One can sure understand how Aoki would think he was an excellent choice to represent them before the CFZ. But Salduba has another side to his business. Less prestigious but more lucrative," Jed emphasized, letting his words sink in.

Duncan straightened himself in his chair. "A more lucrative side?"

"We both know prostitution thrives in almost every city in the world. Here in Panama, prostitution is often part of a larger network of sex trafficking, drug trafficking, money laundering, and the official corruption that allows them all to persist. Our friend Salduba appears to be involved in all of it. He is, first of all, the owner of a nightclub called the Golden Island Club or rather, I should say, he owns a Cayman corporation that owns a BVI corporation that owns the Golden Island Club. He attracts young women from the poor regions of Panama, Colombia, the Dominican Republic, and Costa Rica, but mostly Colombia. Once the girls sign a contract restricting them to work only at his club, he flies them in. Before 2008, he'd get them a visa available for "escorts" once they arrived, but the government abolished that visa category in 2008 under pressure from the United States and human rights organizations. Now the girls get visas as 'entertainers,' as if that makes a difference. Whether they come as escorts or entertainers, however, the system is the same. The girls dance or strip at the club, the customers watch the shows and, if they want to leave with a girl, then they pay a fee to the club to allow the employee to leave early. After that it's just two consenting adults having some fun in a hotel or push-button."

"What in God's name is a 'push-button?'"

"It's what the locals call a motel where you can drive up, push a button to open a garage door, drive in the garage, and close the door all without gettin' out of your car. You put your entry fee into a kind of slot in the wall of the room. Once you pay, you can use the room for an hour or two and drive away happy without anyone ever havin' seen you."

"So Salduba's running a whorehouse, engaging in sex trafficking?"

"There are whorehouses in Panama and God knows poor girls bein' forced into prostitution, but Salduba's too clever to risk anything so blatant. Everyone knows what's really going on, but he can't be prosecuted for smuggling, since the girls are either Panamanian or enter legally, can't be held liable for trafficking because the girls are technically not being coerced by anything other than their own desperate circumstances back home, and can't be arrested for pimping because he's just getting paid to let an employee leave early to do whatever she wants. Moreover, if anyone asks, and no one does, he has copies of their passports, entertainer visas, return tickets home, and a contract to show that he's doing nothing wrong."

"All right, I get it. Salduba's not exactly an Eagle Scout."

"Hold on, friend. I'm just gettin' started. His main competition comes from girls who enter Panama on tourist visas and seek out their own customers at the casinos, bars, and nightclubs around town. The independent girls keep their own schedules and don't have to split any of the profits with the clubs. So, what does Salduba do? He pays off the immigration police to raid clubs, casinos, and bars and sweep up the competition. Although most independent girls are in Panama legally as tourists, they cannot engage in prostitution and have a hard time explaining to the police what they're doing in the club if it's not to pick up johns for a fee. So they're held in immigration cells under threat of prosecution and deportation for prostitution. Sometimes that's when an immigration lawyer from Salduba's firm shows up and tells the girls that he can get 'em off but it will cost a thousand dollars each. If they pay the fee, they're released. If they don't pay up, they are deported and their passport is stamped to prevent them from returning to Panama for five years. Since they are scared to death of losing the only job that pays as much money as prostitution, almost all pay up. In fact, girls keep a stash of bills in reserve so they can pay and get back to work that night. Salduba, of course, takes his cut and gives the rest to immigration officials in on the deal."

"So," Duncan said slowly, "he screws the competition, keeps his own girls from thinking they should go solo, and makes a profit all at the same time?"

"Yes, sir," Jed replied. "He even had his friends in immigration raid his own club. Because he had passports, correct visas, and contracts, his girls were fine. The independents who made the mistake of hangin' out at *his* club that night, however, well, they had a rough time, indeed. All deported, without exception. Not a bad system, huh?"

"And why doesn't anyone go to the police?"

"You're such a naïve boy, Mr. Luke. The immigration authorities here have all the power. If a girl complains, she gets deported on charges of prostitution. Not easy to challenge the system if all the witnesses are in Colombia."

"I understand," Duncan said. "But does his after-hours job have anything to do with the problem Aoki and Bingham face?"

"Well, not directly," Jed explained. "Salduba's criminal activities go far beyond the sex trade. He's suspected of using some of the girls coming in from Colombia as mules to smuggle drugs into Panama and girls going home to take cash back to drug traffickers there. But I'd say his most lucrative business is official corruption. You know about his background with the CFZ and the Panama Canal. You can see that he's been perfectly placed to represent foreign companies, like Aoki, eager to bid on the expansion of the canal, the Free Zone, and related projects. We don't know how extensive his influence is, but we know he has a hand in many applications. Just like he did with Aoki, once a company is well into the process, he demands an extra fee for his efforts. Then he launders the money through his nightclub and his Cayman company. After Salduba takes a cut, the money ends up in the offshore bank account of the government official responsible for approving the deal."

"So Salduba had reason to be pissed when Aoki questioned the need for the fifty thousand dollars?"

"You can imagine that his credibility with government contacts depends on a reliable cash flow."

Duncan rubbed the stubble on his face with his right hand. "You think Salduba paid someone off to make sure that Aoki's qualification was held up at the same time he paid to make sure that his Korean client's qualification went through?"

"I'm fairly certain. Of course, we don't have the evidence to confirm our suspicion and we certainly don't know who Salduba paid off in the CFZ. It wouldn't be Rodriguez himself. It's probably someone a level or two lower."

"So there's really no incentive for Salduba to help Aoki, is there?"

"None, unless Jorge Rodriguez can get his uncle interested in why Aoki's qualification materials have been rejected. If he did, then Salduba might find religion real quick and get Aoki qualified just so no one would suspect him or his CFZ contact of corruption."

Duncan drew another set of concentric circles on the bottom of his yellow legal pad and then wrote and underlined the following words: extortion, corruption, prostitution, drugs, money laundering, and tax evasion. As much as this guy disgusted him, his job wasn't to prosecute Salduba. It was to get Aoki qualified. If

Salduba could make that happen, he'd deal with him but at least he now knew to be cautious.

"Thanks," Duncan said at last. "You've been incredibly helpful. I think I'll get in touch with Salduba anyway, but I'll play dumb, of course. If the meeting with Fernando Rodriguez comes through, I'll make sure Salduba knows so he'll sweat a little. Maybe you're right and that will put Aoki back on track."

"All right, but be careful there, my friend. Salduba's not above hittin' back if he feels cornered and, remember, you'll be in his town. So keep in touch, man, will you? I hope we find some time to get together when you're down here."

"Thanks. Don't worry. I'll be careful with Salduba. And, if I have any time, I'll be sure to call you. Thanks, again."

"Sure. Oh, and remember Panama City ain't Beverly Hills. Crime is skyrocketing and there's been a rash of kidnappings; tourists getting hijacked by small bands of robbers. They take not only the cash in his wallet but force the poor sucker to withdraw as much money from ATM's as he can. So whatever you do, don't go out in the countryside alone at night. It isn't worth it. And I'd hate to get a call from you askin' for a late-night ride back to the hotel." Jed laughed as he ended the call.

Duncan paused to consider the intelligence he had just received and then tapped out an email to Rodrigo Salduba. After introducing himself, he described the purpose of his visit and the details of his arrival and contact information while in Panama. He mentioned Rob Bingham and M.D. Corrales, adding they hoped to meet with Salduba and other relevant parties. He closed by asking that Salduba leave a message for him at the Marriott.

Duncan read over the email. He liked the phrase "other relevant parties." He hoped the wording was threatening enough to set off alarm bells in Salduba's mind but ambiguous enough so Salduba wouldn't, as Jed put it, hit back. He pressed Send and immediately felt weary to his bones. Since early Monday morning in Tokyo, he had slept three hours max. He couldn't count on getting any sleep on the plane. He decided that he would eat something, call a taxi for an eleven thirty ride to LAX, and try to sleep until around ten thirty. An hour was plenty of time to shower, dress, and check his bag one last time to make sure he had everything he needed for the trip. He reached into the freezer and found a cheese-and-jalapeno tamale he had picked up at the Virginia Avenue farmers' market. As he warmed the tamale in the microwave, he sipped from a bottle of Negra Modelo. He was looking forward to meeting Rodrigo Salduba.

Then he looked up at the kitchen clock. It was almost six o'clock. Time to call his Sammy. "Hello, Sam," Duncan purred when Sam answered the phone. "How are you?"

"Fine."

"How was school today?"

Silence. "It's winter vacation."

"Oh, that's right, sorry. Listen, Sam, I'm . . . well . . . I'm so sorry that I missed our time together on Saturday and didn't call on Sunday night from Japan." No response.

But," Duncan continued quickly, "but, I have a present I brought for you from Japan. I'll bring it on Wednesday night. I promise." Except for Sam's soft breathing, nothing.

"Are you mad at me, son?"

"No," he said quietly. "Well, maybe. A little. Why did you have to go to Japan again? I thought you were going to be a teacher."

"Well, ah, let's see. I . . . I need to do some extra work and so sometimes can't see you so . . . ah . . . so I can . . . ah . . . get some help persuading your mom that it would be okay for us to have more time together." Silence.

"I don't understand," his son said. "That sounds stupid to me." And Duncan had to admit missing time with Sam now in order to have time with Sam later did sound pretty dumb.

"Well, look, I know you're angry and that's . . . well . . . that's okay. I made some mistakes. Do you remember what we used to say about mistakes?"

A syncopated beat and Sam chirped, "Everyone makes mistakes, *especially* Dad?" Sam loved being reminded that he was not the only one who struggled.

"Yeah. That's right, *especially* Dad. I'm really, really sorry, but, you know, even Kobe Bryant misses sometimes and his teammates still pass him the ball, right? They give him another chance, don't they? That's all I'm asking," Duncan pleaded. As soon as the words left this mouth, he regretted what he had said. He had used a metaphor and understanding metaphors was terribly difficult for Sam.

A long silence followed before Sam declared matter-of-factly, "But you can't shoot like Kobe Bryant, Dad." Duncan was about to agree when he heard Gracie tell Sam it was time to hang up.

"I hear your mom calling, Sammy. Good-bye. Talk with you tomorrow," he said before gushing, "Remember: I love you!"

"Okay, Dad. Good-bye."

Duncan let out a long sigh. He knew Sam loved his parents, but he could count on the fingers of one hand the times he'd heard Sam say those magic words. Was that his autism or something else, something he'd inherited from his overly reserved, taciturn father? Duncan shifted his eyes back to the kitchen cabinet where the half-empty bottle of Sauza beckoned. He needed something to help him sleep a few hours and he had promised himself to start exercising soon, so what was the harm?

THIRTY-SEVEN

....

TUESDAY, DECEMBER 21
PANAMA CITY

The Copa Airlines Boeing 737 lifted off from Los Angeles just after two o'clock in the morning. Rob had been fortunate to find three seats still available on the day of departure, particularly so close to Christmas. Many Americans and not a few Canadians vacationed in Panama at this time of year, and connecting through Los Angeles was the only way to travel from wintry western North America that did not require a layover in San Salvador or Mexico City.

Rob usually flew economy, not wanting to waste CESD's money on a business class ticket, but he was relieved to discover that economy was fully booked. Duncan Luke was a big man well into middle age whose face had looked flushed and sickly that afternoon and even worse when he arrived at the airport. Brightcrimson lines riddled his eyes; his large hands trembled when he held his ticket out for inspection. Rob hoped a business class seat might allow the lawyer to sleep a little during the six-hour flight. His mother's future, as well as his dream project, depended on Duncan's wits in the next thirty-six hours. At such short notice, Rob couldn't get three seats together. Without a word, Duncan collapsed into his seat. M.D., who wore a black-and-white running

suit and tennis shoes and looked flower-market fresh, dismissed
with a shrug Rob's suggestion they ask a stranger to trade seats.
So Rob spent the next six hours dozing and wondering what the
next two days would bring.

Shortly before ten o'clock in the morning in Panama, the pilot's announcement of an on-time arrival woke Rob. He glanced at
Duncan, who was sitting in the row ahead and across the aisle.
Duncan's head was thrown back, his arms folded against his
chest, his mouth slightly open, and his eyes shut. A rivulet of
drool had descended half way down his chin. Rob glanced back
across the aisle at where M.D. had been sitting. The seat was
empty. Where was she? Before he could pivot around, M.D.
stepped through the drapes separating the economy section,
stopped before her row, and did a series of leg and calf stretches.
Seeing Rob staring at her, she nodded perfunctorily and spun
around to do another lap through the plane. Rob shook his head
rapidly several times the way a dog shakes off water, rubbed the
sleep from his eyes, and turned to look out his window.

The azure waters of the Pacific Ocean gleamed in the morning
sun. The plane banked left and the ocean blue blended into the
earth tones of the shore, which gave way to the olive-green tropical vegetation around the airport. Rob could make out the Pan
American Highway in the distance and beyond that, rows of red-
and-silver rooftops. The pilot turned hard right, straightened the
plane out, and dropped through the light cloud cover. The 737
bumped twice on the concrete runway, slowed, and rolled up to
one of the gates at the northern satellite of the main terminal of
Tocumen Airport. The plane passed the construction site of what
would be the Muelle Norte terminal and halted with a jolt at the
gate. Rob unbuckled and jumped up. He started to help M.D. take
down her roll-on from the overhead compartment, but she waved
him away. Rob and Duncan readied their luggage and the three

Americans walked in silence off the plane. Rob led the way through immigration and then customs.

As they came out of the restricted area and into the small modern arrival hall, Rob spotted Jorge waiting to welcome them. Jorge was six months older than Rob, but his short, wiry body and boyish features made him look several years younger. The two friends embraced, beaming at each other. Rob stepped back and introduced Jorge to Duncan and M.D.

"I'm pleased to meet you. Welcome to Panama," Jorge said. "I have a van parked in the lot outside. We'll go directly to the Marriott so you can check in to your rooms. It's only about fifteen minutes to the hotel."

"Were you able to speak with your uncle?" Rob asked.

"Yes, I did speak with him. But let's not talk here. Let me explain when we're in the van, if you would." Jorge led the group out of the arrival area. As they left the air-conditioned hall, Rob felt a blanket of hot, moist air envelope him and caught the faint smell of jet fuel. Jorge directed them across the street to the covered parking lot where he quickly located his white Chevy van. Duncan, M.D., and Rob placed their luggage in the back and climbed in. Jorge started the vehicle. Its air conditioning blasted out cool, dry air. Jorge backed out and headed to the hotel. The others sat quietly, waiting to hear about his conversation with his uncle.

"I must tell you that my uncle was initially very reluctant to discuss anything to do with the qualification process," Jorge began. "He is not directly involved but has delegated the responsibility to others in the CFZ administration. As you can understand, he is very sensitive to situations that might be misconstrued as corruption. But I explained very carefully that you were only asking him to consider the possibility there had been some error, a miscommunication or misunderstanding between his staff and Aoki, that had resulted in Aoki's submission being rejected. I also reminded him—at your suggestion, Rob—that the CFZ administration and the Panamanian people would benefit by having as many qualified bidders as possible. He promised to review Aoki's file today and meet with you tomorrow morning at eight so any error could be corrected by the noon deadline. He expressly said he could not guarantee a different outcome, but I know my uncle very well. He will do his best to find out the truth."

"Thank you," Rob said. "That's all we can ask."

"It is my pleasure. If Aoki is a qualified company, they should have the right to bid for work. And if assisting Aoki can save CESD, then I am even happier because our work is very important to me as it is to you."

"Yes, that's terrific news," Duncan declared. "Where would the meeting be?"

"In his offices at the CFZ administration in Colon."

"So we could make our twelve thirty flight to Los Angeles?"

"I would think so, yes, easily. Of course, I had hoped you'd stay longer, but understand if you have to return so quickly."

They pulled up in front of the hotel. Rob was again struck by the Marriott's cold stone- and-glass façade, which made it seem more like one of the surrounding banks than a resort. He loved the lobby, however, with its graceful arches, mahogany furniture, and black marble floor. After they registered, he heard Duncan ask for messages and saw the pony-tailed young woman at the front desk shake her head in response. He watched as Duncan checked his BlackBerry for emails. The lawyer looked at Rob and M.D., "Well, no surprise, I guess. There's nothing from Rodrigo Salduba."

"In that case," Rob said, "why don't Jorge and I take M.D. and you out in a couple of hours. We'd like to show you what CESD has been able to accomplish."

"Fine with me," Duncan replied. "I could use a shower and a couple of hours of sleep but, after that, I'll be ready to go. Sound good to you, M.D.?"

"Sure, I'd enjoy seeing some of the country while we're here," she said. "I'll meet you down here at one thirty. In the meantime, I'll report to Ghislaine. She'll be pleased we are meeting with Fernando Rodriguez tomorrow."

Duncan shifted his weight from one leg to the other and cleared his throat. "It's fine to tell her that we have a meeting, but I wouldn't go into too much detail. No need to raise her hopes yet."

M.D. blinked twice at Duncan. "I'm not going to mislead Ghislaine," she announced. "She's not only my boss, she's my friend."

"I'm not suggesting that you mislead her. I'm just suggesting it might be wise to manage her expectations at this point."

"Thanks for your advice," M.D. said curtly, her mouth twisting in annoyance. "I'll certainly consider it. By the way, and it's just a *suggestion,* you might think about emailing an update to Takaya-ma-san."

Rob could see Duncan stiffen for a second and then relax with a chuckle. "All right, M.D. That's a good idea. I'll leave Ghislaine to your good judgment and I'll take care of Aoki. See you both in two and a half hours. Oh, Rob, I take it that there's no need to dress up this afternoon?"

"No. It'll be a steam bath outside, and we'll be on our barge. Shorts, a T-shirt, and tennis shoes are as dressed as we get."

"Perfect. Thanks. I'm looking forward to seeing the Canal."

THIRTY-EIGHT

....

TUESDAY, DECEMBER 21
PANAMA CITY

Ten minutes later, M.D. had put away her clothes in the closet and chest of drawers, splashed some cool water on her face, and lay down on the bed. She picked up her cell phone and dialed Ghislaine's mobile.

"Hello, M.D.," Ghislaine said in a voice more raspy than usual.

"Hi, Ghislaine. I wanted to report in. We've arrived in Panama. Jorge is taking us out to Lake Gatun this afternoon. Rob is eager to show us their work. No word from Salduba, as expected, but we have a meeting at eight tomorrow morning with Jorge's uncle."

"That's great news. Did Jorge say if his uncle would help Aoki?"

"No. In fact, Jorge said that his uncle initially felt uncomfortable even discussing the issue, but once he'd heard the facts, he agreed to review the file and to meet with us." M.D. recalled Duncan's admonition and added, "I don't think we can get our hopes up yet. It's too early for that."

"I know it's still early. You're beginning to sound like Duncan Luke."

M.D. made a mental note to think more carefully in the future before accepting Duncan's advice on how to handle her boss.

"Sorry, I just wanted to make sure that I wasn't misleading you."

"I understand." The line went silent for a moment and then Ghislaine murmured, "Could I ask you a personal favor?"

"Certainly. What is it?"

"I'm worried about Rob," Ghislaine said and stopped for a moment as if she were unsure how to proceed. "It's been almost three weeks since he lost his father, but he hasn't said much to me about it. He didn't shed a tear at the funeral or at the celebration of Robert's life. I think he may be numbed by guilt."

M.D. crinkled her eyes in puzzlement. "What makes you think that?"

"Oh, in the weeks prior to Robert's death, Rob didn't hide how disappointed he was in his father's behavior. Then Robert died so suddenly. I don't think Rob had a chance to reconcile his feelings about his father. I think he's suppressing his emotions as a kind of punishment for feeling ambivalent about Robert's death."

Good God, M.D. said to herself. She didn't feel at all comfortable with this conversation. Who knew Ghislaine Bingham was a pop psychologist?

"He's not as mature as you are," Ghislaine continued, "and, like all men, he thinks he's immortal. Can I tell you something in confidence?"

"Of course," she said while silently hoping Ghislaine would not reveal too much. She was raised to keep her work separate from her personal life and felt others should as well.

"When he was younger, he struggled with a minor learning disability. He's much, much better—most people don't even notice anymore—but he still mixes up syllables when he's feeling a lot of stress and he doesn't always grasp the meaning of more sophisticated words right away."

"Oh, I hadn't noticed," replied M.D. feeling increasingly ill at ease at being made privy to Rob's struggles. She would have been appalled if her mother had ever disclosed anything remotely as private about her.

"Anyway, Rob was also small for his age until he shot up at fourteen, so he compensated for his size and his learning disability by challenging himself physically. You know, backcountry skiing, kite boarding, scuba diving, whatever. What began as an escape for him has become a passion, a part of who he is . . ." Ghislaine paused. "I don't normally care since he's so fit and clear-headed," she continued. "But I worry that his guilt might cloud his thinking and lead him to take some foolish risk out on the Canal or on the streets of Panama City. I want you to look out for him. Will you do that for me?"

M.D. closed her eyes and took a long slow breath.

"Thanks for confiding in me," she replied evenly as she opened her eyes. "I understand now what happened in the meeting yesterday. I'm a proud logophile, but I know I overdo it sometimes. I'll try to be more sensitive in the future. As for the rest, Rob's a grown man twice my size. I'm not sure what I can do to keep him safe or even what you're asking of me. Still . . ." She sighed. "I promise I will watch out for him if that would make you feel better."

"Oh, thank you. I can't tell you how relieved that makes me feel. But don't change yourself for Rob. I know he respects you and if he sensed you were holding back because of him, he'd be devastated. I'll talk with you tomorrow morning L.A. time, after you've met with Rodriguez. Enjoy the trip out on Lake Gatun. I'll be interested in your assessment of CESD's work. Thank you so much!"

After saying good-bye, M.D. remained on the bed staring up at the ceiling. Normally she would jump at the chance to help her mentor, but the call had left her feeling vaguely irritated. She felt supremely confident when faced with business problems that she could analyze at a distance, but just the opposite when confronted with people's emotions, especially her own messy feelings. The conversation with Ghislaine had rubbed an old bruise she thought had healed years ago. She detested Robert for what he had done to Ghislaine, but she was also sorry that Rob had lost his father. Still, at least *he* had his father for twenty-three years; *her* father had deserted her before she was born. To this day, no one—not even her mother—had ever bothered to ask how *she* felt growing up without a dad. And the truth was, if anyone had asked, she would probably have started to sob.

THIRTY-NINE

....

TUESDAY, DECEMBER 21
LOS ANGELES

Ward awoke with a splitting headache from the three Grey Goose martinis he had consumed the previous night at Nic's in Beverly Hills. Swallowing a glass of water from the carafe he kept by his bed, he reached for his phone to call Ron Danko in London.

"Ron, It's Ward Bingham."

"Oh, Ward. Hope your return to L.A. was smooth. No news yet from São Tomé, but I expect the approval of your investment will come in tomorrow or Thursday at the latest."

Ward ground his teeth. "There's been a complication," he said slowly. "I need you to slow things down. I don't want anything approved for another month."

"*WHAT?!*" Danko exclaimed. "You can't be serious. My contacts at the Ministry will think we're mad. I've worked my bloody tail off getting this deal for you and now you want to throw it away?"

"I *am* serious and I don't have time to explain. I am locked in a power struggle with Ghislaine for control of BIG. If you want us to invest in Gulf then I need to win that fight. And to win, I need you to slow things down. Do you understand me? I know you have good connections. Use them," he commanded.

Ron did not respond for a few seconds. "All right. I'll see what I can do, but I can't make any promises. And if we do get the government to delay and the deal later falls through, I will still expect to be paid the one million dollars as a breakup fee. Is that understood?"

"I'm not asking you to scuttle the deal. I'm telling you that I need to have it delayed for a month. That's all."

"Are we agreed that BIG owes me one million dollars even if the deal falls through?"

Ward cursed under his breath. "Okay. Yes. We're agreed as long as you don't cause the deal to fail and you do your best to prevent it from falling apart. Now I've got another call to jump to and you've got to get on the line to São Tomé. If you have any issue with the government, call me tomorrow morning."

Ward terminated the call. Frustration drove his right hand down with a loud crack onto the dark wood of his bedside table. Dealing with his stepmother and half brother had begun to feel like playing Whac-a-Mole. Each time he thought he had smacked them down, they popped up again to taunt him. But they were gravely mistaken if they believed they could outlast Ward Bingham. His hero, Napoleon, was right. "Victory belongs to the most persevering," and Ward would not relent until he had won, even if it meant hammering a few more heads along the way.

He had tried to insert a wedge between Rob and his mother, but that ploy didn't seem to be working. There had to be someone else close to Ghislaine he could strike at. And he would have to strike in a way that only Ghislaine would realize that she was the real target. His recent trip to London came to mind. He called the London office and asked to speak to the office administrator, Gloria Merit.

"It's Ward, Gloria. Thanks for setting up the meeting last week. Unfortunately, I've concluded that our business levels can't support four people working on Eastern Europe. What's the name of the youngest analyst in that group, the one whom Ghislaine hired? Azra Begic? I know it's almost five in the afternoon, but could you call her in and tell her we're very sorry but she needs to move on by the end of the year? Yes, of course, offer the normal severance package and career counseling services. No, I don't think it will hurt morale. I think it will boost morale once the others know that they're not at risk. Yes, Gloria, I realize it's just before Christmas," Ward said, exasperation creeping into this voice, "but she's Muslim, isn't she?"

FORTY

....

TUESDAY, DECEMBER 21
LAKE GATUN

Rob arrived in the lobby a little early. He wore forest-green swimming trunks, a loose-fitting tan Under Armour HeatGear T-shirt and a pair of waterproof sandals. Although his outfit contrasted with the elegant furnishings of the hotel lobby, he had learned from experience that his swim gear worked well for outings on Lake Gatun, where he often spent as much time in the water as onboard. At precisely one thirty, M.D. and Duncan walked from the elevators toward him. Rob noticed with relief that Duncan had managed to rid himself of the dark circles under his eyes in the course of his two-hour nap. Wearing a sweat-stained Dodgers cap and sunglasses, his smiling face looked five years younger than when they had arrived that morning. M.D. seemed lost in her own world, but her pleated khaki shorts, olive-green sleeveless T-shirt, and black sport sandals told him she was no stranger to the outdoors. A ponytail stuck out the back of a well-worn scarlet-and-gold USC cap, but whatever relaxed air her headgear conveyed was belied by the black aviator sunglasses that concealed her eyes. She greeted Rob and Duncan with a curt nod.

Slinging his daypack over his left shoulder, Rob asked cheerfully, "Does anyone need sunscreen?"

"I've put some on, thanks," Duncan replied. M.D. just shook her head.

"No? Okay then, let's go. Jorge's outside in the van." They stepped outside the front door of the Marriott and into the muggy Panamanian afternoon.

Once Jorge had pulled the van out of the hotel driveway, Rob, who was riding in front, shifted himself to face Duncan and M.D. Over the hum of the air conditioning, he explained where they were headed.

"We'll be traveling north out of the city along the east side of the Panama Canal on Avenue Omar Torrijos to a small city by the name of Gamboa. It's only about twenty-five kilometers from here and the road is pretty good so we should be there in about thirty-to-forty minutes. The CESD boat and its pontoon are both docked at Gamboa. We'll take the boat out on Lake Gatun to give you a sense of our clearing and harvesting procedures. We have time for a short dive, so you'll have a good idea of our operations by the time we're finished. We should end up by four this afternoon and be back at the hotel no later than five o'clock. Does anyone have any questions?"

"No, that sounds good to me. We'll have time to have dinner and get organized for tomorrow's meeting. Okay with you?" Duncan asked and glanced over at M.D., who shrugged and turned to stare out the window.

"All right, then," Rob said and pivoted around. "Enjoy the drive out."

Just after two o'clock, the van drove onto the dusty main street of Gamboa and quickly pulled up at the dilapidated town docks. Two craft with the letters CESD in faded black paint on their sides bobbed up and down on the muddy water: a twenty-five foot shallow-bottomed motorboat equipped with a small crane; and a square pontoon boat with a rain shield. Three squat muscular young men in tattered shorts and flip-flops were preparing the pontoon to embark. Dirt streaks ran down the chipped white paint on both vessels. The CESD boats swayed in the breeze among the fishing skiffs and the larger canopy-covered motorboats that ferried eco-tourists to Monkey Island.

The CESD party stepped from the air-conditioned vehicle into the oppressive afternoon air—warm, thick, and heavy as a blanket. The group followed Rob and Jorge onto the motorboat. Jorge took the helm, started the engine, and backed the vessel out from the dock. Once the boat had cleared the docks, he headed it into the middle of the turbid channel leading from Gamboa to the waters of Lake Gatun. The pontoon followed close by. The Americans watched in silence as the jungle-green shoreline paraded by them. Cormorants and toucans, frightened by the drone of the engine, croaked and squawked as they took flight. The wind brought some relief from the heat as well as the scent of damp decay from the shore.

About thirty minutes later, Jorge slowed the CESD boat to a crawl and maneuvered it around a dozen trees protruding from the lake's surface. Some were poles, some had branches stripped of all leaves, and others were as verdant as their cousins on shore. The pontoon slid along behind about a hundred feet away. Duncan and M.D. rested on a wooden bench facing Rob, who stood before them in the bow.

"The trees that break the surface are only a small fraction of those that were covered with water when Lake Gatun was created in 1904," Rob explained, pointing out toward the lake. "We believe there are hundreds of millions of board feet of lumber lying in these waters and there are over thirty different species of trees.

Some of the trees are huge, over eleven feet in diameter at their base."

Jorge brought the boat to a stop, placed the engine in neutral, and threw a small anchor overboard to prevent the boat from drifting in the wind. Several hundred feet behind them, the pontoon had also halted, and one of the men was donning diving gear.

"We face a number of challenges in clearing and harvesting the timber," Rob continued. "We use divers to harvest the trees. But the murky water makes identifying the highest value trees a difficult task. To improve efficiency, we use underwater sonar to locate good prospects for harvesting and GPS tracking equipment onboard to track the diver underwater as we communicate with him by means of an earphone and mouthpiece attached to a helmet. Once a diver locates a tree, he starts up a handheld hydraulic chainsaw that uses an extract of vegetable oil for fluid in order to safeguard the environment. There." Rob pointed back to the diver on the pontoon. "You can see our diver holding one of our saws. As you'd expect, the chainsaws are far less efficient underwater. They are also often not long enough to cut through very wide trees with one pass. The diver is wearing a tank, but only as a safety measure; we drop an oxygen tube down with him to allow him to work without surfacing. Before cutting the tree, the diver attaches a special air bag to the tree at the stem." Behind Rob, the diver splashed from the pontoon into the water fins first.

"Once the log is cut," Rob continued, "it floats to the surface and we tow it, along with other logs we cut that day, to our shore base, an old ranch that's located on the lake front up a dirt road from Gamboa. We passed it on the way out just a few minutes ago." Rob turned and pointed back along the tree-lined shore to the south and east.

"At our base, we use a winch to haul the logs out of the water and up a dirt ramp to a drying area. It takes several weeks for the logs to dry out. In the rainy season, which just ended, drying takes even longer. Once they are ready, we process the logs using a portable sawmill. We analyze the quality of the wood and, so far, the quality has been excellent. Right now, we truck the product to local buyers. Some of them export the higher-value timber, like mahogany, and others sell the less-valuable wood for use in construction or manufacturing here in Panama."

Rob looked from Duncan to M.D., who both sat listlessly in the humidity, and then down at the filthy deck by his feet. Putting his hands on his hips, he considered what he wanted to say next. He didn't want to sound overly pessimistic in front of Jorge, but he also didn't want to give M.D. the impression that he was as simpleminded as he had seemed in his mother's office.

"The good news . . ." he began when suddenly he saw the two men on the pontoon began to wave frantically. Rob looked at Jorge, who put the radio to his mouth and spoke in rapid Spanish, which was returned by the men on the pontoon.

"The oxygen pump has broken again," Jorge yelled to Rob.

"Shit! Tell the diver to surface immediately," Rob commanded.

"That's the problem. He can't. His foot is caught in some thick roots. He has switched to breathing from the scuba tank, but it holds only fifty cubic feet of pressurized air and the way he's struggling the air in the tank won't last more than an hour, if that." Rob stared at the pontoon for a moment. An image of the trapped diver struggling below the surface flashed in his head. He saw himself beside the diver. He knew what to do. He barked to Jorge.

"Tell the men on the pontoon to try to calm the diver down. I'm coming to cut him loose, but I'll need to share his air."

"What are you doing?" Jorge bellowed.

"No time," Rob gasped and dashed into the cabin, grabbed a pair of fins, a mask, and a sheathed boating knife, and sprinted back to the side of the boat. He threw off his tan shirt, kicked off his sandals, and with one long stride leapt into the moss-green waters of the canal. When he surfaced, he had the sheathed knife in his mouth. Flipping on his back, he pulled on the fins and mask. Then he spun over and began to churn toward the pontoon.

"If the water's too cloudy to identify a tree," Duncan shouted, "he'll never find the diver!" Jorge glanced at Duncan and squinted out to where Rob was plowing through the water.

"I don't know . . . wait! Yes, look, he's swimming to the pontoon first to locate the oxygen line leading to the diver. He'll follow that down!" Jorge yelled and pointed to the pontoon, which Rob had just reached. They watched as he located the oxygen tube, took an enormous breath, and plunged beneath the surface. A minute later, Spanish exploded over the radio to Jorge, who listened intently. "Rob's found the diver. They're sharing air. He's trying to cut the diver loose." Several more minutes passed. The radio crackled, passing birds cawed, and the wind rustled through the leaves of branches of long submerged trees.

"What if he gets caught in the same roots? What if his knife isn't sharp enough to cut himself free?" M.D. cried to no one in particular and leaned over the railing. More minutes crept by. M.D. and Duncan exchanged worried looks. Both turned to face Jorge. Jorge shook his head and looked at his watch. Silence fell like a pall over them. Then the radio boomed with more Spanish and, a second later, Rob breached the surface of the water like an orca. A moment later, the diver's head appeared. The diver slowly swam to the pontoon, where his comrades hoisted him up. Rob waved and swam back to the CESD boat. A few minutes later, he pulled himself onboard, his chest heaving from the exertion.

"Now *that* was fun," he finally gasped. M.D. rolled her eyes and threw a towel at him. Jorge embraced him, and Duncan clapped him on the back.

Fifteen minutes later, dry and breathing regularly, Rob stood up and said with a grin, "Now, where was I? Oh, yes, the good news. Well, the good news is that there are a number of positive social and environmental externalities that stem from this project. We employ local people, many of them indigenous and almost all quite poor, and they receive good pay and training. Every underwater tree we harvest and sell is, at least in theory, a tree on land saved. With time, the extraction of trees will improve the safety of navigating the parts of the lake near the shore, which should generate commerce and in the distant future may increase land values."

"And Rob," Jorge interrupted. "You've forgotten to mention your mother's generosity." Jorge turned to Duncan and M.D. "When Ghislaine learned about our plan to apply to the Panamanian government for a concession to harvest timber from Lake Gatun," he explained, "she offered to give fifty thousand dollars to a charity established several years ago by the wife of the Vice President for the purpose of fostering rural economic development. To make sure the funds would be used wisely but also in a way that would benefit CESD, she instructed that her gift was to be used solely for the purpose of training poor women from communities along Lake Gatun to make handicrafts and small pieces of furniture from the wood that our operation would harvest. Ghislaine wanted to do something good for the people but also create a small market for our lumber. My mother has told me several times how much the Vice President's wife appreciated your mother's gesture, especially since she made the offer even before we received the concession."

"Thank you for your kind words." Rob smiled at Jorge. "Yes, I suppose her gift is also a positive result of the work that we have been doing here. But there is bad news, too," Rob added as he glanced nervously at M.D., whose eyes remained hidden behind her glasses. "To put it bluntly, we are losing money on each log we harvest, process, and sell, less on the more valuable species like mahogany but more on the others. If we could find a way to increase both the rate of harvesting as well as the yield of high-value logs, we could generate cash to build a kiln, a storage area, and a permanent sawmill in the Colon Free Zone. With those facilities, we could transport the logs shortly after harvesting to our location in the Free Zone and process them in a few days rather than a few weeks. Except for the lowest-value timber, we would not sell to local markets but would offer our timber to export markets, where we could get better prices. Until we can find a way to increase our harvesting rate and the ratio of high-value to low-value logs, however, we will continue to lose money," Rob concluded with a wince.

"Do you have any questions?"

Rob heard M.D.'s foot impatiently slapping the boat's metal hull. She seemed to have trouble breathing as the stifling air mixed with the exhaust from the boat's idling motor.

"How much of the initial one million dollars have you burned through?" M.D. gasped, wiping her forehead with the back of her hand.

"We have about five-hundred thousand left. At our current rate of operation, we lose about seventy-five thousand dollars a month, so that means we have a little more than six months before we have to find new funding or shut down."

"Does Ghislaine know this?" she demanded. "After all, it's mostly her money that's flowing out the door, or should I say running into the lake?"

"I make quarterly reports to my mother and to Ward as president of our other main shareholder, Bingham International," Rob declared, folding his arms against his chest. "And, yes, of course, they're aware that we've been losing money. But remember, part of what Bingham and my mother are seeking to achieve here is intangible, namely, a good reputation for the company as an innovative contributor to the fight to eliminate rural poverty in Panama."

"Oh, you can't be *serious*." M.D. shook her head. "Since when did positive externalities pay the rent? And when you run out of money what will happen to this little company of yours, your employees, and the women whom Ghislaine's money is training in handicrafts and all the others who have come to depend on you?"

The young woman stood up with her hands in her back pockets.

"Did it ever occur to you and Jorge that one million dollars might be much better spent in Panama on a business run by experienced people, one that had a real chance to survive and would generate both profits for its investors and lasting benefits for its employees rather than just the occasional adrenaline-charged, completely asinine adventure for its . . . its thrill-seeking managers?" M.D. didn't wait for Rob to reply. She turned and stalked away toward the stern of the CESD vessel. Rob and Jorge exchanged glances and shrugged.

Duncan, who had remained silent, stood up and stretched.

"God, it's hot out here, isn't it? I think it's time to get back to the hotel. You may not be tired, but the heat and humidity are killing me. With any luck, we'll be able to persuade Jorge's uncle that Aoki should be qualified. If we can and if Takayama-san does the right thing, Ghislaine and Rob will be the principal shareholders of BIG. At that point, CESD's future will look entirely different than it does now."

"You mean not completely without hope?" Rob mumbled, grimacing at the thought that Jorge's and his dreams for CESD could be ruined. He glanced back toward the stern. M.D. stood there staring at him, her arms folded against her chest.

"Yes." Rob sighed. "Let's get back. It's almost five." As Jorge steered the boat toward Gamboa, M.D. turned to lean against the stern rail and cast her eyes out at the receding banks. Duncan reclined on the bench in the bow, his hat over his face. When the boat docked at Gamboa, they disembarked without a word and climbed into the welcome cool of the van. On the drive back, Jorge and Rob talked in subdued tones. Both M.D. and Duncan closed their eyes and leaned back in their seats.

Thirty minutes later, they pulled up to the Marriott. "Good luck tomorrow morning," Jorge said to Duncan. "As you can well understand, my uncle does not want me at the meeting. He is very concerned about the appearance of corruption, and my presence at the meeting would surely generate rumors of improper influence."

"I completely agree," Duncan nodded.

"Good. Thank you for understanding. Now my uncle is an extremely punctual man, so please do not be late. The drive from the Marriott to his office takes about an hour and fifteen minutes. To be safe, you should leave no later than six thirty tomorrow morning"

"You don't have to worry, Jorge," M.D. promised in a no-nonsense tone of voice. "I will make sure Duncan is on time."

"Ah, good. Thank you," Jorge said and glanced nervously at Duncan. "As for the return," Jorge continued, "I would expect the meeting to take no longer than an hour. You can be back at the Marriott by ten thirty at the latest, pick up your things, check out, and then make your twelve thirty flight to Los Angeles."

"Thank you for everything," Rob said. "I'll speak to the concierge and arrange for a car to pick us up at six fifteen. I'll call you when we've finished our meeting tomorrow."

"It's been a pleasure to meet you all. I hope to see you tomorrow before you return to Los Angeles. Rob, we'll talk tomorrow." The two friends shook hands and then embraced warmly.

The three Americans waved to Jorge and walked into the hotel lobby. Duncan and M.D. waited in silence for Rob as he arranged for the car.

When Rob rejoined them Duncan said, "I know we're all tired and we have an early day tomorrow, but I think we should have a quick dinner tonight to go over what we plan to say to Jorge's uncle."

"Great idea," Rob said. "Why don't we meet back down here at seven thirty? I know a pretty good seafood restaurant nearby, Restaurante del Marisco. Does that sound good to you, M.D.?"

"Sure," she replied indifferently. "See you both at seven thirty." Without looking at either man, she pivoted and strode toward the elevators.

"Any idea what set her off this afternoon?" Duncan asked, scrutinizing Rob.

"We hardly know each other, so I have no clue. She's extremely loyal to my mother. Maybe she thinks I'm taking advantage of Ghislaine? I don't know."

Duncan shrugged. "Probably just the heat. I felt like my head was under a broiler. Any need to dress up tonight?"

"None at all. This place is totally casual, but the food is excellent. I'll be wearing cargo pants and a long-sleeved sports shirt."

"That's good since all I have to wear are my jeans from the plane and a clean sports shirt. See you later, then. I could use a couple of good fish tacos and one or two Cadillac margaritas to help me sleep tonight. I guess Fernando Rodriguez is our only hope to resolve the Aoki mess."

Rob watched Duncan wobble toward the elevators and flinched when the lawyer tripped slightly over his own feet. How would this jet-lagged, hungover, middle-aged attorney possibly convince a skeptical Panamanian bureaucrat to qualify Aoki and in so doing save his mother's and his own future?

FORTY-ONE

....

TUESDAY, DECEMBER 21
PANAMA CITY

Rodrigo Salduba loved the views from his spacious corner office on the tenth floor of the Torre Delta. The floor-to-ceiling windows behind his desk looked down on the fashionable Via Espana, with its banks and hotels, casinos and office buildings, cars, and pedestrians scurrying along in the late afternoon heat. Glancing out the windows to the right, he could just make out the gold-and-green neon sign of the Golden Island on the Avenida Aquilino de la Guardia. He turned and surveyed his office furnishings, a mixture of custom-made teak and mahogany furniture from Colombia, rugs from India, Central Asia, and Pakistan, and art from contemporary Panamanian painters, like Ciro Oduber and Juan Manuel Cedeno. On the wall to his far right hung his treasure, a huge, floor-to-ceiling Kuna mola tapestry depicting two multihued rainbow birds.

With a heavy sigh, Salduba forced himself to focus on the handwritten report from the man he had sent to Tocumen Airport to spy on Duncan Luke's party. His man had reported the arrival of Luke, Rob Bingham, and M.D. Corrales on the Copa flight from Los Angeles. A young Panamanian had greeted them and transported them to the Marriott in a dirty white Chevy van

243

with CESD painted in black on the side. With that information, it took little time for his paralegal to find the corporate records of Canal Environmentally Sustainable Development and to conclude that the young man who met Luke was almost certainly Rob Bingham's local partner, Jorge Rodriguez, the nephew of Fernando Rodriguez, the General Manager of the CFZ administration. Salduba growled again to himself: *Mierda!*

His mobile rang and his shoulders immediately tensed. It was José Mercedes, his donkey-like contact at the CFZ.

"Hello, Rodrigo? It's José. I know you told me not to call, but it's urgent. Fernando Rodriguez has scheduled an appointment tomorrow morning with an American named Duncan Luke and some colleagues from a company called Bingham International to discuss the Aoki situation. What is worse, Fernando has asked to review the Aoki file himself. *Esto es una catastrofe,* Rodrigo!"

Salduba bristled at José's braying lack of composure.

"No hay necesidad de preocuparse, José. I have the situation under control."

"But what if Aoki amends its earlier submission? With Fernando watching, we cannot again claim the application contains defects."

"Doesn't your office suffer from periodic power outages? Make sure you have one tonight. Tomorrow, tell Rodriguez your phone and Internet service connections were down overnight. You received no amendments from Aoki. Nothing. Now, do not call me again."

Salduba slammed his mobile down and began to parade back and forth behind his desk, growing more and more concerned. The meeting *cannot* happen. If Aoki were qualified, his reputation for getting things done at the agency would suffer, jeopardizing the hundreds of thousands of dollars he made each year from clients with business there. Normally fastidious about his appearance, he threw off his linen jacket and loosened his black silk tie. *How do I prevent Luke from meeting with Rodriguez?* He couldn't just have him killed on the streets of Panama City tonight. Luke was a *Norteamericano* and so his death would involve the police, the U.S. Embassy and awkward questions that might lead back to him. Besides, his client had directed that they not be hurt. No, he needed a more subtle strategy.

His eyes turned to a headline on the front page of *La Prensa* sitting on his desk: *"Expresa Secuestros Un Flagelo."* Yes. Yes, that might work, but how would he lure the Americans from their hotel?

The office intercom interrupted his train of thought. "Magdalena is here to see you, Señor Salduba," his secretary said.

"Ask her to wait just a moment, please," he barked, irritated at the unexpected interruption.

"Yes, sir."

"Magdalena," Rodrigo sighed to himself. He regretted having been so generous with her over the years. Yes, she was lovely, but so was the Kuna tapestry on his wall. Unlike a work of art, Magdalena had a mind and she believed she was free, not his possession to do with as he pleased. She had questioned his decision to have the independent girls who came to *his* club to steal from *him* deported! She had indeed forgotten that she owed her life to him and that he could always take it away. Still, having Magdalena killed after she had shared his bed for so many years seemed ungrateful, even unjust, and he considered himself a man who judged others fairly and meted out penalties proportionate to their crimes. What would be a fair-minded way to say good-bye to Magdalena? Should he send her back to Colombia and allow the general's son to determine the punishment she deserves for sins committed long before she came to him? Yes, that would be a just fate. Salduba hit the intercom button.

"You can ask Magdalena to come in now."

"Yes, sir," his secretary said. Salduba sat down and leaned back in his chair, put his hands behind his head, and waited for his lover.

A moment later, Magdalena entered his office. Salduba caught his breath at the sight of her in a strapless turquoise dress tailored to the contours of her body. Her copper-colored hair draped over a red sweater that casually covered her bare shoulders. Noticing she wore the necklace of black pearls and matching earrings he had given her last year, he felt something catch in his throat. Could he really bear to live without this elegant creature who had graced his life for so long? Perhaps he had been rash in his judgment of her?

"Thank you for seeing me," Magdalena said as she sat down opposite his desk. Her business-like manner caused Salduba to sit up straight and fold his hands on his desk.

"I have come to ask how I can persuade you to help me. When I try to speak with you at home about my future, you always evade me. So I am compelled to disturb you at your office."

She hesitated for a moment to throw a lock of hair back over her shoulder and looked Salduba directly in the eyes.

"Rodrigo, I am truly grateful for everything you have done for me, but you know that the escort visa expired many years ago and my latest tourist visa has also run out. Many people know I am your woman," she began to plead. "Some of them are your enemies. What is to prevent one of them from having me picked up and deported from the only country I have known for the last eight years? I am scared. I know you protect me, but even you cannot be everywhere. Please try to understand my feelings."

"Dear Magdalena." Rodrigo held his hands out in front of him. "I do not know why you worry. I will talk with my friends at immigration. We will get you another tourist visa."

Magdalena's eyes flashed and she bolted up from her chair.

"I do not want another *tourist* visa," she declared, slashing her fist through the air between them. "I will be legal for three months and then we must do this all over again. Have you heard *nothing* I've said?" she raised her voice and brought her fist down on his desk. "Do you have *no* feelings for me at all?"

Yes, he had feelings, but he had grown weary of her. There were others, perhaps not as naturally beautiful or as natively intelligent, but younger and more willing to please.

"All right." He exhaled. "If you help me with something I need done tonight, I will get you your permanent residency."

Magdalena brought her hands to her mouth in disbelief. Grinning, she scurried around the desk to embrace Salduba.

"Oh, *te quiero, te quiero,* Rodrigo. *Muchisimas gracias,*" she crooned. "I would do anything for you. You know that. What am I to do, my love?"

"There are three Americans who wish to see me. However, I do not wish to meet them. I need you to keep them from making trouble for an American client of mine. Your English is now very good. I want you to call them tonight at their hotel, pretend to be my assistant, and tell them I have agreed to meet with them at my home in Las Cumbres. You will go to the Marriott Hotel in my car at seven thirty tonight, meet them, and escort them to Las Cumbres."

Magdalena's brow furrowed. "But Las Cumbres is thirty minutes out of the city and, in any case, you do not live there."

"No, dear Magdalena, but the car will be stopped there by several of my acquaintances who will first pretend to be police and then robbers. They will kidnap the Americans and detain them until tomorrow at noon when they will no longer be able to cause me any difficulty."

"I see." Magdalena frowned. "But, what will I do when the Americans are robbed?"

"These men will not touch my driver or you, of course, because you are not rich Americans. They will tell you both to lie down in the car and not to look up or follow them. After they have left, you can return to your apartment, *mi amor,* where I will be waiting for you and we can make love as we used to when we first met."

Magdalena bit her lower lip and again looked down into Rodrigo's eyes.

"I do not wish to hurt anyone."

"No one will be hurt. We only want to scare them and see them depart as quickly as possible. And you will get what you've wanted for so long—a future here without fear."

"But won't these Americans complain to the police about their kidnapping? What if they describe me to the authorities or mention my name and yours?"

Salduba smiled up at Magdalena. So smart! He would miss the sharpness of her mind as much as the silkiness of her skin.

"Do not trouble yourself with such thoughts, *querida.* I will make sure that our American friends find their passports at the hotel and are obliged to leave the country soon thereafter."

Magdalena tilted her head slightly to the right and looked into Rodrigo's eyes.

"I understand and cannot wait to make love with you tonight. Tell me, who is the American you wish me to call, *querido?*"

"His name is Duncan Luke. Here is his number," Salduba said as he wrote the number on a scrap of paper. "He is a lawyer staying at the Marriott with two other Americans. One is a young man, Rob Bingham, and the other is a young woman whose name is M.D. Corrales."

"I see. I have the names in my memory now," Magdalena said. She looked down at her watch. "It is already after five. I need to go home to change and call this Duncan Luke. *Hasta esta noche, mi amor.*"

"*Hasta luego, Magdalena. Que te cuides esta noche, querida.*"

FORTY-TWO

....

TUESDAY, DECEMBER 21
PANAMA CITY

When M.D. returned to her room, she tore off her shirt, dumped her sweaty clothes on the floor, and jumped into the shower, letting cool water flow over her. Refreshed, she dried herself and put on the terry-cloth robe she found hanging in the closet. She glanced at the clock. It was only six forty-five. Throwing herself on the bed, she folded her hands on her chest and closed her eyes. Why had she exploded at Rob and Jorge this afternoon? After all, CESD wasn't her company nor was her money or career at risk. She felt indebted to Ghislaine for her guidance and encouragement, but Ghislaine hardly needed M.D. to protect her interests. The whole project was a moronic waste of time and money in a country that had so many much more pressing needs, but Rob and Jorge meant well even if their ingenuousness doomed them to fail.

She opened her eyes and rolled onto her side. Her mood had been black ever since the call with Ghislaine this morning. Admit it, she told herself. Ghislaine's expression of concern and affection for Rob was more than mildly irritating and had done more than remind her of the father she had never known. M.D. loved her mother and knew that her mother loved her. But as many times as her mother had declared her pride in her daughter, M.D. could not remember a single instance when she had whispered *I love you.* M.D. closed her eyes again and felt a few tears slide down her cheeks. She let her breath out slowly to release the tightness in her chest. She looked over at the clock through blurry eyes. What was the line from that Carly Simon song? Something like, *in the end we all get dropped by our mothers / we all get black and blue?*

All right, she commanded herself, rubbing the moisture from her eyes. That's enough self-pity for one evening. She examined the white blouse and jeans she had laid out. It would be their only night in Panama, why not dress up a little? She would feel better. She put the jeans and blouse away in the closet and took out a mocha linen pants suit and a sky-blue blouse. She slipped on her light-brown canvas shoes and brushed her hair so that it framed her face. As a final touch, she tied an earth-brown and sky-blue silk scarf casually around her neck. Grabbing her black leather backpack, she took one last look at herself in the mirror and then left the room to join Rob and Duncan.

FORTY-THREE

....

TUESDAY, DECEMBER 21
PANAMA CITY

M.D. saw Rob and Duncan speaking animatedly when she stepped from the elevator into the lobby. She walked over to them and chirped, "Hello, guys. What's going on?"

"Hi, M.D.," Duncan said. Then his eyes widened. "If you don't mind my saying so, you look terrific."

"Thanks." She smiled. "I'm sorry about my sour mood this afternoon. I don't know what came over me. I . . . I guess I just got carried away again."

"It's been a tough couple of days for us all," the lawyer replied, touching her arm gently. "Anyway, we have good news. I received a call about thirty minutes ago from Salduba's assistant, a woman by the name of Magdalena Vasquez. She apologized on his behalf for not contacting us sooner, but he had been in meetings all day. He's free to meet with us tonight at his home. She's coming to the hotel at seven thirty to take us there. That is, uh, if we all agree it's the best course of action."

"That's surprising," M.D. said. "Why do you think Salduba is contacting you now?"

"I don't know." Duncan shrugged. "Maybe he really was in meetings all day. Or maybe he learned that we have an appointment with Jorge's uncle tomorrow and wanted to get back on our side. Whatever the reason, I do think it's worth meeting with him. You two don't have to come along if you'd rather go to dinner."

"Don't be crazy. Of course, I'm coming with you. Ghislaine would be furious if I didn't." M.D. looked up at Rob with raised eyebrows.

"I'm in," Rob said.

"All right, then. Thanks. I can use the company. Just remember that we have every reason to distrust Salduba as well as his assistant, Ms. Vasquez. "

A few moments later, a tall, breathtakingly beautiful woman strolled through the front doors of the hotel. She wore a steel-gray long-sleeve silk blouse and black pleated palazzo pants. A strand of ivory pearls hung from her neck.

"Excuse me, sir," the woman said to Duncan with a Spanish accent. "Are you Señor Duncan Luke?"

"Yes, yes, I am," Duncan stammered. Regaining his composure, he continued. "You must be Magdalena Vasquez. Please call me Duncan," he said holding his hand out to take hers. "These are my colleagues, M.D. Corrales and Rob Bingham."

"It is my pleasure to meet you. Please call me Magdalena. Now, if it is not too much trouble, would you please follow me? A car will take us to Señor Salduba's home in Las Cumbres, about thirty minutes from here."

"I have a short call I need to make at nine o'clock," Duncan interjected, remembering that would be six o'clock in Los Angeles and time to speak with Sam. "Will I be able to use my cell phone at Mr. Salduba's home?"

"Oh," Magdalena replied. "I would hope you would be back here by nine o'clock but, if not, I'm sure you will be able to make your call from Señor Salduba's home. This way, please."

Magdalena led Duncan, M.D., and Rob to a black Lexus sedan parked in front of the hotel. Magdalena sat next to the driver. Rob went around the rear of the car and stepped in the backseat behind the driver. M.D. ducked in beside Rob and Duncan followed her.

"Please, *señores* and *señorita,* make yourselves comfortable," Magdalena said as the driver pulled the car out of the hotel driveway and out into the flashing neon lights of Panama City. Within a few minutes, the car turned right onto the Via Simon Bolivar and headed out of the city toward San Isidro and Las Cumbres.

After about twenty minutes had passed in silence and the buzz of traffic and the flash of neon lights of downtown Panama City had faded into a gloomy quiet, Magdalena announced, "We are almost there." The Lexus passed a lonely Pizza Hut on its right and a hospital to its left as it sped into the dark countryside. M.D. noticed Duncan was studying Magdalena's profile in the glare of the few road lights they passed, while Rob stared out the window at the night perhaps worried over the fate of CESD. A few minutes later, the driver turned left off the main highway onto Via Las Lajas. The black of night closed in around them, broken only by the sedan's headlights.

"Where are we?" M.D. asked.

"Do not be alarmed," Magdalena replied. "We are almost there." M.D. was about to demand that Magdalena tell them exactly where they were when a siren pierced the air. Flashing headlights came up behind Salduba's sedan. The driver slowed the Lexus and pulled off on the dirt by the side of the road. He switched off the engine. As the police vehicle drew up behind them, its headlights ceased strobing but remained trained on the sedan, bathing it in bright light. When the police silenced their engine, the buzz of insects in the tree branches above their car filled M.D.'s ears. She looked at Rob.

"This doesn't feel right," she whispered.

Rob shook his head.

"Must be a case of mistaken identity. Don't worry." He shifted his weight forward as if readying himself to spring out the door.

"This is a wealthy area," Magdalena explained, looking over her right shoulder. "The police often stop unfamiliar cars. Please be patient and there will be no problems."

"Good evening, *señores* and *señoritas*," said a voice from behind the sedan. "We ask your cooperation. If you do as we say, no one will be harmed."

Duncan, Rob, and M.D. all turned to see who was talking.

"Please do not turn around!" the voice shouted. A second, more powerful spotlight flooded the car from the left. The three Americans covered their eyes and faced forward as they had been instructed. "Thank you. Now, would the gentleman sitting behind the driver do us the favor of coming out of the car?"

"Don't get out, Rob," Duncan commanded. "Magdalena, what's going on here? Are these police? Can we trust them?"

"You are Americans and friends of Rodrigo Salduba," she whispered. "I don't think you have anything to fear from the police. I would advise you to do as they ask."

Duncan paused for a moment. "All right. Get out, Rob, but move very slowly."

"Don't worry. I will." M.D. watched out of the corner of her eye as Rob opened his door and stepped out of the sedan. She saw him turn toward the rear and peer out to his right. A powerful spotlight was immediately directed at Rob's eyes.

"They're not police! They have a large black van, masks like you see at the local Mardi Gras and a gun," Rob yelled.

"Quiet!" commanded a voice from behind the spotlight. "Do not speak again, or someone will be harmed," the voice growled. "Now, please move over to the van with your hands in front of you. Then put your hands against its side, *señor*, and spread your legs so that we can search you. Please do not take your eyes from the van, *amigo*."

Rob walked slowly to the van with his arms outstretched in front of him. A short, burly man stepped behind him and pushed him forward against the side of the van. The stocky man quickly ran his hands over Rob's clothes, took his passport, cell phone, watch, money clip, and wallet.

"What the hell are you doing?" Rob shouted and pivoted toward the man. The robber shoved him back against the van.

"I have asked you before, *señor*, please do not shout," commanded the deep voice behind the spotlight. "We are poor Panamanians and you are rich Americans. We do not wish any trouble, only your money and other valuables. If you cooperate, you will be back at your hotel very soon. If you do not," the voice paused for a moment, "the evening will become more difficult not just for you but also for your lovely companions. Do you understand, *señor*? I have asked once and will not ask you again."

Rob gritted his teeth. "Yes, I understand."

"Excellent. Now, would the man on the right please get out of the car?"

Duncan opened his door and climbed out. M.D. observed him try to screen his eyes from the van headlights and the spotlight. As the light shifted onto Duncan, she could see the three masked men more clearly. The tallest had a bird mask with a large beak and a plume; he seemed to be holding a weapon in his right hand. Standing next to the bird was a well-built man wearing a white-

and-black monkey mask with gray fringe. He had some type of hand gun stuffed in his belt. The third, a wiry man not as tall as the bird, wore a jaguar mask with a black feline face and whiskers. He held the spotlight that blazed in Duncan's eyes.

M.D. watched Duncan walk over to the van with his arms held out in front of him and stand spread-eagle against its side as the monkey relieved him of his passport, BlackBerry, money, and watch.

"Excellent," said the jaguar. "Now it is time for the young lady in the back to join her friends. Please get out of the car, *señorita*."

M.D. slipped across the backseat and lifted herself out of the sedan. She too shielded her eyes against the headlights of the van and the brilliance of the spotlight to her right. She saw Rob and Duncan by the van, hands out, legs apart, leaning against its side. The shapes of the three masked men standing to her right were just visible through the glare.

"Please walk with your hands above your head and join your friends, *señorita*, and no harm will come to you," the jaguar directed.

M.D. raised her arms and walked slowly over to the van. She stood with Rob on her left and Duncan on her right. She faced the van and let her arms drop to her side.

"Now, *señorita*, please be so kind as to put your hands on the van so my colleague can search you," the jaguar commanded.

M.D. put her hands on the metal side of the van. The sulfurous exhaust from the sedan still lingered in the otherwise fragrant night air. She took a breath and, speaking as calmly as she could, said, "There is no need to search me, *señor*. As you asked, I will cooperate. There is a small backpack resting on the backseat of the car. Everything that I have is in there, except for the watch on my left wrist, which I will gladly give to you." M.D. held up her left arm so the three armed men could easily see what she was doing, unstrapped the watch with her right hand, and threw it over her shoulder. "You now have what you want," M.D. continued. "Let me repeat that there is no need to search me. If you were to insist on doing so, I would feel offended and cannot be held responsible for my actions."

The jaguar examined M.D. from where he stood. "Yes, I see that you have nothing concealed. Thank you, *señorita,* for your gracious warning." He chuckled. "For someone no bigger than my twelve-year-old son, you have courage." Then, in Spanish, he instructed the monkey to find M.D.'s backpack in the sedan and to bring it to him.

While the monkey walked to their car, Rob muttered to M.D., "You are either the bravest woman I have ever met or completely crazy." M.D. ignored him. She spread her legs shoulder width apart and bent her knees slightly to lower her center of gravity. Coiled like a spring, she waited for what she feared might come next.

....

FORTY-FOUR

TUESDAY, DECEMBER 21
LAS CUMBRES

When the monkey returned with M.D.'s backpack, the jaguar's voice rang out from behind the spotlight once more. "And now, I would be grateful if the woman in the front seat would stand with her friends by the van." When first Rob and then Duncan had stepped out of the car, Magdalena felt the tension in her shoulders begin to ease. As M.D. moved out of the car and over to the van, Magdalena told herself that it would be over soon. The Americans would be taken away, held, and released tomorrow. No one would be hurt. She would return to her apartment to celebrate with Rodrigo the success of his plan and the security of her future in Panama. Now she was being ordered to get out of the car?

"*Señorita,* please do not make my comrade come to get you," the jaguar insisted. "He is not as patient as I am."

"*Ay, no,*" she whispered to herself. Her head began to throb. There must be some mistake. Rodrigo had said that she would be told to lie down in the car, that the robbers would leave her to return to him. She did not move. The monkey approached her side of the car. Magdalena looked over at Rodrigo's driver and beseeched him with her eyes to do something. He turned his head away. The monkey tapped his gun against the window. She slumped against the door for a moment as nausea overcame her. Quietly sobbing, Magdalena pushed the door open and stumbled out. Just before she reached the van, she tripped over a root in the dirt and nearly tumbled the last few steps toward the space between M.D. and Duncan. Without looking at either of them, Magdalena closed her eyes and let her forehead fall with a thump against the cool metal of the side of the van. The monkey came up behind her. He grabbed her wrists and stretched her arms out until her hands touched the van. Magdalena did not resist as he first cut free her necklace with a sharp knife and then tore her ring from her finger. Once he had pocketed the jewelry, he reached down and yanked her legs apart and back so that she was spread-eagled against the side of the van. Stepping into the space between her legs, the monkey pressed up against her. He ran his hands along her arms, over her breasts, down her sides and legs, and finally up the inside of her legs. Then he did it again. And then, again. Magdalena screamed, *"Detenerlo por favor. Detenerlo."*

Magdalena's cry triggered an explosion of movement from M.D. She spun around to her left and drove the crescent of her foot into the back of the monkey. He grunted with pain and reached back to where M.D. had landed her blow. Jumping away from Magdalena, he turned toward M.D. Before he could raise his hands, however, M.D. had regained her balance, whirled around again, and struck upward at his throat with a spear fist. He gagged, grabbed his neck with both hands, and crumpled to his knees.

As soon as the bird saw M.D. strike his comrade, he sprinted over to help him. He raised his pistol and brought it down hard toward the back of M.D.'s head.

"No!" yelled Rob as he leapt head first in between M.D. and her attacker. The bird's pistol struck Rob across his forehead. Rob groaned and crashed to the ground. M.D. dropped down beside him.

"I can take care of *myself,* you fool," she shouted. The bird raised his pistol again to strike M.D. Duncan stepped around Magdalena and extended both of his arms to shield M.D.'s head from the blow.

"*Bastante!*" the jaguar bellowed. The bird looked up, hesitated for a second, and then shrugged. He put his gun in his belt and walked over to help the monkey to his feet. "Enough," the jaguar said more calmly. "Did I not warn you that someone would get hurt if you did not cooperate? Now the young man will have a headache for days and a scar for life. We do not mean to hurt you, my friends. Why can you not do as I say?"

Duncan pulled Magdalena behind him so that he stood between her and the robbers. Her hands covered her face. Her body shook as she wept.

M.D. screamed at the jaguar. "We gave you no trouble until this animal assaulted Magdalena. What kind of men are you? I thought Panamanian men respected and protected their ladies."

The jaguar laughed. "My brave *señorita,* we do respect and protect our ladies and even a *Norteamericana* like you. But this woman is neither Panamanian nor a lady. She is a Colombian whore. But enough; it is time to go. Please help your friend to his feet and turn around with your hands once again against the van. One of you has already suffered tonight. It is of no consequence to me if others are made to suffer as well."

"Duncan," whispered M.D. "Should we do as they say?" Duncan nodded to M.D. and Rob that they should do as the jaguar had ordered. M.D. helped Rob to his feet, unwound the silk scarf from her neck, reached up, and tied it around Rob's head to staunch the blood dripping from the wound in his forehead. They turned and faced the van with their hands stretched out before them. Duncan took the arm of a dazed Magdalena and guided her so that she too faced toward the van. The monkey bound their hands in front of them with duct tape then walked around to the back of the van to open the doors. The bird pulled at Duncan with one hand and gestured with his pistol in the other for the rest to follow the monkey to the back of the van. They climbed inside.

The back of the van was empty and smelled vaguely of fertilizer. M.D. sat cross-legged on the floor of the van against the far wall next to Rob while Duncan and Magdalena sat opposite them. There were no windows except one between the cargo bed and the front seat and it was covered in thick black plastic. When the van's door slammed shut, darkness enclosed the four victims.

"How are you, Rob?" M.D. whispered into the blackness.

"Oh, I'm fine except for the hammer stuck in my forehead."

A smile crept across M.D.'s face.

"First bravery and now humor. If you keep this up, I may be forced to reconceive my predisposition about you."

"M.D." Rob murmured. "Please. My head hurts enough already."

"Okay, Rob," M.D. sighed. "Like I said, I can't control myself sometimes. Sorry." She leaned back against the inside of the van.

"Where in God's name do you think they're taking us?"

"Well, they're clearly not the police," Duncan declared sarcastically. "My friend Jed at the U.S. embassy told me about a recent epidemic of express kidnappings where the bad guys are looking for quick money not a ransom. They pull their victims into a car, take all their belongings, force them to withdraw as much money as possible from a series of ATMs, and then dump them somewhere far from the city. He told me to avoid going out to the countryside at night. I guess I should have listened more carefully to him."

"I'm not sure that explains what happened to us," M.D. said. "Where would they find ATMs out here in the country?"

"I agree. This feels like something else. The one with the jaguar mask seemed to know you, Magdalena."

Magdalena had stopped weeping, but the shock had left her shivering. Duncan turned to her and whispered, "Are you able to talk? Do you have any idea where they might be taking us? Are we in serious danger?"

Magdalena's head ached. Rodrigo had betrayed her after all. She felt lost, cast off by Rodrigo and not at all sure the Americans would protect her if they knew that she had been a willing accomplice to their kidnapping. "I don't know who these men are or where they are taking us, but I do not believe you or your friends are in any danger."

"What about you?" Duncan asked.

"I do not think these men will hurt me, but no matter. My life will soon be over," she murmured.

"I don't understand," Duncan hissed. "What do you know about this?"

Before Magdalena could respond, however, the jaguar shouted to Salduba's driver in Spanish to remain in the car for fifteen minutes. A moment later, the van rocked as the three men climbed into the front seat. The engine ignited and the metal bed vibrated beneath the four captives. The van pulled out, turned around, and sped away. The dull roar of the motor made further communication impossible, leaving Magdalena to dwell on the vengeance that awaited her in Colombia.

FORTY-FIVE

....

TUESDAY, DECEMBER 21
PORTOBELO

The van jerked to a stop and the driver killed the engine. M.D. guessed they had been driving for almost two hours. The back doors opened and the bird signaled to Rob to get out. With his hands bound in front, Rob slid on his backside over to the open door, threw his legs out, and jumped down. Duncan, Magdalena, and M.D. followed. M.D. sensed that the air had become even warmer and more humid than when they had last been outside. The sweet-sour scent of the jungle filled her nose. All around her, insects whirred and clicked. She turned around and an enormous bay lay glistening below her in the moonlight. They stood below the remains of what seemed like the ruins of an old fort or castle.

The jaguar took out the spotlight, switched it on, and dimmed the beam. A half-moon-like glow spread across the hillside. He gestured with the spotlight that the prisoners should follow him. Climbing a trail that ran through the ruins, he led them up a grassy hillside. The bird and monkey followed, each carrying a backpack on his shoulders and a pistol in his belt. As they hiked up, M.D. could hear Duncan wheezing and panting behind her. Just before they reached the crest of the hill, the jaguar stopped at what appeared to be a cluster of partially collapsed stone buildings. When the others joined him, he turned right into the ruins and stood before the entryway to a bunker made of blackened rock. The chamber was built into the hillside facing the bay below. The jaguar pushed back a thick wooden door, directed the spotlight around the room, and entered. Then he turned and motioned for the others to follow him. The spotlight illuminated a rectangular enclosure with tall stone walls through which grass and roots had grown. The dirt floor was partially covered with vegetation seeded from the surrounding hillside.

"And now, my friends," the jaguar said, "we wish you a pleasant stay here."

"No me puedes dejar asi," Magdalena cried as she bolted for the door. The monkey caught her wrist as she ran past him. She wheeled toward him, raised her wrist to her mouth, and bit his hand until it bled. The monkey screamed but did not release her. With his free hand, he slapped Magdalena to the ground. Duncan, who was closest to the monkey, pivoted, leaned forward, and with a loud grunt rammed his right shoulder into the kidnapper. The monkey sprawled backward against the wall. Knocked off balance by the collision, Duncan stumbled forward. The bird stepped around Duncan as he lunged past and chopped down on his neck with his pistol. Partially breaking his fall with his bound hands, Duncan's chest thudded onto the dirt. Air rushed from his lungs with a loud "umph." The lawyer rolled over slowly and groaned. The monkey jumped to his feet and folded his forearm around Duncan's neck in a chokehold, dragging him away from the door. Duncan coughed and gagged for air. When the monkey had released his hold, the jaguar stepped over to where Duncan lay gasping for air. Moving with the speed of a soccer player, the jaguar planted his boot in Duncan's ribs. Duncan howled in pain.

"I have lost patience with you. Please, no more stupid things," the jaguar ordered. "We will leave you water, several plastic tarps, and a small knife to free your hands once we have departed. Now," he said looking at Rob, M.D., and Magdalena and gesturing with his pistol in Duncan's direction, "please do me the favor of sitting by the old man."

They walked over and squatted around Duncan, who lay in a fetal position, holding his elbows to his sides and still gasping for air. The bird removed four large bottles of water from one of the backpacks and dropped them on the ground. From the other backpack, the monkey withdrew two folded dark-green plastic tarps and tossed them down. The men wearing the bird and monkey masks stepped outside. The jaguar took a small knife from the backpack and threw it down to his left, well away from where his captives sat. The knife thumped on the floor of the bunker. He backed toward the door, the light receding with him.

"*Adios, mis amigos,*" the jaguar said as he swung the wooden door closed. A metal bolt clanked as it slid into place. M.D. heard the others breathing but could see nothing, not even her hand in front of her eyes.

FORTY-SIX

....

TUESDAY, DECEMBER 21
LOS ANGELES

Ghislaine neared the door of the Verandah Room at the Beverly Hills Peninsula Hotel and glanced around. Behind her several hundred guests of the Los Angeles World Affairs Council, which was holding its annual Salute to the Consular Corps reception, exchanged holiday greetings in a dozen languages. While most of the guests wore the somber colors of western business attire, women in crimson kaftans and matching head wraps or peach kimonos and men in gold-and-brown batik dashiki's or embroidered white barong tagalogs gave the gathering a multicolored, international flavor Ghislaine normally relished. But tonight she had already spoken with the Consuls General of Belgium, Argentina, and Thailand and was eager to return home to soak in a warm bath.

"*Hola*, Señora Bingham. So nice to see you here." Hector Diaz, Honorary Consul of Panama in Los Angeles, greeted her warmly.

"How are you, Señor Diaz?" Ghislaine responded as she took his hand briefly in hers.

"I am very well, indeed," he replied with a slight bow. A tall, stooped, crow-like man with a thin mustache and graying hair, Hector Diaz had emigrated from Panama to the United States several decades ago, built a successful construction business in Orange County, and served as the honorary representative of Panama in Los Angeles for the past five years.

"I hope your son's venture on the Canal is thriving. I lobbied extensively on behalf of CESD, as you know, and so was very pleased when the Canal Authority awarded their concession to it. It is the largest investment in Panama from a Los Angeles company in years and my friends in the government are hopeful that other projects will follow. They have not forgotten your generous contribution to the charity of the Vice President's wife and would be pleased to assist you again. As would I," he leered at Ghislaine.

"You are too kind," Ghislaine replied, looking away and stealing a glance at her watch. It was eight o'clock. "Rob's company is still in the start-up phase," she continued, "so we're not yet certain that it will succeed. In fact, he's in Panama now."

"You must be very proud of your son," Diaz effused, and leaned forward to whisper in Ghislaine's ear. "As I mentioned to you at your celebration of Robert's life, I was very sorry to hear of the death of his father. Such a tragedy. If there is . . . anything I can do for you at this time of sorrow," he said looking in Ghislaine's eyes. "I hope that you will not hesitate to call upon me." Ghislaine almost gagged at the overpowering scent of his aftershave and looked briefly away.

"Thank you for your condolences. By the way . . ." Ghislaine returned his gaze without a glimmer of warmth. "I didn't see your lovely wife. Is she here tonight?"

"Ah," Diaz replied with a sigh, "unfortunately, she is not. She had to fly to Panama this morning. Her brother was robbed and beaten in a terrible incident just two days ago. Panama is a very safe country compared with large cities in the United States, but violent crime has increased in recent years because of the evil influence of the *narcotraficantes.*"

"I am so very sorry. Please give her my best regards when she returns. And now, I must apologize, but I have to go."

"May I walk you to your car?" Diaz persisted and extended his hand to take Ghislaine by the arm.

"No, you may not," interjected a deep voice with a faint Russian accent. "Ghislaine promised that pleasure to *me*, my friend." Andrei Kronsky stepped between Diaz and Ghislaine. Diaz looked down into the cold eyes of the powerfully built Russian.

"Of course," Diaz finally said with a nod. "Good night to you both." Kronsky returned the brief bow, then took Ghislaine by the arm and walked with her out of the Verandah Room.

"Aren't you glad to see me?" Andrei asked with a smile. "Do I not receive even a small holiday kiss for once again rescuing you?" After years of a sterile marriage and the trauma of Robert's leaving her, Ghislaine had at first enjoyed the attention Andrei lavished on her, but now his behavior began to suffocate. She stopped and faced the Russian.

"Andrei, I don't need you or anyone else to rescue me. And you didn't have to be so rude. I may need Hector's help in the future."

"So, you do not need my protection? That is not the impression that you gave me when we were together in Santa Barbara. Have you forgotten so soon?"

"I don't know what you're talking about," Ghislaine replied crisply. "Now, I'm tired and need to go home."

"Would you allow me to escort you back to Beverly Glen?" he asked and leaned forward to whisper, "I long to hold you again."

"Please, Andrei. Please, stop it," Ghislaine ordered. "I . . . I asked you for time to consider your proposal and you agreed not to pressure me." She paused and continued in a softer tone, "Now, dear friend, let me go. I need to rest."

"Of course," the Russian said and, taking her by the shoulders, kissed her lightly on both cheeks. "I wish you a Merry Christmas and, especially, a very, very Happy New Year. I will be at your New Year's Eve party. Perhaps we can make our New Year's resolutions together?" He smiled. Ghislaine sighed and shook her head in exasperation. Then she leaned forward and kissed him lightly on the lips.

"Good night. I'll see you on New Year's Eve," she called as she stepped away toward the hotel's lobby.

Waiting for the valet to bring her black 720i BMW to the front, Ghislaine pushed thoughts of Andrei Kronsky from her head. She held her elbows in her hands and stared down at the pavement rather than admire the brightly lit Christmas tree in the lobby or the garland of colorful lights hanging over the hotel entrance. If Hector Diaz's brother-in-law was beaten, could Rob and M.D. be in danger? She hated to bother Rob, especially at this late hour. He was twenty-three, after all, the same age she was when she married Robert. But he was still her son, and Hector Diaz's story had deepened the vague sense of dread she had felt earlier when she spoke with M.D. She longed to hear her son's voice.

Settled in her car, she turned right onto Little Santa Monica and then darted left onto Wilshire, cutting off a red Porsche. Activating the Bluetooth, she pressed the speed dial for Rob's cell. She began to chide herself for being foolish. How would she explain the reason for her call? After four rings, however, she gripped the steering wheel more tightly. After eight rings, a recorded, metallic voice indicated the subscriber was outside of the service area. She immediately swerved right across two lanes on Wilshire. One of the three cars she cut off honked loudly and long. Careening right onto Comstock, she pulled over in the dark quiet by Holmby Park. She tried M.D.'s cell phone. Again, the same mechanical voice told her to try again later. Ghislaine felt it difficult to breathe. She Googled the Marriott Hotel, Panama, and pressed enter on the hotel's telephone number. When she asked to be connected to Rob's room, a pleasant young man informed her that he had seen Mr. Bingham and his two guests go out with a friend earlier in the evening. They had not yet returned.

"But I can't reach my son on his cell phone," she snapped.

"Do not concern yourself, Señora Bingham," he assured her. "Young men are often out late here and the mobile phones do not work well in our nightclubs. I will leave a message for Mr. Bingham that you called. I am sure that you will hear from him tomorrow."

Ghislaine told herself she had no reason to fear anything had happened to Rob, but she still felt deeply shaken. The anxiety of not knowing where Rob was compounded the stress from her struggle with Ward. Every muscle in her body ached with tension. She yearned for her safe haven, her space of physical and emotional release. After pulling up the driveway and parking in front of her home, she found Mi-young Park's number in her BlackBerry and pushed the green button.

"Mi? Hi, it's Ghislaine. I know it's late but is there any way you could come over tonight?" she asked plaintively. "I'm in need of your healing."

"I am so happy you called," Mi said in a soft, high-pitched voice. "It has been too long a time. I will cancel my eight thirty appointment and be at your home by nine o'clock."

"Perfect. I can't thank you enough."

Thirty minutes later, Mi-young Park was setting up her portable massage bed in Ghislaine's bedroom as Ghislaine undressed in the adjoining bathroom. When Mi had the massage bed prepared, she turned off all the lights except a dimmed lamp by the bed and called out to Ghislaine, who returned wearing a white silk robe.

"What would you like to listen to tonight?"

"Do you have the Gregorian chant? If so, I'd love it. And, Mi," Ghislaine said as she put six fifty dollar bills down on the bed table, "this is for tonight. You know I often fall asleep during sessions with you. If you could just roll me onto my bed when you're done and let yourself out, that would be great." Ghislaine leaned over to set her radio alarm to wake her up early.

"Yes, of course. Thank you." Mi switched on the small CD player she brought as part of her equipment and inserted the CD Ghislaine had asked for. Ghislaine slipped off her robe and lay face down on the massage bed, pulling the single sheet over the small of her back. Mi squirted some oil in her hands and rubbed the oil to warm it. The scent of lavender, chamomile, and sage wafted up. She went to work first on both sides of Ghislaine's neck, shoulders, and upper back. As she did, Ghislaine closed her eyes and began to take long, slow breaths until her breathing matched the rhythm of Mi's hands. Gradually, all thought passed from Ghislaine's mind and flowed into the strong, warm, familiar touch of her Korean confidante.

"Your neck and back are very tight. You should call me more often," Mi complained gently and increased the pressure.

"Oh," Ghislaine groaned. "That feels so good. Oh, Mi, you know how I hated being condescended to by Robert as if I were just a dumb socialite. But at least when he was alive, I didn't feel like an antelope running from a pack of lions. Hector practically invited me to bed with him tonight and Andrei, whom I adore for having saved me when Robert left, now expects me to marry him. Why do men assume all women not only need but desire their protection? Aah," Ghislaine breathed out slowly as Mi continued pressing down.

"I think no man can understand a woman like you," Mi said softly after a moment and paused. "Not the way a woman could.

Not the way *I* can." Ghislaine reached back with her right hand. Mi took it, leaned down and pressed the back of Ghislaine's hand to her cheek for an instant.

"I don't know what I would have done all those years with Robert if I hadn't had you to comfort me." Ghislaine sighed.

"Thank you," Mi whispered and released Ghislaine's hand. "Giving you pleasure will always be my greatest happiness." After a few minutes more, Mi adjusted the covering sheet to expose the lower left side of Ghislaine's body. She worked the various groups of muscles running from the small of her back down to her foot. After she had finished the lower left side, Mi again shifted the sheet and set about the lower right side. The masseuse began to pant lightly. Beads of sweat formed on the back of her neck.

"Time to turn over," Mi murmured after about forty minutes. Ghislaine rolled over silently under the suspended sheet. Mi pulled the sheet down over Ghislaine's breasts, oiled her hands, and began to knead the biceps and other muscles first in Ghislaine's right arm, hand, and fingers and then in her left. Standing directly behind Ghislaine, the masseuse worked her upper neck and shoulder muscles again, increasing the pressure until Ghislaine moaned as the tension trapped there evaporated. Mi then put her hands underneath the sheet and massaged Ghislaine's pectoral muscles with downward strokes of her fingers that ran lightly over Ghislaine's hardening nipples. "You are so very beautiful," Mi breathed in Ghislaine's ear. Ghislaine reached up and pressed Mi's head next to hers for a moment.

"Only as beautiful as you make me feel," she murmured.

The masseuse dabbed more oil on her hands and moved to the foot of the bed. Ghislaine continued to breathe slowly and deeply as Mi rubbed Ghislaine's feet and then her calves, still sinewy from her years of training as a figure skater. The chanting of the monks gradually built toward a crescendo, which was Mi's cue that the session was nearly done. She leaned over Ghislaine's lower body and slowly pushed the fingers of her two hands up and down the top of Ghislaine's thighs, pressing her thumbs into the muscles that ran along the inside of her legs until they met at the moist apex. Mi repeated the stroke again and again as Ghislaine's abdomen began to tighten and heave with each pass of Mi's hands.

"Aaah," Ghislaine moaned finally. Her body quivered and relaxed, like a tree caressed briefly by a passing breeze. "Thank you, Mi. Thank you," Ghislaine whispered without waking from her half-sleep. Mi turned off the music and pushed the massage table over to the bed. She kissed Ghislaine on the forehead, gently rolled her off the table onto her mattress, and spread the top sheet over her naked body. Within a few minutes, Mi had packed up. She turned to check once more that Ghislaine was sleeping soundly before walking down the stairs and out into the night.

FORTY-SEVEN

·····································

TUESDAY, DECEMBER 21
PORTOBELO

When the jaguar locked the door, Duncan's mind drifted to Sam. His son had difficulty expressing his emotions; he even struggled sometimes to identify which emotions he felt. But Duncan knew there was no mistaking what Sam felt on Monday: disappointment, confusion, anger. Duncan calculated it was well past nine o'clock. Sam had again waited for a call that never came. He knew his son's trust in him had frayed; his failure to call tonight would tear it further. If Duncan didn't make it back to see him tomorrow night, he risked losing Sam altogether. He couldn't let that happen. But how would they escape?

Several minutes more passed before Duncan's eyes adjusted to the bunker's darkness. He guessed that the room was about ten feet wide and twenty-five feet long. Once he could see more clearly, he sat up slowly, conscious of the ache in his side, and looked for the knife where he had heard it land. He tried to stand but pain stabbed through his rib cage, and he only managed to wobble to his knees before collapsing against the wall.

"Can you see the knife over there, M.D." He wheezed. "To the right?"

"Yes, I think so." She walked over to the blade lying in the dirt and grasped it with one of her bound hands. Seeing that M.D. had found the knife, Rob lifted himself up and held his arms out. She cut through the tape wrapped around his hands.

"Now let me do you," he said to M.D. as he took the knife from her hand. He freed M.D. and then walked over to Duncan and Magdalena.

"Magdalena, let me have your hands," Rob said as he knelt down beside her. She looked up at him, turned her head away, and stretched out her hands.

Once Magdalena had been cut free, Duncan held up his hands. After Rob cut him loose, Duncan rose unsteadily and stumbled over to the door, willing his mind to ignore the throbbing in his side. If he could break it open, could they make it down the hill without a flashlight? It was worth a try; perhaps the bolt could be dislodged somehow. He shook the door as hard as he could but it didn't budge. Rob joined him and the two of them banged their shoulders against it to no effect.

"All right," Duncan said, "I don't think we're going to break out through here." He turned to face Magdalena. "You said that you didn't know those men, but do you know where we are? You said that we were not in danger but that your life was over. Tell us what you know, *now.*"

Magdalena stared at Duncan through the dimness of the enclosure and then glanced at Rob and M.D. "There is no hope for me," she murmured. "Still, you tried to protect me from those *bastardos.* Can you believe that I am truly sorry for everything I have done to cause you this difficulty?"

"What do you mean?" Rob demanded. "Did you have something to do with our kidnapping?"

"Who are you, Magdalena, and what are you doing here?" Duncan barked. Magdalena held her head in her hands and began to weep again.

"Calm down you two," M.D. ordered and crept over to where Magdalena slumped against the stone wall. "Magdalena, listen to me." She took Magdalena's face in her hands. "We need to know who you are and whether you can help us escape. If you help us, we will help you. I promise."

Magdalena looked up into M.D.'s eyes and nodded.

"I'm sorry for shouting at you," Duncan apologized. "Our chances of escape are much greater with you on our side. Tell us everything you know." Duncan lowered himself carefully in front of Magdalena. M.D. and Rob sat next to Duncan and waited for Magdalena to speak.

"Rodrigo asked me to pretend to be his assistant, to meet some Americans at their hotel, and go with them in his car on the road to Las Cumbres. You must believe me," she implored, "he swore no one would be hurt."

"I believe you," M.D. assured her.

"Thank you."

"Did Rodrigo tell you why he wanted us kidnapped?" Duncan asked.

"He said that you three were causing an American client of his trouble and he needed to have you detained until tomorrow. He assured me you would be returned to your hotel unharmed and could leave the country immediately. He also promised me after you were kidnapped, I would be free to return to my apartment, where he would wait for me." Magdalena took a deep breath. "Now, after eight years, I will be sent back to Colombia where I have no friends and no family and where a man will kill me as soon as he finds me there."

"Kill you?" Duncan exclaimed. "Why would anyone want to kill you? If you've been here eight years, you must have been in your early twenties when you left Colombia."

"Ah, yes, I was. I know you cannot understand what it meant to escape Colombia. Why I am so terrified to return. But can you believe me when I say I am desperate to save you so that you might save me. God knows you are the only ones who can."

"I understand," said M.D. "Tell us why you left Colombia." The three Americans listened as Magdalena described her childhood in the orphanage, her year with the benefactor and the year she spent on her own, her rape, and the attack on the general's son. M.D. reached over and touched her hand. Duncan and Rob shifted their bodies uncomfortably on the ground of the bunker. M.D. saw Magdalena's eyes dart downward and reached out to touch her hand again.

"It's okay. Keep talking."

"A few days later," she continued, "I flew to Panama with a group of five other girls. We were taken to the Golden Island Club, where I was told my job was not to dance and entertain but to entice men to have sex with me. When I tried to tell the head man what the Spanish teacher had promised me, he grabbed my arm and twisted it behind my back. He shouted he would teach me to obey him. He forced me around, lifted my skirt, and bent me over. I struggled but he was too strong. Visions of the rape in Cartagena flew through my head. I screamed. Then from the shadows, I heard a voice commanding the head man to release me. It was Rodrigo. Rodrigo led me away and listened to my story. He seemed kind and gentle and said he would protect me. I . . . I *hungered* to feel safe again. Can you understand?"

"Yes," M.D. replied softly. "I can."

"After a few days, we became lovers. For years, he gave me a life beyond the dreams of an orphan girl. Can you understand that as time passed I no longer thought of myself as a mistress? When we traveled together, he would introduce me as his wife. I began to pretend we were married even in Panama City. Soon I convinced myself the pretense was real. Then ten days ago I . . . I tried to help a young Panamanian girl return to her home. Rodrigo became enraged."

Magdalena stopped for a second and faced M.D. "He tortured her. He threatened me. At first, I did not blame him; no, I hated myself for what had happened. Then a Colombian friend helped me to wake up, to see Rodrigo as he was and . . . to see myself as I was, nothing more than Rodrigo's ornament, a whore. Freed of my fantasy, I wanted to leave him but what could I do? I had no money and was living illegally in Panama. So yesterday I begged Rodrigo to obtain a resident visa for me. He refused at first, saying I had nothing to fear. Then, suddenly, his mood changed and he agreed to help me. I was so very happy. But now I see he planned only to use me to kidnap you and afterwards send me back to Colombia."

"Magdalena," Duncan said looking at Rob and then M.D., "I think we might be able to help you. But we can do nothing for you or for ourselves trapped in here. Do you know where we are?"

"I guess that we are near one of the old Spanish forts on the Caribbean, probably the one near Portobelo, which is about thirty minutes from Colon. I visited the ruins once several years ago with Rodrigo. Although it was dark tonight when we were walking up the hill, I felt that I was near here once before. If I am right, we're locked in a *casamata,* a room the Spanish used to store ammunition and arms a safe distance from the fort below."

"If this is Portobelo, is there anyone who lives nearby?" asked Duncan. "If we made a lot of noise, would anyone hear us?"

"Portobelo is a very small town. If we are in the ruins, no one lives near here. We can try your plan, of course, but I do not think it will work. I saw no one when I was walking up the hill. Did you?"

"No," Duncan replied and sagged against the stone wall. "And even if someone were close, the thick stone and surrounding earth would muffle almost any sound we could make." Duncan remained silent for a moment and then continued, resigned, "I don't have any other ideas. We can't rely on what Salduba told Magdalena. We have to try to find a way out of this place as soon as possible tomorrow morning. If we're lucky, we can find a taxi to get us to Colon in time for our meeting. If not, then Magdalena is our only hope." Duncan turned toward her.

"I believe Rodrigo had us kidnapped because of our appointment with a government official in Colon tomorrow morning. Would you be willing to tell the official that Rodrigo arranged our kidnapping? It might help us get another appointment. More importantly, if they know how Salduba has treated you, they might help you stay in Panama."

"You are kind but know nothing of how powerful men in this country treat women like me. Still, I would gladly help you, if I am still free," she said throwing her hands up in the air. "But you must understand, Rodrigo will have paid the police to arrest me. I will be deported by tomorrow evening. Besides, why would an important official believe the word of a Colombian prostitute against that of a prominent lawyer? Rodrigo used me because he knew no one would listen to me."

As she spoke, Duncan realized Magdalena was right. They could not wait until the police came tomorrow. Besides, if they did, he would miss his flight home to see Sam. They had to break out. But how?

"You're right." Duncan sighed. "Jorge's uncle might not believe you, but you are still the only person who can link Rodrigo to our kidnapping. Our success and your future are bound together."

Magdalena nodded that she understood. "It must be close to midnight by now," Duncan said. "I don't know what else to do at this point except wait until morning. Perhaps daylight will reveal some way out we can't see in this darkness."

"I know we're all tired," Rob said, "but don't you think we should try to sleep in two shifts, with one shift by the door in case our friends come back or someone wanders nearby?"

"I think that's a good idea," M.D. agreed. "Why don't you and Duncan sleep now? You both have been banged up and could use the rest. We'll wake you in three hours. Magdalena, let's sit over here by the door." M.D. reached down and picked up one of the tarps and walked over to the bolted door.

Rob grabbed the other tarp, stepped over to the wall opposite the door, and spread the tarp on the floor. He retrieved two water bottles, handed one to Duncan and stretched out on the tarp, tucking the other water bottle under his head. Duncan lay down next to Rob with his water bottle as a pillow. Thoughts of Sam filled his mind until exhaustion claimed his consciousness.

....

FORTY-EIGHT

TUESDAY, DECEMBER 21
PORTOBELO

Magdalena walked over to M.D. and sat down. "How can I thank you for listening, for giving me hope? I feel like a condemned man who dreams the night before he is to die that his friends will free him before he is killed."

"We will find a way to help you," M.D. reassured her. "I don't know how yet, but I promise you we will." For several minutes, M.D. and Magdalena sat side by side in silence, backs to the door, peering out into the gloom of the enclosure. The moist night air grew cooler. The two young women pulled the tarp over their shoulders like an enormous shawl and leaned against each other for warmth. The buzzing of countless insects pulsed around them. The figures of Rob and Duncan asleep along the opposite wall were barely visible, but soon the heavy breathing of the two men, punctuated from time to time by a soft cough or snort, joined the insect chorus.

"I always hated sleeping with a man who made sounds in the night," Magdalena laughed lightly. "Tonight they comfort me."

"You speak such wonderful English," M.D. said and then switched to Spanish. "But if you wish, we could speak Spanish."

"I would enjoy that very much," Magdalena replied. "Speaking English tires me and your Spanish accent is very pure, like a Colombian's."

"Thank you. My accent should remind you of home. I attended university for a while in Bogotá several years ago."

Magdalena shifted her body to a more comfortable position. "Are you tired, M.D.?"

"No, not at all. Besides, we should try to remain awake."

"Then, may I ask?" Magdalena inquired. "Where is your family? What has brought you to Panama?"

"Well," M.D. replied with a sigh, "that's a long story." M.D. told Magdalena the story of her Irish-American mother and Colombian father meeting in college in California, her mother getting pregnant, her father deserting them, and her mother's family disowning her mother before M.D. was born. She described being raised by her resolute and independent mother to be equally resolute and independent. M.D. spoke of her pride in her career and her loyalty to Ghislaine and about the dispute with Ward Bingham that had brought them to Panama.

Magdalena listened to M.D. without interrupting. When M.D. finished, Magdalena stared out at the darkness surrounding them and murmured, "You are a half-Colombian woman. You could be my younger sister and yet you live in a world completely unknown to me. You are valued for the ideas of your mind not for the pleasure your body can give. You can freely approach any man or refuse any man's advances. You can walk, work, and play without fear of physical assault or arrest. And your employer is a woman? I find it all incredible," Magdalena exclaimed shaking her head in wonder.

M.D. remained silent for a moment before replying, "It could all be gone in an instant. I've worked *so* hard to climb up from the bottom rung while others seem to have been born at the top.

Sometimes I . . . I doubt myself and wonder whether I deserve to have come as far as I have. Sometimes I'm terrified that one slip will send me tumbling down not just a rung or two but all the way back to the grimy, gritty land of strip malls and fast food places where I grew up."

"But surely your boyfriend would not let that happen!"

"I don't have boyfriend. What gave you that idea? I've had lovers, of course, but never anyone with whom I wanted to share my life."

"But, Rob, he is your boyfriend, no?"

"No, of course not," M.D. laughed. "We're business colleagues. Whatever gave you the idea that he was my boyfriend?"

"Why," Magdalena replied, "have you not noticed the way he looks at you, the way he protected you, the way he listens to you with admiration in his eyes? I know something of such things, and his eyes are not the eyes of a business colleague. They are the eyes of love or, at least, of wanting to love. He is handsome, rich, and smart, no? And, a good man, a man who seems capable of the love he wants to give?"

"I really don't know him," objected M.D., sitting up defensively. "But even a good man is still a man. And for thousands of years men have, sometimes consciously and sometimes unconsciously, offered every woman the same bad bargain. In return for security and the resources to make a home for herself and her children, the woman must agree to put the man's wants and work and whims before hers. No man, Magdalena, even a good one, is worth that trade, because in the exchange you give up yourself."

"But a good man would not require you to lose yourself," Magdalena insisted. "He would embrace and support your dreams as his own. His love would make you stronger not weaker. Love is a gift that two people give freely to each other. You make it sound like a business, like commerce."

"That is romantic nonsense," M.D. said and twisted to face Magdalena. "You of all people should know that love exists only in books and films and that what is exchanged between a man and a woman in real life is business. Did Rodrigo embrace and support *your* dreams? He used you and discarded you. You are in this desolate bunker tonight because he feared giving you the key to unshackle yourself from his prison. Look around you." M.D. waved her hand at the stone walls. "So much for love."

"I enjoyed my fantasy life with Rodrigo," Magdalena admitted, returning M.D.'s gaze, "but I know now you are right. He never loved me and I never loved him. We were like actors in a *novela romantica*. I think now . . . how to say it? A part of me has always lived in a place much deeper than my skin. I believe my soul longs for a man who could find contentment in holding me at night, stroking my hair, and, just before he fell asleep, telling me he loved me. That is my new dream. I do not think life would be worth living without the hope of making such a dream real," Magdalena paused, hesitated, and then added quietly, "Tell me about Duncan."

"I don't know him well." M.D. shrugged. "In fact, I met him for the first time only a few days ago. He is a lawyer retained by Ghislaine Bingham to help her defeat Ward Bingham's plans to take over the company where we work."

"He is unusual, yes? He protected you and he tried to protect me from the robbers, so he has courage though not the strength of a younger man," Magdalena explained to the darkness around them. "Despite everything I have done to hurt you, he forgave me and allowed me to redeem myself by helping you. So he is kind but also intelligent. Perhaps, in another time and place . . ." Magdalena began and then her voice trailed away.

"Dear God," M.D. blurted out. "You're not saying that you find him attractive. He must be more than twenty years older than you!"

Magdalena laughed, "Duncan is no older than Rodrigo. One of my girlfriends once told me that I found older men attractive because I never had a father. Could this be true?"

"I don't know. I never really had a father either but, while I like Duncan, I do not find him at all attractive. Still, I envy that you hope to find love. I have always been afraid to give myself to anyone at all," M.D. confessed in a whisper. "I know that one must be able to trust in order to love, and I am terrified that trust is something I may never be capable of."

Magdalena smiled and leaned more heavily against M.D. "Do you believe in destiny, M.D.?"

"No, I don't. Why?"

"Because I feel that fate has led me to the three of you. I do not know what the dawn will bring, but I am no longer afraid of its light."

Magdalena put her arm around M.D.'s shoulders and drew the younger woman toward her as she had many times embraced an orphan child who cried out in the middle of the night. When M.D. leaned her head against Magdalena's shoulder, Magdalena stroked her hair. In a few minutes more, Magdalena rested her head on top of M.D.'s and let the sounds of the night jungle wash over them.

....

FORTY-NINE

TUESDAY, DECEMBER 21
LOS ANGELES

After dinner with two investors in his Middle East and Africa fund, Ward returned to his office around ten o'clock to pick up his briefcase and check phone messages. Elaine had left him notes of two calls. Ward read the first from Rodrigo Salduba with barely contained glee. Salduba reported that, as expected, he had encountered no problems with his assignment and would finish it on Wednesday at noon, Panama time. The second note said Gracie Lewis had called as promised. Ward held the pink slip in his hand for a moment, weighing whether he should return her call. He knew she would ask for money for her son's school. On the other hand, he remembered her as quick-witted, pretty, and ambitious. If she were no longer married, she might be fun to go out with for a while. Recently divorced women always seemed eager to prove how sexy they still were. Ward picked up his phone and dialed Gracie's number.

"Hello?" she answered in a light soprano that did not bother to conceal a note of irritation.

"Hi, Gracie. It's Ward Bingham returning your call."

"Oh, Ward," the annoyance gone from her voice. "I didn't expect you to call so late. Anyway, thank you so much for calling back. How are you? It's been a while since we worked together on financing that BIG investment."

"I'm fine. Thanks for asking. And you? How are you? Still at Goldman?"

"Oh, no. I've been a full-time mom for five years now. My son has special needs and I've devoted myself to helping him and others like him. Frankly, I feel more fulfilled than ever before. And I'm doing okay considering I'm in the process of getting a divorce."

"I'm so sorry to hear that."

"Don't be. It'll be the best thing for my son and me in the long run, but it *is* hard now. His father's trying to avoid paying the support my son needs to keep improving."

"Excuse me for saying so, but he sounds like a real prick. Isn't he a well-heeled lawyer of some kind? How can he object to paying support?"

"That's the problem. As our marriage began to unravel, he all of a sudden decided he wanted to leave practice to become an academic. Quite a coincidence, huh?"

"What an asshole!"

"Naturally, he *said* he threw our marriage under the bus because he wanted to spend more time with our son. So what does he do the first weekend after we've separated? He goes overseas, misses a night with our son, and forgets to call when scheduled."

"I'm so sorry you have to put up with that kind of abuse. You . . . you don't know this about me, but I lost my mother when I was fifteen years old and have missed her every day of my life since then. I appreciate good mothers and can tell you're one."

"Thanks, Ward. That's a really lovely thing to say. Do you . . . do you have children?"

"No." Ward laughed. "Never married, in fact."

"Too bad." Gracie sighed. "You'd be a great father. Men who have sound relationships with their mothers usually are. I made the mistake of marrying a guy whose mother left her two sons to be raised by an introverted father. In hindsight, I don't think either my ex or his nerdy younger brother ever recovered from the trauma of losing their mother. They're probably both schizoid as a result. Anyway, my ex certainly always had trouble appreciating me as a mother!"

"Your son's lucky to have you."

"Thanks, again. You're very kind," Gracie murmured.

"Not at all. Is there anything I can do to help?"

"Oh, I don't want to bore you with my troubles. Besides, I'm calling to ask you for a donation, not to depress you."

"Not a burden at all, but I am sorry to say that our charitable-giving budget has been completely used up for this year. Still, why don't we get together sometime and you can tell me about your son and his school? Maybe I can donate some money next year?

"I would really love that! Thank you. In fact, I know it's short notice, but how about tomorrow night? It's supposed to be my son's night with his father. Unless he screws up again, I'll be free for an hour between seven and eight."

"Wednesday night? I think that will work fine. You're in Santa Monica, aren't you? How about Rustic Canyon Wine Bar at seven?"

"That would be wonderful. I'm looking forward to seeing you, Ward."

FIFTY

....

WEDNESDAY, DECEMBER 22
PORTOBELO

Dawn turned quickly to sunrise and soon Wednesday morning's light blanketed the hillside and crept under the door of the *casamata,* where M.D. and Magdalena lay fast asleep. The whir of insects gave way to the chirps and whistles and caws of jungle birds. Magdalena opened her eyes and looked around. M.D., Rob, and Duncan still slept. She shifted her weight and M.D. awoke with a start. She wiped the sleep from her eyes, stood up, and stretched.

"Rob, Duncan," she called. When the two men did not stir, "Rob, Duncan," she said more loudly. The two men rolled over, sat up, and rubbed their necks and backs.

"Sorry we didn't wake you," M.D. said. "We fell asleep but I don't think it mattered. No one tried the door and I think we would have heard anyone who walked by."

"Can't help it now," Duncan said as he hoisted himself up and massaged his ribs where he had been kicked. "What time do you think it is, Magdalena?"

"Sunrise is around six thirty. So I would say six forty-five."

"Then we don't have much time. At least it's getting lighter in here. We need to examine the walls for any weakness, any small openings or large cracks, and look for any tool or stick or rock that we might use to break out. Use your eyes and your hands to probe for holes. Rob, you take this side," Duncan said and pointed to the long side of the rectangle resting against the hill. "M.D. and Magdalena, you take the two short sides, left and right. I'll start with the door and work along the wall on this side."

After only a few seconds, Magdalena shouted, "Come quickly!" Standing by the corner formed by the short wall to Duncan's right and the long front wall, she pointed up at what looked like an opening just under the roof.

"It must be some type of ventilation system," Rob said. "M.D., why don't you look to see whether there's an identical opening on the left side?"

"Yes, there is!" she exclaimed.

"Rob and M.D.," Duncan ordered, "see if there is any way to climb up the wall to reach the vent on the left. Magdalena and I will check the one over here."

"No way to climb up over here," Rob reported after a moment. "The stone surface is flat and intact. And I think the opening may be partially covered over with soil and grass."

"Going up here also looks impossible without some assistance, but at least the opening appears clear, even if it's pretty small for either you or me," Duncan replied. "Let's lift M.D. up so she can see whether the shaft is large enough for her to slide through and out to the other side.

"I don't think she can reach if we just boost her up," Rob said as he wiped his hand over his face.

"Any suggestions?" Duncan pleaded with the three of them.

Rob looked away for a moment. Suddenly the image of a human staircase flashed across his mind.

"I have an idea!" Rob exclaimed.

"What is it?" M.D. asked.

"I . . . it's better if I just show you. Duncan," he directed, "you're the tallest so stand here with your face to the wall below the opening." Once Duncan was in place, Rob dropped to his hands and knees in front of Duncan and positioned himself parallel to the wall. "M.D., step on my back and then onto Duncan's shoulders, if you can. Duncan, you may have to squat a bit so M.D. can reach to step up. Magdalena, stand behind M.D. to brace her in case she loses her balance and falls back. Okay, everyone? Let's go."

M.D. stepped up and onto Rob's back. She tried to lift her right foot onto Duncan's right shoulder but couldn't reach. Duncan lowered himself about six inches but M.D. still couldn't place her foot on his shoulder.

"Here," Duncan said, turning around and making a stirrup with his hands. "Put your left foot here and your hands on my shoulders. Good. Now, as I lift you up move your hands above me and be sure to lean forward against the wall just above my head. When you're high enough, put your right foot on my left shoulder and then step up with your left foot on my right shoulder." Duncan gasped with pain from the bruise on his side as M.D. climbed over him. Soon, she was standing unsteadily on his shoulders with her hands on the front ledge of the ventilation shaft. Duncan held her feet to his shoulders to steady her. Rob stood up and joined Magdalena behind M.D. in case she should fall.

M.D. lifted herself up to where her head was level with the opening. She reached into the shaft with both her arms groping for a hold. "I think I have a good grip now. I'm going to try to get into the shaft. When I jump, lift my feet up as high as you can, Duncan." M.D. hesitated for a moment and then jumped up from Duncan's shoulders with a grunt. She tried to pull her upper body up and into the narrow passage. Her hands slipped. She reached out wildly for another hold, lost her balance, and fell backward, screaming as she dropped. Rob moved to catch her, throwing Magdalena out of the way. M.D.'s back thumped against Rob's chest and knocked him backward. Rob wrapped his arms around M.D. using his body to break her fall. They landed with a thud in a heap on the dirt floor.

"Are you okay?" M.D. asked as she disentangled herself from Rob and stood up.

"Yeah, uh, fine," he said lifting himself up. "Happy to be your landing pad. What happened?"

"When I stood on Duncan's shoulders, I was able to see that the shaft was clear but about six inches too long for me to reach the outside edge where I could get a firm grip. I tried to find a place in the passage that would bear my weight so I could pull myself up and into the opening. I thought I had a good hold in a crack between two stones, but my hand slipped out when I tried to yank myself up. I'm sorry. Thanks, again, for catching me." M.D. looked up at Rob and reached out to touch his left arm.

"It's all right," Duncan said. "If you were that close to touching the outside edge of the shaft, I think Magdalena should be able to reach it and pull herself up. Magdalena," he said turning toward her, "will you give it a try?"

"Being up so high frightens me but, yes, I will try. We have so little time. I will do as you say. But, please, only very slowly."

Once again, Duncan stood with his back against the wall and Rob knelt down in front of him. Magdalena stepped up onto Rob, gained her balance, and then placed her left foot into the stirrup formed by Duncan's hands. Her hair fell across Duncan's face and he cried out in pain as he lifted her up. In an instant, she was standing on Duncan's shoulders and had inserted her arms and head into the shaft.

"I can just reach the outside edge of the opening," she said, panting, "and think that I can pull myself into it if you lift my feet up at the same time." Rob stood up by M.D. in case Magdalena fell back. He could see Magdalena bounce up from Duncan's shoulders as she boosted the upper half of her body up and into the shaft. Her hips rested on the interior ledge of the narrow stone passage and her feet dangled down the wall just above Duncan. Duncan turned around and stood with Rob and M.D., looking up at Magdalena.

"Oh dear Jesus," Magdalena cried. "I can see the outside wall. It slopes out from where I am and is at least ten feet down to the ground. If I go any farther, I will fall and my head will hit the bottom of the wall. What do I do now?"

Duncan looked at Rob whose eyes darted around the enclosure. "We need something to break her fall."

"What about making a rope out of the two tarps?" Duncan suggested.

"I think that would be a good start, but we'll probably need something around twenty feet. The two tarps are only about four feet square, so about six feet on the diagonal. We'll need something else. I know! Let's use our clothes to lengthen the tarps."

M.D. eyes widened. "Another good idea!"

"I . . . I told you, I may not be good with words, but I'm not bad at solving practical problems." Rob grinned. "Magdalena," he shouted. "Hold on! We're going to tie the tarps and our clothes to your legs and then lower you to the ground."

"Why not make the rope and push it through the shaft so Magdalena can climb down it?" M.D. asked.

"She can't turn herself around to get her legs out first. I think that this is the only way," Rob replied.

Duncan and Rob stripped off their shirts and pants. Duncan tied one of the arms of his shirt around Magdalena's left ankle and the other arm around her right. He made sure the knots were secure. He twisted the body of his shirt and held it out to Rob. Rob tied one of the arms of his shirt around a loop he'd made in the body of Duncan's shirt and then tied the other arm to a loop knot he had fashioned with one of the legs of Duncan's pants. Finally, he tied the other leg of Duncan's pants to a loop knot in one leg of his pants.

"Roll up the tarps in a diagonal, M.D., but make sure that the grommets at the two exposed corners are free."

"Okay," M.D. said, and after few seconds she held them out. "Here they are." Rob took the free leg from his pants and rolled it up. He threaded it through the grommet of the first tarp and tied it off securely. Grabbing his belt, he tied the other grommet of the first tarp together with a grommet from the second tarp. Rob tried pulling apart each of the knots to confirm that they would hold. They did, although Magdalena's weight would be the real test. Rob nodded at Duncan, who looked from Rob to M.D. and then turned toward the wall where Magdalena's legs, now tied to his shirt, were still dangling.

"Magdalena, do you hear me?" Duncan asked.

"Yes, I hear you. I can feel the shirt tied to my ankles. Are you ready? Is it safe?"

"Yes, we're ready now. We've tested the knots and they are as secure as we can make them. When I say go, please start to pull yourself forward through the shaft. As you leave the outer opening of the passage, the line tied to your ankles will gradually tighten as it begins to bear your weight. We will lower you as slowly as possible. Magdalena, you said that the wall slopes out, right? So, as you crawl out of the shaft, use your hands and arms both to slow your descent and to keep your body away from the wall as much as possible. Pretend that you're walking down the wall with your hands. Do you understand?"

"Yes. I think so."

"Okay, Rob, I'm a little taller, but you're a lot stronger than I am. Would you take the rope?" Duncan asked.

"You got it." Rob seized the safety line with two hands and braced himself with his feet against the wall. Duncan stood a little behind Rob and picked up another part of the line in case the rope slipped from Rob's grasp. M.D. stood to the side, watching for any indication that a knot was unraveling.

"Okay, Magdalena. Please move slowly out now," Duncan yelled. As Rob felt Magdalena move forward, he carefully paid out the rope.

"I am crawling out of the shaft now!" Magdalena cried. Rob could feel the rope tighten as it began to bear more of Magdalena's weight. He leaned back against the increasing strain and released the line hand over hand. After what seemed like hours of a very slow descent, Rob's hands neared the end of the second tarp.

"She's not reached the ground, yet, but we're almost out of rope. Did we miscalculate the length?"

"I don't know. Perhaps the outer wall is longer than we thought because it's built on the down slope of a hillside?" Duncan asked out loud.

"What do we do?" Rob asked as he reached within a foot of the end of the last tarp.

"Should we take a chance and just let her go? She can't be more than a couple of feet from the ground and there's no way we can pull her back in at this point."

"No, let's not do that yet. We can get another few feet if you let me hold you around the waist so you can stop leaning away from the wall." Duncan stepped behind Rob, encircled Rob's waist with his arms, and locked his hands together. "Now stand up and hold the rope as high as you can." Rob stood slowly and raised the rope above his head. The muscles in his arms shook with the strain and his face flushed red. Then, suddenly, the rope went slack. Rob released the tarp with a *whoop*. It flew up the wall and out through the shaft. M.D. pumped her fist into the air and ran over to hug Rob. She wrapped her arms around his waist and placed her head against his chest.

"My God, your heart is thumping wildly," she said as she looked up at him, tossed her head back with a smile, and turned quickly away to run to the door. A second later, the three Americans heard the bolt slide free with a sharp, metallic clang. The door swung open.

Light flooded in from the doorway where Magdalena stood grinning. Her face and arms were covered with sweat and black dust from the stones. Here and there rivulets of blood formed where the stone had cut her arms. Her silk blouse and pants were shredded. She stared at Duncan and Rob standing before her in their boxers and handed them the clothesline with a laugh. M.D. ran up to embrace Magdalena, but the sight of her hands, cut in a thousand places from her hand-walk down the stone face of the bunker, and the deep-red welts on her ankles where the shirt had been tied stopped M.D. as if she had been struck by a bullet.

"What have we done to you? Can you walk?" M.D. asked. Duncan and Rob, now dressed, ran over to the women. Duncan took Magdalena in his arms and hugged her. "You are an incredibly brave woman. You didn't make a sound. Why didn't you cry out something, anything?"

Magdalena's eyes welled with tears. "I did not want you to stop. I could not bear the thought of being taken by the police. I was the only one who could free us. The cuts and bruises look worse than they feel. They will heal. *Mis queridos amigos.*"

Duncan took Magdalena by the shoulders. His eyes softened as he looked directly into hers. "All right then. We need to get down the hill as quickly as possible. It must be almost eight o'clock. Do you think you can jog down?"

"I will try."

"Good," Duncan said. "Rob, throw the tarps in the room and shut and bolt the door. Let's go. We don't have a second to lose."

FIFTY-ONE

....

WEDNESDAY, DECEMBER 22
LOS ANGELES

The local public radio station woke Ghislaine at five thirty. She had set the alarm early so she could exercise and be ready for M.D.'s call after the meeting with Rodriguez, but she could still feel Mi's fingers running over her skin and lingered in bed to enjoy the memory. . . . She rose a few minutes later, tied back her hair, and slipped on her purple cotton unitard. After sipping some water from the carafe on her nightstand, she laid her navy blue yoga mat on the rug.

Standing, Ghislaine stretched her neck, back, legs, and ankles, feeling only a tweak of pain in her right ankle from the injury that had ended her skating career. After stretching, she jogged, ran, and then sprinted in place for five minutes, swinging her arms and bringing her thighs up parallel to the ground. Puffing and perspiring as she finished, she wiped the sweat from her forehead and lowered herself to the mat. Controlling her breathing and closing her eyes, she performed a series of yoga poses, starting with pelvic tilts and progressing through cow and cat, downward-facing dog, and pigeon. Moving onto her hands and knees, she carefully positioned her left wrist to avoid aggravating another old injury from falls on the ice, and finished her routine with push-ups until she could feel the muscles in her arms and chest burn.

At exactly six o'clock, she rose from the floor and rolled up her yoga mat. She decided to shower quickly, but she kept her Black-Berry nearby. A few minutes later, Ghislaine patted her body dry with an enormous beige bath towel, wrapped a smaller towel around her head to dry her hair, and rubbed organic honey-almond moisturizing cream into her skin. Putting on a terry-cloth robe, she noticed that the red message light on her BlackBerry began to flash. Picking up the cell phone, she sat down in the lounge chair that rested in the corner by one of the two bedroom windows, punched in her password, and scrolled up to see a message from Ron Danko to Ward and her. Ghislaine cursed as she read that the São Tomé and Príncipe government had indefinitely postponed consideration of Bingham International's investment in Gulf of Guinea due to political infighting. *Merde.* So much for Rob's plan to use the Gulf deal to force Ward to increase the company's value.

Ghislaine was about to call Danko when she saw an urgent message from Gloria Merit, the London office administrator. Gloria asked that Ghislaine contact her immediately. Ghislaine tightened her grip on the BlackBerry and tapped the London Office number.

"Gloria? It's Ghislaine? Why the urgent message?"

"I . . . I thought you'd want to know, about Azra, I mean, since you recruited her to the firm," Gloria said.

"What about her? When I spoke with her early last week, she seemed fine, a little concerned about her work levels, but otherwise in good spirits."

"Well, I think you know that Ward visited us late last week to review the performance of the professional staff. He had a meeting with everyone on Friday and said he didn't think business warranted keeping everyone on the Russia and Eastern Europe team. He called me late yesterday and told me he'd decided to let Azra go. He instructed me to tell her she needed to move on by the end of the year."

Ghislaine pressed the fingers of her right hand against her temple.

"Good God," she cried. She felt a cold sweat break out on her forehead. First Danko's email and now Azra's firing. "*Ward,*" she swore under her breath. "How did she take it?"

"She sat there as if she'd been cast in stone, completely rigid," Gloria replied. "Poor thing couldn't speak. Didn't even ask a question when I reviewed her severance package. She just got up and said, 'Thank you,' and walked out like she was in a trance."

Ghislaine closed her eyes and tried to imagine the young Bosnian woman's face.

"I'm so sorry. Is she in the office today? Can you transfer me to her?"

"That's why I called. She didn't come in today and didn't call in sick," Gloria's voice faltered and cracked. "As soon as I discovered she was out, I called her flat and her mobile number to make sure she was all right. When she didn't answer at either, I became concerned so I sent our office boy, Johnny, over to her flat to check on her and . . ." Gloria began to sob.

"And what?" Ghislaine demanded. "*What?*"

"Johnny rang her flat and she didn't answer," Gloria said, sniffling and trying to regain control of her emotions. "So he buzzed the flat manager and told her we were worried about Azra. The flat manager opened Azra's door with one of her keys. They found her, thank God," Gloria cried, "lying on her bed, barely breathing, a half-empty bottle of sleeping pills beside her and a note apologizing to her family for failing them and God. Emergency medical services responded immediately. They got her to vomit up as much as they could and then they took her to St. Thomas' hospital. That's where she is now, poor girl."

Ghislaine felt her throat grow taut.

"Thank you, Gloria. You and Johnny saved her life. Would you send her flowers from me and let me know when she's well enough to talk? Tell her I will speak to Ward about keeping her on and, if we can't, I will make sure she finds a position with another firm quickly. And, for her sake and for ours, keep quiet about how she was found, will you?"

"Of course, I understand. I haven't told anyone but you, and Johnny is under strict orders to keep mum."

Ghislaine held her head in her hands after she disconnected the call. Then she remembered Rob and M.D. were in Panama with Duncan. She stared at her watch. It read seven thirty. Ten thirty in Panama. The Rodriguez meeting should have ended by now. M.D. should have called. Ghislaine felt sure Ward lurked behind the delay in the Gulf deal just as he had fired Azra as a warning to her. Could Ward have learned that she had approached Takayama-san for his support, that she had sent Rob, M.D. and Duncan to Panama to win him over? Ghislaine's fingers trembled as she first called M.D.'s cell phone and then Rob's. Neither one answered.

FIFTY-TWO

··

WEDNESDAY, DECEMBER 22
PORTOBELO

M.D. and Rob led Magdalena and Duncan down the path through the ruins. Portobelo Bay lay below them in the distance, sparkling in the morning sun. Sailboats at anchor bounced up and down on the turquoise Caribbean. Within five minutes, a road running parallel to the bay appeared just below them. The ramshackle buildings of a village stood to their right. The blackened ruins of a Spanish fort rested beyond the road, overlooking the bay. When they reached the road, no car or truck appeared, so they set off at a slow trot toward the village. Duncan huffed as he fought to keep up with the others.

The village was deserted. Only a few stray dogs basked in the sun. They stopped at the first building they came to, a tiny, two-story dirt-stained white stucco house with faded red tiles on the roof. Brightly colored paintings of enormous tropical snakes framed the forest-green door.

"Magdalena, would you see whether anyone is home and, if so, whether we could borrow a phone? We'll need a taxi, if there is such a thing around here," Duncan wheezed and then bent over to catch his breath. Magdalena nodded and rapped on the door. In a second, a short, heavyset woman with a round wrinkled face, milk-chocolate skin, and stringy gray hair peered out at them. She wore a cotton dress of brilliant blues and reds and worn black leather sandals.

The woman gaped in surprise at what stood in front of her: two men and two young women, faces caked with dirt and sweat, wearing filthy, tattered clothes in which they had almost certainly spent the night. She stepped behind the door seeking protection from the strange spirits who had appeared this morning. Leaning her head out into the space between the door and the doorjamb, she raised her eyebrows as if to say, "Speak, if you are human and capable of talking."

"Good morning, *señora*. We are so very sorry to disturb you," Magdalena apologized in Spanish. "But we have a problem of great urgency. Do you have a telephone that we could use? Is there a car or taxi that we could hire?"

"*Con el dinero baila el perro,*" cackled the woman.

"With money, the dog will dance," M.D. interpreted for Rob and Duncan. "Anyone have any money? They took everything I had." Rob and Duncan shook their heads. The woman didn't need a translator to understand.

"*Que perdida de tiempo!*" she shouted and began to shut the door.

"No, please a small moment only," Magdalena begged. The woman stopped. Magdalena leaned over and rolled the left leg of her pants up above her knee. The woman gasped at the sight of the wound around Magdalena's ankle and gasped again as she lifted her pant leg even farther to reveal a thin scarlet garter wrapped around her thigh. Sewn onto the garter was a small pocket made of pink lace. Magdalena unbuttoned the pocket and withdrew a tightly folded stack of one hundred dollar bills. She held one up to show the woman. Duncan and Rob gaped; M.D. grinned and squeezed Magdalena's arm.

"Now," Magdalena pointed at the woman, "a phone first and then a taxi. And quickly," she commanded.

The woman squinted at the hundred-dollar note and back at Magdalena. Without a sound, she wheeled around and disappeared into the home. Soon she was shouting to someone to bring their mobile phone immediately but first to call a taxi. "*Rapidamente, rapidamente,*" she ordered. In a minute, a gangling teenage boy emerged with a mobile phone in his right hand. His left hand brushed back the long hair from his face and then picked sleep from his eyes.

"I've called the taxi," he yawned. "He will be here in ten minutes. Here is my mobile. Please do not break it," he begged. "I would die here without it."

"Thank you. We will take good care of it," Magdalena said. "Here, Rob, you wish to call Jorge, no?"

"Yes, thank you." Rob took the phone and noticed the time. "It's nine o'clock already," he said as he punched in Jorge's mobile number. "I'm turning the speaker on so you can hear what he says."

"How can we ever thank you, Magdalena?" Duncan whispered and squeezed her arm. She beamed up at Duncan and then winked at M.D.

"How strange life is! One day ago, I did not know who you were and now you are the only friends I have in the world," she declared. Before Duncan or M.D. could respond, Rob began to speak.

"Hello, Jorge. It's Rob."

"Where are you?" Jorge yelled. "What the *fuck* have you been doing? My uncle just called and was furious with me. His staff told him that they received nothing from Aoki this morning. When you did not arrive on time for the meeting with him, my uncle's secretary called the Marriott to speak with you. Someone at the front desk told them you and Duncan had left last night with two Colombian prostitutes and had not returned. My uncle has lost all confidence in my judgment. What the *hell* is going on?"

"Hold on," Rob pleaded. "Salduba had us robbed and kidnapped to make sure we would miss the meeting with your uncle. We didn't leave with two Colombian prostitutes. One of the two women was M.D. The other was Salduba's girlfriend, who pretended to be his assistant sent to take us to a meeting with him. We spent the night locked in a stone bunker outside of Portobelo."

"My God!" Jorge exclaimed. "Is everyone all right?"

"Yes, we're tired and a little beat up but okay. Look, is there any way that we can see your uncle now? Salduba's girlfriend is with us. She will swear that Salduba was behind all of this."

"Is his girlfriend named Magdalena Vasquez?"

"Yes. How did you know?"

"Because my uncle's secretary told him the hotel clerk recognized one of the two women. The clerk said Vasquez is a well-known hooker."

"Listen," Rob implored Jorge. "This guy on your uncle's staff is full of shit. Salduba must have paid him off to get him to say these things."

"Rob, my uncle is very disappointed in me. I cannot put my relationship with him at risk again. Tell me truthfully, is Magdalena Vasquez a Colombian in Panama illegally? Was she brought here to work in the clubs?" Rob looked at Magdalena, who cast her eyes down at the dirt beneath her feet.

"Yes," Rob murmured into the mobile phone. "She was brought here from Colombia years ago by Salduba to work in his nightclub."

"Jorge," Duncan interrupted, "I understand what Rob has just told you must be difficult to absorb. It's still hard for us to grasp. But the truth is, the robbers locked Magdalena up with us. She risked a great deal to help us to escape. We trust her and believe that Fernando can trust her, too."

"You must try to understand my uncle's position," Jorge begged them. "Would you believe the word of a prostitute rather than that of a former official and well-known lawyer? And what if my uncle were to trust her, what could he do? His staff found deficiencies in the Aoki submission and Aoki has done nothing to correct them. He cannot overrule his staff without risking charges of corrupt influence by his nephew being made against him. Put yourself in my place," Jorge demanded. "Would you even consider asking a relative in high government office to meet with someone like Magdalena?"

Duncan looked back at the lime-green and chili-pepper-red snakes framing the door of the woman's home. He wondered whether such snakes actually existed or whether they were the product of the artist's imagination. And who conceived of such fantastic creatures and painted them with such creative abandon?

"Duncan?" Rob asked.

"Sorry," Duncan apologized. "I'm exhausted. Jorge, thank you for what you have tried to do for us. I regret very much that helping us has harmed your relationship with Fernando. Please tell him that we're extremely sorry for missing the appointment but that we were robbed and detained last night and did not escape until just now. Tell him that we don't know why Aoki did not send anything to his office, but we will follow up as a matter of courtesy. You don't have to say anything about Salduba or about our suspicions concerning your uncle's staff."

"Okay. I will do as you say. Please understand I'm very sorry I can't do more with my uncle. You know I wish to help your mother and you, Rob, so if you can think of any other way to approach him, please let me know. In the meantime, let me come pick you up and bring you to the hotel. Perhaps we can think of something else while we drive back."

"Thanks, Jorge. But we have transportation here that's ready to take us back to the hotel."

"All right. Please let me know if there's anything else I can do."

"Thanks. I'll talk with you later, my friend." Rob clicked the mobile phone closed.

Magdalena barely lifted her eyes from the ground and whispered, "I told you that this would happen. I wish I could wash away my past like the dirt from my feet, but I can't. And, if I cannot help you, will you still help me?"

M.D. put her arm around Magdalena's waist.

"We found a way to escape from the *casamata,* didn't we? You said it was your destiny to be thrown in with us. I'm beginning to believe that perhaps it was. We'll find a way to persuade Fernando and to protect you."

"Yes," interjected Duncan, "I don't know anything about destiny, but I do know that, after everything you've done for us, we'll keep you safe from Salduba. I give you my word." As soon as the words left his mouth he remembered his promise to be with Sam tonight. How in the world would he keep both promises?

FIFTY-THREE

....

WEDNESDAY, DECEMBER 22
PORTOBELO

A few seconds after the call with Jorge had ended, a canary-yellow van pulled up. The old woman stepped down from the front seat and walked over to Magdalena.

"*Señorita,* here is your taxi to take you to Panama City as I promised," she smiled and held out her hand. "Three hundred dollars, please, *señorita.*"

"Two hundred dollars and *not a cent more.* That's twice what a taxi would cost," Magdalena scolded her. "The two hundred dollars pays for the use of the mobile and the car, correct *señora*? The driver will not ask for more?"

"All right, *señorita.* I accept two hundred dollars. The driver is my oldest son and a good boy, unlike my youngest, who wastes his entire day talking on the mobile. He will take you where you wish."

The driver opened the side door. Duncan and Rob waited for M.D. and Magdalena to climb in the backseat before they stepped up and sat in the middle seat. The driver slid the door shut and swung up into the driver's seat. He honked his horn and waved to his mother. The next moment, they were bumping and rocking along the road back to the Colon-Panama highway. When they reached the highway, the van sped up and soon the white noise of the engine enveloped the four companions as each sat with eyes closed, lost in a fog of exhaustion.

After twenty minutes, Magdalena began to sing to herself the words from "A Yellow Submarine."

Startled by Magdalena, M.D.'s eyes opened. "What are you singing?"

"You know, 'Yellow Submarine.' It was my favorite song as a girl. I used to dream that I lived on a yellow submarine with all my friends and without a care in the world. With this song, I escaped the orphanage. Perhaps," Magdalena said, "riding in this yellow van with my new friends reminded me of the song. Would not it be wonderful to sail away together?"

"Yes, it would." M.D. sighed. "Perhaps we could even sail the submarine through the Canal, harvesting trees along the way."

Duncan's eyes sprang open. He twisted around to face M.D. "What did you say?" he demanded, placing a hand on her leg.

"What? Oh, I was just enjoying Magdalena's dream. We were talking about the Beatles' song 'Yellow Submarine.' Why?"

"I'm not quite sure. When I heard what you said, something flashed across my mind." Duncan closed his eyes and struggled to recapture the vision of a yellow submarine floating down the Panama Canal, a vision that had fluttered for a moment just beyond his consciousness. Then he heard Taka's boisterous laugh. That was *it*.

"M.D.," Duncan said waving his hands, "do you remember the memorandum you wrote about Aoki? There was something in it about submarines, wasn't there? Do you recall what it was?"

"Yes, Aoki is working with some Japanese government agency to build prototype robotic submarines for use in underwater mining. Why?"

"Rob," Duncan said twisting to face Rob, his voice rising and his hands shaking. "You said that CESD's main problem was the inefficiency of harvesting timber using divers, right?"

"Yes, that's right."

"What if the harvesting could be done with some kind of robotic submarine equipped with a special cutting device and sensors or even a camera that could see what kind of tree it was cutting? Wouldn't that increase both the quantity of trees harvested and the yield of high value timber?"

"Yes," Rob agreed cautiously, "but, even if such technology existed, which I don't think it does, it would cost a fortune."

"What if Aoki had already developed and built a robotic submarine for far more difficult work, like deep-sea underwater mining? The marginal cost of applying that knowledge to your situation and of building or, even better, retrofitting a prototype submarine would be minimal. Besides, you said yourself you would need a larger kiln, a warehouse and other facilities if your efficiency improved. Aoki could build all of those for you as part of the package. And with its global trading network, it could find markets for all of the timber you produced and make money on the marketing end."

"But what about the divers and their families," Rob objected. "Part of our mission is to increase employment and, if the submarine works, it will take away their jobs. And we'd have to think about the harm that a submarine could do to the environment. Using divers seems to be much more environmentally sustainable."

M.D. inhaled sharply. "Rob." She gently but firmly squeezed his arm. "If this works, there may be fewer dangerous jobs doing the diving, but wouldn't there be many times the number of jobs created for workers in the kiln, the warehouse, and in marketing? And if Aoki has developed the submarine for deep-sea use under mandate of the Japanese government, wouldn't it be logical to assume that the technology has been tested against rigorous environmental standards?"

"Uh, I guess you would be right on both counts. Sorry, I wasn't thinking."

"No, you raised good questions."

"The key," Duncan interjected, "is whether there'd be enough in this idea to excite Takayama-san so that he would forget our failure to help him qualify and, more important, support Ghislaine over Ward. We won't know until we talk with him, but at least we have some hope now."

"*Some* hope," M.D. cautioned, "but Aoki doesn't own the technology and must decide by December twenty-seventh whether to exercise its option to license the technology from the Japanese government. Remember, they've been studying the costs and benefits of such a license, but it was uncertain what Aoki would decide, particularly given the fragile state of the world economy."

"By December twenty-seventh?" Duncan shook his head. "Jesus, that's only five days away. No, actually less, because the twenty-seventh in Japan is *four* days from now. Well, we still have a little time. Even if they are leaning against a license, the opportunity with CESD in Panama might be enough to tip them the other way."

"Okay. So, do you have a plan?" M.D. asked, arching her eyebrows. Duncan glanced at the time on the dashboard clock. It was ten o'clock. They would be back in Panama City in about thirty minutes. Could he still make the twelve thirty flight? Perhaps. If the kidnappers had delivered their passports to the hotel by the time they returned and *if* he went straight to the airport from the Marriott. But then he'd have to leave Magdalena to fend for herself against an enraged Salduba.

Duncan closed his eyes and tried to steady his breathing. After a few seconds, he slowly shook his head. He couldn't abandon Magdalena, not after everything she'd done for them. They'd still be in that fucking bunker if it weren't for her. Besides, he'd given her his word. Of course, he'd given Sam his word, too. Damn! He would have to email Gracie, apologize again, and explain what had happened. She couldn't blame him for being kidnapped. But he knew that no explanation would make a difference to Sam. All he would know is that his dad had disappointed him again. Oh, Sammy, he moaned, you were right. He was no Kobe Bryant. What should he do? Duncan bit his lower lip until he tasted blood.

"Duncan?" M.D. inquired again. "Do you have a plan?" Duncan licked his lips and then looked around at his friends.

"It makes no sense for all of us to return to the hotel, especially Magdalena," he began slowly. "She should stay out of sight while I try to think of some way to protect her." Duncan smiled at Magdalena and touched her left hand. "Thank you, again, for everything you've done."

"I don't understand what you say about harvesting trees from the Canal, but I am happy to help," the Colombian replied and placed her right hand over Duncan's.

"Here is what I propose," Duncan said rubbing his free hand over the stubble on his face. "There is a type of hotel here called a push-button. They are used by couples who want some, uh, short-term privacy and sometimes by criminals as a hideout. I understand that they are very discreet. We should find one near the airport and rent a room. After we check in, Rob will return to the hotel by noon to pick up our clothes and computers and check us all out. With luck, we'll find our passports and maybe our credit cards at the hotel. If not, we'll be screwed and have to reconsider the plan. While Rob's gone, I'll make some calls to people I know here to see what we can do to help Magdalena. Once Rob returns with our things, I'd like M.D. to do some more research on the use of submarines in timber harvesting; perhaps there's some precedent we can give Aoki. And, Rob, you should start some projections on the growth and profitability of CESD under various assumptions concerning increases in the quantity and quality of timber harvested. Are we agreed?"

"I think that's a good plan," M.D. said, "except I'm going with Rob to the hotel. Ghislaine told me that she didn't want any of us to be left alone and, besides, I'd feel better if I gathered my things myself. I can't do any research until I have my computer anyway."

"I don't see any reason why you shouldn't stay safe in the push-button," Rob objected.

"None except Ghislaine told me to make sure none of us was left alone," M.D. shot back, chin thrust forward.

"Okay, okay, guys," Duncan said holding his hand up. "Rob, I think M.D. has a point about no one traveling alone. Besides, I'm sure that M.D. will be fine as long as you're there to protect her."

M.D. groaned.

"You should have been a politician," Rob laughed.

"All good?" Duncan asked. "Magdalena, could you ask the driver to take us to a push-button near the airport, and then we'll need him to take Rob and M.D. back to the hotel."

"Okay," Magdalena said. "*Por favor, señor, nos illevara al push Campo Amor via Tocumen y luego al hotel Marriott.*" The driver's eyes widened at the command.

"*Claro, señorita,*" he said as a toothy grin split his face.

FIFTY-FOUR

....

WEDNESDAY, DECEMBER 22
PANAMA CITY

At just after ten thirty in the morning, the yellow van pulled into one of the short driveways at the Campo Amor. The driver pushed an intercom button and the garage door slid open. He drove in and the garage door closed behind him. Magdalena stepped out of the van and walked over to a door on the left wall of the garage. She opened it and went inside. A moment later, she came out and gestured to Duncan. He climbed out of the van and Magdalena handed him a card with the name and telephone number of the push-button. Duncan passed the card to Rob.

"Be safe, you two," he said. "Call as soon as you reach the hotel." The driver opened the garage door and backed the van out.

Duncan turned and entered the room. Immediately in front of him was a heart-shaped bed with cream-colored sheets and a blood-red velvet cover. On the wall behind the bed hung an enormous picture of a voluptuous dark-skinned woman, whose limbs entwined a muscular man with coal-black hair and a handlebar mustache. A four-foot-wide floor-to-ceiling mirror hung on the wall opposite the bed and just to the side of the door. In the far left-hand corner, an open door revealed a bathroom. In between the bathroom and a table rested a flat-screen television. On the other side of the bed a writing desk leaned against the wall; a red-shaded lamp squatted on the desk, and a wooden chair nestled underneath it. A telephone had been positioned on the desk, as had a travel magazine, a telephone book, and an old issue of the Spanish edition of *Penthouse*. To the right and above the desk, there was a small sliding partition, like the door of a tiny dumbwaiter. A slow salsa tune played from the speakers in the corners by the bed. Duncan blinked in amazement.

Magdalena rolled up her pant leg once again and removed a hundred dollar bill from the scarlet garter. She slipped past Duncan, grazing his chest, opened the partition, and placed the bill on the ledge inside the sliding door. Closing the partition, she declared, "That money should pay for the rest of the day."

"Thank you, again. You are truly amazing. Do you want to order something to eat? To rest? I have to make a couple of calls."

"What I want most of all is to shower and then to bathe. Do you mind? I feel like the dirt of the past day has crept beneath my skin, and I would like to clean the small cuts on my hands and the scrapes on my ankles."

"Not at all. You've earned it."

Magdalena smiled and tossed a lock of hair out of her eyes. "You are a true gentlemen," she said. "A few days ago, I feared for my future and dreamed only of making a life here in Panama. Then I awoke from that vision realizing that I meant less to Rodrigo than one of his paintings. Today I can see no further than tonight, but I am no longer frightened. You have given me this gift, Duncan, you and M.D. and Rob. Do you not feel as though we have known each other for many years?"

"Yes, I do," he nodded. "Sometimes a day full of struggle can form a friend for life. I think that the intensity of the shared experience is what matters, not its duration."

"I am glad that you feel that way, too," she smiled as she walked to the bathroom.

"Oh, before you shower," Duncan stopped her just before she closed the door. "I wanted to ask you about something that has been bothering me since last night. Do you think Salduba really planned to have us freed at noon? I understand the deadline to help Aoki will have passed by then, but wasn't Salduba concerned that we would go the police and file a complaint, giving his name and yours as well?"

Magdalena nodded. "This also bothered me. Rodrigo told me not to worry, that he would make sure that you were obliged to leave Panama as soon as you returned to the Marriott."

Duncan caught his breath. M.D. and Rob were on their way to the Marriott now. "Obliged? What do you think he meant by that?"

"I am not certain, but he has very good connections with the police. Perhaps he instructed the police to threaten to arrest you for being with me," she laughed and pulled her hair back from her face with both her hands. "Anyway, we have escaped so it is of little concern to us now, no?"

"I guess you're right," Duncan said slowly. "Enjoy your shower."

"I will not be long. I promise you," Magdalena tilted her head toward Duncan, then turned and closed the bathroom door.

Duncan repeated in his mind the phrase "obliged to leave the country," hoping to trigger some idea of what Salduba had planned. Jed had made it clear that Salduba wouldn't hesitate to strike back at those who challenged him. While Duncan waited, he looked for a way to turn down the volume of the salsa music. He finally found the knob by the television set and turned the music off. A few minutes later, the phone rang.

"We're here," said M.D. "We had a little trouble without any identification and looking beat up, but luckily one of the young men at the front desk remembered us. He asked the bellman whether anyone had left a package for Rob, you, or me and, sure enough, someone did leave three envelopes at the hotel this morning and my backpack. We have all of our passports, cell phones, and credit cards. When he saw the contents of the packages, our friend at the front desk guessed that we'd been robbed. We told him that you asked us to check you out. He was kind enough to give us the key to your room so we could bring your belongings to you."

Duncan felt the muscles in his shoulders relax. "That's a relief. I guess Salduba really didn't want to do anything to keep us hanging around Panama. Listen, you'll find five thousand dollars in traveler's checks hidden in a shirt in the middle drawer in my room. Don't forget to bring them along."

"I won't. We're heading up now to the rooms to gather everything. We'll stay together, just in case."

"Thanks. Don't let your guard down. Instruct the front desk not to tell anyone you've returned to the hotel. I know that you guys want to clean up and change, but don't waste any time, okay?"

"Sure. And, just to be safe, I'll ask for a new room for the next hour where we can move our things and clean up. I'll tell them not to put our names on it. I'm sure that won't be a problem."

"Great idea," Duncan said, amazed at the resourcefulness of his two young colleagues. "But call me when you're about to leave the hotel," he ordered. "I don't want to be out of contact for too long. We're not safe yet."

FIFTY-FIVE

....

WEDNESDAY, DECEMBER 22
PANAMA CITY

Duncan scrolled his phone log and found the number for the U.S. embassy. He called and asked a young woman to connect him to Jed Barbour.

"Hello. This is Jed Barbour," said the familiar voice.

"Jed! It's Duncan."

"Duncan, man it's great to hear from you. I was hopin' you'd call, but when I didn't hear from you yesterday or this mornin', I figured you'd come and gone. Any chance we could have dinner tonight?"

"I have to leave tonight, but I do need your help now, if you have a moment," Duncan's voice echoed with fatigue.

"What's wrong, buddy?" Jed asked. Duncan spent the next fifteen minutes telling Jed what had happened since he had arrived. When Duncan had finished, Jed exclaimed, "Wow, you sure do settle into a place fast. I can't believe you're at Campo Amor. What's it like?"

"I'll send you pictures, but first I need some advice. How do I help Magdalena? We'd still be up in that Portobelo bunker if she hadn't been so brave. She doesn't trust the police, and I don't blame her. Is there any way that the U.S. government could assist her, if she agreed to testify against Salduba, for example?"

Jed was silent for a moment. "I hate givin' friends bad news, but you've probably already realized that there aren't any good answers. Magdalena won't qualify for the Witness Protection Program. Salduba's a bad guy, but there's no indication he's violated U.S. law or, if he has, that the crime would be one of the few that justify putting a witness against him into the program. Then there's Magdalena herself. To qualify, her testimony against Rodrigo would have to be both critical and credible. I think my good friends in the Office of Enforcement Operations would decide in the blink of an eye that she'd fail the second test. Anyway, would she really want to be relocated to some small town in the Midwest, where the winters are brutal and the most excitin' thing to happen during the week is the change in the window displays at the local Walmart?"

"No, that wouldn't be what she'd want," Duncan admitted. "But I've got to do something to protect her. What about asylum under the Trafficking Victims Protection Act? Years ago I prosecuted someone for bringing young girls to the United States as prostitutes. While it was hard to get the girls to trust the police and even accept that they were victims, they did eventually apply for and were given asylum under the TVPA. I know that Magdalena initially came to Panama legally, but I'm sure we could come up with something Salduba did to her after her arrival that would qualify as coercion or fraud."

"I've seen you work a case and know you could persuade an immigration judge that Bin Laden deserved a green card, but the sad secret is that TVPA isn't there to protect victims. It's really a tool to help U.S. law enforcement prosecute traffickers who've violated U.S. law. The TVPA doesn't protect someone like Magda-

320

lena, who is trafficked outside the United States and then seeks refuge in the United States."

"Jesus Christ, Jed," Duncan growled. "Everyone cries out to protect victims of predators like Salduba, but the local laws have loopholes large enough to drive a truck through and our own laws aren't really designed to protect those who need help the most! If Magdalena stays in Panama, Salduba will have her tracked down and deported to Colombia or, who knows, taken somewhere and murdered. I can't let that happen. There's got to be a way to protect her."

"I understand your frustration, but let's be objective for a moment, okay? She's an illegal alien here and a woman whom the police will regard as having violated the law prohibiting prostitution. No matter how brave she's been and how much she's helped you, we can't make all of that disappear. We don't have any authority in Panama; Christ, we can't even put her in one of our safe houses without screwin' up our relationship with the police here. If she won't go to the police, and I'm not suggestin' that she should, then she can't stay in Panama. If she can't stay here and can't go to the States, the choices are pretty limited."

"Goddammit, Jed. I *promised* to help her!"

"Okay. Okay. Hold on for a second. Does she have her Colombian passport?"

"I don't know. She certainly doesn't seem to have it with her, but I would think she could get it. Why?"

"Well, then she can go back to Colombia or she can go someplace where Colombians can get in without a visa."

"She'd rather die than go back to Colombia. I haven't told you everything about her, but she suffered some pretty severe trauma there. It's why she left in the first place. And she made at least one dangerous enemy. There's got to be another way!"

"All right. If she doesn't want to return to Colombia, she'll probably want to change nationality as soon as she can. If that's the case, and you didn't hear this from me, there are two Caribbean countries where you can, in essence, purchase a passport by makin' an investment in the country. Dominica and Nevis-St. Kitts are the two legitimate ones; the Internet says that there are others, like Suriname and Guyana, but they're scams. Dominica's economic citizenship program runs around seventy-five thousand dollars for the investment and another twenty-five thousand in fees, lawyers, and the like, so it's not cheap."

"I don't think she has that kind of money. I'd give it to her if I had it, but I don't have a hundred grand either."

"Hmm. Here's another way to go. She could get permanent residency in the Dominican Republic or in Paraguay and, in a couple of years, citizenship. If she has her Colombian passport, she should qualify for residency in either country and, once she has that, she can get a job there. The Dominican and Paraguay usually require a copy of the birth certificate and a police report from the home country. She won't have those, of course, but all she needs is a well-connected immigration lawyer and he'll solve that problem, if you know what I mean. I wouldn't think the whole thing would cost more than five thousand dollars. Come to think of it, that might be the quickest and cheapest way to get her settled someplace safe. I'd go with the DR. It's only about a thousand miles from Panama, and they're at least three or four flights on Copa to Santo Domingo every day."

Duncan closed his eyes and considered Jed's advice. No perfect solutions, he decided, but she would be safe and that was what mattered most. His mind raced on to what had to be done. She needed about five thousand dollars for the residency. That was easy; he had that much in traveler's checks and would sign them over to her. She needed a flight to Santo Domingo and a place to stay for a couple of weeks while she filed her papers and looked for an apartment and a job. Again, that would be simple. Once Rob and M.D. returned, they could look up flights to Santo Domingo from Panama City and inexpensive but comfortable hotels. He could pay for them with his credit card. She would have to get her passport and probably a tourist visa from the Dominican Consulate here. Could that be done today? It would have to. She could show proof of sufficient funds and a hotel booking so it shouldn't be an issue. Perhaps they could pay for some type of expedited processing? Yes, he thought, it's not perfect but it would work. And she'd be safe. Perhaps they could even visit her after a few months.

"Jed, you've been incredibly helpful. I think you're right; the DR makes the most sense as a place to settle her safely. How can I thank you, my good friend?"

"Oh, it's a pleasure to be of service, man. She must be a special lady if you're puttin' yourself out like this."

"She is special, and incredibly courageous," Duncan declared and then paused. "Listen, there's one more thing that's bothering me about Salduba. Magdalena said that he'd arranged things to force us to leave the country quickly once we got back to the hotel. Any idea what that could mean? Could they have accused us of breaking the law for being with Magdalena?"

The line went silent for several seconds. "I don't know what he meant," Jed answered slowly. "Sorry. The police don't normally arrest johns for being with girls 'cause no one wants to scare away the sex tourists. Of course, they could have threatened you with prosecution to get you to leave the country without filing a complaint, but it's hard to see what they could do now."

"Okay, thanks. It's probably nothing to worry about. I'll call you in a couple of days when the dust has settled."

"Take care, buddy."

Duncan rubbed the back of his neck. He had been terrified he wouldn't be able to rescue Magdalena. But he had a plan now. The hair dryer whined through the door to the bathroom. She would be a few more minutes. He stood up and stretched. Fatigue filled his large frame. A quick nap would revive him and clear his mind for the work ahead. Consciousness left him as soon as his head hit the red silk pillow.

....

FIFTY-SIX

WEDNESDAY, DECEMBER 22
PANAMA CITY

He strode across the broad cobblestone square in front of the Cathedral in Santo Domingo. The island breezes whirled around him and provided relief from the sweltering midday sun. As he approached the church, he searched the area in front of the main entrance to the cathedral, but saw no one. And then, Magdalena, wearing a white linen dress, stepped out from behind one of the massive columns and strolled from the shadow cast by the roof of the portico into the light of the square. She hesitated only a moment before she ran toward him. He could not move, paralyzed by the sight of her beauty. She reached out to embrace him. He longed to touch her but could not move his arms. No matter. She rested her head on his chest. Her hair smelled of gardenias. She turned to face him. Her almond eyes holding his gaze, she raised herself on her toes and kissed him lightly on both cheeks. And then, more firmly, she kissed him on the mouth as she began to unbutton his shirt. He could not believe the sweetness of her lips. He pressed his lips against hers and opened her mouth with his tongue. He felt himself becoming aroused. He wanted her but not like this, not in front of a church, not for all to see. He struggled to restrain her hands but they would not be held. She had undone his shirt and was beginning to kiss his chest. He panicked. "Stop!" he shouted.

Duncan opened his eyes. A mist of sweat covered his brow. Lying on her side next to him was Magdalena, covered by a white cotton towel that stretched from her breasts to just below her waist. Her long right leg draped over his thighs. Her mahogany eyes gazed at him with concern.

"Why do you wish me to stop?" she whispered. "I thought you would want to make love."

I do, Duncan thought, but, no, I can't. I'm not ready. Not yet.

"I'm filthy and must stink terribly," he said. "Plus, I'm twenty years older than you, and we've known each other for less than a day. You can't really want to make love with me."

"Yes, I can," professed Magdalena. "I like a man who looks and smells like a man and not like some *chulo*. Twenty years difference is nothing and we agreed, did we not, that twenty-four hours together can be everything? What matters is how two people feel about each other."

Duncan felt an icy fist grow in his stomach. He shifted uncomfortably.

"Magdalena, you don't know this but it's only been two weeks since my wife and I separated. And I'm still, well...the breakup of my marriage has made feeling anything difficult for me right now."

"Ah, I did not know you were married, but it is of no importance if it has ended. Besides, you did not seem troubled a moment ago," she teased, her eyes twinkling. "It was your tongue in my mouth, no? Did you not dream of making love to me? Are not our dreams the pictures of our deepest desires? I am certain that I can, what is the word in English, un-numb you if you would let me."

"Oh." Duncan sighed and ran his left hand through her shiny hair. "Yes, I did want you in my dream." He paused to stroke her cheek. "I'm sure with a little time together, you could un-numb me. I just need time."

Magdalena's eyes crinkled and her brow furrowed. A lock of her long brown hair fell over her eyes. She swept it back over her ear.

"Every other man I have known could not keep his hands off me," she said, her voice rising. "It made no difference if they felt good or felt bad, if they were sick or were healthy, if they were making love for the first time or the thousandth. None of them could wait to touch me. And now the one man I want for myself asks me to understand that he can't make love with me now because he doesn't feel good inside." She rolled on her back and, shaking both hands at the ceiling, shouted, *"Es increíble!"*

Duncan rested his head on his right hand.

"I'm sorry," he said. "But the most important thing to me now is to make sure you're safe. If you still want me once you're free, then I can't imagine I would want anything more than to be with you. But first I need to know that you are someplace where Salduba can do you no harm. Will you listen to my plan?" Magdalena rolled back to face Duncan. She crossed her arms and rested the side of her head on the pillow.

"All right, Duncan. Please explain to me your plan."

Duncan explained what Jed said about finding a country where she could easily establish residency and, someday, obtain a different nationality. Both Paraguay and the Dominican Republic were candidates, but the latter seemed a better choice. The procedure for obtaining residency was less expensive and faster. He told Magdalena he would gladly provide the money for the airline ticket, hotel, and short-term living expenses. "So," he finished with a proud nod, "all you need is your Colombian passport and, by this time tomorrow, you'll be safely in the Dominican Republic."

"Well, I do have my passport. I keep it in a black garter on my right leg. I never go anywhere in Panama without both money and my passport," she said. "But, *mi querido,* while I appreciate greatly your friend's advice, I cannot follow it."

Duncan shook his head rapidly several times. He had laid out a road map leading to safety for Magdalena and she wouldn't follow it? Perhaps she didn't understand everything that he had said. "Let me explain again."

"You do not need to explain it again. I understood perfectly everything you said. I agree I cannot stay in Panama and cannot return to Colombia. But I also cannot go to the Dominican Republic."

"Why not?" Duncan cried.

"Because I am going to the United States with you," she declared.

Duncan's head jerked back. "Did you say . . . ?"

"Yes, I did."

"But . . . but, you can't," he protested. "You need a visa to get in and you don't have one."

"You just told me that you had a friend at the embassy. Could he not arrange for a tourist visa for me? If we could get a visa for the Dominican Republic today without any assistance, then surely with your friend's help we can get one for the United States."

"I can't ask my friend to do anything improper," Duncan objected.

"No, you could not. I understand. But you could ask him to assist us in obtaining a tourist visa legally, could you not?"

Duncan paused. There had to be a way to expedite the processing of a visa for the United States, and Jed would know all about it.

"Okay," he agreed. "Perhaps there may be a way to receive a tourist visa today, but such a visa would only allow you to stay for a limited period of time. You'd have to leave again or risk deportation. Where would you go? The whole point of going to the Dominican Republic is that you could become a resident quickly without risk of being sent back to Colombia. That wouldn't be possible in the United States."

Magdalena sat up on the bed and pulled the end of the towel over her thighs.

"I have known at least ten women who have gone to the United States on a tourist visa and stayed for years. You cannot tell me that I could not do the same."

"But where would you stay? How would you live? What would you do, Magdalena?" Duncan asked gesturing in exasperation with his left hand.

Magdalena's lips pursed.

"What a silly man you are! I would stay with you. Did you not just say that you wished to spend time with me? I would make a home for you. If we pleased each other, which I am certain we would, we would have a life together. That would make you happy, no?"

Duncan sat up cross-legged on the bed and ran his hands through his tangled black hair. He tried to imagine what life with Magdalena would be like. For a moment he saw himself arriving home from teaching to find her at his apartment, an apartment warmed by her smile and filled with the scent of gardenias. She would welcome him with an embrace and then they would cook together, sharing their days. Later they would drink wine and eat and talk into the night. Or hold hands in silence listening to the distant roar of the waves. Not right away, but perhaps after a month or two when they had grown used to each other and he had lost his fear, they would make love, falling asleep in each other's arms. Yes, that would please him. A noise suddenly came from the other bedroom. What was that? Ah, it was Sam, unable to sleep, reciting to himself statistics from the most recent Lakers game. How could he have forgotten Sam?

"Let me tell you something important about myself," he said looking directly into her eyes. "I have a son. His name is Samuel. He is a wonderful child, but he is also a boy who has trouble communicating with other people, even understanding other people. He is in a special school to help him, but his problems will not go away for many years, perhaps ever. He lives with his mother now, but he will soon stay with me part of the time."

Magdalena reached out to touch Duncan's cheek.

"I do not know your Samuel and I am not sure what problems he has. But I was raised in an orphanage with countless brothers and sisters. Many had seen horrible things, their mothers raped and fathers blown apart, or had unforgiveable things done to them. In some of them their fear ran so deep they refused to talk or even to be touched. Still, they were my brothers and sisters and I loved and cared for them as best I could for as long as I could. I know I could do the same for Samuel."

Duncan pressed Magdalena's hand to his cheek. He heard the determination in her voice. Yes, he thought, Sam would be fine with Magdalena, and Magdalena would be wonderful for Sam. But how long would it take before Sam told Gracie about Magdalena and Gracie discovered that Magdalena was staying in the country illegally? He had to find a way to bring her home with him legally or she'd be sent back to Colombia. Duncan closed his eyes and forced himself to concentrate. She wouldn't qualify as a trafficking victim, but what about another kind of asylum? He strained to remember what he once learned about asylum cases. Women who feared gender-based violence in their country of origin like genital mutilation or an honor killing could qualify. Even if a woman couldn't show a well-founded fear of future persecution, she might receive asylum based upon severe past persecution or at least avoid deportation based upon a probable threat to her life if she were returned to the country of origin. But would the beating and rape Magdalena suffered be enough to show past persecution? Would Magdalena's fear of retaliation by the general's son be sufficient to show a threat to her life? And, he agonized, how could he prove her story was true when it took place so many years ago? STOP IT, he commanded himself. Stop the endless thrust and parry of pros and cons. Years ago, he had laughed when his French girlfriend at Stanford had left him because he was *"trop equilibre."* Until now, he had never understood how one could one be too stable. But suddenly he realized that being too balanced, too relentlessly judicious, buried the passions, both petty and profound, that made him human, that made him not just worthy of love but capable of it. He took a deep breath and opened his eyes.

"Yes, I know you'd do the same for Sam," he said still holding her hand to his cheek. "And I know you'd love living with me near the beach in Playa del Rey."

"You live near the King's Beach!" She exclaimed.

"Yes," Duncan smiled at the girlish delight in her eyes. "The King's Beach. But my apartment is a really small castle. All right, dear Magdalena, I will call my friend at the embassy and get you a tourist visa. Once we're the United States, we'll apply for a visa that will allow you to stay legally based upon what happened to you in Colombia and your fear of returning. You don't know this about me, but I'm a pretty good lawyer and a professor at Loyola Marymount University. I've never believed in destiny before, but I suddenly feel that my whole professional life has prepared me for one reason--to help you. I will fight for you, Magdalena," Duncan promised, "as long as it takes to win."

Magdalena stroked Duncan's cheek; then a puzzled look crossed her eyes.

"I am grateful, dear Duncan, but why would such trouble be necessary? I have read that there are more than ten million *ilegales* in the United States. No one would care if there were one more."

Duncan lowered his eyes.

"Sam's mother and I are arguing about how much time Sam will spend with me," he said softly. "Once you and I are living together, she will hear about you from Sam and her lawyers will discover that you're in the United States illegally. They will put that in papers filed with the court to show that Sam should not be allowed to live with us. The immigration authorities would find out and send you back to Colombia."

Magdalena removed her hand from his cheek. Her eyes wandered past Duncan.

"Is it true that a judge would take a son from a father just because the father wished to live with a woman who also loved the son but did not have the right papers?" She looked directly at Duncan. "Could anyone be so cruel?"

Duncan gazed at Magdalena before lowering his eyes once again. He did not respond.

"And these lawyers, they would find out about my past, would they not? So, even if I were allowed to stay legally, your wife would tell the judge that her son should not live with a woman like me?"

Duncan did not reply but took Magdalena in his arms and held her head to his chest. She began to weep.

"I wanted to give you more of myself than I have given any other man," she whispered. "But I know what it feels like to be an orphan and I will *not* orphan your son." Magdalena slowly released herself from Duncan's arms, slid off the bed, and walked into the bathroom. Duncan watched her, speechless, spent. Two minutes later, the bathroom door opened. Magdalena was wearing her stained and torn clothes. She ran to the front door.

"Magdalena, please wait. It's not safe to leave here. *Please,* let me help you," Duncan begged. He swung his legs off the bed and started to get up.

"Please stay where you are," she implored Duncan wiping tears from her eyes. In an instant, she bolted through the door.

FIFTY-SEVEN

···

WEDNESDAY, DECEMBER 22
PANAMA CITY

M.D. and Rob rode up the elevator with the keys to their rooms and Duncan's as well as a key to a new room under the name of John Smith. They agreed to pack up their rooms, grab Duncan's stuff, and bring their luggage to the Smith room, where they would quickly clean up before returning to the push-button. In a few minutes, they had cleared out the old rooms and opened the door to the new one.

"This is the first time since we were pulled over last night that I feel safe," M.D. called over her shoulder as she walked past Rob and into the new room. "Can't you just sense the fear draining from your body?"

"You never seemed scared to me," Rob replied as he closed the door. "Quite the contrary."

In the small corridor that led from the door past the bathroom on the right and into the bedroom, M.D. turned around and looked up at Rob. "I'm not very good at giving compliments, but I want to say before we get caught up in the business of the next forty-eight hours, I think you've been remarkable. You've been brave, inventive, and, for someone who is usually so serious, funny. Here, bend down and let me take a look at that gash on your head." Rob leaned down to where M.D. could take his head in her hands and examine the cut. "It's stopped bleeding, but you'd better wash it with warm water and soap. You might need a stitch or two when you're back in Los Angeles, but I guess you'll live."

She smiled, released his head, and patted him on the chest the way a little girl might pat the belly of a beloved golden retriever. Rob looked at her right hand on his chest, grasped it with his left hand, and placed it on his shoulder. Just as he stepped forward to wrap his arms around her, M.D. stuck the heel of her free hand against the middle of his chest.

"What do you think you're doing?"

"I'm . . . I'm sorry. I just thought . . ."

"I know what you thought," she interrupted, "and I understand. We've been under a lot of stress and now much of that is gone. But I think it would be a big mistake for us to confuse relief with desire." Then she turned away and, gesturing toward the bathroom, said, "Why don't you shower while I pack up? Then I'll clean up and we can get back to Duncan and Magdalena."

"Okay," Rob said to M.D.'s back. "Ah, and thanks for the compliment. It means a lot to me, coming from you."

"Sure," M.D. replied, looking over her shoulder. "I meant every word."

Rob sighed, stepped into the bathroom, and closed the door. He stripped off the sports shirt, cargo pants, and tennis shoes he had worn since last night and turned on the shower. Shutting the glass door behind him, he stepped underneath the stream of hot water. He scrubbed off the dirt and sweat and gently washed the wound on his head, grimacing at the sting. When he was thoroughly clean, he closed his eyes and let the water pour over him. After a minute, Rob rubbed his eyes open. He turned the hot water to cool and, a few seconds later, he rotated the dial again and let cold water cascade over him. After a few seconds more, he turned off the shower and dried his body. Failing to find a robe, he took the damp towel and wrapped it around his waist.

While Rob showered, M.D. threw off the filthy blue blouse and dirt-stained linen pants suit she had been wearing since last night. She tossed her day-old clothes into a plastic laundry bag, sealed it, and tucked the bag in her suitcase. After she had pulled on a robe that was hanging in the closet, she stretched out on the bed to wait for Rob to finish his shower. Her eyes crept closed.

The opening of the bathroom door jarred M.D. awake. She slid off the bed and, still half-asleep, staggered toward the small corridor leading to the bathroom. As she approached Rob, she saw his eyes drift down from her face and widen. She followed them to where her untied robe dangled half-open. She hastily folded her robe closed and muttered, "Sorry about that. I'm pretty tired, I guess." Stepping sideways past the half-naked Rob, careful that they should not even brush against each other, she closed the bathroom door. Dropping her robe, she stepped underneath the shower and turned the valve on without noticing the setting. As the frigid water spilled over her head, she jumped away, banged her shoulder into the tile wall and screamed, "Goddammit!"

FIFTY-EIGHT

....

WEDNESDAY, DECEMBER 22
PANAMA CITY

Twenty minutes later, M.D. had dressed and Rob and she were about to walk out the door of John Smith's room. "Hold on," she said. "We promised Duncan to call him when we were ready to leave." She punched in the number of the room at the push-button. "Hello, Duncan. It's M.D. and Rob on the speakerphone. We're about ready to leave."

"All right, guys," a groggy voice came across the line. "Have you got everything?"

"Sure. We have everything that was in our three rooms, plus the passports, credit cards, cell phones, and my backpack."

Duncan pinched the bridge of his nose, struggling to focus. He could see M.D. with her backpack emerging from the elevator last night and then the monkey taking it from Salduba's car and handing it over to the jaguar. He had never understood the attraction for women of an accessory that was too small to be useful and too large to be elegant.

"Duncan?" M.D. asked. "Are you still there?"

"Yes, I'm sorry. Just bone tired. Did you say that you had the backpack? I thought that they had taken it from you?"

"They did," M.D. replied, casting a quizzical look at Rob, who shrugged his shoulders. "You must be exhausted. Don't you remember?" she asked the way a mother would remind a child at bedtime of the events of the day. "We told you they brought it back here along with the envelopes containing our other stuff."

Duncan blinked several times. Why would they have returned the backpack? It had no value.

"M.D.," he shouted sitting up on the bed, "search your backpack! NOW!" he bellowed.

M.D. rolled her eyes, cursed the unpredictable temperament of the middle-aged lawyer, and walked to the bed where the backpack lay. Unzipping the main compartment, she reached in and found nothing. Then she opened the side pockets. Nothing in the right pocket, but in the left pocket her forefinger touched several tiny plastic bags buried at the bottom.

"Shit," she exclaimed as she withdrew three small sealed plastic bags, each of which contained a teaspoonful of a grainy, off-white powder. She yelled at the speaker, "They planted cocaine or at least something that looks a lot like it."

"Good God. Flush it down the toilet, fast! And get out of there! It's almost one o'clock so Salduba will know we've escaped and could have police at the hotel any minute. GO, GO, GO!" Duncan commanded. "Call me when you're out!"

M.D. raced to the bathroom, threw the three tiny plastic containers into the toilet, and flushed twice to make sure they were gone. Rob grabbed Duncan's luggage and his own and opened the door for M.D. The phone in the room rang. Rob looked at M.D. and shook his head. M.D. ran out of the room with her roll-on. She was about to call the elevator when Rob emitted a low whistle.

"Over here," he insisted, and motioned with his head to the staircase. "This leads to the side of the hotel, not to the lobby."

M.D. nodded and followed him down the five flights of stairs. They emerged into an alley at the side of the Marriott and walked briskly to Ricardo Arias Street. To their right around the corner was the entrance to the hotel. Rob held his hand up. They peered around the corner. Three police cars, lights blinking, were parked in the driveway of the hotel. He waved to M.D. and the two of them turned left at the corner of the alley. They walked quickly away, staying as near to the line of buildings as possible. When they reached the next intersection, they flagged down a taxi and sped off, glancing back on occasion to make sure they weren't being followed.

....

FIFTY-NINE

WEDNESDAY, DECEMBER 22
PANAMA CITY

After M.D. had called from the taxi to say that they were safely on their way, Duncan fought to hold back his fear for Magdalena's safety and his remorse at missing his visit with Sam. Could he possibly have fucked things up any more? He groaned and sat up. His eyes drifted across the bed, which looked like a huge box of Valentine's Day candy, to the mirror. He saw a doughy middle-aged man sitting cross-legged with his hands folded in his lap. The man-in-the-mirror had watery eyes, unruly black hair, dark circles under his eyes, and wrinkles squirming across his brow like rattlesnakes. His shirt pocket was ripped and his jeans were streaked with black soot. The man in the mirror resisted the temptation to order a beer and a shot of Sauza. Instead, he rubbed his face, took a deep breath, and slapped his cheeks twice. He needed to focus on what he could do to protect Magdalena, to get home to Sam and to help Ghislaine, Rob and M.D. With a deep sigh, he forced his regret at what may have been lost into a small closet of his consciousness and closed the door.

It was already one o'clock. Rob and M.D. would be there soon. He would email Gracie and shower while M.D. researched submarine use in underwater timber harvesting and Rob analyzed how a dramatic yield increase would affect the company's operations and profitability. They would have to call Ghislaine with some kind of report and then reach Taka from the airport before their flight back to Los Angeles at seven. Neither one would be happy at his failure to help Aoki qualify. He hoped Aoki could be convinced it would reap even greater profits by transforming CESD's business with the robotic submarine technology they could option.

But first, he would call Jed again. There wasn't much he could do to protect Magdalena now, but perhaps Jed could call in a favor with the local police, tell them he would appreciate hearing if they picked her up. Knowing the U.S. embassy was interested in Magdalena might at least keep the police from mistreating her and give him time to get her a good lawyer to keep her from being deported before he could return to Panama. Duncan got Jed's voicemail. Duncan left a message telling him that Magdalena had rejected their idea of settling in the Dominican Republic and asked him to request that the local police pass on any news they might receive about a Colombian national named Magdalena Vasquez. He knew that his friend would understand his reasons.

Duncan heard the garage door move. His heart leapt to his throat and he ran to the door and threw it open. When he saw M.D. and Rob getting out of a taxi with their luggage, his shoulders slumped. Duncan held the door open for them.

"Jesus," Rob said as he put Duncan's luggage on the bed. "That was close. Why would they have planted cocaine on us?"

"To make sure we left Panama without making a fuss about being kidnapped," Duncan replied. "Magdalena told me Salduba had arranged something that would force us to leave rather than file a complaint. The police would have searched the backpack, found the cocaine, and given us a choice of an early flight home or arrest on drug charges."

M.D. looked around the room. "Where is Magdalena?"

Duncan closed the door behind him and leaned back against it with his hands in his pockets. "She left about an hour ago. I had worked out a plan with my friend at the embassy. He said she could get a tourist visa for the Dominican Republic this afternoon, fly to Santo Domingo tonight, and within a few days apply for residency. She would have been safe there. She would have been safe there," he repeated in a hoarse monotone.

"Then why did she leave?" M.D. demanded.

"She wanted to come to the United States with us," he explained and then corrected himself, "with me, I mean." Duncan hesitated before continuing, "I agreed to help her get a tourist visa and apply for asylum once we were home. I explained she couldn't stay illegally because my wife and I are fighting for custody of our son and my wife would use her illegal status against us. When she heard that, she realized that, even if she received asylum, the past eight years of her life could be used to keep my son from living with us. She ran out weeping."

"I'm stunned," M.D. declared.

"So was I. I left a message for my friend at the embassy asking him to contact the local police and express an interest in her. If she is arrested, they will at least treat her with respect and let him know her whereabouts. He'll call me and then perhaps there will be something we can do."

"You don't understand. I am surprised she would ask to go home with you, but I'm dumbfounded that you would let her leave after all she's done for us."

"Wait a minute," Duncan said, holding his hands up in front of him. "Now it's you who doesn't understand. I didn't *let* her go. I wanted to take her with us or at least get her to the DR."

"Here's what I understand," M.D. cut Duncan off with a chop of her hand. "As a young girl the people she trusted most bartered her off to an old man in exchange for his paying for her education, not for her own future, but to benefit the mission of those who betrayed her. Rather than being outraged, she emerged from that horror story in a state of shock still believing so strongly it was her destiny to help the orphanage that she should sell herself to do so. Can you imagine? When that decision resulted in her being beaten and gang raped, she suffered a true crisis of faith. She lost all her moorings. In that traumatized condition, a woman pimp preyed upon her vulnerability and sold her to Salduba. In Panama, she was at the point of being raped again when Salduba saved her. To rationalize sleeping with a man she knew deep down was a thug as well as to escape from the continuing terror of absolute powerlessness, she created a fantasy where she believed he was a saint to whom she was married."

"What do you mean a 'fantasy'?" Rob asked. "Surely she must have known the truth." M.D. shot Rob a withering look.

"The truth? Don't you understand? Sometimes the truth is so terrible that the line between hope and falsehood blurs and we tell ourselves lies just to survive. Magdalena lived a fantasy until this past week when the saint tortured someone she'd tried to help, deported her closest friend, and ordered her sent back to Colombia to almost certain death. Oh, not to mention that one of his hired guns practically raped her again."

"But she didn't seem in shock or nervous. She . . . well, she seemed cool, confident when we met her," Rob interjected.

"Oh, Rob! Not every wound is visible. She's a smart, strong woman, you can see that. And she has a good heart. But you heard her weep last night at all the loss she's suffered. Then, today, she is saved, miraculously, once again. This time, however, it's not a lecherous old man, a treacherous pimp, or a cold-hearted

343

predator. No, it's by someone who promised to protect her, someone she wants to believe truly likes and respects her. So this morning she conjures up another illusion, one of a safe and loving future with that man. When she suddenly realizes fulfilling her dream would hurt that man and his son, she couldn't bear the guilt and fled, probably convinced she didn't deserve the love of a decent man anyway. The pain must be unbearable."

Duncan dropped on the bed and looked up at M.D. "All right, all right. I don't disagree. I've prosecuted traffickers and learned something about the psychology of their victims. But Goddammit! She *chose* to leave. She could have gone to the DR. We wouldn't have abandoned her there."

"I don't think that you should be too hard on yourself," Rob interjected with a sideways glance at M.D. "You did your best to find a solution to an impossible situation. I like Magdalena and we all owe her a lot, but offering her a path to safety that may have been different than what she wanted wasn't betrayal."

Duncan remained silent for a moment. He reached over with his right hand to rub the stress out of his left shoulder. "I'm sorry, M.D., that you feel I let her down," he shook his head. "I know we all have come to care a great deal about her. Let's hope that we hear something soon." Another pause to let out a deep breath. "In the meantime, as difficult as it will be, we have to get to work or everything we—including Magdalena—have gone through will mean nothing. Ghislaine has probably been expecting a call for some time now, but I'd like some preliminary results from your research before we speak with her. We should leave for the airport in two hours or so, right after our call with Ghislaine. I'll call Takayama-san before we get on the flight. I'm going to get cleaned up. Do you have any other thoughts?"

"On the way over here, I picked up a voicemail from Ghislaine from earlier today," M.D. said. "She sounded frantic that we hadn't called to report on the meeting with Rodriguez. If you don't want to call her now, I should send her an email, telling her we were delayed and proposing a time to talk."

"That makes sense. Why don't you say noon Los Angeles time?"

M.D. nodded and returned to her computer. Duncan picked up his BlackBerry and composed a short message to Gracie. Thirty minutes later, after he had showered and changed clothes, he checked for messages and found Gracie's reply, bold and in all caps. He cringed as he read her response.

"PANAMA? KIDNAPPED! I FRANKLY DON'T KNOW WHAT TO BELIEVE ANYMORE. YOU SAY YOU QUIT PRACTICE SO THAT YOU COULD STOP TRAVELING AND SPEND TIME WITH SAM AND THEN YOU FLY OFF TO TOKYO AND PANAMA, DON'T CALL WHEN YOU SAY YOU WILL, AND MISS TWO OUT OF YOUR FIRST THREE VISITS WITH HIM. HOW *COULD* YOU BE SO IRRESPONSIBLE?

NOT ONLY HAVE YOU INCONVENIENCED *ME* BECAUSE I HAD MADE PLANS FOR TONIGHT, BUT YOU'VE HURT SAM TERRIBLY. WHEN YOU DIDN'T CALL LAST NIGHT, HE BECAME VERY QUIET AND THEN VERY HYPER. HE KEPT TALKING ABOUT KOBE BRYANT. IT WAS A STRUGGLE TO GET HIM TO SLEEP. WHEN I TOLD HIM A FEW MINUTES AGO THAT YOU'RE NOT COMING TONIGHT, HE EXPLODED INTO A RAGING TANTRUM. I FINALLY HAD TO CALL JENNY RICE FOR ADVICE. WE AGREED THAT I SHOULD DRIVE SAM UP TOMORROW TO VISIT HIS GRANDPARENTS FOR THE REST OF THE WINTER BREAK IN THE *HOPE* THAT A CHANGE OF SCENERY WILL CALM HIM DOWN.

I KNOW IT'S THE HOLIDAYS, BUT I HAVE NO IDEA WHERE YOU ARE OR WHEN YOU'LL BE BACK AND HAVE TO THINK OF SAM FIRST. WE'LL RETURN BEFORE THE NEW YEAR. I'LL LET YOU KNOW THEN WHETHER SAM IS READY TO SEE YOU."

Duncan lay down on the bed with his back to M.D. and Rob and read the message over and over until tears blurred the bold, black letters. He couldn't bear to spend another ten days without seeing Sam, not when his son was so profoundly angry with him. But, *wait.* Gracie said she wasn't leaving until tomorrow. He still had some time. He would be back late tonight, drive over first thing in the morning, and beg her for an hour with Sam. Yes! She couldn't refuse him an hour, not during the holidays. He'd bring the Yokohama Baystars cap, take him to breakfast at Izzy's Deli, and they could celebrate an early Christmas. He'd make things right with Sammy tomorrow. Somehow.

SIXTY

....

WEDNESDAY, DECEMBER 22
LOS ANGELES

After she was unable to reach Rob or M.D., Ghislaine hurried to the office hoping to find a message there. Nothing. She tried to busy herself with her morning emails but soon was pacing around her office in a futile effort to chase from her mind images of Rob and M.D. lying hurt somewhere in Panama. The chance to banish from her soul Robert's condescension, Ward's contempt and her own self-doubts was not worth this agony. She would never forgive herself if her ambition had endangered her son and young assistant. Plagued by recriminations, she failed to notice a message had arrived on her computer. When her eye caught the tiny gold email icon staring back at her, she felt weak and collapsed in her chair. Clenching and unclenching her left fist, she clicked the email open with her right hand. When she read that they had been delayed and wanted to talk at noon, her left hand unwound and fell to her lap. Then, almost immediately, it rose and slammed on the desktop.

"Completement irresponsable," she hissed to herself in equal parts anger and relief. When M.D. called her at noon, Ghislaine exploded.

"*Where* have you been? I have been waiting for more than a day for you to contact me."

"Uh, sorry, Ghislaine. By the way, Rob and Duncan are with me. I have you on speaker. We'd like to bring you up to speed on what's happened since we spoke yesterday. Do you have time to talk now? It's pretty complex, so we'll need at least forty-five minutes."

"Yes, yes, I have the time," Ghislaine growled. "But first tell me, are you all safe? Why couldn't I reach you?"

"Yes, we're all here and safe. We're missed our flight out, but we're planning to return to Los Angeles tonight. The last twenty-four hours have been . . ." M.D. paused. "Challenging, to say the least. Let me explain."

"Good God," Ghislaine exclaimed when M.D. had finished. "Are you sure you're safe where you are? Is there something I can do from here?"

"Thanks, mother," Rob replied. "We're all right, but if something happens to us before we can get on the plane tonight, contact Jorge immediately, will you? He'll know what to do."

"Of course, Robbie," Ghislaine replied and then paused. "Well, I'm glad that you're not hurt, but this is a *total* disaster. It's obvious Duncan should never have contacted Salduba."

"Wait a minute . . ." Duncan started to object.

"Well, we can't change the past," M.D. cut him off and continued quickly, "but we do have a strategy that might get us where we want to go with Aoki."

Ghislaine drummed her fingers on her desk. "All right, please go on."

"You know of CESD's current operations and the reasons it's losing money. What you may not remember is that Aoki has partnered with the Japanese government to develop submarine technology to extract minerals from the ocean floor. Our idea is that Aoki and CESD could join forces to harvest trees from Lake Gatun using Aoki's submarine technology to increase dramatically the quantity and quality of timber extracted. I've done some preliminary research and there is at least one Canadian company that is exploring the concept of using a submersible device to identify and cut underwater trees. Rob has done some rough analysis of the effect on CESD's operations of a sizeable increase in productivity. Rob, why don't you explain what you've found?"

"Sure," Rob said. "What I've found is that a twofold increase in productivity would allow us to break even and a fourfold increase in productivity would generate enough cash flow to justify the construction of a warehouse, saw mill, and kiln, all of which could be done by Aoki. We don't know the effect of Aoki's technology on our operations, but we hope that it could result in at least a fourfold increase in our yield."

"Well, is that it?" asked Ghislaine.

"Yes, that's our strategy to persuade Aoki to support you against Ward," M.D. announced, a tinge of pride coloring her words. "We know that Takayama-san is likely to be pretty upset when he finds out that we didn't get Aoki qualified, but we think a partnership with CESD might be attractive enough to move him to our side."

"*Bagatelle,*" Ghislaine bellowed. "You think offering Aoki a partnership with CESD in Panama and the chance to put up a few buildings will convince them to support me against Ward? When they have just lost the chance to make *millions* on a concession from the government?" Ghislaine shook her head furiously. And then she stopped herself. Robert had for years denigrated her ideas in just that way, leaving her fuming in frustration. She had wanted a chance to prove herself better than Robert. Well, she now stood on the cliff of a crisis. Would she be content to curse the sky or would she be brave enough to leap? And if she jumped, would she soar or crash?

"Ghislaine? Are you there?" asked M.D.

"Yes, I'm here," she snarled. "Give me a moment to think!" What, she asked herself, would she do if presented with the opportunity M.D. had described? Another few seconds passed before she slapped her hands together. She had it.

"The only way this may work is to think more globally," she announced. "Aoki operates worldwide and will find a deal with CESD attractive only if they conclude that it may lead to similar deals in other countries. You need to find out how many underwater forests exist in the world, where they are located, and whether they're being exploited. You need to persuade Aoki that the partnership with CESD in Panama is a kind of pilot project that can be replicated in many places. Only then would there be a chance that the opportunity to work with CESD would tip the balance toward acquiring the technology and toward supporting me."

"Ghislaine, this is Duncan. We think your idea is superb. We will describe the opportunity to Aoki in exactly those terms when we speak with them this afternoon."

"No you won't," ordered Ghislaine, determined more than ever to take control from the lawyer who had brought them to the brink of failure. "You should know better than to expect to be able to persuade Aoki of anything important unless you're there in person. Besides, there isn't time to prepare a convincing presentation to Aoki for this afternoon. You can explain the concept to them and ask them to explore the possibilities of modifying their technology to harvest timber." Ghislaine rose up and leaned on her desk. "Then you must say that you will fly to Japan and meet with them in person on Friday. That will buy us time to prepare and will impress upon them the importance of what we have to say. Remember, the deadline for deciding whether to license the technology is Monday. If you don't get over there by Friday, they'll make that decision without taking into account our proposal." Duncan bowed his head and massaged his temples. The two young Americans exchanged worried glances. M.D. placed her hand on Duncan's fleshy shoulder.

"Duncan?!" Ghislaine shouted. Duncan's head snapped up.

"Look, I've been traveling constantly for the better part of six days, across multiple time zones and into and out of at least three different climates. But even if I weren't too exhausted to go back to Japan, it's not possible to get to Tokyo in time for a meeting on Friday."

"Actually," M.D. interrupted as she tapped on the keys of her computer. "I'm looking at a travel website now. We arrive in Los Angeles at just after midnight tonight. There's a flight from Los Angeles to Tokyo leaving at one thirty tomorrow morning. It's a flight to Haneda, not to Narita, and arrives at five in the morning on Friday. You could sleep on the flight over and have plenty of time to meet with Takayama-san on Friday during the morning and early afternoon. I know that you'll want to get back as soon as possible on Christmas Eve, but there are plenty of flights leaving Tokyo for Los Angeles on Friday afternoon."

"Good work, M.D.," Ghislaine said, triumph in her voice.

"I won't go," Duncan declared flatly. "I need to get home tonight for . . . for family reasons."

"Now you listen to me, Duncan Luke," Ghislaine interrupted. "You failed to accomplish what I sent you to Panama for. You owe it to me to do everything you can to clean up the mess you've made, and if that means flying back to Tokyo to meet with Takayama-san, so be it."

"I won't go. We'll prepare a presentation tomorrow in Los Angeles and do a videoconference with Takayama-san tomorrow, late afternoon, which will be his Friday morning. That will be good enough."

"Not good enough for me!" Ghislaine roared. "And *not* good enough to be paid a *cent* for your work either, let alone a bonus."

Duncan kneaded his hands together until his knuckles turned white. He looked at M.D. and Rob, who both furrowed their brows and stared back at him. He closed his eyes for a moment and saw M.D. attacking the monkey and Rob straining to slow Magdalena's descent from the ventilation shaft. He heard Web's gravelly voice remind him not to place too much importance on any single day with Sam. And then he saw Sam's black curls through the rear window of Gracie's Saab station wagon as it pulled out of the driveway on its way to San Francisco. He tried but could not lift his hand to wave.

"Duncan!" Ghislaine boomed. "Did you hear me?" Duncan's eyes slowly open.

"All right, all right," he growled. "I'll try to set up a meeting with Takayama-san in Tokyo for Friday in the late morning or early afternoon. I owe it to Rob and M.D., who have done every-thing and more to help me. If BIG goes to Ward, their careers are finished too. As for my family, I'll . . . I'll take care of my family issues in a few days."

"Good," Ghislaine declared. "It's now almost one o'clock here and I need to leave for a lunch and you need to get to the airport. Rob, M.D., you land late tonight, so let's talk early tomorrow morning."

"Yes," said M.D. and Rob simultaneously.

"Excellent. Well, have a good trip, Duncan," she called cheer-fully.

"Hold on, Ghislaine. If I'm going to do this for you, I need you to buy me a first-class, round-trip ticket to Tokyo leaving on the flight M.D. found and returning on a flight Friday afternoon. I need the ticket ready for pickup at the first-class counter at LAX when I arrive tonight around midnight. I also need a room booked and paid for at the Peninsula Hotel."

Ghislaine replied evenly, "Of course. I'll call Monica right after lunch and have her make all the arrangements." And then, the lilt in her voice carrying more than a dollop of sarcasm, "Anything else you'd like me to do for you while I'm at it?"

"Sure. Have a bonus check ready for fifty thousand dollars. And one more thing," Duncan rejoined. "Raise a glass of wine with your lunch to wish me luck with Takayama-san. I'll need it."

....

SIXTY-ONE

WEDNESDAY, DECEMBER 22
LOS ANGELES

"Dear Ward," Salduba's cryptic email began. "You will be pleased to know that lunchtime has passed here in Panama City, but no one showed up to eat. Regards, Rodrigo." Ward appreciated the lawyer's sense of humor and wanted to reply with a quip of his own but restrained himself. Rather, he deleted the message from his inbox and then permanently deleted it from his deleted items file. When he finished, he dialed the Sephardic Home for the Aged and asked to speak with Khala Sawari.

"Oh, Judah," his old nurse exclaimed. "How the days have flown by. I can't believe it's Sunday!" Ward had noticed for some months now that Khala's mental faculties were weakening, but she had never before lost track of the day of the week. He couldn't bear that the last thread from the fabric of his mother's family had begun to unravel. Surely Rebecca Schwartz would know of some therapy that would help Khala. Ward would pay whatever it cost.

"No, dear Khala," Ward said quietly. "It's only Wednesday, but I wanted to invite you to a special lunch on January ninth, to celebrate."

"Well, I'm not sure I'll be free on that day," Khala squeaked a protest. "It's such a long time from now."

"I know," Ward said. "I'm sorry, but I will be traveling until then. I'll tell Rebecca to keep your calendar open for me."

"Oh, that would be nice. What are we celebrating?"

"That I have finally fulfilled my mother's promise. The business her parents started will be in her son's hands in a matter of days."

"Oh, Judah. That's wonderful news. I look forward to seeing you on . . . oh, dear . . . what day was it again?" Ward felt his throat tighten and tears begin to form in his eyes.

"Sunday, January ninth," he finally managed to say. "But don't worry, Khala. I'll take care of everything. Good-bye." Ward set the receiver down gently, as Khala used to lay him down for a nap, turned, and gazed out the window at a sky full of mist. Several minutes passed and then his assistant rang him.

"It's Gracie Lewis," Elaine announced. "Do you want to take the call?"

"Yes," Ward said. He wiped the tears from his eyes and punched the button to connect Gracie.

"I'm really sorry," Gracie apologized. "But I can't meet you after all. My son's father left on a business trip without telling me and when he finally did contact me to cancel, I couldn't get a babysitter."

"God, what a jackass! I feel so sorry for you and your son. But wait, I thought he was an academic? He's gone on a *business* trip? Overseas again?"

"I know. I know. Don't get me started. I'm just *so* relieved to be rid of him. Can we re-schedule for sometime early next month? I will be away for the holidays but would like to see you when I get back."

"Of course, I have plans to go skiing and travel to London over the next two weeks, but I'll call you when I've returned."

"That would be great. And thank you for being so . . . so gracious. I look forward to seeing you in a couple of weeks. In the meantime, have a great holiday season."

"Thank you, Gracie. And happy holidays to you and to . . . oh, what's your son's name?"

"His name is Samuel. Sam."

". . . and to Sam, then. I look forward to meeting him someday soon."

....

SIXTY-TWO

WEDNESDAY, DECEMBER 22
EN ROUTE TO LOS ANGELES

Dressed in the tan cotton pants, blue shirt, and blazer he had intended to wear to the meeting with Fernando Rodriguez, Duncan lowered himself into his aisle seat on the Copa flight back to Los Angeles. A deeply tanned, middle-aged American man in shorts and sandals sat dozing in the window seat next to him. He wore a T-shirt with the words "I DIG YOUR CANAL!" written in script over the body of a dark-haired beauty dressed only in her smile. Duncan glanced at the man's shirt and felt a volcano erupt inside. He leapt to his feet and thrust his face inches from the man's. The stench of stale tequila on the man's breath further fueled his rage.

"You fucking asshole!" he shouted jolting the man awake, his right finger aimed like an arrow at the passenger's heart. "Do you have any idea how much damage men like you do to helpless women in Panama? The girls you use, they are someone's daughter, someone's girlfriend," he hissed, his voice cracking.

A frightened look passed over the man's face. He began to reach for the flight attendant call button.

"Oh, you're an imbecile!" Duncan barked and turned away. "I can't stand to be anywhere near you."

Hearing Duncan's outburst behind and to his right, Rob swiveled around. M.D., who sat directly ahead of Rob, unbuckled and rose from her seat ready to restrain Duncan to keep him from being kicked off the plane. Both stared at the lawyer as he walked back toward them, found an empty aisle seat opposite M.D., and stared out the window to his right. M.D. reached across the aisle and squeezed Duncan's arm. Without returning her gaze, the lawyer placed his hand on hers in thanks.

Thirty minutes later, the plane had launched itself into the sky. When Duncan felt his heart stop pounding, he leaned back in his seat and forced himself to review the call with Taka. When he had reached his Japanese friend on his cell phone, it was eight o'clock Thursday morning in Tokyo, and Taka was being driven to work. He had already learned that Aoki had failed to qualify for the CFZ project and so he greeted Duncan with none of his customary warmth. As Duncan relayed to him the details of the kidnapping, however, Taka expressed alarm. When Duncan explained to him why he believed Salduba had instigated both Aoki's debacle and the kidnapping, he boiled over with fury, threatening in rapid succession to sue Salduba, to have him disbarred, to have him thrown in jail for a thousand years. Duncan allowed Taka's wrath to subside before reminding him that Magdalena was the only person who could link Salduba to the kidnapping and to Aoki's failure to qualify. At that point, Duncan revealed that Magdalena had disappeared and would, if by any chance she did reappear, be regarded by the Panamanian police as an illegal immigrant who had violated Panama's laws against prostitution. Duncan could hear Taka suck his breath back through his teeth.

"So, Duncan-san, *mattaku shikata ga nai*? There is nothing we can do in this matter?"

"I will keep trying to find a way to get Aoki qualified, but I don't have any ideas at this point how to accomplish that goal. In the meantime," Duncan continued quickly, "we believe that there might be an enormous opportunity for Aoki in the work that CESD is doing."

"We are not in the business of environmental cleanup and have no desire to become involved in small-scale development work," Taka snorted.

"Give me five minutes to explain our idea. I think you will find it interesting. In fact, I believe so much in the potential of a partnership between Aoki and CESD that I am flying to Tokyo from Los Angeles in order to meet with you on Friday to discuss it in detail."

"If you are willing to return to Japan so soon after having just visited us, then this idea must be interesting indeed. Please continue."

Duncan summarized the current state of CESD's business, including its low productivity and, hence, low profitability. He began to describe the results of Rob's preliminary analysis showing what a dramatic increase in yield would do to the company's cash flow and operations.

"Yes, yes, I understand what you say," Taka interrupted. "Please tell me what relationship this has with Aoki?"

Duncan responded by reminding Taka of the work that Aoki had been doing with the Japanese government on the use of submarines to exploit deep-sea mineral deposits. Before he could link that work to the problem faced by CESD, Taka interjected, "So, you think that our technology might be used to improve the rate of timber harvesting? *Omoshiroi*. I will ask my staff to investigate and report to me by tomorrow on their preliminary conclusions; however," Taka paused, "we at Aoki have many attractive ideas to explore and limited time and resources. Why should Aoki choose to spend time and money on a partnership with CESD?"

"I can think of several reasons, such as a share in the profits flowing from CESD, the opportunity to build the infrastructure needed for CESD to ramp-up operations, the chance to market CESD timber around the world, and acquiring operating experience in Panama that could be leveraged into other business in Panama."

"I see," Taka said. "Your idea has some attraction, but your timing is unfortunate. We must decide by Monday whether to license the submarine technology from the government. Frankly speaking, our analysis is not so optimistic about the short-term profitability of underwater mining, and our preliminary decision is not to spend any more money on this project. I very much doubt that including an underwater forestry business in Panama as part of our analysis of the costs and benefits of the license would change our conclusion."

"Perhaps not," Duncan replied quickly, "but the benefits flowing to Aoki from the underwater harvesting of timber would not be limited to Panama. There are many other sites around the world where underwater forests exist, waiting to be harvested. While there are a few companies attempting to harvest submerged timber, they are small and none has the worldwide reach, stellar reputation, and substantial financial resources of Aoki. We believe that Aoki should see the Aoki-CESD venture in Panama as a pilot project that, if successful, could give Aoki a sizeable competitive advantage in this new global industry."

"I understand," Taka said slowly. "This idea is more appealing than it first appeared. Perhaps it could affect our decision on the submarine technology after all."

"I should add," Duncan continued, "that it was Ghislaine Bingham who had the vision of a worldwide venture and who insisted on my presenting it to you."

"Ah," Taka murmured. "Ghislaine Bingham is an unusual woman, to be sure."

"Yes, I believe she is. I apologize, but it's time to board my flight to Los Angeles. I will arrive in Tokyo tomorrow in the early morning and stay at the Peninsula Hotel again. With your permission, I will call upon your office tomorrow at eleven o'clock. In the meantime, I would be very grateful if you would ask your staff to investigate the ideas that we have discussed. I will have some further information to present to you on Friday," Duncan promised. Before ending the call, he added, "Perhaps after our discussion of this possible partnership, we can again discuss the situation at Bingham International and Aoki's position regarding Ward Bingham's proposal?"

"Of course, of course," Taka said. "I look forward to seeing you tomorrow in Tokyo. Please get some rest on the flight."

Duncan felt relieved that Taka had been so open minded. The groundwork had been laid for the discussion in Tokyo, but now they had to focus on the details. Duncan rose from his seat and asked M.D. to move over to the window seat. He sat down in the aisle next to her and gestured for Rob to join them.

"I know that you're both exhausted," he said in a half-whisper, "but we're nearing the finish line and must accomplish a great deal in the next twenty-four hours. Rob, I need you to complete your analysis of the effect of increased productivity on CESD, or at least make it as complete as possible. I know you've done an analysis based on a fourfold increase, but let's be aggressive. Take the analysis up to tenfold."

"Okay. Once the fundamental variables and calculations are locked into the spreadsheet, I can generate the numbers based upon multiple assumptions."

"Good, thanks. M.D., could you come up with some information on where else in the world there are significant harvesting

opportunities, some rough estimates of the size of those opportunities and, if you can, some comments on how they differ in
general respects from what CESD is finding in Lake Gatun?
Showing Aoki that it can scale up this business in multiple sites
around the world is critical. Since we have limited time, I would
focus first on Asia, second on Africa, and third on Latin America.
I wouldn't worry about the Canadian possibilities; Aoki has little
advantage there compared with the local companies."

"I'll see what I can find. I won't have time to polish the data,
but I'll indicate the sources of my information so that Aoki can
check it if they want."

"Do as much as you can. They may well make their decision to
license or not license the technology based on what you and Rob
tell them," Duncan said. He hesitated a moment before continuing. "Now, to change the subject, do either of you recall Magdalena's saying Salduba was acting for an *American* client when he
asked her to help him have us kidnapped?"

"Yes, I do," M.D. said.

"And I do, too. Why?" asked Rob.

"Because I can't think of any American client who would want
us out of the way other than Ward Bingham," Duncan whispered.
The two young Americans sat stunned for a moment.

"You don't really believe he would have us kidnapped, do you?"
Rob asked.

"I'm not saying that he did. But I can't think of any other
American client who would have had a motive. Is there any way
we could get a look at the last week's bank records to see whether
any funds flowed from the company to Salduba, and at company
phone records to see whether any calls were made between L.A.
and Panama? Can you get that done without alerting Ward?"

"I'm pretty friendly with Alan, the office manager," said M.D.,
"and Ghislaine hired him. I think he'd be willing to take a look at

recent bank transactions. And the company supplies a cell phone to each of its executives, so I would think he'd also be able to get a printout of recent calls. But I can't believe that Ward would use a company account to pay Salduba, can you?"

"Not if he had thought through the implications. But perhaps he didn't have any choice or was just arrogant enough to believe no one would ever find out, especially now that he thinks he's in control of the company. It's worth a try, don't you think?"

M.D. and Rob both nodded.

"Good," Duncan continued. "The meeting with Takayama-san is Friday morning at eleven o'clock in Tokyo. That's six o'clock on Thursday afternoon in Los Angeles. We should plan to talk no later than nine thirty in the morning Tokyo time. You'll have to call me at the Peninsula. In order to make that call worthwhile, I'll need to have whatever materials you have prepared for the meeting by email no later than an hour before. That doesn't leave you much time between now and then to get everything done, but that's all the time we have. Agreed?"

"Yes," they both said.

"So here is what I suggest. You obviously can't go to the office to work. I think you should take the shuttle to the Marriott at the airport, check in, get some rest, have your laundry done, and then wake up as early as you can to start work. Get a small conference room with secure wireless access to the Internet and teleconferencing equipment. I'd like to have you both available by teleconference for the meeting with Takayama-san."

"Okay. Will do," M.D. said. Rob nodded in agreement.

"Thanks," Duncan said, reaching out with both his hands to touch the arms of his colleagues. "I owe you dinner and drinks when all this is over. I know a good Oaxacan restaurant near the Santa Monica airport. They have almost as many kinds of mole sauces as they have tequilas."

When they arrived at LAX, they quickly passed through immigration and customs. Rob and M.D. wished Duncan good luck and headed for the shuttle to the Marriott. Duncan ran up to the departure level to grab his ticket, rushed through security in the priority passenger lane, and sprinted to the gate to catch his plane to Tokyo. The final boarding announcement had just been made when he arrived at the gate, sweating and breathing heavily. He boarded, set his briefcase and roll-on in the overhead compartment, and collapsed in the first-class console. While he waited for the doors of the plane to close, he switched on his BlackBerry and scrolled down for any urgent messages. There was one from Jed around nine o'clock Los Angeles time, reporting only that he had no information yet. The doors of the plane closed.

Once the plane was airborne, Duncan asked for three glasses of red wine and a plate of cheese and fruit. Wolfing his meal down, he ordered a double cognac and two bottles of water. The water went in a side pocket of the console and the cognac went down in one gulp. His throat burning, he reclined and lengthened his seat so that it became a narrow bed that almost, but not quite, accommodated all of his seventy-six inches. Rolling over into a semi-fetal position on the side opposite his bruised ribs, he pulled a blanket over him. His mind hurtled through the wine and cognac to all the possible reasons why Jed had not heard anything. Had Magdalena been deported to Colombia? Was she in a cell somewhere badly hurt? And Sammy, he sighed. I'm so sorry. Stop it, he commanded himself. You need to sleep. Tomorrow promises to be the longest Christmas Eve you'll ever experience.

SIXTY-THREE

....

WEDNESDAY, DECEMBER 22
LOS ANGELES

As a misty Wednesday sky evaporated into the softening light of a December dusk, Ward looked out the window of his office and imagined the celebration he would have with Khala in January. She would recount stories of his mother, rekindling his own memories of her. Leila would spring to life again, gaze proudly at her son, and thank him for restoring to her family what his father had stolen many years before. The ring of his BlackBerry at five o'clock dashed his daydream. When he saw the call was from an unknown number in Japan, his pulse began to race.

"Good afternoon, Ward-san. This is Takei. I hope that this is a convenient time to talk. Since I am calling from a public phone in the Imperial Hotel, I have only a few minutes."

"Yes, Takei-san," Ward responded sitting back in his chair. "How may I help you?"

"Actually, I am calling once again to offer you some useful information. Takayama-san called a surprise meeting of a group of Aoki managers this morning, including Emoto and myself. He reported that our attempt to qualify in Panama had failed."

Ward grinned. "That is very good news for BIG and for us."

"Yes, it is. But I would not call you if there were not more," Takei-san continued with impatience creeping into his voice. "Takayama-san said Duncan Luke accused our lawyer, Rodrigo Salduba, of kidnapping him and two executives from BIG who had traveled to Panama to assist Aoki."

"What! Kidnapped?" Ward exclaimed, rocking forward in his chair. Would Salduba, a lawyer after all, really have gone that far? "That's a shocking allegation."

"Yes, I agree. So you had no knowledge of these matters?"

"No, absolutely not! I spoke with Salduba as you suggested, but I can't believe he would resort to kidnapping. Besides, taking hostages for money is not unheard of in Central American countries. How do we know that this Duncan Luke is telling the truth about Salduba's involvement? Did he offer Mr. Takayama any proof?"

"No. He said that the only person who could testify against Salduba had regretfully disappeared."

"Ah, I see," Ward exhaled slowly. "Well, that is an unfortunate development. Is there anything else?"

"Only that Duncan Luke is visiting Japan again tomorrow, and we are to meet with him to discuss a new way of cooperating with CESD."

"*What?!*" Ward thundered into his BlackBerry as he jumped from his chair. "I knew nothing of this."

"That is why I am calling," Takei-san responded calmly. "CESD is proposing a partnership with Aoki to use submarine technology to harvest timber lying underwater in lakes around the world. Takayama-san has organized a meeting tomorrow at eleven o'clock to discuss the matter with Luke-san. Once that meeting has concluded, Takayama-san will undoubtedly wish to discuss the request from Luke-san that Aoki assist Ghislaine-san in her dispute with you."

Ward leaned on his desk with one hand and gripped his cell phone tightly with the other. "And how do you think Takayama-san will respond?"

"It is very difficult to predict. He will have to consult with our board of directors on such a matter. And the board will undoubtedly ask my opinion since I am the manager responsible for the Bingham International relationship."

"I see," Ward replied, aware that Mr. Takei was being overly coy. "And, if I might ask, is your opinion still that I am best suited to run the company?"

"My view *was* that you would be a far more effective leader than Ghislaine-san, but I have since had time to reflect on the question. I now believe your leadership would be to Aoki's benefit, provided," the Japanese executive paused, "that I serve as vice chair on the BIG board of directors, to assist you in maximizing the potential of the Bingham-Aoki relationship."

"But Takayama-san is the Aoki representative," Ward protested. "You know that I have no power to change whom Aoki appoints."

"Yes, I understand it is Aoki's decision. However, if you were to insist strongly that it would benefit both companies to have the responsible Aoki manager on your board as vice chair, I do not think Takayama-san would object, given his many other duties. Besides, you would find me a more, how shall I say it, accommodating board member than Takayama-san, and we could continue our personal partnership to our advantage as well as that of both Aoki and BIG."

Ward sat down on the edge of his desk. "Mr. Takei, I very much appreciate the suggestion. I don't know why I didn't think of it before."

SIXTY-FOUR

....

WEDNESDAY, DECEMBER 22
PANAMA CITY

Rodrigo Salduba searched his pockets for the keys to his office as he strode into the lobby of the Torre Delta around nine o'clock. He intended to call his Korean client to congratulate him on having qualified and ask that his bonus be wired immediately. Salduba waved to the guard on duty, who nodded perfunctorily and quickly returned to watching a televised soccer game between two local clubs. Riding up in the elevator, he cursed again the incompetence of the three men he had hired to kidnap the Americans and the police officers whom he had paid to escort them to the airport under threat of arrest for cocaine possession. Still, he consoled himself, Duncan Luke and his colleagues had failed to meet with Rodriguez, the deadline for Aoki's qualification had passed, and the Americans had departed without complaining to the U.S. embassy of their treatment. As for Magdalena, the police would soon find her, almost certainly cowering in the apartment of one of her girlfriends, whose names he had supplied to the authorities.

Salduba entered his law firm's suite and opened the door to his office. "*Maldito*," he spat out when he saw that the cleaning lady had left his lights on again. Then he stopped, shocked by the sight of a woman's dark head darting beneath his desk. "*Que haces aqui?*" he shouted and sprinted toward her. A tall woman with short black hair and thick glasses wearing a cleaning service uniform shot up from behind his desk. Her hat flew off her head as she dashed away from him. Salduba reached out, seized the woman's left hand, and yanked her face down onto his desk. With his free hand, he grabbed her hair and jerked upward and then downward as hard as he could. But instead of slamming her head onto the desktop, his strength ripped the woman's hair from her head. Shocked, he stood open-mouthed, gazing at the black mass in his hand. The woman shrieked in fury. Then he felt a sharp stab in his left side and buckled over, grabbing for the wound. A moment later, the woman cried out, "*Bastardo!*" and he felt his right temple explode in pain.

SIXTY-FIVE

....

FRIDAY, DECEMBER 24
TOKYO

D uncan's flight touched down at Tokyo's Haneda Airport just after five thirty on Friday morning, twelve hours after it had taken off from Los Angeles. He had slept about half the flight and spent the remaining hours staring at *True Grit* on a movie screen without bothering to use the earphones. Due to his early arrival, he emerged quickly from immigration and customs. As he walked out, he switched on his BlackBerry and then swore at himself for forgetting it wasn't configured to operate in Japan.

Thirty minutes later, Duncan checked in to the Peninsula Hotel and soon found himself standing in a room identical to the one he had left only four days before. He felt lightheaded from the jet lag and slightly queasy. Three hours remained before his nine thirty call with M.D. and Rob. After undressing and putting on the hotel's thick bathrobe, he called housekeeping and asked them to have all his clothes cleaned and back to him by nine o'clock.

Turning on his laptop to check his emails, he saw a message marked urgent from Jed, asking him to call as soon as possible. A wave of nausea flowed through him as he glanced at the phone on the nightstand. He started to pant and a light sweat broke out on his face. Calm down, he commanded himself, forcing his body to breathe more slowly. After a moment, he managed to push the buttons that would connect him to the U.S. embassy in Panama. A minute later, the voice of Jed Barbour echoed halfway across the world.

"Hello, Duncan. Are you in Los Angeles?"

"No," Duncan replied hoarsely and then, trying to keep the fatigue out of his voice, he added, "you're not going to believe it, but I'm in Tokyo."

"*What?* Tokyo? What the hell are you doin' there, buddy? Oh, never mind. I'm sure you must have a good reason to fly around the world again. Listen, I've got some news about your friend."

Duncan felt a lump grow somewhere deep in his lower chest.

"Is she all right, Jed? What did you hear?"

"Well, you're not gonna believe it. Around eight thirty last night, she comes to the building where Salduba works. She's got on a short black wig and glasses and is wearing the cap and baggy uniform of a cleanin' woman. She's carrying a wooden case full of cleanin' supplies. The security guard was watching a soccer game on television, so he didn't bother to do more than just glance up when she passed him. After riding the elevator to the lawyer's floor, she enters the men's bathroom off the corridor outside the lawyer's office suite. In that bathroom, there's a door that leads to a closet and at the back of the closet, there's another door that's always locked. A sign on the door says DANGER. ELECTRICAL CLOSET. But that door actually opens directly into the lawyer's office. On the other side, the door is hidden by a huge Kuna tapestry. Salduba must have had all this laid out as a kind of escape route or perhaps a way to usher girls quietly into and out of his office. Your resourceful friend not only knew about the secret door but had a key to it. Are you following me so far?"

"Yes. I'm following you. But where is she? How is she?"

"Hold on, buddy. I'm gettin' to all of that. Anyway, she lets herself into her friend's office and opens his safe. How she knew the combination is anyone's guess, but I'm thinking this is one smart lady. She must have been with him many times when he opened it in the past and simply memorized the combination. Anyway, your friend is in the process of helpin' herself to fifty thousand dollars in cash and some papers from the safe when, you guessed it, Salduba returns to make a call to a client in Asia. My colleagues are not sure what happened, but there was definitely a struggle. To defend herself, your friend apparently grabbed scissors from the desk and stabbed the lawyer in the side. Then she clobbered him over the head with a paperweight, knocking him out. Rather than running right out, though, she opens his fly and cuts off about an inch of his dick with the scissors. He's unconscious but starts to bleed down there, of course, so it seems she tied his pocket scarf around what was left of his weenie as a tourniquet. Can you believe it?"

I can believe it, Duncan thought. "Where is she? Is she okay?"

"No one knows for sure. She left a trail of blood that led to the secret door and the bathroom. They don't know yet whether she was hurt somehow in the fight or the blood was only Salduba's. If she was hurt, it couldn't have been bad 'cause the blood stops in the bathroom. Anyway, she left the building the same way she came in. Salduba regained consciousness around a half an hour later. He called his doctor for help and the doctor called an ambulance to take him to a hospital. The doctor later reported that Salduba had lost a lot of blood and was dazed and confused from the concussion he suffered. After patchin' him up, the doctor gave him a sedative. The hospital staff called the police, as they are obliged to do when it appears that a crime may have been committed, but the police couldn't question him until this morning.

When they did, Salduba told them what he remembered of the robbery and the fight. The police did some forensic work at his office today, spoke to the guard in the lobby and the doctor, and pieced together the story I've just told you."

"Jed, Goddammit, do you know where she is?" Duncan shouted into the phone.

"Not exactly. The police are supposedly searchin' for her, but with that kind of money and a twelve-hour head start, she could be anywhere by now. Anyway, here's what I think happened. I think she hired a car to take her across the border into Costa Rica sometime early this morning. She'd need a visa but, if she had planned her escape yesterday, she could have received one from the Costa Rican Consulate in Panama City. Or she could have stopped to get one at the Costa Rican Consulate in David, a Panamanian city just south of the Costa Rican border. She might even have used her newfound financial resources to obtain one under the table at the border itself. It's not unheard of."

"Why do you think she's in Costa Rica?"

"Are you holdin' your hat, buddy? Today at around three o'clock in the afternoon, the Panamanian Anti-Corruption Commission received a fax from a business center in the departure lounge at Juan Santamaria International airport in San Jose, Costa Rica. The fax contained three handwritten pages from a notebook your lady must have taken from the lawyer's safe. The pages detail payments the lawyer made over the past three years to two officials at the CFZ administration. The coversheet said, 'From Rodrigo Salduba, Salduba & Asociados.' She has a sense of humor, too, huh? Anyway, you'll be delighted to know that the Anti-Corruption Commission has launched an investigation into Salduba and his friends. The CFZ also announced it will conduct its own investigation. Moreover, given the appearance of corruption,

Fernando Rodriguez has reopened the qualification process and declared that he will supervise it directly."

Duncan's mind reeled. Magdalena was safe. Salduba was under investigation. The qualification process reopened. In the time that it took him to travel halfway across the world, the world had indeed turned completely upside down.

"Where could she be?" Duncan whispered into the phone.

"Like I said, we don't know for sure. We do know there were at least a dozen international flights from San Jose between three and five this afternoon, about half of them to places like Honduras or Venezuela, where no visa is required for a Colombian. Once she's there, she could immediately transit to yet another visa-free destination or take a day and get a visa for almost anywhere. She has the money to do what she wants. The Panamanian police could seek the help of the Costa Rican authorities to try to track her down, but they're focused on Salduba now. Magdalena just isn't a target anymore, even if they believed what Salduba told them about her, which they probably don't. She's gone, Duncan. But be happy for her, because she's safe."

Duncan stared down at the carpet for a long time. Jed waited patiently before saying, "Look, I know that you're worried about her, but she'll be fine. Anyone who is savvy enough to make a copy of the key to the lawyer's escape route, smart enough to memorize the combination to his safe, and strong enough to beat the shit out of him is not gonna have any trouble. She's safe, man. It's what you wanted for her, right? Just not the way you planned it. She did it her own way and did you a huge favor at the same time by takin' care of that bastard."

Duncan rubbed his eyes. "You're right," he said quietly. "It is what I wanted for her and I'm even more in her debt than before. I just wish that there was some way I could repay her."

"I hear you, buddy. Listen, I'm sorry, but I've got to go. I'm leavin' on a red eye to the States to join my family for Christmas. Take care of yourself in Tokyo, will you? Shoot me an email when you're back in L.A."

"Sure, Jed, I will. And, thanks again, for everything. Give Haley and your beautiful girls a hug for me."

"I'm happy to oblige you on all counts. You take care now."

Duncan hung up the phone. It was seven thirty in the morning. While he showered and cleaned up, he needed to think through the implications of what he had just learned. Thirty minutes and a long, hot shower later, Duncan felt revived enough to order breakfast. He was starved and for some strange reason craved Canadian bacon, which he ordered along with two poached eggs, some rye toast, and a large pot of coffee with some hot milk on the side. At eight thirty, he began to skim through the emails from Rob and M.D. They had both done an excellent job in a very short period of time on the information needed for the presentation to Aoki. In a postscript to her email, M.D. said she needed to speak with him about the phone and bank records. His clothes arrived back at nine o'clock, cleaned and pressed. He dressed and sat staring out the window at the bare cherry trees in Hibiya Park.

At exactly nine thirty, the phone rang. "Hello, Duncan? It's M.D. and Rob."

"Hi guys," Duncan replied. "I hope that you had at least some rest last night, although by the look of your reports you couldn't have slept very much."

"M.D. called me at five o'clock this morning. She said she couldn't sleep, so I had to get up," Rob laughed.

"Five o'clock this morning in Los Angeles was already eight o'clock in Panama, where we just came from, remember?" M.D. bantered back.

"Since we don't have a lot of time, let me just say, I think, Rob, your analysis of the beneficial impact on CESD of the various assumed increases in productivity is terrific, and, M.D., your report on other opportunities around the world to harvest underwater timber is extremely well written and informative. I don't have comments on either one. Let me suggest that you don't go into detail for the Aoki team on the call, but summarize your findings and conclusions. They may ask questions, but, more likely, they will want to study your reports after the meeting and handle any questions by email. Since their deadline on the license is Monday, do you mind being available over the weekend? I know it's Christmas weekend, but I think your input would be helpful. Is that okay?"

"Yes, of course," Rob said.

"Sure," M.D. replied. "You know them much better than we do."

"Good. Now, what did you learn from the bank and phone records?"

"Well," M.D. began, "things don't add up, so I thought we should discuss what I found before I sent the records to you. I called Alan at home to ask for the record of all payments made in the past year to payees in Panama. He said there might be a lot because of CESD, but he would get me what he could. I then asked him if I could get a list of the calls made this week from the company cell phone assigned to Ward. He wasn't very happy about being asked for information about Ward, but I reminded him that Ghislaine had hired him and that we needed to stick together now more than ever. I also suggested he could ask for a list of all international calls, so it wouldn't look like he was targeting Ward. He said that he would need a little time but could contact the cell phone company for the records."

"Good work. Did Alan get back to you?"

"He just did. The company made only two payments in the last twelve months to someone in Panama, other than to CESD. The first was a payment in March of last year of fifty thousand dollars to the charity Jorge mentioned when we were on Lake Gatun. The second payment, you'll be delighted to know, was made on Monday, fifty thousand dollars to Rodrigo Salduba, Salduba & Asociados."

"That's great. Is there a record of who requested the payment and for what reason?"

"Yes, Ward made the request. Accounting has an invoice from Salduba for legal advice on tax and investment issues in Panama."

"Okay. So we've linked Ward to Salduba just before our trip to Panama."

"Wait a moment," Rob interrupted, "how could Ward have known on Monday that we were going to Panama? We didn't meet with Ghislaine until Monday afternoon and didn't leave until very late Monday night. When did he authorize the payment, M.D.?"

"The authorization is dated Monday, but there's no time indicated. The payment was processed at the end of the day, like all payments."

"Maybe someone informed Ward you were traveling to Panama, and he immediately contacted Salduba?" Duncan asked.

"Yes, that's one possibility," M.D. responded, "but the phone records tell an even more perplexing story. There were only two international calls made this week on the phone assigned to Ward. One of them was to Salduba on Monday morning, not Monday afternoon. So Ward must have known about our plan to visit Panama before we met with Ghislaine."

"But that's not possible," Duncan objected.

"Perhaps not. I don't know how to explain it otherwise, unless it's just a coincidence that Ward had contacted Salduba, of all lawyers in Panama, for advice at exactly the same time as we were planning to travel there to help Aoki. Anyway, the other international call Ward made was placed around two a.m. on Monday to a number in Japan."

"What?" Duncan exclaimed. "Did you say he called a number in Japan early Monday morning?

"Yes, that's right."

Duncan leaned forward, elbows on his knees.

"That would have been Monday late-afternoon in Tokyo. After my meeting with Takayama-san. He and his two colleagues knew it was likely I would be going to Panama for Ghislaine; in fact, Takayama-san wished me a pleasant trip."

Duncan thought for a moment.

"M.D., would you please fax a copy of the phone record and printout showing the payment of fifty thousand dollars to Salduba? There's a fax machine here in my room."

"I'll send it right away."

"Thanks. And could you email Takayama-san the CESD materials you sent me, indicating that they are for the meeting today?"

"I'll take care of that," Rob offered. "Is there anything else?"

"Yes, there's a lot more." Duncan summarized for them what he had just learned from Jed.

"I'm so relieved Magdalena is safe," M.D. said.

"So, we're home free?" asked Rob. "I mean, Aoki has another opportunity to be qualified."

"No, I don't think we can rest easy yet. Takayama-san may not know what happened in Panama in the past twelve hours and, besides, the partnership with CESD is still a good business idea that should be pursued, particularly if they have any intention of licensing the submarine technology. It can only help us persuade Takayama-san and his board to support Ghislaine."

"Duncan," M.D. interjected, "I'm sorry, but I have to tell Ghislaine what's happened in Panama and what we've found in the bank and phone records. She's already called me three times today asking for a status report. After seeing how she reacted when we delayed our call to her from Panama, I don't want to keep her in the dark. She would be furious if she discovered I didn't give her the information as soon as I had it."

Duncan walked over to the window and looked down at the commuters rushing along the sidewalks below. He hated the idea of providing Ghislaine with ammunition he knew she could not resist using before he could think through how best to take advantage of it. Yet while he recognized the familiar urge to protect a client against herself, he knew M.D. was right. Ghislaine would feel M.D. had betrayed her if M.D. didn't report her findings immediately.

"There's not much time before the meeting with Aoki. Can you wait until we've finished that meeting and then call Ghislaine? You can tell her we wanted to make sure that we had all the relevant information before briefing her."

"Okay. It's already almost five o'clock here anyway. Another hour or so won't make any difference."

"Thanks. Now I've got to get ready for the meeting. Talk with you in about an hour."

Duncan hung up the phone. He stared at the receiver for a moment and made up his mind. He quickly dialed one last number, the office of his divorce lawyer, Web Allen.

"Duncan!" Web shouted. "How are you? Where are you? How's the work for Ghislaine coming?"

"Web, I was in Tokyo, as you know. Since then, I've been to Panama and now I'm back in Tokyo, all in the space of about ten days. I can't thank you enough for the referral and look forward to returning the favor someday, perhaps just before you're ready to leave for your next vacation."

"Jesus. I had no idea that the matter would be that involved. I'm sorry."

"Don't be. It's the fatigue complaining. Listen, I have a quick question for you. You said at Outlaws that a judge might find I was intentionally avoiding my support obligation because I left my practice and started teaching at about the same time my marriage began to fall apart."

"Well, it's more complicated than that, but, yes, there is a risk. Why?"

"What would it take to reduce that risk significantly, short of going back to private practice? For example, what if, instead of taking a full-time teaching job for around seventy thousand dollars, I had decided to leave practice to serve as general counsel for a company? Would the risk be the same? Would it depend on the size of the salary?"

Web hesitated for a moment. "I'm not sure what you're up to, but the short answer is yes, it would depend on the salary. If you made, say, two hundred and fifty thousand plus a possible bonus, I doubt a judge would see becoming a general counsel as a drastic change from private practice, even if the compensation you received was substantially smaller than the one-point-five million you were making before. Besides, I think even Fran Cooper would have a hard time finding you were intentionally avoiding support if you had a job paying two or three times what she makes."

"And what would be the level of support I'd have to pay under those facts? It wouldn't be twenty-five thousand a month, would it?"

"No, it wouldn't even be close to that amount. The precise figure would depend on a lot of factors, but I'd guess you'd end up paying around five thousand dollars per month, perhaps a little less."

"Thanks. That's all I wanted to know."

"What's going on? Why are you in Japan?"

"I can't tell you now. I'll be in touch after the holidays. Take care." Duncan hung up the phone, picked up his briefcase, and strode out of the room. Outside the hotel, the late December air reddened his cheeks and chilled him to the bone. He had forgotten that the blue blazer and cotton pants he had packed for Panama would afford no protection against the Tokyo winter, but he decided to walk the three blocks to the Aoki office anyway. He couldn't wait for the meeting to begin.

SIXTY-SIX

....

FRIDAY, DECEMBER 24
TOKYO

Knowing the Japanese prized punctuality and considered tardiness a sign of disrespect, Duncan arrived at Aoki's offices at precisely eleven o'clock. Within a minute, a uniformed office lady walked into the reception area, bowed, and motioned for Duncan to follow her. She led him past the elevators and through double-glass doors. Turning left down a long corridor, she walked past several seemingly identical conference rooms, one of which, Duncan guessed, was the one where he had met with Taka and his colleagues only five days before. Opening the last door on the corridor, she ushered Duncan into an empty room furnished with a rectangular table and ten chairs. A telephone with a large round speaker lay in the middle of the table.

"Would you like coffee or tea?" she warbled.

"*Ocha, onegai-shimasu,*" Duncan replied, startling the young woman. Realizing his terrible Japanese accent had confused her, he added in English, "Green tea, please." Relieved, she bowed and left the room. Duncan walked to the side of the table opposite the door and stood behind the middle seat. Thirty seconds later, Taka burst into the room, followed by Emoto-san, Takei-san, and two younger men whom Duncan did not recognize.

"Duncan-san," Taka boomed. "What a surprise and pleasure to see you again so soon. You remember Emoto and Takei. This is Wada and this is Kimoto." Taka nodded toward the two younger men. "Wada is an engineer. He has been working for several years on the underwater mining project, including the cost-benefit analysis we prepared to decide whether to license the technology. Kimoto is head of our Forestry Products division."

The two Japanese came over to Duncan, bowed, and offered him their business cards.

"Please, sit down," Taka said gesturing to the chair in front of Duncan. The effects of the hotel coffee disappearing with each second, Duncan was happy to oblige. The five men from Aoki sat opposite Duncan, with Taka in the middle flanked by Emoto-san on his right and Takei-san on his left. Two young women entered, placed a cup of green tea in front of each of the men, and left the room with a bow.

"Please, have some tea," Taka waved at the teacup in front of Duncan. "Did you have a pleasant flight?" Taka inquired with a twinkle in his eye.

Duncan sipped his green tea.

"Yes, thank you. I am always happy to return to Tokyo, even after so brief an absence."

"An absence filled with many adventures it seems. We have much to discuss, but I do not wish to keep your Los Angeles colleagues waiting. Do you have the number we should call?"

Duncan handed Taka a slip of paper with the number of the conference room where M.D. and Rob were waiting. A moment later, Wada-san had dialed their number and connected them to the conference call.

"Hello, M.D., Rob. This is Duncan." Duncan turned to Taka. "Let me introduce my colleagues, M.D. Corrales and Rob Bingham."

"Good morning, this is Takayama from Aoki in Tokyo. Let me introduce four colleagues of mine who are here today, Emoto, Takei, Wada, and Kimoto. We have received this morning by email the information you so kindly prepared for this meeting, but have not had a chance to review it in detail. Perhaps you could summarize your findings for us?"

As Duncan had asked them to do, Rob and M.D. briefly outlined the reports. When they had finished, the room fell silent.

"Thank you for your presentations, Corrales-san and Bingham-san. We cannot offer any definitive responses at this time. However, we do have two comments." Taka looked over at Wada.

"Hello, this is Wada speaking. First, based upon our preliminary study, we think that your estimate of the possible gain in productivity from using the submarine technology may be too conservative. We estimate that it may be possible to increase productivity as much as twenty times."

Duncan tried to keep his face from betraying any emotion, but he could hear Rob's barely stifled "wahoo" come across the line from Los Angeles. Wada then turned to Kimoto.

"This is Kimoto. Our second comment is the number of opportunities outside of Panama to engage in underwater forestry surprised us. We will continue to study them carefully. Thank you for the valuable information."

"You are most welcome," M.D replied.

"As you know." Taka looked at Duncan. "We must decide by Monday whether to license the technology that would permit us to enter into some cooperation with CESD. Frankly speaking, many at Aoki have been skeptical of the benefits of exercising our option, but this new opportunity may change their opinions. In any event, our team will continue to work today and tomorrow morning and report by Saturday afternoon on their recommendation. Our company's management will meet on Saturday evening to make a final decision."

"Mr. Takayama, this is Rob Bingham," Rob interjected. "I wanted to tell you that Ms. Corrales and I will be available over the weekend. Please do not hesitate to contact us if there is any further information we can provide."

"Thank you." Taka continued, "Now, we know that it is the holiday season in Los Angeles and do not wish to keep you from your families. If we decide to license the technology, then perhaps we can communicate again in early January and arrange for a convenient date to meet in Japan to refine the productivity analysis and conduct a more detailed examination of the top three to five opportunities for exploiting underwater forestry in Asia and Africa."

"We would be delighted to do so, Takayama-san," M.D. said.

"We appreciate very much your consideration of our holiday and look forward to working with you on this project," Rob added.

"Good-bye and Merry Christmas," Taka said.

"M.D. and Rob," Duncan interrupted. "I should be finished here in no more than an hour. Could you hang around until then? I'll call you when I'm free."

"That's fine. Talk with you then," M.D. said.

After Wada clicked the speaker off, Taka instructed Wada and Kimoto on what they needed to accomplish in the next twenty-four hours. He then thanked them for their participation and dismissed them.

"Now." He turned to Duncan. "I wish to discuss our qualification problem in Panama. When we met in Tokyo on Monday, we requested you to ask Ghislaine-san whether she could assist us with our problem. I understand that you discussed this matter with her and traveled to Panama with Corrales-san and Rob

Bingham-san. We received on Wednesday morning here the communication from Panama that you sent on Tuesday afternoon. We were very pleased to read that you had been successful in obtaining a meeting on Wednesday morning with the head of the CFZ administration to discuss our qualification materials. So, you can understand that we were shocked on Thursday morning when you called from Panama to tell us that you had been kidnapped and could not meet with Rodriguez-san. And we were even more surprised to hear you say you strongly suspected our former lawyer may have arranged the kidnapping to prevent you from meeting with Rodriguez-san." Taka paused to drink from his teacup.

"Do you know our Japanese proverb, *kishi kaisei?*" Taka asked. "It means 'wake from death, return to life.' This morning, we awoke from the death of our business in Panama and found that it had returned to life. Emoto reported this morning that the CFZ administration notified us it had received information about possible corruption in the qualification process and, as a result, the process would be reopened in January in order to ensure a fair and transparent result. Did you know this?"

"Yes, I did." Duncan nodded. "I spoke this morning with a friend of mine in the U.S. embassy in Panama who informed me the process had been reopened."

"Do you know how this happened? Were you involved in any way?"

"No, I was not. However, we believe Magdalena Vasquez, whom I told you about when we spoke yesterday, was responsible. Let me explain what my friend told me," Duncan offered. He related to the three Japanese executives what Jed had told him, leaving out the more graphic details of the fight between Salduba and Magdalena.

"So we have this Magdalena-san to thank for our return to life?" Taka asked.

"Yes, I believe so. But she has vanished, so you may have to wait to thank her."

Taka paused for a long time before resuming.

"*Guzen desu ne!* What a coincidence. If Salduba-sensei had not tried to rob you of your meeting with Rodriguez-san, you would never have met Magdalena-san, and if you had never met Magdalena-san, she would never have robbed Salduba-sensei of the evidence that has given us another chance to qualify."

Taka slowly shook his head, still unable to believe his company's good luck. Finally, he turned to Emoto-san.

"If you have no other questions, I think that we have finished our discussion of Panama now. Please return to work. Fate has given us another chance and we must not fail."

Emoto-san rose, briefly bowed to Duncan, and let himself out.

"Well," Taka continued, "our problem in Panama has been solved thanks to Magdalena-san and you, but we still have the question of Bingham International. Although we may now succeed in Panama, I regret that your meeting with Rodriguez-san did not take place as you had hoped. A clear demonstration of the influence of Ghislaine-san in Panama would have helped to persuade our board to support her. Now many will say simply it was luck and not skill."

"Yes, it has been a lucky but also strange series of events," Duncan said and leaned forward on the table. "I had assumed that Salduba acted to protect his Korean client after he received my email telling him that I was coming to Panama. Then I remembered Magdalena had said Salduba was acting not for a Korean client but for an *American* one."

Taka's eyes narrowed. "An American client?"

"Yes. I could think of only one American who would have an interest in preventing us from succeeding. That American would, of course, be Ward Bingham."

Taka turned to Takei-san with a puzzled look on his face.

"But this is irresponsible!" Takei-san exclaimed in a high-pitched voice. "You are insulting Ward-san based on mere speculation."

Taka looked back at Duncan.

"Takei is right. I can understand your suspicion, but our board will not believe claims against Ward-san that you cannot prove."

"But I have proof," responded Duncan as he pulled out from his coat pocket the copy of the bank records and passed it to Taka. He then took out a second sheet of paper and handed it over. Taka looked down at the two documents and then up at Duncan with his eyebrows raised.

"The first document," Duncan explained, "is a copy of a Bingham International bank record showing a transfer on Monday of fifty thousand dollars from a bank account to the Law Offices of Rodrigo Salduba. The second piece of paper is a record from the phone company showing a call from Ward's phone on Monday morning to Salduba's number in Panama. So, we know that Ward paid Salduba fifty thousand dollars after calling him Monday."

"But Ward-san could have called Salduba-san for many reasons," Takei-san interrupted. "Perhaps he wanted him to do some legal work for the company in Panama."

"Yes," Taka said slowly as he considered the situation. "Takei must be right. You did not arrive in Los Angeles until after Ward-san made his call. So, it was not possible for Ward-san to know on Monday morning of your trip to Panama."

"Yes, that is what I thought too until I saw this." Duncan removed the last piece of paper from his pocket and handed it to Taka. "This is a record of a call made by Ward around two a.m.

Monday, which would have been Monday late afternoon in To-kyo, *after* our meeting. It's a Japanese cell phone number. Do you recognize it by any chance?"

Taka looked at the number and flushed. He turned slowly to Takei-san and passed him the piece of paper. The Japanese execu-tive's hand quivered as he examined the phone record.

"This is my cell phone number," Takei-san admitted, "but it is not what you suspect. Ward-san called me to discuss the upcom-ing board meeting and his desire that the board approve the pur-chase of the shares held by Robert Bingham's estate. Naturally, I only listened and did not say anything about our meeting on Monday or about Panama."

Duncan stared at Takei-san.

"So it was just a coincidence that Ward called you, in the mid-dle of the night, to discuss the upcoming board meeting when you had learned hours earlier about my trip to Panama? And it was just a coincidence that a few hours later Ward called *your* lawyer, Rodrigo Salduba, and wired him fifty thousand dollars?"

Takei-san jumped up and shouted, "Remember, *I* did not call Ward-san, *he* called me and he could not have known *anything* about our meeting. Besides, Salduba-sensei is a well-known law-yer in Panama. Ward-san could have contacted him about CESD or some other investment."

Takei-san turned to face Taka.

"Takayama-san, if you do not believe me, I cannot continue at Aoki and must resign immediately."

Taka glowered at Takei-san.

"*Tsukue e modotte, matte kure!*" he barked.

Takei-san bowed stiffly and left.

When the door had closed behind Takei-san, Duncan turned to Taka.

"Forgive me, but I don't understand. You don't believe him, do you? And, after what he's done, why didn't you accept his resignation?"

"No, I don't believe Takei." Taka sighed, shaking his head slowly. "Still, I cannot allow him to resign without proof of his inappropriate conduct. Anyway, leaving the company is too good for him. I will speak with our director of personnel and arrange to send him to a truly intolerable location. We have an office in Sudan that might suffice."

Taka gazed down at the conference table in front of him for a moment and then looked up at Duncan.

"I must apologize for Takei. His misconduct caused your colleagues and you great trouble."

"With respect, let me remind you that *Ward* was the one who actually contacted Salduba and paid him to sabotage Aoki's qualification. And since he used company funds to pay Salduba, Aoki actually contributed ten thousand dollars to Ward's scheme to damage Aoki's own project."

"Yes, I know." Taka sighed. "We know now we cannot trust Ward-san. On the other hand, even if we support Ghislaine-san, he will remain a major shareholder and will continue to make trouble for her, for the company, and for us. You have shown us for the first time that Bingham can provide good opportunities to Aoki, but Bingham is also a big risk. In my opinion, the company needs both Ghislaine-san's vision and Ward-san's energy to succeed. But left alone, they will continue to fight each other and as a consequence the company will fail."

Duncan contemplated what Taka had said. Ghislaine and Ward would never be friends, but they might stop fighting if they had roughly equal power in the company and, more important, could be convinced that feuding posed a greater risk to their interests than entering into an uneasy truce. The two men looked across the table at each other. Several more seconds passed before Duncan spoke.

"I have an idea for your consideration. Here is what I propose," Duncan said.

As Duncan explained his idea, Taka's eyes grew large as lanterns. When Duncan finished, Taka leaned forward and slapped both hands on the table.

"Let me discuss your proposal with my board. If they approve of your strategy, I will contact Ghislaine-san and Ward-san, as you suggest."

Taka rubbed his hands together and laughed. The two men rose and bowed slightly to each other. As Duncan stepped in front of Taka and out the door, Taka clapped him on the back.

"Have a safe trip back to Los Angeles, Duncan-san! Merry Christmas. Merry Christmas!"

Once again, Duncan headed to Narita Airport in an Aoki limousine. He asked the driver if he could make a call to the United States from the car phone and was soon connected to M.D. and Rob. He relayed all that had happened during the meeting with Taka and his colleagues, leaving out the discussion at the end about the future of Bingham International.

"Then I can tell Ghislaine the Japanese cell phone number was Mr. Takei's?" M.D. asked.

"Yes, you can tell her that, but you should remind her that Takei-san denied Ward had called about Panama. You also need to point out that the payment made to Salduba was supported by an invoice for legal services. As much as my gut tells me Ward knew about Aoki and Salduba, we don't have any *definitive* evidence that Takei-san told him about my meeting with Aoki or that Ward retained Salduba to obstruct our efforts. You should also tell her Takayama-san will not present circumstantial evidence to his board, even though he is suspicious. The bottom line is he will consider everything we've told him, consult with his board, and inform us sometime over the weekend if Aoki wants to partner with CESD and if they will support Ghislaine against Ward. You might also tell her I advise against saying anything to Ward until I get back and we can map out a plan of action."

"I will tell her, but I can't guarantee she'll listen once she hears that Ward contacted both Takei and Salduba. I think she'll explode," M.D. warned.

Duncan felt the adrenaline of the last twenty-four hours flow from his body.

"I understand," Duncan said in a hoarse voice laden with fatigue. "I'm just giving advice. I don't always expect clients to follow it."

"I hope you get some sleep on the plane," Rob chimed in. "We'll be in touch once we know of Aoki's decisions."

"Thanks," Duncan said. "Whatever the outcome, it's been great working with you two these past few days."

"We feel the same way," said M.D. "Take care. Travel safely."

SIXTY-SEVEN

....

THURSDAY, DECEMBER 23
LOS ANGELES

Rob disconnected the speaker and stood up from the small table in the conference room where they had worked the past day. M.D. packed up her briefcase as Rob zipped up his backpack. They grabbed their roll-ons and walked to the door.

"If I weren't so exhausted, I'd invite you to dinner tonight to thank you for everything you've done," Rob said just as they reached the door. M.D. turned, looked up at his face, and smiled.

"Thanks, but I'm pretty tired, too, and I still have to call Ghislaine." She paused when she saw a cloud pass over Rob's face and added, "Perhaps you'd give me a rain check sometime?"

"Of course," Rob beamed. "Anytime you want."

They walked in silence to the taxi stand, the sound of cars speeding along Century Boulevard roaring in the background.

"Why don't I drop you?" Rob asked. "It's . . . it's on my way."

M.D. hesitated a second before she accepted, "I'd like that. Thank you."

As they rode to her condominium in Santa Monica, M.D. remembered the conversation she had with Ghislaine about Rob's lack of reaction to his father's death. After all that had happened between them, she felt she should say something to Rob, even if it betrayed Ghislaine's confidence.

"Rob, could I share something with you that Ghislaine discussed with me, but only on the condition you won't tell her?"

"Sure. You have my word."

"Okay," M.D. said. She looked down at the space between them and continued. "Ghislaine is worried about you. She thinks you feel guilty that you were estranged from your father when he died, that you regret deeply you didn't have a chance to reconcile with him and now never will," she ventured. "She's concerned that your remorse might lead you to, well, ignore risks that could result in your getting hurt skiing or kite-boarding or even in Panama. And she may be right to worry; after all, you did risk your life to rescue the diver, and you threw yourself between that Panamanian kidnapper and me."

Rob turned and faced M.D., his soft eyes crinkling in bemusement.

"Thanks for telling me. I know my mother is worried, but what she doesn't know is that I spoke with my father at least once a day after they separated. I didn't try to hide that from my mother, but I saw no reason to talk about it either, and she never brought it up. My relationship with my father was always a little strange; he was in his fifties and sixties when I was growing up. He treated me more like a grandfather would than a dad. But I always felt close to him. When he moved out, I wasn't angry, though I had a difficult time understanding the choice he made. I just thought I couldn't condemn him outright without knowing everything about his relationship with my mother and, I have to say, I knew very little."

Rob hesitated. "I don't think any child can ever know enough to pass judgment on how their parents act toward each other, as much as the child may want to."

M.D. stared into Rob's eyes and then out the window at the coral trees on San Vicente Boulevard. Ghislaine had completely misunderstood Rob's reaction to his father's leaving her. If a mother as devoted as Ghislaine could misjudge her son's feelings, perhaps Rob was right. No child could possibly understand a father or mother—let alone their interactions—sufficiently to judge them. Was it time, she wondered, to speak with her mother about her father, maybe even to contact him? As soon as she asked herself that question, another thought burst into her mind, an idea that terrified and captivated her at the same time, like the churning surf she had gaped at as a young girl from the safety of the sand. If she might consider letting her father back into her life, could she imagine allowing a man into her heart?

As the taxi pulled up at her apartment at the corner of Third and San Vicente, M.D. found the air between Rob and her had suddenly thinned. She couldn't breathe. Throwing open the door, she put her feet on the curb, ducked her head out, and gulped down the fresh air. Feeling better and embarrassed that she might have appeared to be running from the car, she abruptly twisted around, leaning back with her left hand to squeeze his shoulder. Contorted, half out of the car and half in, she doubted she could have made the moment any more awkward if she had tried.

Rob, however, didn't take his eyes off her hand. He gazed at it, started to cover her fingers with his, and then stopped.

"As for why I protected you in Panama," he said, locking his eyes on hers. "You know, well, there are emotions other than guilt."

"I know," M.D. murmured, feeling slightly lightheaded.

"Good. Merry Christmas, M.D."

"Merry Christmas to you." She returned his smile and then dropped her eyes from his gaze.

"I better unwind myself before I hurt my back," she called over her shoulder as she stepped out of the cab. "Oh, and if you want to enjoy the holiday, you might want to stay clear of Ghislaine for a while. Once I tell her everything we've learned, I think she'll detonate like a nuclear bomb."

....

SIXTY-EIGHT

FRIDAY, DECEMBER 24
LOS ANGELES

G hislaine had listened without comment to M.D.'s report late Thursday evening. When M.D. finished, Ghislaine had thanked her, told her to take Friday off, and wished her a joyous holiday season with her mother. As soon as M.D. ended the call, however, Ghislaine had slammed her BlackBerry down on the desk and paced around her home office.

Her young colleague's detailed description of what had happened in Panama, of the conference call with Aoki, and the information in the bank and phone records had infuriated her. The canceled pledge to Children's Charity? Ward. The delay in the Gulf deal? Ward! The unforgiveable treatment of Azra. *Ward!* The kidnapping in Panama. *WARD!* She had angrily dismissed Duncan's caution that there was no proof Ward had tried to frustrate her attempt to assist Aoki. Her instincts had already judged and sentenced her stepson. For the remainder of Thursday night, she had considered how she should act and what she would say to Ward the following day. Buoyed by her success on Wednesday in creating a plan to present to Aoki and her resolve in ordering Duncan to implement it, confidence had flowed into her veins.

She had decided to put all pretense aside. She would play herself on Friday, an enraged and commanding Ghislaine Bingham.

But on Friday morning, she woke before dawn feeling drained. The tide of certainty of the previous night had ebbed. Doubt filled her mind as the early morning light began to flood her room. All she had done Wednesday was extend someone else's strategy to a logical conclusion and insist that it be executed or else. Today she would have to leave the command bunker and fight hand to hand in the trenches. She needed strength. Even though it had only been a couple of weeks since her last one, she craved a shot of her red vitamin.

She'd started injecting herself when Robert had insisted she lose weight after her pregnancy with Rob, which had left her a few pounds overweight. Though the weight fell away quickly, Ghislaine discovered that she loved the way the shots seemed to keep her invigorated. For more than two decades, she had been injecting herself each month. She kept the practice secret, not from the sense she was doing something wrong—she knew the red vitamin was perfectly legal—but she didn't want Rob to worry she had become addicted to the feeling the shot gave her.

Rising and walking over to her bathroom, Ghislaine pulled open the bottom drawer below the sink, removed a half dozen olive-green hand towels, and took out a locked steel-and-plastic box. Placing the container on the granite next to her sink, she dialed the combination on the small tumbler lock in front and lifted its lid. Then she washed and dried her hands thoroughly and extracted from the container two alcohol swabs, a ten milliliter vial of cobalamin, and a packaged sterile syringe. She carefully wiped the top of the vial with the first alcohol swab. After unwrapping the sterile syringe, she removed the plastic cover from the needle and inserted the needle into the vial. When she'd pulled out slightly more than one milliliter of the scarlet liquid, she tapped the syringe to make sure all the air bubbles were gone, adjusted the plunger so exactly one milliliter remained, and withdrew the needle from the vial. Sitting on the side of her bathtub, she sterilized a portion of her upper thigh with the second alcohol swab. After the alcohol had dried, she pinched the sterilized area of her thigh muscle together so that it made a small mound of flesh and plunged the needle into the middle of it using the same motion she would have used to throw a dart. Having inserted the needle, she injected the liquid vitamin B12 slowly. When she had finished, she flipped the safety cap over the needle and tossed the syringe into a blue plastic sharps container in her lower drawer. She took a deep breath. Although she knew that the cobalamin couldn't possibly have any effect so soon, she nonetheless felt stronger and more alert already.

After showering, she donned her huge white terry-cloth robe and nibbled on the Mexican strawberries and granola that Inez had bought the day before at the Century City farmers' market. She knew it was Christmas Eve day and that the office would close just after lunch. Nevertheless, she was certain that Ward would continue to work into the afternoon. She decided to wait until two thirty to arrive at the office. At two fifteen, she descended from her bedroom in one of her favorite outfits, a Donna Karan black lightweight wool pants and jacket ensemble and a tailored, white cotton blouse. She wore her Tahitian black pearl necklace and matching earrings and carried her Italian black leather briefcase. Dressing well helped to quiet the anxiety brooding within her.

Fifteen minutes later, Ghislaine strode back to Robert's old office to find Ward. Elaine glanced up as Ghislaine marched past her desk. "Wait, Ghislaine, Ward's on the phone," she warned, but Ghislaine waved her off with a flip of her wrist. Without knocking, she opened Ward's door, stepped into his office, and closed the door behind her.

Ward looked up at Ghislaine. Maintaining eye contact with her, he said evenly into the phone, "Look, George, something's just come up. I'll have to call you back on Monday. Yes, I understand. Talk with you then. Happy Holidays, George."

"Hello, Ward. How are you?" Ghislaine said as she leaned against the door.

"I'm not bad. How are you? You seem much better than when we met last."

"Do you mind if I sit there?" Ghislaine asked as she pointed to one of the two sleek office chairs resting in front of Ward's desk.

"Well, actually, I'd love to catch up but it's Christmas Eve and I have plans with some friends. Can this wait until Monday?"

"No, it can't wait until Monday," she snapped and sat down. Looking directly into his eyes, she continued, "I've come to ask you to resign."

"Resign?" Ward sputtered and lurched forward in his chair. "You *must* be joking. I control this company now. I can't believe you still harbor some illusion the company is yours. "

"I'm not here to quarrel with you about Robert's estate. Our lawyers will deal with that. I'm here to ask you why you hired Rodrigo Salduba to obstruct Aoki's qualification in Panama and, in the process, had Rob, M.D., and our lawyer kidnapped?"

Ward's eyes narrowed, but his face remained impassive.

"Don't be absurd," he replied after a moment. "You've been under a lot of stress the past few weeks. You're clearly out of your depth. You should leave now before you embarrass yourself any further."

Embarrass *myself,* Ghislaine fumed. We'll see who's embarrassing whom.

"Do you deny calling Mr. Takei around two a.m. Monday just after his meeting with my lawyer where Takayama-san asked for my help in solving their problem in Panama? Do you not admit calling Rodrigo Salduba later on Monday morning and sending him fifty thousand dollars to ensure our plan to help Aoki would fail? *Come on,* Ward," she growled. "It's time to stop pretending. You've undercut the company's relationship with our partner Aoki and committed a crime by asking Salduba to bribe a government official and stage a kidnapping. You've not only embarrassed yourself, you've endangered the company that Robert and I built!"

Ward gazed at Ghislaine's face, normally alabaster-white and satin-like, but now taut and flushed with fury.

"I don't know what you mean," he replied calmly as he massaged the back of his neck. "Yes, I called Mr. Takei early in the morning on Monday, but I was jet lagged and he's our Aoki liaison. I talk with him at least once a week. Yes, I phoned a lawyer by the name of Rodrigo Salduba later on Monday morning, but he's a well-known Panamanian attorney and I needed some advice concerning our investment in CESD. And, as you have undoubtedly learned, lawyers don't work for free so, yes, I wired Salduba fifty thousand as a retainer, for which he sent me an invoice. If you'd care to check with accounting, I'm sure they have it on file. I fail to see how any of that hurts my relationship with Aoki or amounts to criminal behavior. I've heard nothing from Takayama-san about any of this, and he would certainly have called me if he were concerned."

The depth of the deception momentarily stunned Ghislaine; then she lashed out.

"It's Judah, isn't it?" she growled.

"*What* did you call me?"

"Your Hebrew name. Judah. Robert told me years ago. It fits doesn't it? So jealous of your younger half brother, you arrange to have him kidnapped and lie brazenly about your crime. Don't you know your Old Testament?"

"You fucking Belgian anti-Semite!"

"I'm not the one who could never stop talking about how much he loved his Catholic boarding school and WASP fraternity, who hid his mother's heritage his entire life," Ghislaine retorted. Ward flushed and stood up, banging his fist on the table.

"Get out!" he bellowed. Ghislaine rose from her chair and leaned forward, pointing at Ward.

"If you don't resign, I'll . . . I'll go to the government. You'll be investigated and charged. You have a choice: resign now or face an investigation!"

"Ghislaine," Ward responded in a menacing tone, "I've answered your ridiculous, in fact, slanderous questions. If you wish to go to what you call 'the government,' please do so by all means. You have no evidence to support your wild claims because none exists and, even if it did, you would soon realize that any investigation would damage the company as much or more than me. And now," Ward said as he walked over to open the door to his office, "leave or I'll call security and have you escorted out in front of the entire office."

Ghislaine felt the blood drain from her face and her shoulders slump. She immediately straightened herself and stood to face Ward.

"This is not the end. I promise you that," she warned.

"You're right about that, at least," Ward retorted. "I've decided to move up the board meeting to consider my proposal for the buyback of all of the estate's shares. I'll send out a notice later today. The meeting is now scheduled for Monday afternoon at five o'clock. Today is not the end, Ghislaine, but Monday will be. I'll expect you to have cleaned out your office by the end of the year. Good-bye and Merry Christmas."

Ghislaine turned to leave but stopped just before the door.

"You may not care about risking the reputation of this firm," she hissed back at Ward, "but I do. Our name is why clients give us their money to invest and why our partners agree to the investments we make in their companies. Our reputation is everything and the people who work here depend upon us to protect it. You are so sure that Aoki will support you. Aoki may be a Japanese company uncomfortable with the notion of a woman running Bingham International, but it is also a Japanese company that prizes teamwork, trust, and tradition. I represent those values. Go ahead. Call the meeting for Monday. I can't wait to see your face when I win. And when I do, *that* will be my Merry Christmas *and* my Happy New Year."

A half hour later, Ghislaine stood in front of the desk in her office at home. Ward had lied boldly and well, she had to admit. She had labored for years to build the company. She couldn't believe that her future, the legacy she wanted desperately to leave to her son, depended on the whim of a Japanese businessman whom she barely knew. Did Takayama-san really value teamwork, trust, and tradition? She hadn't a clue and she detested the feeling of helplessness mounting in her chest.

Stop! She heard her maman shout. *You are not impotent. You are only as vulnerable as you allow yourself to be.* Yes, her maman was right. She still had time. She needed a plan to win Takayama-san's support. Standing before her pine desk, she asked herself, what did the Japanese want out of Bingham? She felt certain Takayama-san had to be worried enough about Ward to want someone at the company who could stand up to him. She knew that she could rein him in if she were given the chance. But Takayama-san and a group of gray-haired Japanese businessmen would never consider her capable of controlling Ward. She needed a man on her side, someone whom Takayama-san trusted and she could rely on. Rob would be perfect, but the Japanese would consider his youth as much a disadvantage as her sex. Who else? Takayama-san respected Duncan Luke. To be sure, Luke had refused her once before when she had asked him to use his influence with Takayama-san. But this time, she would not be asking him to influence anyone. She would be offering him a job.

SIXTY-NINE

....

FRIDAY, DECEMBER 24
LOS ANGELES

Duncan's plane landed three hours before Ghislaine walked into Ward's office. He had slept almost the entire trip, not able to stay awake for even a sip of Courvoisier. After an hour wait to pass through immigration and customs, he climbed into a taxi to take him home. As he checked his BlackBerry, he felt his muscles grow taut anticipating a deluge of messages from Ghislaine. His shoulders relaxed. No one from BIG had tried to contact him. There was nothing to be done anyway, he thought. Everything was in Taka's hands.

Duncan paid the taxi driver and climbed the staircase to his apartment. Once inside, he set his roll-on and briefcase down just inside the door. He sniffed the stale air and opened a couple of the windows facing the beach. Brisk, salty air streamed in. The corner of his eye caught sight of the Yokohama Baystars baseball cap he had bought for Sam hanging on the doorknob. Had it been only two weeks since Gracie had locked him out and Sam had run screaming from his embrace? Only two days since Magdalena had disappeared? He began to heave with sobs at so much loss in so little time. After a few minutes, he quieted himself and grabbed a blanket from his bed. Lying down on the couch, he wrapped himself in the blanket and closed his eyes. Wondering when he'd see his son again and worrying about Magdalena, he fell fast asleep.

The ring of his BlackBerry woke him around four in the afternoon. He didn't recognize the number on his screen and touched the answer button. Ghislaine Bingham's smoky voice filled his ears.

"Hello, Duncan. I hope that I haven't disturbed you. Did you have a good flight back?"

"Yes, thank you," he responded hoarsely. After a slight hesitation, he rushed to explain, "I didn't call you because M.D. told me that she would give you a full report last night."

"Oh, she did, she did," Ghislaine assured him. "I wanted to thank you for everything you've done for the company and me. You've been extraordinary."

Duncan sat up on the couch and looked down at his phone. Was this the same woman who, for ten days, had been treating him like a day laborer whom she could chew out at will?

"That's very kind of you to say. I hope that we'll have good news in a day or so from Takayama-san. If we do, I still want to discuss that bonus with you."

"Well, yes, of course. I'm always happy to listen. In the meantime, another issue has come up that I'd like to discuss with you. Could I take you to dinner tonight?"

After nearly two weeks of eating on planes and hotels, he didn't feel like going out, but the change in Ghislaine's tone piqued his curiosity.

"That's a wonderful offer, but I've been gone for almost ten days in a row and would really like to cook at home. Besides, it's Christmas Eve. You must have a dinner or a party to go to, don't you?"

"I do have a party later tonight and I'm not much of a cook, but if you tell me what you're making, I'll bring a bottle of wine and we can talk over an early dinner. How would that be?"

"Well, that would be fine. I hadn't given much thought to dinner, but something light would be good, I think. How about a mushroom risotto and a wild arugula and roasted red pepper salad?"

"That sounds delicious. Would six o'clock be convenient?"

"Yes, that would be great. See you then."

Duncan spent the next hour and a half cleaning himself and the apartment and running down to the local market to buy what he needed for dinner. Spurred on by the sparkling sunlight of a cool but cloudless December day, he felt less weary, and the jet lag gradually released its grip on his mind.

Just after six o'clock in the evening, Duncan heard someone mount the outside stairway. He opened his front door to find Ghislaine Bingham shivering in a long gray coat and holding a bottle of red wine with hands gloved in brown leather.

"I'd forgotten how cold it can get by the sea," she said, stepping into the apartment. "Here," she handed the wine to Duncan. "It's a Zinfandel from Sonoma. I thought it would go well with the risotto. Oh, I can smell the red peppers." She inhaled. "You must have roasted them yourself. Where did you learn to cook?"

Duncan hesitated. The truth was, his brother was too young and his father too distracted to cook when his mother deserted the family, so Duncan taught himself and gradually came to enjoy it. But he had no intention of sharing his private life with Ghislaine Bingham.

"Oh, here and there, a lot in law school," he half lied. "I found cooking a great distraction from all the reading. Anyway, roasting the peppers is easy to do and they actually taste like red peppers, unlike the mush that's been stewing in a jar for months," he said. "Here, let me take your coat."

When Ghislaine removed the jacket, Duncan saw that she was dressed in a black wool- and-satin cocktail dress and wore a multi-strand white pearl necklace and white pearl earrings. She looked gorgeous. He shrugged off the feeling that he was underdressed in his blue polo shirt and brown chinos. While Ghislaine wandered over to the large windows, he hung her coat in the closet. She gazed out over the broad Playa del Rey beach and to the ocean beyond.

"Shall I open the wine now?" he asked. "I thought we might discuss the issue you mentioned before dinner."

"That's a wonderful idea," she said. "You have a spectacular view, by the way."

Duncan went into the kitchen and returned with a corkscrew and two wineglasses, which he placed on the small dining table behind the couch. He opened the wine and, as he was about to serve Ghislaine, she called over from the windows, "Only a mouthful for me, please." Duncan poured a splash of the black-cherry liquid into her glass and filled his more than halfway. He walked over to the windows, handed Ghislaine her glass, and touched his lightly against hers.

"Here's to a favorable response from Takayama-san," he toasted.

"Yes," she replied, "to a favorable response."

Ghislaine quickly swirled the wine around the tulip-shaped glass. Then, in one continuous motion, she poured the liquid into her mouth, allowed the wine to run over and around her tongue, and spat the wine out into the glass.

"I'm sorry," she apologized. "I love the sight, smell and taste of wine, but I can't drink even a little of it without feeling intoxicated and becoming silly."

"No need to apologize," Duncan said. "But I happen to like feeling silly once in a while. I hope you won't mind if I enjoy the wine."

"Not at all," she replied as she placed her glass down on the tiny coffee table. "Shall we talk about Bingham now?"

"Sure," he said and emptied his glass. He lifted the bottle and served himself more of the wine.

"I met with Ward today," she began. Duncan's heart sank, but he remained silent, staring into his wine. "I asked him to do the right thing for himself and for the company."

"Which was?" Duncan murmured.

"To resign, of course. Don't you think what he's done is enough reason for him to leave the company?"

Duncan could see from the flash in Ghislaine's eyes that she didn't expect disagreement, but he could hardly imagine doing anything more stupid than asking Ward to resign before it was beyond dispute that he would have no choice.

"I don't believe it matters what I think now," he said and swallowed another mouthful of Zin. He felt the warmth of the wine course through his veins. "What did he say?"

"He refused and practically dared me to go to the police, knowing that I couldn't risk the damage to the company's reputation. He is completely without scruples," Ghislaine vented, whipping her hand through the air. "Even if Aoki supports me and I become CEO, I'm terribly afraid for the future of the company. Ward will still be a significant shareholder. He won't listen to me, of course. He's a loose cannon. The company needs someone to keep an eye on him so that he doesn't sink the ship."

"Do you have anyone in mind?" Duncan inquired as he swirled the wine in his glass and marveled at its brilliant ruby hue. He wondered whether this Zinfandel was produced from the small clusters of grapes grown on the gnarled, arthritic-looking old vines planted by pioneers as many as a hundred years ago. What would life have been like in California back then?

"As a matter of fact, I do," Ghislaine said with a smile, and then she frowned.

"Duncan. *Duncan*. Are you with me?"

"Sorry, just enjoying the wine. Yes, I'm with you."

"Good. I was saying that I do have someone in mind to watch over Ward. You're trusted by Aoki and, although I had my doubts at first, I see now you're tough enough to stand up to Ward. Rob obviously likes and respects you and, of course, you'd have my support. I want you to be my compliance officer."

"I see." Duncan sighed as he walked over and slumped down on the Naugahyde couch. After a few seconds had passed, he rubbed his chin.

Clearing his throat, he said, "I understand the risk that Ward poses. But I have no desire to be his babysitter. Besides, he's not the only one who would need watching. What about you? You made a fifty thousand dollar contribution to a charity run by the wife of the Vice President of Panama."

Ghislaine's eyes grew cold and she took a few steps toward Duncan.

"I don't see what that has to do with anything. We make contributions to all kinds of charities."

"Yes, I'm sure you do," Duncan declared, as he put his feet on the small table in front of the couch. "And I'm also sure it was a coincidence this particular grant was made just before the Canal Authority awarded CESD the concession to harvest timber from the canal."

Duncan took a gulp of his wine.

"Look, I'm not saying you intended to corrupt anyone, but you exposed the company and yourself to a bribery claim. More important, why was it left to me, an outsider, to organize the gathering and analysis of information that may well create a valuable opportunity for both companies?"

When Ghislaine looked away, Duncan added, "I have no desire to be employed as a compliance officer. I would, however, consider a role that would not just protect the pie, but grow it as well."

"And what role would that be?"

"I would consider an appointment by the board as a consultant who would oversee the gathering of intelligence relevant to the company's business, as well as the analysis and interpretation of that intelligence both to manage risk and to create competitive advantages. Although I would agree to work exclusively for Bingham, I would not be an employee and would report only to the board."

"You mean you want to be our sword and shield, our KGB?" Ghislaine snorted. "I've never heard of such a thing."

"I'd prefer to think of myself as your business intelligence officer. You'd be surprised how many large companies have a significant number of people charged with exactly that function. Oh, you're right, the role I'm describing is most often spread out over several departments, you know, legal, compliance, government relations, business development, and the like. The problem with multiple people filling these roles is they become territorial, and information that needs to be shared is held in separate silos, undermining the whole objective. But a small organization like Bingham International can avoid that pitfall, especially if the business intelligence function focuses only on the areas of greatest risk and most likely competitive advantage for the company."

Ghislaine took a few steps back toward the windows and then pivoted to face Duncan, hands laced together in front of her. "And what do intelligence officers receive in compensation, may I ask?"

"I don't know what others receive, but I would expect no less than two hundred and fifty thousand, plus bonus opportunity, at the board's discretion, of course."

"But it's *absurd*," she exclaimed with a wave of her hand. "A consultant who is paid like an executive vice president? What value do you add? What opportunities will you create? I was under the impression that I was still executive vice president for business development. What makes you think we need a business intelligence officer as well?"

"Oh, you need one. You can bank on that. Bingham International has succeeded because it was one of the first firms to focus on emerging markets. Those countries often do present great opportunities, but they're not Switzerland. Investing in emerging markets carries enormous legal, regulatory, reputational, and financial risk as well as a business environment in which the right information at the right time can legally create competitive advantages."

"But this is not at all what I intended," Ghislaine blurted out. "I don't need you to develop strategy for my company or watch over me, I need you to help me win Aoki's trust and keep Ward from ruining the company's reputation. Look, I can't offer you two-fifty, but I could see a salary of a hundred and twenty-five thousand plus bonus, *if* you're successful in checking Ward."

Duncan downed the wine in his glass and looked up.

"No thanks, but I would still like to talk about my bonus for helping you with Takayama-san, assuming, that is, he supports you."

"You've got to be joking!" she exclaimed. "Well, this has been a *most* informative discussion. I'm afraid I've lost my appetite. Could you get my coat for me?"

Without waiting for Duncan to respond, Ghislaine stomped over to the door and tapped her foot as she waited for Duncan to get her coat from the closet. When he had handed it over to her, she threw it over her shoulders and opened the door. A chilly ocean breeze flooded into the apartment.

"It's been an unforgettable experience," she called over her shoulder as she marched out.

"For me, too," Duncan replied with a smile. Then under his breath, "I would give anything to see your face when you look under your tree tomorrow morning."

He closed the door behind her, moved to the kitchen, took out a small pot, and poured in a tablespoon of olive oil. After finely dicing half a white onion, he turned on the gas flame under the pot and, when the oil was shiny, he scraped the onions in. They sizzled and gave off a slightly acidic scent. After they had softened a little, he sliced up two small Portobello mushrooms and added them to the onions with a pinch of salt and dried oregano. Then he poured a cup of chicken stock into a glass measuring cup and heated it in the microwave. When the onions and mushrooms were soft but not mushy, he scraped them into a bowl, leaving a patina of oil and mushroom drippings in the pot. He measured out a half-cup of Arborio rice and added it to the drippings, stirring to coat the rice completely. When the rice became translucent, he poured the onion-mushroom mixture back to the pot. Adding a quarter-cup of the hot chicken stock to the rice mixture, he stirred until almost all of the liquid had evaporated. He repeated that step twice more, and the rice grew creamy. With the last quarter-cup, he added a little more salt and pepper and a few strands of saffron. When the rice had absorbed the last of the chicken stock, he added a little shaved Parmesan into the risotto along with a lump of butter. Duncan spooned the finished rice into the bowl that had held the onions and mushrooms to absorb the last bit of their flavor. He lumped a handful of wild arugula on a small salad plate and laced over the greens several bright red ribbons of the red pepper he had roasted and marinated in lemon juice, olive oil, and salt.

Satisfied, Duncan switched all but one of the kitchen lights off. He carried the risotto and the salad over to the table and sat down in the seat he had intended for Ghislaine, the one looking out toward the Pacific. He filled his wineglass to the brim with the rest of the Zinfandel and lit the single candle. After wishing the empty chair beside him a Merry Christmas, he tasted the steaming risotto. The rice grains were still firm and the Portobello mushrooms tasted smoky and sweet. The dry, slightly peppery wine offset the creamy saltiness of the risotto. How odd, he mused, that two such different tastes and textures could complement each other so well.

SEVENTY

....

SATURDAY, DECEMBER 25
LOS ANGELES

Duncan wanted to sleep late on Christmas Day, but memories of past Christmases with Sam and worries over how Magdalena might be spending the holiday kept intruding. Crawling out of bed at nine, he switched on the coffee maker and poured a glass of grapefruit juice. A glance out the front windows told him that the cold, blustery weather of Christmas Eve had blown itself out, allowing a dense fog to creep in. He punched on his BlackBerry but saw that wireless service at the beach was failing him again. Yawning, he turned on his laptop so he could check his emails and access *The New York Times*. As the computer started up, he switched on the KCRW Christmas morning broadcast of holiday songs. A rendition of "God Rest Ye Merry Gentlemen" summoned to his mind the image of his father singing the carol to his brother, Alistair, and him when they were boys in Santa Monica. Ali! He hadn't spoken with his younger brother for at least a month and, of course, the workaholic, reclusive Ali hadn't called him. His brother taught some esoteric math class up at Stanford now and rarely surfaced. Ali didn't answer his cell phone, so Duncan left a message wishing him a Merry

Christmas and promising that he'd be in touch again before the New Year.

When he returned to his computer, he found an urgent email from Taka to Ghislaine and Ward at the top of the email inbox. Taka had entitled the email "The Future of Bingham International." Duncan was bcc'd. He grinned as he read that Aoki had decided to license the submarine technology and partner with CESD and that Aoki, concerned about the future of Bingham International, was proposing a settlement of the dispute between Ghislaine and Ward which, if either did not accept, would result in Aoki's being forced, with regret, to support the other person's position.

Wearing a black unitard and sipping a café au lait, Ghislaine sat in her office at home reading Takayama-san's email. When she saw that Aoki had declined to approve Ward's proposal to buy back Robert's stock for six million dollars, she thrust her fist into the air and exclaimed, "*Mais, oui! On a gagne après tout.*" However, as she continued to read, she unraveled her fist and lowered her hand to cover her mouth. "*Espece de con,*" she murmured through her fingers.

"Our proposal is that the sixty shares of the estate of Robert Bingham be divided into two groups of thirty shares each," Aoki wrote. "The first thirty shares will be considered as separate property and divided equally between his two sons. To avoid the disruption a battle over valuation would bring, the second thirty shares will be allocated to Ghislaine Bingham in proportion to the number of years of her marriage to Robert over the total number of years since Robert founded the company. The balance will be divided by Robert's two sons. The resulting shareholdings will be: Ward Bingham, 40.625 shares; Aoki Co., Ltd., 20 shares; Rob Bingham, 20.625 shares; and, Ghislaine Bingham, 18.750 shares.

416

Ghislaine Bingham will serve as chairperson and Ward Bingham as president."

Ward Bingham bellowed, *"Fuck. Fuck. Fuck,"* as he reviewed the Aoki email on his cell phone. But when he read further that Aoki was insisting Duncan Luke be retained by the board as director of a newly created Bingham Intelligence Group at a fee of $250,000 per year plus bonus, he flung his BlackBerry against the living room wall, shattering the outside case.

By the time Duncan had finished the Aoki memo, two other urgent messages had landed in his mailbox. The first was from Ghislaine to Aoki with a copy to Ward. She wrote: "Your proposal is most welcome and farsighted. I agree and look forward to our company's benefitting from the services of the Bingham Intelligence Group, which I propose we henceforth refer to as BIG. Ghislaine Bingham." The second, sent a few minutes later, was from Ward Bingham to Aoki with a copy to Ghislaine. It read only: "Agreed. Ward Bingham."

Duncan got up from his computer and stretched, grimacing at the pain from the beating in Panama that still throbbed in his ribs. He frothed some warm milk in a mug, poured strong black coffee through the white foam, and sprinkled chili powder and cinnamon on top for bite and aroma. Just as he took his first sip, his cell phone rang. It was Jenny Rice, Sam's therapist. His heart began to beat wildly. He punched the button to answer.

"Hello, Duncan?" Jenny greeted him in her high-pitched Boston accent. "This is Jenny Rice. Sam's therapist. We met once before. I'm sorry to trouble you on Christmas Day, but I'm going out of town later today and wanted to catch you before I left."

"Of course, of course," Duncan gasped. "Is Sam okay?"

"Well, I think you know he's had some tough moments recently. Anyway, I called Sam yesterday to wish him a Merry Christmas. He sounded good; in fact, much better than just a few days before. I think the trip to visit his grandparents has been helpful. In any event, at the end of our short talk, he asked, 'Do you know where my dad is?' I told him that I did and I asked him whether he was ready to see you again. He said he wasn't sure, but he thought he would be soon. He murmured something about how everyone makes mistakes, even Kobe Bryant, whom I believe is a basketball player? I thought the statement demonstrated some real progress in cognitive development. Anyway, as you know, that's about as positive a statement as Sam is able to make right now."

Duncan struggled to speak through the lump growing in his throat and could only manage a husky, "Yes, I know."

"I understand that this is good news for you, but I think that we should go slowly. Rather than meet Sam at Gracie's, let me suggest that the first step would be for you to come to Sam's therapy session in early January when he's back from San Francisco and has settled in at school. The three of us can talk and, if Sam wants, perhaps you can take him to an early dinner. How would that be?"

"That would be," Duncan said, rubbing his eyes, "that would be great. Thank you. Do you think I could call him today or on his birthday? It's in a few days."

"I'd give him a day or two to settle down a little more. Why don't you email Gracie on his birthday and see what she says?"

"Okay. I'll do that."

"Ah, Duncan?"

"Yes?"

"If we make this appointment in January, you *must* be there. Understood? No last-minute cancellations."

"I'll be there," Duncan mumbled.

"So, well, good, then," Jenny said. "We're all arranged. The next session is Tuesday, January 4th at four. I'll see you then. Oh, and

I'll call Gracie now and discuss all of this with her. Happy Holidays."

Duncan rested his head in his hands for a long time. Finally he sat up and wiped his eyes. Over the radio came James Taylor's bittersweet rendition of "Have Yourself a Merry Little Christmas." Duncan lifted himself up and stepped over to the windows overlooking the sand. Through the heavy mist outside and the moisture still in his eyes, he could just make out a solitary figure in a black-and-white running suit jogging on the beach path below. The fog swirled around the lone runner, hiding and revealing him several times as he moved silently along. When the jogger had vanished into the mist for the last time, Duncan wondered where he had come from and where he was going.

....

WEEK OF DECEMBER 27
LOS ANGELES

G hislaine rose in the dim light of the morning of December twenty-ninth, sipped some water, and slipped into her black unitard. Left arm over her head and right hand on her waist, she leaned right to stretch her left side and then reversed the movement. Waist twists, toe touches, and hip thrusts à la Bob Fosse followed until she felt her back and leg muscles begin to warm. Beginning to run in place, the events of the past few days crowded into her mind. She had agreed on Christmas Day to the Aoki proposal to resolve her differences with Ward, betting that Ward would reject the settlement thereby forcing Aoki to support her. When Ward had also agreed to the compromise, she had cursed Aoki and then Duncan Luke, whom she strongly suspected had suggested the strategy.

As she pumped her arms and legs faster and faster, however, she persuaded herself that the Aoki plan, while certainly less than what she deserved after twenty-five years of marriage to Robert and twenty years of hard work, achieved her principal objective: the survival of Bingham International under circumstances in which she would have substantial influence, if not absolute control. She would be able to protect the company's reputation, craft her own future and Rob's, and, not insignificant, no longer have to pawn jewels to fight off Ward. Still, she knew Ward's ambition to destroy her and control the company would not cease with his acceptance of the Aoki plan. She remained in danger. Panting as she raced in place, she wondered again whether Duncan Luke as head of the newly constituted BIG would mitigate the risk Ward posed to her or create new obstacles to the success of her company.

Later, playing with a Greek yogurt parfait, Ghislaine wondered what her maman would have advised. A deep, sandpaper voice, so like her own, echoed in her mind: *Mieux vaut plier que rompre*, it said. All right, Maman, all right, she murmured grumpily. She knew she had, over the years, barricaded herself behind walls of adamancy and mistrust. Each time she fended off an unwanted advance from a skating coach or a director, endured one of Robert's unending complaints, or pretended not to hear an off-color joke that she was "nothing but a pretty face with a fat rolodex," she had added another bulwark to her defenses until she had constructed an emotional fortress.

She longed now to fling open the gates, to discover the person who had crouched behind the walls for so long, to see how fast the new Ghislaine could sprint over an open field. Wasn't that the reason she needed Bingham International? It was her drawbridge to a new life. Perhaps, it was time to try to temper her skeptical, headstrong nature, to trust this Duncan Luke, at least a little, and even to work with Ward. She wanted a chance to find out who Ghislaine Bingham really was. Well, no time better than the present, as her maman would say.

Ghislaine neatly folded her magenta napkin and then, still irritated at being forced to share control with Ward, crumpled it up and threw it down by her half-consumed café au lait. All right, all right, Maman. She would invite both Ward and Duncan to her

New Year's Eve party. She had no illusions that a simple social gesture would extinguish Ward's resentment toward her. But as the new chair of the board, she felt an obligation to find a way to cooperate with him. And, she half-smiled to herself, it would be fun to observe the laconic Duncan Luke in a setting in which talk of the value of business intelligence would make for dull conversation. She strode to her office. It was eight o'clock. She picked up the phone on her desk. As it rang, she tried to picture her darkly handsome stepson at his condominium in Century City.

"Hello, Ward? It's Ghislaine. I hope it's not too early. Listen, I'm calling, first, of course, to wish you the best of the holiday season. And second, to invite you to a small party I'm having here on New Year's Eve. I'd like, Ward, I . . . I *hope* that we can forget our disagreements and usher in a new year that will be a new era for our company, one in which our partnership will grow and the company will flourish as a result."

Ghislaine could hear Ward cough and clear his throat before responding.

"How nice of you to call and I appreciate your kind invitation. Unfortunately, I made plans to ski at Vail for a few days this week and leave on New Year's Day directly from Vail for London. I need to meet with Ron Danko as soon as possible to see whether we can expedite the government approval for our investment in Gulf of Guinea Exploration. As you know, we're counting on that investment for a great deal of our profits in the coming year."

Ward paused and then continued quickly, "However, I, too, hope that the new year will bring with it a spirit of partnership between us and a reborn prosperity to Bingham International. Now that we've both agreed to the Aoki plan, why don't I ask the company's lawyer to draw up an agreement between us, which will memorialize the plan, and a consulting agreement for Duncan Luke? I think he should be able to get drafts to us both by

Wednesday. We can execute them by the end of the week and they will be effective as of January one. Oh," he interjected before Ghislaine could reply, "I'll also ask him to contact Monica to arrange for an arbitration to settle the remaining estate issues as quickly as possible. Is that acceptable to you?"

Ward's unctuous tone sent a chill down Ghislaine's spine. But she forced herself to stay in character.

"Yes, of course. Thank you so much. Please ask our lawyer to send the draft to both Monica and me. We'll get him our comments immediately. I agree that we should try to finalize everything before the end of the year so that we can begin January on fresh footing. I'm sorry you won't be able to join us on New Year's Eve, but have a wonderful time in Vail and good luck with Ron Danko."

Ghislaine paused a moment before inquiring sweetly, "If it wouldn't be too much trouble, perhaps you could report to the board at the January 13th meeting on where things stand with Danko and the Gulf of Guinea investment so that we can reach a . . . a *collective* decision on how to proceed?"

Another grating cough sounded over the line.

"Sorry, I seem to have caught a minor cold," Ward added. "Yes, I'd be happy to report to the board on the thirteenth. Given our agreement, I wouldn't dream of making any decisions without board approval. Please accept my best wishes for an unforgettable New Year."

"Yes, Happy New Year," Ghislaine replied and then muttered "*connard*" to herself as she hung up.

***

Duncan Luke spent the two days after Christmas Day recovering from the physical and mental strain of the previous two weeks. His bulky fifty-year-old body craved long hours of sleep, and with rest the dark smears below his eyes began to fade and his sallow skin regained the normal doughy hue of a man who spent too little time outdoors. Remaining unshaven and wearing the same set of baggy, food-stained sweats in bed and out, he rose late each morning only to prepare and wolf down his version of huevos rancheros and gaze at the online *New York Times*. The afternoons he spent staring out the front window of his apartment at the churning sea. As the hours passed, the soreness on the back of his neck and the right side of his rib cage started to dim, although not as quickly as he remembered similar injuries healing thirty years ago when he had wrestled. In the evenings, he pan-grilled whatever meat, fish, or vegetable he found in his refrigerator, wrapped the result in several large warmed flour tortillas along with some black beans, shredded Monterey Jack cheese, and Cholula sauce and devoured the eye-watering burritos along with shots of Sauza and fresh lime. His stomach full and his mind bleary with fatigue and tequila, he stumbled each night to bed, falling asleep almost before his head hit the pillow.

On Tuesday morning, still hungover from the previous night, Gracie surprised him by sending a short email announcing that she and Sam were home. Duncan walked back into the bathroom and examined his glassy eyes and flushed complexion in the mirror. He ran his fingers through the tangle of his black curls and over the brown bruises on the outside of his arms. Shaking his head in disgust, he pinched a new bulge protruding from his waist. All right. That's enough, he commanded himself. He returned to the kitchen and poured the remaining Sauza down the drain. A sweet-sour, alcoholic scent filled his nose and caused him to gag. No more tequila and lots more exercise, he vowed.

Duncan spent an hour composing a reply to Gracie apologizing again for his unanticipated absences and asking whether he could call Sam, since it was his birthday. To his surprise, Gracie replied immediately that it would be fine. Duncan read her message with relief and new hope that the emotional torrents between them would recede, leaving a tiny land bridge on which they might meet to raise their son. He punched in the numbers of Gracie's home phone. She answered and immediately handed the receiver to Sam.

"Hello?" Sam ventured. "Is this really my dad?" The mistrust clouding his son's voice caused Duncan's heart to drop. His relationship with Gracie wasn't the only one that needed bridging.

"Yes, Sammy," Duncan replied, swallowing a sob. "It's really your dad. Happy Birthday, sweetheart. How are you?"

"Okay." Then silence. Duncan took a deep breath and willed lightness into his voice.

"I . . . I'm really sorry that I missed our time together, Sam. I have a couple of presents to give you the next time we're together."

"Okay."

Duncan exhaled slowly and changed the subject.

"Tell me about your trip to Grandma and Grandpa's. Did you see the Golden Gate Bridge?"

"Where are you? Japan? Again?"

"No! No, Sam. I'm in Los Angeles. At . . ." Duncan was about to say, "At our home," but stopped himself. Take it slow, dammit! "At my apartment on the beach near your school. Did you have some Chinese food in San Francisco?"

No response. Duncan heard Sam breathing softly and knew his son was weighing whether to risk being disappointed again. Duncan closed his eyes and waited for the verdict.

"Yes," Sam replied finally and Duncan felt the tension drain from his shoulders. "We had Chinese food. I didn't eat the vegetables."

Sam spit out the words as if they were the hated greens themselves.

"Why do they always put vegetables in with the noodles? And we went to the Golden Gate Park and I got to ride the carousel five times in a row! And then I played on this huge climbing structure . . ."

Sam continued to jabber away for five minutes, reporting on almost every hour of his trip. Under other circumstances, Duncan might have wished he were more than a dartboard on which Sam flung the details of his life. Today, hearing the singsong squeak of his son's voice brought a wide grin to his face and tears to his eyes.

After speaking with Sam, he telephoned M.D., whose mother was visiting her for the holidays, and Rob, who was skiing black diamonds in Taos with friends, to thank them again for their courage during the Panamanian ordeal. Duncan initially hesitated to inform them of his appointment as head of BIG but ultimately decided that he wanted them to hear the news of BIG's formation directly from him. To his surprise and pleasure, each raved about the idea and not only volunteered but demanded the chance to work together again. Both M.D. and Rob ended their calls by inquiring softly, "You haven't heard anything from Magdalena, have you?" When he replied that he hadn't, both reassured him. "Well, I'm sure she's safe. We'll hear from her soon."

Without liquor dulling his mind, he had trouble falling asleep on Tuesday night but awoke Wednesday morning clearheaded and hungry for fresh air. He decided to work at his office on the LMU campus. After hacking the tough, four-day growth from his face, he headed to work, the cool sea breeze, the smell of salt in the air, and the brilliant morning sun raising his spirits. On his way, he stopped at Tanners Coffee House. With a chocolate biscotti and a Tanners drip in his lap, he drove to LMU to continue preparations for his seminar, "Strategic Intelligence for International Business." His first class was in less than two weeks, on Tuesday, January 11th.

At twelve thirty, recalling the image of his waistline in the mirror the previous morning, he set out on a long walk around the deserted campus, seeking both physical release and a chance to reacquaint himself with the university from which he had been absent for the past two weeks.

An hour later, he returned to his office to find an email from a lawyer for Bingham International, attaching a draft of his consulting agreement. He tapped out an acknowledgment, read through the agreement, and concluded that there were no major problems. Just to be sure, however, he sent it to Web Allen with a note asking him to review it and provide comments by return. He wanted to make sure that the agreement would resolve the dispute with Gracie over the financial terms of their divorce. As he was finishing the email to Web, his office phone rang.

"Hello, Duncan? It's Ghislaine. Where have you been? I tried your apartment, but no one answered and you don't have a machine. And your cell phone is turned off. If you're going to work with us, you need to have an answering service at home and learn to put your cell phone on vibrate. You can't just disappear," her deep voice scolded.

Ah, Ghislaine Bingham, Duncan sighed to himself. Four days and I had almost forgotten what a pain in the ass you can be.

"Hello, Ghislaine," he replied. "Happy holidays to you, too."

"Oh, now don't be upset. You asked for the job; Christ, you practically created it yourself. You must . . . I mean . . . I would think you'd *want* to be available to those who will come to rely upon you."

"Well, I didn't think I started until January first but, of course, you're right. I'll keep my cell on vibrate from now on," he promised. "How can I help you?"

"Well, I'm having a small party on New Year's Eve at my home. I was hoping you could come. It won't be anything too fancy; just some old friends and a few investors in our funds. If you wouldn't mind, I'd like to introduce you as the head of our new BIG."

Duncan shook his head. He loathed parties filled with unfamiliar faces decorated with painted smiles. Yet Ghislaine clearly wanted him to come, and refusing might insult her just as their new work relationship was beginning.

"Thank you," he replied slowly. "I'm still recovering from the past couple of weeks, but I'd be happy to stop by briefly. What time?"

"How about nine thirty? I promise that I'll have you out by eleven."

Shit, Duncan swore to himself. He liked to be in bed by ten.

"Okay. I'll see you at nine thirty. By the way, will Rob or M.D. be there?" he inquired, his baritone rising with hope.

"No, unfortunately, they won't be. You'll have to wait until after the New Year for a reunion of your intrepid team."

"Well, that's disappointing." Duncan sighed. "It would have been great to see them. But, in any event, thank you for the invitation. I'll see you on Friday."

***

At nine forty on New Year's Eve, dressed in a dark-gray suit and a napkin-size red-and-white striped tie, Duncan walked through the door of Ghislaine's Mediterranean mansion. He deposited his charcoal wool overcoat on the portable rack set up at the rear of the entryway and headed toward the party noise. Twisting and turning through the long rectangular music room to the right of the entryway, he swam his way past the black ties and brocades, the red vests and velvets, the starched shirts and sequins bobbing on the ocean of guests. A deeply tanned man with a silver mane was playing on the baby grand piano the famous Kander and Ebb song "New York, New York" for three off-key revelers who substituted "L.A., L.A." for the original words. Two tuxedo-clad men, who had the girth of former football players, huddled by the casement windows opposite the piano and debated the relative merits of the Oregon Ducks and Auburn Tigers, the teams that would play for the national title in less than two weeks. Shiny blue, silver, and gold helium balloons proclaiming the New Year hovered near the high ceiling like miniature zeppelins. If this is a small party, Duncan told himself, I want to make sure I'm at least ten miles away from any of her big ones.

As he walked under the gold-and-silver banner hanging over the entrance to the living room, he saw Ghislaine standing near the French windows on the right. Ghislaine's champagne-colored hair was tied back in elaborate braids and she wore a black satin dress with a long train that had tiny sequins and platinum beads sown into the fabric. She may be a royal pain, Duncan thought, but she is a remarkably beautiful woman. He watched as Ghislaine laughed gaily and leaned forward to whisper something in the ear of a broad-shouldered, confident-looking man with short, graying hair. Suddenly she looked up and her eyes locked on Duncan.

"Duncan!" she called out and waved her hand. When Duncan managed to thread his way to Ghislaine, she held out her hand and said, "How nice of you to come tonight. Let me introduce you to my dear friend, Andrei Kronsky. Andrei emigrated from Moscow a decade ago and founded one of the most successful biomedical companies in Los Angeles. He has been an investor in several of our funds."

Duncan observed Kronsky cock his head and felt the Russian's eyes scrutinize him closely.

"Just give me a minute, would you, Duncan?" Ghislaine said. "I have to say hello to the Counsel General of Belgium before he leaves, but I'll be right back. Andrei, be a dear and keep Duncan company, will you? Oh, thank you!"

Ghislaine moved away toward a group of guests across the room suddenly leaving the men enveloped in an uneasy silence.

"A pleasure to meet you," Kronsky finally said with a curt nod in Duncan's direction. "You're a lawyer, aren't you?"

"I am but I don't practice law anymore. I'll be a consultant to the Bingham board of directors and I'm a professor at Loyola Marymount's business school."

"But still a man of laws." Kronsky snorted. "We Russians believe that laws catch flies but let hornets go free. And while I live here now, I am Russian, especially when it comes to protecting Ghislaine. So my friend," Kronsky said in a tone that made it clear he considered Duncan to be nothing of the kind. "If you see a hornet fly even within a hundred meters of Ghislaine, do not waste time with your laws. Contact me. I will smash that hornet into a thousand pieces as I have others before. And if you are careless and Ghislaine is stung, your laws will not save you from me. Do I make myself clear?"

Duncan stared down at Kronsky and smiled thinly. Russians could be melodramatic but Kronsky seemed deadly serious. Did Ghislaine have any idea how this man felt about her? Just as he was about to respond, Ghislaine returned.

"How are you two getting along?" she smiled.

"I was just telling Duncan how very happy I was to hear that he'd be working with you," Kronsky crooned. "How, like most successful women, you stubbornly refuse to acknowledge that you need the protection of a strong man from time to time."

Ghislaine's face darkened briefly before she laughed and turned to Duncan.

"Like most successful *men*, Andrei refuses to acknowledge that some women are quite capable of taking care of themselves. Now," she said as she kissed Kronsky on each cheek, "if you'll excuse us *cher* Andrei, I want to introduce Duncan to more of our friends."

And, with that, Ghislaine grabbed Duncan's elbow in a vise-like grip and led him away as if she were a mother leading a shy child through a series of elementary school admissions interviews. An hour later, Duncan felt queasy from the stress of smiling at dull eyes and even duller jokes. He took Ghislaine aside.

"This has been an incomparable experience, but I don't feel well and need to get home."

"Oh, don't be such a bore," Ghislaine chided him with a sly smile. "It's not even midnight yet."

Duncan felt the hairs on the back of his neck begin to bristle. He hadn't had a drink for several days and the three glasses of 2010 Pouilly-Fuisse he had quaffed to wash away his inhibitions had worked their magic.

"Look, I said I'd drop by briefly and I did. You promised you wouldn't keep me past eleven and it's now eleven. Thank you for a memorable evening," he snapped and walked back to the entryway.

He could feel Ghislaine striding behind him but did not slow down. When he reached the coat rack, he grabbed his coat. Her hand seized his arm before he could put the coat on. He swiveled to face her. Her eyes blazed at him.

"Don't give me that promise bullshit," she growled. "You should be flattered that I asked you to stay. But you don't like me, do you? Or is it that you envy my lifestyle and friends? Well, I don't give a damn what you think as long as you don't insult me in public."

Duncan threw his coat over his left shoulder, folded his arms, and stared down at Ghislaine. He looked away, shrugged, and then met her eyes again.

"I don't know you well enough to say whether I like you. I know you're smart but not always wise. I know you have energy but not always patience. And I know you possess vision but not always common sense. I hope that we'll have the chance to become better acquainted, because I'd like to know you well enough to like you. I'm sorry if anything I've done tonight offended you. In my world, keeping a promise is not an insult; reneging on a promise is not a compliment."

He saw Ghislaine open her mouth to respond, but he held his hand up.

"Let me finish." He gazed back over Ghislaine's shoulder across the music room and shook his head slowly. "As far as envying you your lifestyle and friends, well, let me just say that not very long ago I lived in a big house packed with lots of fancy things, not as big as your house and not as fancy as your things perhaps, but close enough. And I had scores of acquaintances, not as many as those you call your friends perhaps, but plenty. Do I regret not having the house, the things, and the hundreds of sometime friendships anymore? Not on your life. I'm happier than I've been for years. I have less space, fewer possessions, and only a handful of close friends, but everything I do have I value. Far from envying you, Ghislaine, I . . . well, let's just say I hope all of this," Duncan declared as he waved in the direction of the packed music room, "fills you with as much joy as I will feel when I am home tonight alone."

"All of this does make me happy," Ghislaine retorted and gripped his arm more tightly. "You're Scottish, right? Well, I'm sorry that you've not been able to escape your Calvinist past. Pleasure makes you feel guilty and the guilt keeps you pure? That's the bargain you've made with your soul, the pact you want to impose on everyone else? Well, I have a secret for your officious little brain, Duncan Luke: you're no better than the rest of us. You indulge like everyone else, except you revel in self-important self-denial. By God, you *will* make the perfect compliance officer, won't you?"

"I'm your intelligence consultant, and I'm not the one who can't bear to swallow a thimble full of wine because I might lose all control."

"Intoxication isn't pleasurable for me," she sniffed, dropping her hand from his arm. "Good night and travel safely back to your beachside hermitage."

"And air-kissing airheads isn't pleasurable for *me*," he shot back unable to resist parroting her. "Good night and, yes, I can't wait to be home."

As Duncan drove the thirty minutes back to his apartment in Playa del Rey, he alternately upbraided Ghislaine Bingham for her arrogance and reprimanded himself for his loss of self-control. Not a particularly auspicious beginning for the head of the Bingham Intelligence Group, he brooded.

Arriving at his apartment shortly before midnight, he passed his mailbox and absentmindedly stuck his hand into it. To his surprise, he felt something jammed in the metal enclosure and extricated a small FedEx envelope. What the hell is this? He lumbered up the two flights of stairs to his apartment, opened the door, and switched on the lights. After he clicked on his radio to hear KJZZ ring in the New Year, he examined the outside of the FedEx envelope. The lines for information concerning the sender were blank. He tore it open. A postcard fell out and onto the floor, address side up. With a grunt, he bent over to pick it up.

Whoever had sent the card hadn't written a message or an address on it. Puzzled, he flipped the card over. A cobblestone plaza in which a statue of a man pointing to the horizon dominated the foreground of the picture and a large limestone structure with a red tile roof and graceful arches rested in the background. The words *"Parque Colon y Catedral de Santa Maria la Menor en Santo Domingo"* were written in yellow script across the bottom. He smiled, closed his eyes, and held the postcard up to his nose. He breathed in the faint scent of gardenias. "Magdalena," he murmured, just as the radio struck up Duke Ellington's version of "Auld Lang Syne."

ACKNOWLEDGEMENTS

What Picasso once said about artists is even truer about novelists. We tell an elaborate lie in the hope of helping our readers realize some truth. If *BIG: Beginnings* succeeds at all in convincing readers of the truthfulness of its lies, it is because of the encouragement and advice I have received from my colleagues, friends and family. I would like to mention a few here.

First and foremost, I owe an immense debt of gratitude to Katharine Cluverius, my brilliant editor and an innovative publisher of new authors, for championing the *BIG* series. I also wish to thank Jerry Boak for his sage advice on the manuscript and web design expertise.

I am very grateful to the late Deborah Raffin for reading through two of the earliest of many drafts and for helping to shape the storyline, and to Victoria Preminger for her helpful notes.

My wife, my father, my son, my sister, Hilary, and my friends, Marlee Anderson, Mindy Balgrosky, Nina Hachigian, Virginia Keeny, John Quisenberry, and Alan Schwartz slogged through various versions of this book and conveyed, in the nicest way possible, their constructive criticisms.

The talented screenwriter, Richard Kletter, deserves special mention for his insightful comments and timely words of encouragement.

435

I am thankful to Terry Deal, my copyeditor, and Rebecca Lown, the jacket designer, for their contributions to the book.

Finally, after nearly five years of writing, I am still searching for the words to express the fullness of my love and appreciation for my two children, Danielle and Jordan, and my wife, Katie. They inspire me every day to be a better father, husband, and now, writer.

ABOUT THE AUTHOR

GREYSON BRYAN is an international lawyer who earned his B.A. from Stanford and a J.D. from Harvard, and taught at the Harvard Law School and UCLA. A longtime L.A. resident, *BIG: Beginnings* is his first novel and the first book in the BIG series.

Made in the USA
Columbia, SC
27 April 2017